AN APOCALYPTIC SERIES

The Ushering

AMETHYST

BY

Dan-Dwayne

Cover designed by DSGA
Art elements provided by Pixabay, pixabay.com
No Attribution Required

Dan-Dwayne Spencer
Visit my blog at www.Dan-Dwayne.com

Printed in the United States of America

First Printing: March, 2024
DSGA Publishing

Paperback ISBN: 978-1-961632-00-4

AN APOCALYPTIC SERIES
THE USHERING
AMETHYST
Book 3
DAN-DWAYNE

My thanks to the old King James, Confucius, and William Shakespeare, the old Bard, all of whom Iggarest and Arland loved to misquote.

"Ah, Shakespeare, quite a striking fellow. The things I could blather on about that scallion. If we had time, the tales would go on for hours. But then, there was Dear Ann, his wife. To quote the old bard himself... 'She had very little about her face that was worth sunburning. Methinks she had more hair than wit, but sadly more faults than wealth.' Or was it hairs? I can never remember."

Facing Stoney, I said, "Old friend, don't harken to gossip and foul words concerning me. A great man once said, 'A man who moves a mountain begins by purchasing a wheelbarrow.' As always, I will prevail."

"He made that up, didn't he?" Jimmy asked.

"Either he made it up or Confucius worked at a hardware store," Flower replied.

CHAPTER ONE

Tucker Black
Western, Texas, 1874

A hard west wind blew along the dirt road we called Main Street. After living in the little town of Western, Texas, for five years, it didn't surprise me that this blustering gale deposited a layer of airborne silt and sand on everything it touched. My eyes watered in defense of the gritty onslaught blowing in through the open door of the blacksmith shop. It filled my mouth with the earthy taste of rock bits and the herbal residue of desert sage.

Thankfully, the large sliding door to the shop faced east. Still, I left it half open to expel the heat from the forge and half shut to limit the influx of dust. I headed toward the coal burning forge with a hammered out horseshoe held tight in my blacksmith's tongs when an angel appeared barring my way. Over the years, I have met more than one, both Favored and Fallen. This one I recognized. His flaxen hair glimmered, highlighting his stern face with a reflective halo. The robe he wore appeared to be golden beams of light bound at the waist by a silver belt. Sparks of cosmic lightning danced along the lance he held. Without a doubt, this was Michael, the leader of the Favored.

The angel's voice resonated, powerful as a mighty waterfall. "**Hail, ageless one, marked prophet, and champion of the favored. I greet you in the name of the Elohim, we who you call angels, and exhort you to beware. Abaddon, prince among the fallen angels, has sent an assassin, one of the demonic Thrones, to kill you. Our blessing of longevity will mean nothing if Hell's emissary is successful. Again, I say—beware.**"

Michael tipped his lance toward the earth. In a thunderous and brilliant flash of lightning, he disappeared.

The shadowy oddity I called Mr. Dark announced, "*Now, isn't that just like the angels? Show up and yell some claptrap about the dangers of one demon prince or another, then vanish before you get a word in edge-wise.*" For a moment, a silence came from the corner of my mind where I heard his telepathic voice. "*Don't keep working like you're invincible. Do something. I can't see anything through this dirt storm, but there's no denying it. I feel the presence of a demon. Either it's one powerful mother, or maybe there's more than one. It's close, Arland, even though I can't home in on its exact location—the evil is real close.*"

"Okay then," I paused to look out the door at the black-blizzard raging outside. "Tell me when you know something that's not a gut feeling. I can't send a premonition to Hell, but a demon; that's another thing altogether."

Mr. Dark was right about more than one thing. Despite all my gifts, a demon could still kill me. The angel Reuwel explained it like this. I am called the marked prophet because my eyes are a freaky amber gold, but beyond that, my dark side is an actual, sentient being. I call him Mr. Dark, and most of the time, I ignore his self-centered comments, but he has been helpful on occasions. His bravado only surfaces when I'm in mortal danger. He doesn't want me to get killed because our life forces are linked. If I die, he dies. I also hear his voice as if it were a thought.

"*After your encounter with Abaddon, he is hell-bent on ending you.*"

This time, I didn't stop my work at the forge, barely giving him my attention. "Yep. Nothing new, old friend."

The sound of jingling spurs alerted me to more than dirt filling the doorway. Startled, I jumped back, hand extended, ready to use the *Prophet's Voice* to attack the hellion. Then I realized what I heard. Demons don't wear spurs. Well, not as a rule they don't.

A stranger sauntered in through the brown haze. Wearing a black leather vest, black denim shirt, a gun belt hanging low across faded black jeans, and a bandana covering both nose and mouth; no doubt, this was a gunslinger. The stranger spoke. "Are you the smith called Loudermilk?" It took me aback because the voice was that of a young woman.

Mr. Dark quietly whispered, "*Relax, she's not a demon, but I'm not kidding you. There's one close by.*"

Going back to my work, I answered her, "No. Loudermilk owns this forge. I run it for him." After striking the hot rolled metal I'd taken from the glory hole, I paused. "If you're looking for him, you're the heck out of luck. He's not here." I slammed the hammer down again. "He'll be back next week. He took the misses over to Amarillo for a few days."

"You play nice with Miss Gun for Hire, and ignore the fact a demon the size of Gibraltar is heading this way. Go ahead. Get us both killed, won't ya?"

From the corner of my eye, I glimpsed Mr. Dark's blob like shape as he scurried off to hide in the shadows.

"So...are you the one they call *Arland, The Cursed*?" she asked.

I stopped to look up. "That's what they call me in these parts."

Despite my own youthful look, grueling years of demon fighting managed to harden my emotions. However, when the gunslinger removed her hat and pulled down her bandana. I admit her teenage face, short cropped blond hair, and a hearty layer of trail dust darkening her freckled nose surprised me. Seeing her youth stung my senses for any gunslinger her age would never live to be twenty.

"I don't recall meeting you before, stranger. How the hell do you know my name?" I asked.

"They say there's something special about you; I mean, about your work."

"Who're you kidding? I know what people say behind my back. There's a reason they call me *The Cursed*."

With a dead stare, the stranger let the awkward moment pass. "How good are you at making gun parts?"

Grabbing the horseshoe with the tongs, I laid it at the edge of the glory hole, and replied, "As good as any and better than most."

She pulled a fancy six-shooter from her holster and handed it to me.

As soon as I touched the cold metal, the gift of the prophet alerted me of a supernatural empowerment imbued in the casting. Engraved filigree covered the barrel, and between the scrolling shapes, glowing angel runes emerged. "This thing is a demon killer! The angels forged this."

The stranger stepped back and took a good look at me. One glance at my yellow gold eyes and she stammered, "You...you're not one of *them*, are you?" She pulled a long dagger from her boot and waved it at me. The blade glowed with the aura of angelic magic. Then she paused, taking in my small sinewy frame and the sweat pouring off my brow. "No! You're something different. Demons don't sweat." She returned the knife to her boot. "You're one of the Champions." Smiling, she stuck her hand out in my direction. "I'm one of the angel's Champions, too; I'm pretty proud of the fact the great Archangel Michael himself chose me."

"You don't say. Last I heard, pride was a sin." I ignored her outstretched hand and continued inspecting the gun.

Withdrawing her offer to shake my hand, she let her arm drop to her side. "Shucks, I didn't mean it like that," she said.

"The last thing you needed is to get mixed up with a bragging demon hunter from the distant past. What happened to

trying to get back to the year 1969? Or doesn't that keep you busy enough?" He called to me from his hiding place, but I heard his voice clear as my own thoughts.

"Shut up!" I said it louder than I meant to.

Thinking I was talking to her, she responded to my outburst. "What?"

No way could I expect her to understand about how I live with a split consciousness, or that an act of angel magic flung me a hundred years into the past. So I said, "Don't make a mountain out of nothing. That's something I say when I get excited. You see, I don't know much about reading Angel, but I know Saint Michael's mark when I see it. Looks like he made this himself."

Despite Mr. Dark being an impudent son of a gun, sticking his nose into my business, he was right about us trying to find a way back to 1969. I aimed a harsh look in his direction and laid the gun on the finishing table by the forge. "No ordinary smith can fix this thing. Good thing I'm not ordinary."

Her story sounded good, and she carried an angel made weapon, but still, I didn't know exactly what to make of this female gunslinger calling herself one of the Champions, I scratched the back of my neck before returning to my cooling horseshoe. I asked, "Well stranger, you got a name other than Champion."

"Folks call me Tucker Black."

"Pardon my manners, but that's an odd name for a lady."

"It would be if'n I be a lady. Ladies are frilly and lacy. You see anythin' frilly and lacy about me?"

I gave her another glance and shook my head.

"Ma named me Teresa Ann Tucker. Face it, I ain't no Teresa Ann. Don't know exactly why folks started calling me Tucker Black, but it's stuck ever since."

"She's kidding, right? Let me guess her favorite color and my first try won't count."

Mr. Dark's sarcasm didn't distract me.

She spat on the dirt floor. "So ya know, I don't answer to plain old Tucker. It's Tucker Black. Hear?"

Mr. Dark interrupted my thoughts. "*And you call me impudent. This one's full of herself, insisting on being addressed by two names is a bit much. Get rid of her. Send her on her way.*"

Half talking to the stranger and half to Mr. Dark, "Yeah, I hear you," I said. "Tucker Black, you say. And where did you ride in from?"

"Nowhere and everywhere. Never stayed in one place long enough to make friends or call it home. Figured it be for the best." She put her thumbs in the top of her jeans and looked down her nose at me. "Ya look a bit young to be slammin' iron and chasin' demons. You can't be more'n thirteen—maybe fourteen."

"Trust me. I'm a lot older and definitely stronger than I look." I lifted the smoldering horseshoe with tongs and quenched it in a barrel of oil I kept near the forge. "Leave the gun and I'll see what I can do to fix it." The horseshoe thudded down onto the finishing table.

She laid the six-shooter next to the horseshoe. "No. You don't understand. Besides being enchanted, I can't rightly explain it, but it's like...the gun's a part of me. Most time it talks to me, but like, no one else can hear it. Makes people think I'm crazy, but I ain't."

I closed my eyes and shook my head. Probably, she thought, I didn't understand either, but no one could have understood more.

"Really, I can't be separated from it. I mean, it's not like I'm afraid somebody's gonna shoot it, cause it won't fire for nobody but me." A concerned expression crossed her face. "You gotta fix my gun while I'm here—watching."

"Calm down. I get it. Stick around, and I'll get to it right away." She had no clue I too shared a supernatural dilemma, for Mr. Dark's voice silently stayed in my head as well. I picked up the gun and inspected the swirls and fiery letters, like those in Roger Reynold's talisman's book. They glistened in the firelight. I missed the other teenaged champions from the future, but Roger, my best friend, most of all. Wishing he was there with me to translate those markings, I grimaced. It would be another ninety-five years before I'd see him again. The angels promised I'd live as long as Methuselah and he lived over eight hundred years.

"Ya can fix it, though, right?"

"Yeah, I think I can." I pulled the hammer back. The gun was loaded, but the hammer moved without the tension needed to slam into a shell. "I've got to know...how did you break something blessed by the angels themselves?" She kept staring at it, so I handed her the weapon.

She aimed it at several things around the room, including me. "Don't know. The last few days the danged thing's gone silent, and it stopped firing. Almost got me killed, last time I ran into one of those ugly green devils. Good thing I got my Heaven-made blade." She patted her boot.

"Only the minions are green. Wait till you get a load of a blue one." I sighed. "I'll do it. No one else can. That's for sure." Opening my hand, she gave me her gun back. "Answer one question for me."

She tilted her head and asked, "And what might that be?"

"I'm curious why you keep a broken gun loaded?"

"It's part of the charm. I guess it isn't a six shooter at all cause every time I fire it, another shell just appears in the chamber. It never runs out of ammo." She huffed like a school girl refusing a date. "I've told ya all about myself, but I know nothin' about you. What's your story? Who are ya, really, and what's your gift?"

"*You going to tell her everything? Even about me?*" in his silent voice, Mr. Dark asked.

"There's nothing to tell. Well, not much anyway. The angels say I'm a prophet. My gift allows me to call things into being by using what they call *the Prophet's Voice.*"

"Is that so? Sounds pretty special to me. You get premonitions about those green skinned monsters when they get close?"

"Kind of. I get a warning one way or another," I replied.

"My gun used to tell me when the demons get near, but not lately. Don't know why, but those hellish things are following me. I've had to deal with at least one or two every day this week."

"They don't want you. They what this..." I reached under the finishing table and laid a sparkly silver diadem beside the finished horseshoes. "...a crown of Abaddon. There's four of these, all angel-made and immensely powerful. Those green hellions you're talking about are his demons, and they won't stop coming until that devilish prince has all four of them back."

Tucker Black reached for the crown. "Dang, whatever else they do, they're really beautiful."

I snatched it away from her. "I've been keeping this one away from Abaddon, and... No offence, but I don't know you. There's no way I'd let you get hold of one of the most powerful supernatural objects ever created." Holding the crown up for her to see it, I continued, "There's one catch to these sparkly headbands. Once their magic is tapped, they vanish. Don't know where they disappear to; probably gone to some spirit sensitive place to recharge. Like I said, I don't know."

The savage wind broke one of the loft shutters loose from the hay door, and it banged back and forth on its hinges.

Startled, my nerves shot up to the max level and both Tucker Black and I focused on the hayloft. Behind me, the front door creaked as it opened wide enough for a man to enter. With him, clouds of dirt gushed through. He pushed the door shut behind him and stood before us, all shrouded in a scarlet cloak and hood. At first, I didn't give it much thought, but this guy didn't have a lumbering walk like a man. I'd swear, he glided through the doorway. Oddly, his face remained concealed under that large hood.

"*Now you've done it.*" Mr. Dark yelled. "*You let the enemy catch you with your guard down.*"

I silently replied, "Shut up!" but he was right. Despite all the warnings, I let the gunslinger distract me.

Tucker Black grabbed her boot knife and took a fighting stance. I extended my hands, ready to call upon my prophet's gift...but the figure didn't attack. Instead, it raised its arms and pulled back the hood. I expected it to look hideous, but it wasn't. It appeared to be a handsome, blue-skinned man. Like opening a geisha's fan, golden wings folded out from the sides of his robe.

"*Shit, it's a fallen angel,*" Mr. Dark yelled. "*Your prophet's gift never works on angels. They're too powerful. We're doomed.*"

CHAPTER TWO

The Devil's Assassin

Like all angels, and I've seen my share, this one was more than handsome. If a guy could be called pretty, he was ethereally beautiful. His long black hair cascaded down from under the hood onto his shoulders. Around his blue eyes, he wore lines of black and red Egyptian-like markings. Bare chested and dressed in a black Persian-style kaunakes, a floor length fabric tied into a skirt, and he had a chain wound around his waist.

The angel's voice, although powerful, sounded smooth, pure audible velvet. "**Golden eyed prophet**." He smiled a sharp and jagged smile. "**I know you, for I have sent your ilk to the grave many times before. Despair for Abaddon has condemned you to spend eternity in Hell with him. He longs to inflict pain on you, the likes of which you have never known**."

"Don't be so sure about that. I promise you, he'll not be inflicting pain on anyone today. There are two Champions here. Don't you know when Champions band together we are stronger than anything you can throw at us?"

"**This one?"** The angel pointed toward Tucker Black. **"She has lost her charm; therefore, she is of no consequence. Before long, all the Champions will die."** He eyed Tucker Black. **"Aha, little girl-child, don't look so forlorn. Death is the final challenge every Champion must face.**"

"Demon, you've not met the likes of me. I ain't no pushover," Tucker Black said.

"**You are vermin to be crushed underfoot. You will fall like all who have gone before you...and, Prophet, as for you; today, you will join me in the pit where the worm never dies.**"

From above in the loft, a slimy green tentacle slithered downward, grabbing Tucker Black around the legs and pulling her up toward the loft. The haze cleared enough for me to see the thing ambushing us from above. There in the rafters perched a hideously deformed half-human shape. Its arms transformed into long, slinky, fingerless extensions. A jumble of pointy, jagged teeth filled the demon's mouth, and to my horror, the thing possessed a scorpion like tail, stinger bared, waving over that ugly head.

Caught unaware, Tucker Black struggled against the tentacles, arms pinned and helpless.

The scorpion tail slammed downward. A stream of foul smelling ooze gushed from the stinger, jabbed the air directly above my head, and missed me by inches. Thankfully, I dodged enough, if only barely. The stuff landed on the dirt and sizzled like strong acid.

In all probability, the demon's failure to hit its target stemmed from the fact it had that wicked mouth opened wide; ready to chomp into Tucker Black's head.

I extended my hands and commanded, "Demon, wither and turn to dust."

In the next instant, its tentacles turned gray and cracked. Dust, soft as ash, fell from the loft as the demon dissolved. I covered my mouth and eyes to shield myself from the odious rot raining on me. I again looked up to witness a dozen more huge tentacles smashing through the dusty remains of that demon. They unfolded from the rafters and slinked downward towards us.

Arrogantly, Tucker Black jumped up from where she had fallen, and yelled, "I don't need your help to vanquish these demons. Stand back and watch while I take out the garbage." She went for the fallen angel with her Heaven made knife.

I grabbed up the charmed gun lying on the finishing table and yelled, "The prophet commands; gun, be repaired." At the mere sound of my voice, the thing recoiled. A bullet shot out, followed by the harsh odor of gunpowder. Even though I hadn't aimed the weapon, the bullet found its mark. The demon above us oozed gore from a hole in its head.

The gun fired and fired again. It went off without my aiming or pulling the trigger. The shells flew into the haze of hay, dirt, and demon ash floating in the loft.

Tucker Black stopped in her tracks, pivoted my direction and stood still. A dumbfounded expression blazed across her face.

I'm not sure she even noticed that the largest of the demon's tentacles had shriveled. Then another, along with one poised to land a deadly blow to my head. Like raisins in the sun, they all shriveled. "Tucker Black, don't stand there catching flies with your mouth. There must be a whole herd of demons upstairs. We've taken out three of them and they keep coming."

I fired again. The shell flew this way and that, maneuvering around to find the optimum angle of attack. From above, another one shrieked. It, too, dissolved, but not before hurling a tentacle downward, aimed somewhere behind me.

The sound of a whip cracking pulled my attention back to Tucker Black. A tentacle had hit her shoulder, knocking the gunslinger to the ground moments before it shriveled and dissolved.

After pulling herself back to her feet, she eyed me with an expression I took for skepticism. She said, "I've never seen that before."

"You never saw a slimy green demon with tentacles before?"

"No, them I've seen. I've never seen anyone who can fire that gun besides me." She dusted off her knees.

"You don't have to worry. Have no intentions of keeping it."

"I—Ugh!"

From around his waist, the angel had thrown the chain at her. The thing must've had a curse on it because the links glowed with an eerily green radiance. I watched as it slithered through the air, moving as if it possessed a will of its own. Tucker Black, caught by surprise, lay bound. Despite her kicking and twisting, the angel called his chain back to him, dragging her to what certainly would be a grizzly death.

I leveled the gun at the blue devil and fired again. The angel blessed bullet, although powerful enough to kill a demon, had no effect.

"*Now what are you going to do, hot shot? This thing is going to kill you both...and me, too.*"

Instinctively, I grabbed the crown from the table, raised it toward the demon, and commanded. "Back to Hell with you." Blue lightning erupted from the diadem; it danced through the air and crackled over the devil. A smell of sulfur mixed with a cloud of dirt filled the room.

I waited, unable to see past four feet. Silence replaced the sound of supernatural combat. When the air cleared, and I could see what I had done, both Tucker Black and the fallen angel were gone. I had accidentally sent one of the angel's Champions to Hell along with one of the Fallen.

Mr. Dark exclaimed, "*What did you do? Arland, you stepped in it now, and the stink's going to stick to you like glue. Didn't we need that crown? That was our only way home... And what's more, you just sent one of Saint Michael's Champions to Hell. We're royally screwed.*"

I ignored Mr. Dark, as usual, but then something unexpected happened. I heard the gun's voice. Like Mr. Dark, it spoke in my mind. "*Arland.*" The thing called my name.

It was hard to conceal my longevity through the century to come, and like Mr. Dark said it would, the guilt over what I did to Tucker Black stayed with me. As for the gun, it never fired again after the gunslinger disappeared. Actually, I had to put it away because every time I laid eyes on it...well, the very sight of the thing condemned me for my recklessness.

The next time I saw that gunslinger was in 1969, when I managed to rescue a group of my friends and a host of others from Hell. For Tucker Black, her stay in the devil's pit didn't alter her appearance. Once here, she looked to be nineteen again, and her western garb didn't raise as many alarms as some of the other strange outfits the rest of the multitude wore.

CHAPTER THREE

Western High School, 1970
The Principal's Office

More than eighty years later, and still a rather youthful looking adult thanks to my supernatural gift; I couldn't bring myself to explain my presence to my friends. Instead, I took a teaching job at Western High School in Western, Texas, where they went to school. Although I may never look old, a hundred years left its toll on me.

I had been sixteen when angel magic threw both me and Sarah Hampton back in time. She spent the last hundred years in Purgatory, where time is very different. Upon her return, she remained a teenager.

For me, living more than a century was like the arduous task of ascending a steep staircase, with each step bringing me closer to where I once belonged. The 1970 man in my mirror hardly resembles the teen my friends called

Arland; the years have marked my face with serene maturity. For that reason, no one recognized me. Not until last year, when events and demon intervention forced me to reveal myself to the teenaged team of Champions.

Realizing my identity left them confused and somewhat bitter, particularly Roger Reynolds. Some say that lies sting, but time has taught me that a sweet lie is easier to take than a sour truth. Too bad no one can live a lie forever. When it finally came time for the truth, Roger couldn't find it in his heart to accept my explanation of what happened.

I don't know when exactly, but at some point in my long life, probably at Harvard, I took on a more floral speech. My coworkers called it theatrical vernacular. I think it added to my masquerade as a quirky classroom teacher by the name of Mr. Bertarelli. Upon being outed to the Champions as their friend, Arland Loveless, I tried to not sound so much like their teacher. I failed. Mostly because teachers, in general, are demonstrative, or should I say, aggressively in charge by nature. That and my colorful way of stating things had become a part of me.

Perhaps my inability to change was an excuse for letting my relationship with the team slip into chaos. Yet change has never been easy for anyone, especially when that someone has lived over a hundred years.

Honestly, I've tried to do my best at it, mostly because of Roger. He complained that when I talked with what he called *Berti-speech*, he just couldn't see his friend, Arland, inside the older man. Frankly, I'm not sure it's possible for him to see me in the same light as he did when I was young.

For the good of the team, he put away his anger long enough to help rescue our friends from Purgatory. I only expected to find a few acquaintances there. Those who I knew the demons had kidnapped, but no, we discovered way more than that. Once we saw how many poor souls Abaddon had taken, we couldn't just rescue our friends and leave, so overnight thousands of wayward souls, people from various eras of time, mysteriously appeared in the streets of Western, Texas. Amazingly, the team's secret remained safe because few believed their story. After all, who would?

Well, that was last year when it made national news...for a day or so, before Texas Social Services and a dozen prominent citizens of Western, myself included, knuckled down to the task of finding homes for these wayward innocents, those people rescued from the outer-ring of Hell. Among their number—a female gunslinger named Tucker Black. Even though no one except the team of Champions knew about our adventure to Hell and back, the gunslinger's return marked another wrong made right.

The passing of time had been a blur up to December 1970; mostly because since September, I accepted the position of principal here at the high school. I may never get used to being called—Principal Bertarelli.

Taking this job wasn't exactly in my plans, but because of the sudden disappearance of three key faculty members: the previous principal, the school secretary, and the school librarian, the WISD school board, all but forced the position up on me. Behind all the hype, I believe they couldn't find anyone else willing to take this position, but like the good-hearted shmuck I am, I accepted with a smile...it was far better than trying to explain that the missing faculty members were all demons in disguise, or how my teenage friends and I sent them back to Hell, where they belonged.

Living a hundred years and still appearing to be only in my thirties would have been an impossible feat for a normal man, but there is little about me to claim normality. Each battle with a demon shoved me through life to places I would rather have not gone. Becoming the principal of this school was no exception, but I couldn't refuse it. This new job title put me in a unique position to aid my teenaged friends as they forge ahead in the war for the Favored against the Fallen.

I have become the guardian of their secret; supernaturally empowered, they are the tip of Saint Michael's spear in the battle against evil.

This day started as many had. Despite the supernatural weirdness that surrounded my daily life, things were as usual. Miss Wilson, my secretary, a darling woman, stood across the school office from me; totally occupied with her particularly noisy mimeograph machine. With each turn of the handle, the click-clacking spirit copier spit out purple notices to the faculty, informing them that student grades must be turned into the office before the end of the day. After

4:00 p.m. rolls by, I would finally be able to catch my breath again—Christmas Break will have officially started.

Just outside my office, I stood by her desk, when, in a moment of foreboding, my breath caught in my throat. Involuntarily, I stepped back. Almost mocking me, flame like flickers of light animated the letters painted in gold on the window glass set into my hardwood office door. Reaching forward, I placed my hand flat on the glass pane and tapped into my prophetic gift. An icy dread ran through my arm and images of fire, brimstone, and cankerworms the size of whales filled my head. Amidst it all stood a blazing hell-horse, flaring nostrils blowing fire, and astride it rode a hideous, red she-devil.

I shuddered. Hell was a memory better forgotten. Thankfully, the air in the school office didn't reek of cadaverous flesh and rot, instead the unmistakable odor of mimeograph fluid filled my nostrils. Stepping into my office, I closed the door behind me. Before sitting at my desk, I glanced up at the high ceiling and the one of a kind Tiffany light fixture illuminating the room. Smiling to myself, I admired the angel motif designed into the colored glass. The fortune I amassed during my lengthy life allotted me some expensive pleasures. One of them was my propensity for collecting relics and objects attributed to angelic intervention—this included books and a variety of antiquities like Joseph's silver diviner's cup, among other things.

Another extravagance I allowed myself was in how I furnished my new office. Two ebony finished chairs sat facing my seventeenth century desk, and beyond them, a matching round conference table dominated the room. In its center, an artfully crafted cruciform cross design contrasted with the black wood.

On my desk, a white feather trimmed with gold hung from a hook under a bell jar. Staring at it, I smiled. For over a hundred years, I carried that incorruptible angel feather in my pocket; to this day, it still gives me hope every time I look at it.

I spun my chair around to look out of the window behind my desk. Mr. Dark's gravelly voice filled my mind. "*It's about time people notice your accomplishments. This promotion is way overdue.*"

In silent meditation, I replied. "This all landed in my lap. I would prefer being a history teacher."

"*What you want is to be a sixteen-year-old kid again and battle demons with your friends.*"

I'll never be one of them—never again." I rested my chin on my clasped hands. "Before the angel magic hurled me back in time, Roger Reynolds used to be my best friend, but now he's cold as ice. I don't see that changing."

"*And what about Sarah*?"

Sarah Hampton was the most popular girl in school, crowned prom queen, and every schoolboy's dream girl. "If you haven't noticed, I'm not a teenager anymore. My feelings for Sarah have changed." With a heavy sigh, I said, "Truth is, I gave up on that relationship way before I ever admitted it. If I'm honest with myself, the infatuation lost its spark about ninety years ago."

"*Don't give me that. I listened to you pine over this girl for a century, and now you say you don't love her?*"

"Back in 1869, my bungling sent her to the edges of Hell, not unlike what happened to Tucker Black. I admit it. I loved her back then, but after seeing her again a hundred years later, I realized how completely I'd moved on. She will probably marry some high school football hero and live happily ever after."

"*You're right. Why would anyone love you?*" He grunted out a grave laugh.

"Shut up, Mr. Dark! Go hide in some shadow and shut up."

Silence came from the part of my mind his voice emanated from, and I relaxed. A yawn uncontrollably forced its way out of my mouth, and I watched my breath freeze in mid-air. Realization opened my eyes wide when the temperature in the room dropped by at least twenty degrees. That meant only one thing; an angel had entered the room. I hesitated to swivel my chair around to see.

"**Marked prophet of legend, Arland Loveless Bertarelli, Son of Norman, you are needed once again.**" The resonating voice flooded me with reluctant memories.

There, before me, stood the angel I knew as Reuwel. With only inches from the ceiling, his regal stature demanded respect. His divine clothing glimmered as if it were sheer light. Six impressive wings adorned his back, and his hair, long and chestnut brown, emitted a golden radiance, casting a halo around his refined features.

"This is unexpected. What crisis prompts a visit from my guardian angel?" I asked.

"The fallen one called the *Morning Star,* is angered by your intervention. He amasses his most powerful agents of evil, the unholy *Favored Five.* They plot against you."

"Angel, they are no longer the five, for Abaddon has been vanquished. That leaves only four."

"Hear my words and beware, for the horsemen ride to bring chaos to this world and usher in a reign of darkness."

My forehead furrowed in concern. "Ride? What do you mean, ride?"

"They are indomitable spirits and command a wealth of angel magic. The cursed Baalist Queen of Israel, Athaliah, rides a white horse. Once the daughter of Jezebel, she defied God and killed countless numbers of the house of David trying to end his bloodline. She now has become the harbinger of the night. He who sits on the throne of the Fallen has christened her *Pestilence.* Beware her gnarled and emaciated touch. It withers human flesh. At her belt is the unholy arrow Nimrod shot toward heaven to defy God. In this arrow, Nimrod forged a spirit called an Eidolon, an entity powerful enough to cause worldwide pandemics and untold deaths."

"She must be stopped." I hammered a fist onto the desk. "I'll call my friends together. We can send her back to the fires of Hell. Or, if need be, I still have Gabriel's sword, imbued with the essence of death. It can kill an immortal."

"Beware, she doesn't come alone. With her comes the principality called Adora, daughter of Aod and concubine of

Beelzebub. She rides a red horse and wields the flaming sword that once marked the entrance of Eden. This sword severs the soul from the body. It is proclaimed she will decimate hundreds of thousands with her cursed blade. Within her bosom burns a fiery coal from the altar of Cain. It drives her murderous will, but if the light of it falls on mortal kind, the voices of the dead will drive them mad. The angels now call her *Gewalt*; mortals will call her War. Prepare yourself, war is at hand."

"Before now, we've stopped two demons at the same time; we can do it again."

"**The black horse brings the demon once known as Abimelech; now the angels call him Famine, the greatest plague to befall the Earth. He earned his place in Hell after he killed his seventy brothers to claim his throne. The Morning Star has given him the *Scales of Condemnation* to judge the heart of man, and with his judgement, terror. Yea, for the heart of mortal man battles with his soul, and ever since Adam's downfall, it has desired the things of darkness.**"

I should have been scared to death at the mere thought of these horsemen, but the anger in my heart blinded my judgement. "The devils are the ones who should be frightened of us—the Champions of the favored angels."

"It is you they come for first...Arland Loveless Bertarelli...then all humanity will follow."

"Oh, that's more than a little upsetting. I don't like this." Mr. Dark's voice cut through my mind. *"Devils on hellfire's steroids tracking us down. It's time to retire."*

I didn't have time for Mr. Dark's cowardly blubbering. "What does the fourth one bring?"

"Death! Dominikus, who was Ishtar the fallen, is now the death angel! Filled with Beelzebub's hate, she is the most powerful of them all. For in her right hand, she carries the black *Sword of Retribution*, and in her left, the cursed noose that hung the traitor Judas. That relic has been infused with an evil spirit known only as an *Apathy.* Its ugly claws dig into a mortal's heart and buries itself there; turning gold to rust, it withers the most virtuous heart."

"Got it. Don't look at the noose," I said.

"Prophet, she comes astride a hideous horse-like beast. We angels call it a pale horse, for it lacks substance. It was born of Mephistopheles' curses. Astride her hell-beast, no mere mortal can harm her. Infused with hatred and rage, her hands will spread her imperious anger, vaulted pride, and irrational thoughts among Adam's kin. She desires mortals to wallow in prejudice and bigotry because these are the tools of mankind's destruction. The people will turn on one another and die. Prophet, again I say beware! Never have you faced foes so great. Armageddon is at hand."

"A flaming sword, an insidious flame, an inglorious arrow, a cursed noose... How can we possibly...and what did you mean by the favored—" Before I could finish, Reuwel vanished in a blinding light followed by a deafening boom.

"Typical. Saddle us with the impossible and leave."

Contemplating the task the angel handed me, I leaned back and propped my feet up on the corner of my desk.

"*Really a fun guy, that one.*" Ridicule was Mr. Dark's way. "*Bet he puts a damper on every party he's invited to.*"

"Without his warnings, the Champions would... We would be at a huge disadvantage."

"It's a good thing your old gang hasn't changed their habits. You know where those teenaged demon hunters will be eating lunch. If you hurry, they will most likely be all together and you can tell them all about this, or...you can finally tell the angels to go take a hike. Let them find a new Champion for their centuries old war with the Fallen. I think that's the best idea we've had in the past hundred years."

"What do you mean—our idea?" I sat up. "Those are your thoughts, not mine. I didn't give up an eternity of heavenly bliss, so I could sit in this office and play at being the principal of Western High School. We've been given a job to do, and it's going to get done."

"*And what if the others don't rally to your call? You're not one of the gang anymore and you've had more than your share of goof-ups.*"

His words conjured images in my memory of those I've failed—those once dear to me—both fallen Champions and my innocent friends killed by demons. The thought galled me. This bitterness, although it wasn't courage, drove me to find justice for their sacrifices.

Standing, I placed my fists squarely on my desk. "Then I'll go it alone."

"*Bad idea. You're always jumping right into the fire. You call me selfish when it's you who's always risking your life, and mine, too. Remember, I have a dog in this fight.*"

"So now it's a fight. I thought you didn't want to fight."

"Touché! Round one goes to the chump, who's about to be demon fodder. At least tell the team about the impending disaster. I think the angels would appreciate it."

"Okay already. I'll tell them."

"Today!"

"Yes, today."

"No, take backs."

"Shut up, Mr. Dark...just shut up."

CHAPTER FOUR

A Hot and Dry December Day

In most of the country, December is a time when the land plunges into freezing temperatures. Snowfalls entice people to ice-skate, sled, and ski between snow-laden trees. For them, the term white Christmas has true meaning. They huddle in their lodges and around fireplaces awaiting the time when the Earth stirs from its frigid slumber and green buds peak through the frozen white crust left from where God breathed across the land. Not so for those of us who lived in West Texas.

Here, most December days were warm enough for the football jocks to practice outdoors in tank tops and shorts. Although we might get an occasional dusting of snow after Halloween, not one kid owned a sled because the ground remained warm enough to melt away any flakes that might fall.

We roller skated on hardwood floors inside air-conditioned buildings and the farmers harvested the surrounding sea of cotton all the way into January. Short sleeve shirts and a lightweight coat usually sufficed. In especially warm years like this one, the restaurants even kept their patio seating open through Christmas.

I shut the door to my one-year-old, 1969 Jaguar MK2, moved my rearview mirror, and looked myself in the face. To garner trust from my contemporaries I had cut my shoulder-length chlorine blond hair, which used to be pulled back in a ponytail. This new Sebring haircut, although trendy, gave off a corporate vibe, more to the liking of the collegiate community. It made me appear more professional. My freaky amber eyes, which usually hid behind tinted contact lenses, were concealed behind dark teardrop aviator style sunglasses. I straightened my tie and tweed sports jacket before readjusting the mirror. Putting the car in drive, I headed out.

Moments later, I pulled into the McDonald's parking lot, and hesitated, dreading the cool reception awaiting me. For some long minutes, I sat there and watched my old friends. They were sitting at their customary table on the patio, where a wrought-iron fence separated them from the asphalt.

Roger Reynolds bravely waved his French fries in Jimmy Dugan's face, knowing all the while Jimmy possessed *the Strength of Samson* and could rip his arms out of socket with the flick of a wrist. Of course, Roger, who possessed *the Wisdom of Solomon*, would have calculated the exact amount of pestering Jimmy could take before he retaliated with a predictable backhand.

Rose McFarlane, Jimmy's girlfriend, who possessed the angelic power of transfiguration, and for the time she touched any broken object, could restore it to the original form. I was proud of the fact that this past year she had quit smoking and made Jimmy give up his cigarette habit, too.

Next to Rose sat Rebecca Villarreal. She wielded no angelic power, but had a splinter from Jacob's Ladder, otherwise known as *the Ladder of Ascension*. Any ancient artifact became a supernatural weapon in her hands. The Angels had blessed her with an acrobatic fighting style, and on more than one occasion, she had proven her worth facing one of the Fallen.

Sitting at McDonald's, this group of chosen teenagers appeared so normal. Together, the girls pointed and laughed at the boy's antics. Jimmy threw French fries at the girls, and Roger pestered everyone.

I smiled, more than willing to trade my wealth, position, and experience for another day of being one of the gang. I stepped out of my car and headed toward their table. Roger glanced my way, his face contorted into a sour expression.

As I approached, Roger scowled and nodded my direction. Everyone turned to look, and upon seeing me, their conversation came to an abrupt stop. I leaned on the wrought-iron fence, and opened my mouth to relay the message the Seraphim Reuwel gave me when Sarah Hampton and her faithful entourage, Dee Dee and Dina, burst through the patio doors. Giggling, they sashayed over to the table wearing their cheerleading uniforms. It was quite obvious why the boys at school dubbed them the Sirens—because the girls' bobbing miniskirts and shapely legs silently called to them.

Sarah was the only other student in the school who knew about me and this team of gifted teens. So far, she had kept our secret—even from her posse. Sarah made her snub unmistakably obvious as she tilted her nose up at me before she and Dina took a seat at the table next to the teenage demon hunters. However, Dee Dee slid over next to Roger and brazenly laid a ruby-red kiss on his cheek.

I gave Roger a nod and broke the silence. "I see you and Dee Dee are dating."

"That's right, Mr. Principal Man. Not that it's any of your business."

"Yes. You are correct. It is none of my business. I suppose you think your old principal has nothing better to do than come here just to pester you." Roger wasn't the only one who could be sarcastic. I exhaled heavily and stood there for an awkward moment. "I knew I would find all of you here, and needed to be sure you,"—pointing at Roger, Jimmy, Rose, and Rebecca—"are in my office as soon as you get back to school."

"Oh lover, looks like you're in trouble with the man." Dee Dee's voice echoed her glib expression.

"Is that right, Principal Man? Am I in big trouble?" he pressed his lips into a grim straight line. "And what if I decide I have better things to do?" Everyone else sat speechless.

"My dear fellows,"—leaning over the fence, I handed Jimmy the white angel feather taken from my desk—"It's important."

Jimmy's eyes grew wide, and he nodded. "Whatever you say, Mr. B. We'll be there. I knew something was up. Today, I almost ripped..." He glanced over at Dee Dee and Dina. "I mean, the Mustang's door almost came off in my hand. Bad things simply happen, right?"

I casually replied, "Right." After pausing, I took a card out of my pocket and scribbled a note on it. "If you need to get your car fixed, take it to Mr. Scott, who teaches the auto tech class, and give him this." I handed Jimmy the card. "He, or his students, will repair it right away."

He took the card. "Thanks, Mr. B., but the door still shuts. I may take it by there after Christmas holidays."

Dee Dee acted like Jimmy said nothing out of the ordinary. She kept stroking Roger's cheek and rubbing the edge of his ear.

With an arm firmly around his curvaceous blonde, Roger retorted, "Bad things? Yeah, they're totally coincidental if you live in a fantasy land." He played with a strand of Dee Dee's hair. "As for going to the principal's office, speak for yourself, Jimmy. I haven't decided yet."

I turned and walked back to my car, but behind me I heard Jimmy's scolding voice, "Numbnuts, if I say you'll be there, then you'll be there."

Roger didn't reply. He must have known better than to test Jimmy's patience any further. I closed my car door and sat for a few moments watching them, before I turned my Jag toward the school.

Like a secret handshake, handing Jimmy my angel feather signaled the presence of demons. Once again, the Elohim needed their champions to come to their aid. Even though the team would surely bicker about my presence, I hoped their need would overshadow their personal mistrust.

CHAPTER FIVE

Bitter Feelings

I pulled into the school parking lot, and there in my space stood Tucker Black. Since finding herself in 1970, I couldn't help but notice how she had changed. Still decked out in black, she had traded in her 1880s gunslinger persona for a fashionable western leisure suit, full quill ostrich cowgirl boots, and a crisp, clean 100X felt cowboy/cowgirl hat.

I stopped the Jag half in the parking space, and she sauntered over to my rolled-down window. The remarkable thing about both her and Sarah was how they still fit in with the other teenagers after being trapped in Hell for years. To everyone at the school, Sarah had only been missing for a day or so, but Tuck was an oddity, transplanted into the twentieth century from a long-ago era.

When she leaned over, her polyester jacket blew open, and the shoulder holster with her charmed gun peeked out from under her arm. Angel magic had transformed her six shooter into a snub nosed police special. "Saint Michael told me you needed some help."

"I should have expected you to show up. Trouble lifts its dastardly head and you appear." For the first time, I got the feeling that the angels weren't solely waiting for us to make the first move. They were assembling a bigger team. "Tucker Black, how do you feel about attending high school?"

"Well, Doc, I don't go by Tucker Black any more. It's just Tuck. Everybody these days has what they call a nickname. I figure I gotta catch up with the times."

"My dear girl, whether it's 1874 or 1970, I think you are exactly what you are supposed to be. Don't discount what God has made you by putting on airs." I paused, carefully choosing my next words. "Still, I need a hand with a demon problem. You and that charmed gun of yours would be profoundly helpful. How about enrolling in my school?"

"What? Me learnin' spellin' and figures? I ain't no good at schoolin'. Sorry Doc, it's not for me. I'll lend a hand, but on my terms."

"Considering the hellstorm coming at us, I can't turn down any offer of help. Walk with me to my office, and I'll introduce you to the rest of the team."

She nodded and stood back while I pulled up into the parking space.

Leading the way, I spied Mr. Dark as he silently scurried along the ground, dodging from shadow to shadow.

Like clockwork, right as the fifth period bell rang, the four teenaged demon hunters pushed their way into my office. I had already sent Mr. Lancaster, the teacher who took over my classes, a notice of their impending absences.

There, sitting at the conference table, waited Stoney Abara, the Spanish teacher who, like Rebecca, would fight demons with an array of relics. I saw him as the great enigma, for he remained the most peculiar of us all. Not only was Stoney a formidable fighter, but also the first educator at Western High School of African descent. His command of languages many times made me question whether he possessed the angelic gift of tongues.

Next to him sat an empty chair for me, then Tuck and Nurse Felisha Cumberland. She was a beautiful woman with perfect skin and a flawless face. People thought she was no older than thirty, but like me, she was over a hundred-years-old. Her special qualities didn't stop there, for she held the gift of healing in her hands.

Felisha, who I called Flower, actually mentored me when I came to her as a teenager and she helped me understand my own unique empowerment. Even to this day, she remains the only person, other than myself, who the angels gifted with extreme longevity. Her complicated lifetime held even more ambiguity than mine.

After removing Gabriel's Sword of Life and Death from its hiding place, I laid the weapon in the center of the decorative inlay, I joined them at the table. Jimmy put the angel feather on the sword's blade.

"Who's this?" Jimmy asked. "Are we recruiting from The Women's Professional Rodeo Association?"

"Team, meet Tuck," I said. "You might have seen her when we raided Hell and set Abaddon's slaves free. She was one, who we rescued."

"Sorry," Jimmy said. "I was kinda busy bustin' demon chops with one hand and climbing Jacob's ladder with the other."

"Needless to say, she is a Champion, and, like the rest of us, has a supernatural gift," I said.

Everyone hesitated. It was Rose who spoke up, "Welcome to the team, Tuck. What is your gifting?"

Tuck said nothing. She simply pulled the police issue, snub-nosed 45 caliber revolver from its holster. The angelic markings on the gunmetal glowed with an eerie blue light.

Everyone in the room got quiet. "It makes a mess of those green monsters," she said.

Rose stammered... "uh, yeah, I bet it does."

I glanced out through the window in my door at Miss Wilson's desk, in hopes she hadn't seen Tuck pull her gun. Thankfully, she was still pouring over her mimeograph machine.

Mr. Dark sent me a telepathic message, *"Don't worry about that. This is Texas. Everybody carries a gun here. She'll fit right in."*

"They don't at school." I whispered back.

Flower looked up and asked, "What did you say?"

"Me? Oh, I said her gun will be a useful tool."

Tuck removed her hat and scratched her head. "Thanks, I think." She eyed the rag-tag group with scrutiny.

"Doc, they look like you ordered them to wear porcupine breaches. You sure they know how to work as a team?"

"Tuck," I replied, "give them time. You'll see, they can be very effective. They rescued you, remember?"

Nothing I said removed the skeptical look from her face.

"What the hell are porcupine breaches?" Roger cynically shook his head. "Just who are you, anyway? I'm guessing you're a danged cowgirl who ropes ghosts at breakfast, hogties demons before dinner, and then rides them sidesaddle after lunch."

Roger's mood hadn't improved in the last forty minutes—neither had his wit. He slapped his hands down on the table. "Enough of the introductions! Arland, you called us here, get to it. What's the freaking big emergency?"

It was my hopes they would respond to Tuck better than they did. She, and that charmed gun, could be a powerful asset to the team. However, Roger's point was well taken. "Right. I'm going to let Nurse Cumberland open this meeting."

Before leaving for the restaurant, I'd filled her in on what the angel said, and thought maybe she would have a better chance than I of pulling the teens together as a team. Motioning to Flower, she stood, hesitated, and gave me a doe eyed look...I can't exactly explain it, but recently I've seen it on her face more, and more often. She stood and tapped on the table to get everyone's attention. "Have any of you ever heard of The Four Horsemen of the Apocalypse?"

They looked at each other in bewilderment...all except Roger. "Yeah. So what? I've read about them in *the Book of Uriel*."

Tuck leaned my direction and asked, "What, in the name of Saint Michael, is the Book of Uriel?"

Roger blurted out the answer, "It's the journal of an angel named Uriel and it contains secret angelic knowledge and magic."

"That and the fact it has a powerful talisman attached to the cover," I added.

"Yeah, speaking of that talisman," Roger said. "I think you still have it. How about returning it to me? If I had it, the angel magic would work twice as well."

"Miracles, Roger. The angels don't call it magic; they call what they do miracles." Flower corrected and leveled her eyes on him. "Okay, Roger. What do you know about The Four Horsemen?"

With a smirk, he said, "Everyone knows about them, right?" He looked from face to face, all expressing the same blankness. "Come on, guys, really? You don't know?"

I sent a harsh gaze in his direction. "If they knew, Flower wouldn't have asked you to explain. Suppose you clue everyone in?"

"Just goes to show how lost you guys would be without me." He stood and took the floor. "All right, where to start? The Four Horsemen of the Apocalypse are wicked Elohim with extra special gifts. There's not much more about them in the Book of Uriel except that they're hugely powerful and supposed to bring a shitload of trouble before the great tribulation and the end of days. They kill like three-fourths of the total population of the planet and cause a devastating war where even more get killed."

Flower walked over to where Roger stood and put a hand on his shoulder. "Thank you, Roger. Yes, those are the ones I'm talking about."

Rebecca waved her hand to catch Roger's attention. "Did you say they kill like seventy-five percent of all the people on the planet?"

With a grimace, Roger nodded his reply.

With everyone talking over everyone else, the room went up in an undecipherable roar.

Flower cleared her throat, this time loudly. She needed everyone's attention before continuing. "As we speak, they are coming to Earth."

Her announcement started a louder uproar than before.

"Get quite...SHUT UP, for heaven's sake!" I yelled. "Listen to what she has to say."

"Thank you, Arland." Pausing, she tapped her fingers on the tabletop to insure her control of the room, "Like I said, they're coming...or they may already be here."

"What? We don't know for sure?" Roger's sarcasm heightened to a new level.

I took over the conversation. "What we do know is that Beelzebub has made Ishtar one of them. Furthermore, she's hell-bent on starting that hideous war Flower is talking about. It's called Armageddon."

"Hold on!" Jimmy spoke up, "Let's say they *have* arrived on Earth. They could be on any continent, island, or in any city." His eyes moved from person to person. "And there are only seven of us. How can we cover that much territory and fight off four of the most powerful and corrupt Elohim ever thrown at us? Even with our gifts, we aren't that powerful."

Flower looked my way, as did everyone else. I stood to my feet to make my point stronger. "The angel was clear about this point. We won't have to find them. They will come to us... or specifically me."

Roger rolled his eyes. "Oh, I see you need my help to pull your butt out of the fire."

"I don't have all the answers." Perhaps it depended on whose perspective Roger *wanted* to look at, but ultimately I had to agree...Roger was right. I certainly couldn't take on all the horsemen alone. "I know that if we put our minds to it, we'll come up with a way to conquer this enemy. We always have and we always will. The angels haven't let us down yet, and they're depending on us to hold back this darkness."

Roger stood. "This is stupid. We're supposed to fight four immortal, magical beings without a plan. We don't even know where they are or if they are even on Earth. All we know is that they have targeted you, and you alone." He made a huffing noise. "Say we find them. What then? Do we even know what to do or how to vanquish them? No."

I stood mute, and no one else answered.

"Exactly! We're clueless." He thudded a fist down on the table. "I'm done. I have a date tonight with Dee Dee, and I'm not missing it for some mystical goose chase that could lead us to Timbuktu." He headed for the door.

Stoney called out, "Roger, sit back down and hear this out. You may change your mind."

With his hand on the doorknob, the redheaded boy I once called my best friend turned to us and flatly said, "I'm quitting. If you don't know what that means, I'll spell it out for you. I'm D-O-N-E, done! Let the angels find another chump to pick on. I want a normal life filled with normal people, and the biggest adventure I have to worry about is when will Dee Dee and I ride *The Runaway Mine Train* rollercoaster at Six Flags Over Texas." With that, he slammed the office door shut behind him.

Stoney spoke first, "Well, that's unfortunate. The team will be far weaker without Roger's gift."

"Ain't he as cheerful as a dead pig in the sunshine?" Tuck chimed in. "Let him go. With that kind of attitude, he'd hobble the whole team."

Rose spoke up, her voice quivering, "Roger can cast angel magic, and he knows all kinds of things about supernatural stuff none of us know. We need him."

"And who's going to interpret any angelic words that we encounter?" Rebecca added. "He came in handy the day we vanquished Abaddon. Remember when we tripped that warning charm on the concrete steps going down to the boiler room? Not to mention that we would have never figured out why Abaddon's lackeys turned the school's boiler into a shrine."

"I don't know." I shook my head, partly in disgust and partly in despair. "We have to face the fact that the Creator's

Favored Angels are still depending on us to stop these mega-demons."

With the conversation focused on evil spirits, a startling knock at my door made the lot of us jump.

CHAPTER SIX

George Johnson

Through the glass, we could see it was George Johnson, the student everyone called *The Arkansas Kid*. Rail thin, almost six-foot-tall, curly black hair, skin the color of chocolate milk, and he always looked like he wore his shorter brother's hand-me-downs; his pant cuffs usually hung two inches above his ankles. Not only was his clothing somewhat ragged, but I had rarely seen him wear a belt. On second thought, maybe he never did.

I motioned for him to enter, and he slowly stepped inside the office, closing the door behind him. In his hand, he held a length of rope about four feet long.

"Principal Bertarelli, I need to talk to you privately," he said.

Stoney hurried over to him and took the rope. "Where did you get this?"

"That's why I need to talk to Principal Bertarelli." He looked over at me and added, "You're going to think I've lost my mind, but I swear I haven't."

For a moment, Stoney stared at *The Kid*, then at the rope before turning to us and saying, "The last time I saw this, it was in the possession of *The Council of Angelic Elders*. This relic is the rope that bound Saint Sebastian when the heretics shot him full of arrows." He examined it more closely. "If this rope is wrapped around a mortal, the person cannot be killed. No matter the severity of their wounds, he will quickly recover."

"Are you sure this is a relic and not simply a piece of ordinary rope?" Flower asked. "One piece of rope looks so much like another you could be mistaken."

"Arland, Miss Flower is right," Tuck said. "I've roped my share of cattle, and I don't think I could pick a charmed rope out of a bunch of lariats if Beelzebub himself was on my tail."

"No...I'm certain," Stoney said. "If you look closely, there are tiny strands of gold fibers woven into the braiding. This is not ordinary—this is a holy relic." Stoney handed it to me. There could be no doubt, scattered throughout the fibers were strands of gold.

I pointed toward Roger's empty chair. "Come, George, sit with us and explain where you got this rather special piece of rope." As the principal, it didn't feel right to address him by his nickname.

After hesitantly sitting, he met my gaze and explained. "Last period, when the bell rang, I went to the school cafeteria for lunch, like I always do. I stepped through the swinging doors and there he was, a giant with six wings spread out on his back. On top of that, I swear he glowed." George laid the rope on the table.

"Believe me when I tell you, I've met this angel before." I assured him. "You're not going crazy."

"Maybe, but this next part is super freaky. Everyone in the room stood still as statues, and I guess I did too because I was scared enough to run but couldn't. When I could move again, he gave me this rope and said to bring it to you. Said you'd know what I'm to do with it." The boy heaved a sigh and stuttered. "He... He told me I was chosen."

Rose leaned his way and gently said, "We believe you, and we each have a similar story of our own."

He gave a half smile as Rose told him about how in the summer of 1969 we came to the Kansas hippy commune called Happy Hollow, and how it was a sanctuary for those who are privileged enough to commune with the angels. She also told him our most closely guarded secret. We were all chosen to champion the favored angels in this ongoing war against the fallen ones.

George passed the rope around the table, letting everyone get a look at his gift. It had made its way over to me, and I sat there inspecting the sparkly gold threads woven into the cordage. After pulling at the fibers and making them fray, I watched as the stranding ends automatically, without human intervention, reformed into a tight coil. It left no doubt in my mind; this was indeed a spirit blessed artifact.

"You're telling me," George said, "that each of you has been chosen to be a champion in a supernatural war? And that everyone of you has some kind of supernatural gift or power to fight these... What do you call them, devils?"

"Yeah, you can call them devils," Jimmy said.

Tuck replied, "Green slime monsters works for me."

Rebecca folded her arms against the table and leaned on them. "Technically, I think they are demons, but the word *devils* fit pretty well, too."

"So, if I'm chosen, then what supernatural power do I have?" George asked. "That giant angel didn't say anything about a power."

"That's the difficult thing about angels. They don't exactly give out operating manuals when they bestow their gifts," Nurse Cumberland said. "We all had to learn about our gifts on our own. It's possible that the rope is your gift, and you don't have another...only time will tell."

"Yeah, it's kinda trial and error," Rose added. "You try something and maybe it'll work, and maybe it won't. It was Mr. B., who helped me work out mine. He figured it out before I did."

Rebecca chimed in, "I don't understand why the angels make it so hard. They could give some kind of hint about the gifts they hand out, but no." She looked over at George, and I could have sworn she blushed. "I remember Arland saying that he was going crazy, not knowing why he heard voices in his head, and mentioning how he saw things that weren't there. It all made him sound like a psycho. Of course, it was his prophetic gift kicking in."

"Wait. I don't get it." George turned to me. "Principal Bertarelli, did Rebecca call you by your first name?"

Still holding the rope, I glanced around the table. It was apparent no one was coming to my rescue. I said. "Yes...yes. Well, we're old friends—she and I."

"That's an understatement, if'n I ever heard one." Tuck chuckled.

Not giving George time to come up with more questions, I stepped over to him. "Slide this rope through your belt loops and tie it off like a belt. The angel gave it to you for a reason."

He nodded and did as I asked. "You think my life may be in danger and that angel knows it?"

"Maybe, I don't know. My gift doesn't let me see everything that's about to happen and even when it shows me the future, most times it only gives me bits and pieces I have to put together myself." I put a hand on his shoulder. "Like I said, I recognize the description of the angel who came to you, and I trust him. His name is Reuwel, and he never does things without a reason." I caught his gaze. "Wear the rope. Never let it leave your person."

The unmistakable look of fear flashed across George's eyes. He answered in silence, nodding while threading the rope through his belt loops.

"You all better get to class, and, George, keep everything we talked about to yourself. Mum's the word." I looked out through the glass pane in the door to see that Miss Wilson, my secretary, had returned to her desk. Deciding not to bother her, I scribbled a note excusing his tardiness. "Here, give this to your teacher." I handed it to him as he walked out the door.

"This one I don't feel good about. Get rid of him." Mr. Dark complained. *"Tuck's got a gun. I get it. That's a weapon we can bank on, but this guy's got a sparkly rope. Tell me you don't think that's a weapon. Nope, throw this one back. We need weapons to fight these horsemen."*

CHAPTER SEVEN

An Unexpected Alliance

After everyone left, Miss Wilson entered my office and said, "Mr. Bertarelli, don't forget you have an appointment later today with the parents of that boy who went missing the night when all those people appeared out of nowhere. Their names are...." She started looking through a stack of papers in her hand.

"Their names are Loveless, Norman and Irene Loveless. Yes, I remember."

"Okay, as long as you remember. Well, I have to go upstairs to Mr. Thompson's class and deliver a schedule to a new student. I'll only be gone a few minutes."

"No worries. I have work to finish before they get here."

She went back to her work, and I closed my door.

What was I supposed to say? We need a plan to save the world from four demented angels hell-bent on destroying the world as we knew it. Or maybe something like, I don't have time for my neurotic dad or my narcissistic mother?

"This is going to be awkward. You, counseling your own mother and father, good thing they have no idea you are that boy who disappeared, their son, their bundle of bouncing joy, the...."

"Stop it, Mr. Dark! You're starting to sound like Roger. When his ginger angst rolls at full steam, his rant can go on and on."

I went to the table, stuffed the feather in my pocket, and picked up Gabriel's Sword. Taking it to my desk, I replaced the feather under the glass where it belonged before opening the top right drawer and staring at the magical crest drawn on plain old cardstock. Holding the weapon, with a firm grip, I stabbed the sword into the card. I say into it because instead of going through the paper, the sword flattened out and became a part of the picture. The crest itself was two swords crossed at the tip of a spire and surrounded by a scrolled filigree design. I watched the weapon slide into the empty space in the picture. There it would stay until a time when I again would reach into the two-dimensional surface and withdraw it.

Gabriel, in his wisdom, placed his angelic sword in this unique hiding place to conceal it, and keep it safe from the Fallen. That was until it was gifted to me. To my knowledge, the blade I held in my hand was the most powerful angelic weapon ever forged, and this crest, no bigger than a five-by-seven photograph, was the perfect hiding place for such a powerful artifact. If a demon were to wield it against us, it would be all but impossible to defeat.

Mr. Dark's call brought me out of my rumination. "*That's right. Put that thing back in its hiding place. You have a glass panel in your door, and all you need is for someone...anyone passing by to see you waving an angel blade around your office.*"

"Shut up. I'll do as I please."

"*Oh really, then why not take out those charmed knives blessed by the Leper King of Jerusalem...and the Talisman of Uriel. You could wear it around your neck on a chain. I know. Better still, you could strut around your office waving that long tent spike Lady Jael used to nail the warlord's head to the ground. That would be fun.*" There was no denying it; sarcasm oozed from his every statement. *"Why hide your relics if you're going to play with them like they're toys?"*

"Don't be so absurd. Oh, wait." I paused. "I see. That's your excuse for sarcasm. Well, it failed."

"**Do you usually talk to yourself when you're alone**?" A man's voice, baritone, and smooth as silk, came from the doorway.

Caught unaware, I jumped with a start. My door stood partially open and a gentleman wearing what looked to be a black Victorian style vest and long-coat stared at me through the glass insert. He pushed the door open and stepped inside. Thin silver chains decorated his bowler and golden angel wing charms were tucked in his hatband. Despite being indoors, he hid his eyes behind dark, round sunglasses.

Glancing out through the open door to Miss Wilson's desk, she was nowhere in sight. "I'm sorry. Today is an extremely busy day. Please go back out to Miss Wilson's desk and wait for her to return. She will make you an appointment."

"Your efficient secretary has been called away so that you and I can have a private conversation." He paused, taking off his sunglasses, and our eyes met. **"Don't despair, dear boy; she's fine. I only arranged her timely absence, not her demise."**

Casually, he withdrew a lace-trimmed handkerchief from his sleeve and wiped the seat of one ebony chair before sitting. I expected him to tuck it away in the same manner, but instead, the handkerchief vanished from his fingertips.

My first thought was that he might be a magician who wanted to perform at an assembly. Wearing that costume, he certainly fit the part of an entertainer. This was probably his way of weaseling in for an interview. He crossed his legs and leaned back. A pleasant, disarming expression graced his face.

Oddly, the room was getting somewhat warmer than usual. I'm sure he could see the confusion on my face. "Sir, I have no idea what you're talking about? Who are you?"

"Really, Prophet?" he laughed. **"Use your gift and see."**

If he knew I was a prophet, then this was no street magician. I held my hand out toward him and closed my eyes. My mind pulled away the disguise, and an image slowly came into focus. In reality, he was the most beautiful angel I'd ever seen. His chest was sculpted from a single translucent gemstone, every muscle faceted, reflecting a myriad of kaleidoscopic colors, and all glimmering like diamonds. His arms and legs shined as bright as polished platinum, and the feathers in his wings were crimson tipped with gold.

In my vision, he wore a linen toga with one arm exposed. It belted at the waist with golden bands and draped gracefully across his lap. At the neck, the fabric gathered in a ring over his left shoulder, and hung down his back. His white, satiny hair flowed down over his shoulders. Amidst his splendor, the most startling feature was his eyes. They glowed like emerald gemstones set above a blazing fire. Despite his radiance, he couldn't hide the overshadowing darkness my prophet's vision identified.

With a startled expression, my hand lowered to my side, and I stepped back from my desk. When my vision faded, again he appeared to be a man, but doubtless, he was one of the Fallen masquerading in human form. I had to stay alert, eyes open, and on my guard.

"*Oh, shit.*" Mr. Dark's voice roared in my mind. "*He's one of them. Cast him back to Hell before he has a chance to harm us. Do it now.*"

Conflicted, I tried to think while silently replying to his demands. "My gifts don't work too well on the angels, or have you forgotten? Now shut up and leave me alone."

This odd member of the Fallen tipped his hat, and said, **"You may call me Iggy, short for Iggarest."** He gave me a smile littered with sharp little teeth. **"I'm not one who stands on the ridiculous pomp and pageantry other angels do. I suppose it's because I've lived among mortals for so long. They are my prize, you know, my minions."**

"Really! Iggy? I'm not calling you Iggy. I may call on the stone and brick of this building to vanquish you." My declaration didn't faze him. More confused me than his words. I couldn't imagine why a Fallen would be approaching me without leading a horde of demons in its wake, but since he made no threatening move, I listened.

"Dear boy, relax...sit and hear my tale. We have much in common, you and I. One might even say our interests are aligned like the stars on midsummer's eve." A sparkling, verdant glint escaped from behind his glasses. **"We are allies."**

"I don't need help from a Fallen. That would be ridiculous and reckless."

Nonchalantly examining his fingernails, he turned his hands one way and the other. "Prophet, I think you have a visitor."

Turning on my heels, I faced the door. Right outside the threshold stood a man who, to my knowledge, I never met before. Then my prophet's vision took over and I could see what no one else could. This was a poor husk of a man inhabited by a grizzly three eyed demon. The cadaverous human skin, stitched in place to contain the imp hidden inside, hung off its slimy green frame. It spoke in a jaded harmonic voice, "Marked Prophet, you must die." The horror lumbered toward me.

I lifted my hand to vanquish the demon when Iggarest spoke up. **"Oh, allow me. No sense having a supernatural showdown right here in the school."** He waved his hand toward the abomination and it exploded, blowing demon guts all over the walls of my office. **"That was messier than I anticipated. Here, let me clean this up for you."** He waved his hand again, and the walls were spotless.

"I don't remember asking for your help." With caution I opened the right hand draw on my desk where I kept my most powerful relics.

Iggarest continued, **"I told you I was on your side."** He paused and exhaled a pretentious, audible sigh. **"I agree. You have no reason to trust me other than I saved you an hour's work and a lot of explaining to your staff and that nice Miss Wilson. Trust me; we are on the same side."**

My hand stopped inches from the card, and I gave my guest a quizzical stare.

"Let me explain. I was once an archangel, Same as Michael, Raphael, and Gabriel, but when I sided with that majestic worm named Lucifer, I was cast out of heaven with him. And there lies the problem. Only one can be the supreme dark lord of the angels, and to my chagrin, Lucifer got *The Crown of Power* and ascended to that throne."

He flipped the ebony chair around, resting his forearms across the top of its backrest, and straddling the seat. **"As for me, well, Lucifer's jealousy is legendary... Indeed, his is almost as severe as that of your so-called friend suffering from *Solomon's curse*."**

Since I had no idea what Solomon's curse was, I let his remark pass. After pausing, he continued, not skipping a beat. **"Anyway, I digress. After I helped Lucifer, he took the crown and gave me the scraps of power no other angel wanted. I stood by and watched as less deserving of the**

Fallen were granted greatness—especially the unholy five who he favors most. They were given armies of demons to rule over. I was given mere humans. Not all humans, mind you, but a select few who languish in the unforgivable—the seven deadly sins, and the abominable who have risked committing the unatonable heresy. Dare I say it...I rule over the foolish and the stupid. Yes, they are my minions."

I pulled my chair around and eased into it, so I could keep an eye on this unlikely ally. "I fail to see how that makes us allies," I said.

He tilted his head and raised an index finger. **"Ishtar and I are at odds. She wants to annihilate mortals like vermin. Our kind doesn't call her Queen of the Dead for nothing. Alas, recent changes in the hierarchy of power disturbs me...it disturbs me greatly! Morning Star, our simpleton of an archangel, has promoted Ishtar and changed her name to Dominikus. He anointed her with... Well, you wouldn't understand the mechanics of it all, anyway. Let's just call it mega-magic."**

"You're wasting your breath. I know this already—my prophetic gift revealed this much to me." His condescending attitude galled me. However, I didn't think I'd ever heard the term *mega-magic* before.

"Comme ci comme ça. **The point is, if she succeeds, there will be no more humans for me to rule over. My kingdom will literally be...eradicated. If I am to retain power, I have no choice but to side with my enemy's enemy."**

"I still don't see how you can be any help to our cause. Your agenda is still to enslave people in the darkest of sins." I looked in my top left desk drawer and sorted through the relics I'd collected over the last century. First, I grabbed *Deborah's Dart*, the long, sharp tent peg Jael used to save the nation of Israel; but my hand brushed against one of the daggers blessed by The Leper King of Jerusalem. This weapon could sever immortal sinew from immortal bone. I took the dagger out and laid it on my desk. "'Frankly, methinks thy tongue out venoms all the worms of the Nile.'"

Iggarest's right eyebrow raised an inch as he eyed the dagger, and yet the timbre of his voice didn't change. **"Ah, Shakespeare, quite a striking fellow. The things I could blather on about that scallion. If we had time, the tales would go on for hours. But then there was Dear Ann, his wife. To quote the old bard himself... 'She had very little about her face that was worth sunburning. Methinks she had more hair than wit, but sadly more faults than wealth.' Or was it hairs? I can never remember."**

I picked up the dagger and waved the blade at him. "Get said what you came to say and get out."

"No need to go all militant on me. I'm here to offer my help." His expression took on the air of boredom. **"You would have no way of knowing, but I am, after all, still an angel of imperial rank, and I hear things. My proposal of... What shall we call it? A treaty? Yes, let's call it a treaty."**

"Hold it right there. If I hear you right, you want me to keep your tiny kingdom from falling apart. A treaty goes both ways. What do I...I mean, we Champions, get in this deal?"

"For my part, I can share information in hopes that I foul Ishtar's plan and put things back the way they were. If

I'm successful, then you keep fighting on the side of the Favored; Lucifer continues his conflict with Father; and I get all the unforgivable and vengeful souls."

His insidious smile grew wider. He must have been weaving an enchantment of some sort, because his words felt more persuasive. **"It's a win-win for everyone except Ishtar, the archangel's pitiful excuse for a lieutenant. The problem is, I fear that this time, the Queen of the Dead's plan may succeed. Never before has he let her send the remaining *Favored Four* into the world to annihilate mortals. This time she has the power to challenge the Master's Champions in out-and-out combat. And by the way, she really doesn't like you, old bean."**

"I don't know. For now, I'll have to think about your offer. You'll have to forgive me if I can't find it in my heart to trust a Fallen."

"And so you shouldn't, dear boy." He stood and walked to the door. **"Don't trust me and especially that red-headed friend of yours. No, he is one you definitely don't want to trust."** Looking at me from over his shoulder, the angel hesitated. **"Ponder my offer. If I were you, I would trust only in my own strength, and from what I hear, you are quite formidable. I hope you don't mind my asking, but how did you manage to obliterate one of lucky Lucifer's favorites?"**

Refusing to answer, I simply pulled Gabriel's sword out from its hiding place in my desk drawer.

"Oh, I see. You have Gabriel's pretty pointy. Last time I saw that, I was at the receiving end of Gabriel's wrath. If I

were you, I would keep it tucked away in that drawer. You won't be needing it while I'm around. Still, in this game of who's got the power...the stakes are high, and as commander of Hell's favorites, Ishtar just doubled down with four aces. However, I confess, with pretty pointy there, you might actually have a chance of stopping one or two of the four. Sadly, with all your supernatural skills and that sword, confronting them all at once would be disastrous." With both hands atop his fancy cane, he leaned toward me and lowered his voice. **"You need me, Brother Bertarelli."** With that, he stepped through the doorway and vanished from sight.

Not knowing exactly what to do, I stood there, stunned, holding Gabriel's sword and deliberating over my choices. Nothing I experienced in the past century prepared me for my encounter with Iggarest.

Ms. Wilson entered the school office, so I quickly hid both the charmed dagger and the sword behind my back. She must have finished her errands and returned. In general, secretaries know more than they let on and I'm sure by this time she knew I kept a sword in my office. Either that or she was completely blind. Even so, I would rather not allow her to see me standing comatose at my desk, holding two lethal weapons. No telling what conclusion she might jump to.

I could see her through the glass pane; she gave me a demure wave before gathering a stack of mimeographed papers and taking them to her desk. I sighed and said a prayer, hoping she would remain oblivious to what evil I and my teenaged team of demon fighters were about to face.

"Mr. Dark, old boy, are you there?" I cleared my throat before continuing, "Remind me to get a similar-looking sword and mount it over the door for decoration."

"*Oh, you're right! One sword isn't enough. That Fallen might come back and you could defend us with a sword in each hand. I have a better idea. Let's plaster them all over the walls. That way, you will have one close whenever you need it.*"

"Seriously, if someone were to get a glance at me holding Gabriel's Sword of Life and Death...well, I think having a dummy hanging on a plaque would explain where I might have gotten it. And they would be none the wiser, because having a dull one would alleviate the danger quotient."

"*I get it. What you're saying, minus all those big words, is you want a decoy? So, if anyone accused you of having a dangerous weapon in school, you're off the hook.*"

"Precisely!"

"*My idea is better.*" Mr. Dark paused for a moment. *"Knock, knock, any rational person at home in here? This is a Fallen we're talking about. Better to not take chances. Can you put up some kind of magical defense thing around your office? Better yet, let's take a sabbatical and get as far away from here as possible. The Fallen don't make it a habit of popping in for tea and crumpets. These guys don't play around...they kill people."*

"I don't cast angel magic. That's Roger's wheelhouse. As a prophet, I only command animals and the elements: wind, fire, and earth."

"*Boy, we sure could use that redheaded loudmouth right now. Maybe, if you get on your knees and beg him to come back to the team, he would? I think that's a great idea, don't you?*"

"There's one point you have right."

"*Oh, which one? Getting the hell out of here, and hiding on an island in the blue Pacific Ocean, far away from horse riding, Hell-spawned, homicidal mega-demons? Or begging Roger to come back to the team?*"

"You're right about the Fallen not playing around. If one of them is serious enough to betray his Archangel, then the danger is greater than any of us realized. I need a plan of action before we get caught off guard."

CHAPTER EIGHT

The Emissary of Evil

After shoving Gabriel's sword back into the magical crest where it hid, I grabbed up the picture and tucked it away in the left inside pocket of my tweed sports jacket. Iggarest saw which drawer I kept it in, but he didn't know about the magical crest. It's possible that he wouldn't realize the sword in the picture was the real thing, but why take the chance? Anyway, I felt sure he would return to my office looking for it in my absence. This way was safer.

For the time being, I stashed the charmed dagger back into the drawer. It would be out of sight—at least for the present. I needed to talk to someone about Iggarest's intervention, and with Roger on the warpath, it limited my choices.

Darting out of my door and past my secretary's desk, I headed across the hall to Nurse Cumberland's office. Miss

Wilson called out after me, “Mr. Bertarelli, don’t forget about your five o’clock appointment.”

“Thank you, Miss Wilson.” Behind me, the door closed on my words.

I burst into Flower’s office to find her counseling with Sarah Hampton. Surprised to see a student, I reconsidered the purpose of my immediate visit. After spending a century in the outer ring of Hell, Sarah had been through enough. As far as what the rank and file of normal people knew, she had only been missing for a day or so. I knew better.

Hell was not a pleasant place. In fact, it was downright repulsive. Thankfully, she remembered little of what happened there, but I didn’t want to be the one to trigger her memories. The last thing she needed to hear about was a fallen angel visiting the high school. And worse, she might let it slip to her posse, Dee Dee and Dina. Most students were ignorant of this supernatural war; a conflict into which Flower and I were drafted, and Sarah was accidentally thrown into.

“Pa...Pardon the interruption, Nurse Cumberland.” I stammered. “If...If this is a bad time, I can—”

“No, it’s all right...” it was Sarah’s turn to stammer, “...Mr. Bertarelli...I mean...Arland...uh, Mr. Bertarelli. I don’t know what to call you anymore. It seems like only yesterday when... I mean, you were a year younger than me,” Sarah said as she took a cigarette out of her purse. She lit it, looked over at me, then threw it on the floor and stepped on. “Okay, I put it out. Can’t seem to kick the habit, you know. I guess I’m a bit nervous.”

I could have made a big deal of it, but instead I ignored the smoking faux pas and addressed her question. "Jimmy calls me Mr. B. However, Roger insists on calling me Principal Bertarelli, but you don't have to. Please, don't make it harder than it was before you knew my true identity. If Mr. Bertarelli feels right, then that will do."

"I was talking to Nurse Cumberland here about my experiences in... You know where."

Hand on the doorknob and one foot out into the hall, I replied, "Oh, well, I shouldn't interrupt, then."

Flower gave me a raised eyebrow, and said, "Arland, stay. Not only has Sarah been telling me about the adventure you two had in the distant past, but she has come to me with some interesting information to share." Nurse Cumberland held up a super realistic drawing of a vicious demon astride a fiery-maned horse. Ironically, the exact one I saw in my vision. "Sarah drew this in Miss Willard's art class. I thought you should take a look at it."

I took the drawing in my hand, and the room spun under my feet. The colors dizzily swirled together. I staggered sideways. Both Sarah and Flower helped me to sit in one of the vinyl chairs lining the walls of her office. In midair before me, the fire laden, blazing-red horse appeared. This time, it looked like it was burning without being consumed. The hell-horse reared up and raked its hooves across the top of the cavern where it stood. Seeing the beast standing before me was more frightening than witnessing it in my Prophet's Vision, for the sockets that should have held its eyes were lacking the colorful brown irises and black pupils. Its eyelid slid over a solid orb radiating with the afterglow of what looked like an atomic explosion. Even from the distance I stood, the beast's breath huffed out with a gust of scorching heat. Smoke billowed from its nostrils, filling the air with the foul stench of brimstone.

A woman's voice, shrill and hollow, reverberated within the surrounding walls. **"Prophet, your spying will do you no good. I see you and I know your weakness. Fear me, for I'm coming; first for you and then for all humanity."**

My surroundings were becoming more real. The air grew thick. I choked on the morbid, cankerous odor of rotting flesh. The acrid smell of brimstone turned my stomach, and, for a moment, I thought I was actually in Hell with this demon rider. I dropped the drawing and gagged; clutched at my throat and gasped for air. As suddenly as it had appeared, it vanished. The pleasant fragrance of Flower's lavender candle replaced the stench of rotting flesh and refrigerated air replaced the searing heat.

"Are you okay? What happened?" Sarah asked.

"Your drawing triggered his prophetic gift." Flower blotted my forehead with a tissue, wiping away the beads of sweat. "Arland, what did you see?"

"The principality on the red horse, Gewalt, I saw her. She spoke to me. I think... No, I'm sure I actually saw inside the realm of Hell where she rides from. She told me to stop spying on her."

Sarah blurted out, "You saw into Hell? You actually saw past the realm of Purgatory into the inner kingdom?" Urgency flooded her question.

"I...I think so. It's hard to know when it's a vision—if that was a vision. It sure was real. Anyway, the rider spoke to me like we could see each other." I sucked in more fresh air. "Yes, definitely...she could see me and I could see her."

"Her?" Flower asked. "The rider of the red horse is a woman?"

I rubbed my head. It ached after my traumatic experience. "Did I not mention that part? I guess I didn't." Sometimes it's best to not tell everything the angels tell me. It can get pretty depressing, but in this case, there was no option. "All but one of the horsemen are women, or were women when they were mortal." The room stopped moving around, and my vision returned to normal. "You've heard of this demon before, only in another form. The rider called War is the new and improved Witch of Endor. She was the daughter of a priest until she became the mistress of Satan."

"Oh! Hell no!" Sarah exclaimed. "You guys barely vanquished Jezebel. That hussy nearly killed you all. How are you supposed to fight a supercharged, demon-loving sorceress, riding a hell-beast?"

"The angels will help us," Flower replied. "They may not do it personally, but they always make a way."

"*Not true,*" Mr. Dark's thoughts rang out loud and clear in my mind. *"Arland, our last encounter with Abaddon was painful and unfortunate. It's a good thing she can't remember what happened to her. She would have to be put in an asylum."*

Directing my silent thoughts back at him, I replied, "For once, we agree. It's a blessing she can't remember." I gave Flower a quizzical glance, and said, "Maybe having a window into Ishtar's headquarters will pay off." I brazenly met Sarah's eyes. "How did you come to draw this picture?"

"I don't know," Sarah explained. "There I was in old lady Willard's...I mean, Miss Willard's art class. She told us to draw anything we wanted to and so I started a charcoal sketch. It kind of grew from one corner, across the page, to the other side...like I had no control over what I did. When Miss Willard saw my drawing, she went off, saying how masterful my technique is, and right in front of everyone, declared me to be some kind of self-taught genius. But, Arland, this was something else—it's like I didn't draw this."

Flower interjected, "*Psychography*."

"Psyo-what?" I asked.

"It could be Psychography. It's also called *automatic writing*. I guess in this case it would be *automatic drawing.*" From the way she talked, Flower sounded like an expert. As for me, I felt like a lost lamb.

"What? That leaves me as clueless as I was before," I admitted. "I don't know what you're talking about."

"Have you ever heard of people writing, but the words come out of their subconscious? ...Or maybe, they come from someplace else?"

Baffled, Sarah and I shook our heads. I finally said, "If I'm hearing you right...it's possible for people to draw images from across the veil of death."

Flower continued, "Yes, in this case it is drawing, not writing, but the principle is the same."

"Wait a minute," Sarah demanded. "No dead person showed me anything. I drew it from my imagination."

"Right...and you have always drawn like Leonardo da Vinci," I said.

"No need to get sarcastic. I get your point." Sarah picked up the picture again and said, "It is good, isn't it?"

Flower remarked, "Good? Sarah, it's amazing!" She paused. "I wonder which of the angels worked through your hands to create it?"

"That we may never know," I said.

A familiar and captivating voice called out from the doorway. "**Oh yes, you will. My dear boy, it's not that hard to figure out.**" He gazed down at Sarah. "***Ooh La La*, Oh my. *c'est beau, Regarde comme c'est beau!* My dear, you are lovely.**"

He being an angel, I would have expected his French accent to be excellent. But, no...it sounded similar to a southern gentleman trying to impress with a half-baked Parisian pronunciation. The only thing worse was his leering at Sarah, like she was a pastry on a plate.

"Iggarest, put your tongue back in your mouth. You're going to get devil drool on the floor. Now, explain. Are you saying you drew this?" I asked.

"For your information, a gentleman never drools. And as for me drawing this picture... Oh no, I gave this exquisite young thing the ability to draw it. She simply used her new gift, and viola, there it was."

"You gave Sarah an ability?" Flower looked up at me, perplexed. "Who is this? If he's an angel, he lacks the noble and radiant air Reuwel has."

"Iggarest claims to be a fallen angel with a grievance against his dark lord, Morning Star. He wants to help us fight The Four Horsemen."

Flower didn't flinch at the words fallen angel. She'd certainly met her share over the years, one of which had fallen in love with her. But Sarah started gasping and pushing away in terror.

Flower grabbed her hand, and using her gift of healing, calmed her down.

"One of the Fallen gave this ability to me?" She started rubbing her hands and arms as if she could erase the gift. "I don't want it. Take it away!"

"**Dear child, a supernatural gift cannot be returned like a pair of socks. Once given, it is yours—forever. It's an angelic rule.**"

"Iggarest, somehow I get the impression you don't care much for rules." I patted my pocket where I stashed Gabriel's sword.

"**Oh, that's what you did with Gabriel's pretty pointy. I took the liberty of looking in your desk drawer for it, but alas, it wasn't there.**"

"See! I knew it!" Mr. Dark spit the words out into my brain.

Ignoring my dark side, I reached into my pocket to draw the sword from its hiding place.

"**No need for dramatics, dear boy. It will do no good at all, for I haven't lied. I can't take back the gift. It's hers for as long as she lives.**" He flipped his fingers outward directly in Sarah's face. "**See, nothing happened. I dare say she will make a fortune as this century's greatest artist, though.**"

Sarah gasped and almost passed out. "Don't touch me or else Arland will send you to Hell, where you belong!" she bellowed.

"**That, too, is impossible. I know all about the power of the marked prophet. He has great prowess over demons, but angels; that's a different thing altogether. Everyone will be fine as long as he keeps Gabriel's pretty pointy in his pocket.**"

Sarah took some deep breaths and asked, "What good is this gift? I may be able to draw both hellish angels and demons, but I don't see how that helps us defeat The Four Horsemen."

"**Oh dear, and I thought you all were working as a team. Pardon my silly assumption.**" His words dripped with sarcasm. "**Didn't you see how your drawing affected your prophet? In his hands, it became a window to the nether world. Your gift is integrated with that of Arland Bertarelli. Together, you are more than either of you are alone.**"

"No, you don't," I declared. "Sarah has nothing to do with this war. She is an innocent."

"**Principal Bertarelli, she is not a little girl, she is a woman of eighteen.**" He turned to Sarah. "**Happy birthday, young lady; I do believe this is your birthday, is it not?**"

Sarah blinked and glanced over at me, blushing. "Yes, it is. But that has nothing to do with this. I don't want a gift that was created in Hell by a fallen angel."

"**What's done is done. Consider it a birthday present.**" He gave us all a wicked grin and vanished, leaving behind the faint scent of brimstone.

Sarah wept, and Flower grabbed her hand. Instantaneously, Sarah calmed down. I knew without a doubt Flower must be healing her emotions and giving her a healthy dose of hope. Something she had done for me on more than one occasion.

"I best leave you ladies to... Well, at any rate, I'll be in my office if you need me." With that, I exited. Before I got across the hall, I ran into Dee Dee and Dina.

"Mr. Bertarelli, have you seen Sarah Hampton?" Dina asked. "She missed cheerleading practice, and normally, after school, she waits for us by the soda machine outside the cafeteria door. But she didn't meet us today. I'm...I mean, we're worried."

"She's in the nurse's office." I blurted the words out before I thought.

"I knew she was sick." An alarm sounded in Dee Dee's voice. "The only time she's ever skipped out on cheerleading practice was when she was abducted by those aliens."

I stopped in my tracks and turned on my heels. "What aliens?"

Dina popped her friend on the shoulder with her geography book. "Dee Dee, Sarah told us not to say anything about that."

I gave them my most stern, authoritative look. "Girls, what aliens? What did Sarah tell you?"

With a sheepish expression, Dee Dee confessed, "Sarah told us that she and all those people that appeared out of nowhere last year… Well, they all had really been abducted by aliens. She said they were slimy and green, with tentacles instead of arms."

I suppose Sarah had to tell her posse something, to explain where she'd been when she went missing, and that was as good a cover story as any. "Oh, is that right?" Not exactly sure how to respond to their tale; I must have chewed my words. When I finally coughed them up again, I pointed to Flower's office. "Okay then. Well, like I said, Sarah is in with Nurse Cumberland."

The girls giggled at my reaction and trotted off, miniskirts bouncing, into the nurse's office.

Shaking my head, I made my way to my own office. Mr. Dark skittered out from under a filing cabinet, and like two joining blobs of ink, he attached himself to my shadow.

"*Let me get this right. Sarah was abducted by aliens, and one of the fallen has gifted her with a supernatural power. Does that make her one of the Champions or something else—something sinister?*"

"I don't know, old friend. I don't know."

CHAPTER NINE

Old Regrets

"If you don't know, who does? You're the prophet, remember. You're supposed to know things before they happen." Mr. Dark made it a habit to berate me every time he found an opportunity. Usually, his manner was stern and cynical. This was no exception.

"Clearly, it doesn't work like that all the time," I replied. "If you can make sense of these flashes I'm getting, then be my guest and help me."

"Oh, no. this is far worse than I thought. If you're asking me for help, then we are in some real deep shit. Do you seriously think one of the Fallen simply dropped in to say hello to Sarah Hampton? It's not likely he strutted over to her and out of the goodness of his heart said hi there little girl, want a birthday gift? No, you don't, and I don't either!"

"Cut it out! Stop mocking her! She didn't ask to get mixed up in any of this."

"Oh, you're quick to put me in my place, but not Iggarest. Like an idiot, you stood there making nice with the enemy. What were you thinking? You know, this can't turn out well. Cash in your early retirement from this job and let's go somewhere tropical, where there are no fallen angels dropping by just to say hi."

On my desk, the interoffice intercom buzzed. I pressed the flashing light before speaking. "Yes, Miss Wilson?"

"Norman and Irene Loveless are here to see you, sir. Should I show them in?"

"Mr. Bertarelli, please see us." Irene Loveless spoke loud enough for me to hear her without an intercom.

Miss Wilson added, "These are the parents I told you about. Their son was...um, is Arland Loveless. You remember him? He's one of the missing boys. He and Christopher Ross are the only students the police still can't find."

Her words brought back the memory of little Christopher being devoured by a demon in the midst of Hell—another soul I failed to save. Despite my feelings, I had to shake off the despair and play the part of the school principal. "Yes, Ms. Wilson. Please show them in," I said.

Norman and Irene came into my office, and I found myself face to face with my own parents. I was that boy who disappeared by an act of angel magic. Of course, they knew nothing of those happenings and they would never recognize me because I appeared to be a middle-aged man. Even if I tried to explain how could they understand their son went from being a teenager to an adult, in what to them was overnight?

My words caught in my throat as I spoke, "Mr. and Mrs. Loveless, please, come in and find a seat." They went straight for the antique ebony-black chairs.

Mr. Dark's voice rang through my head. "*I'm back. Went down the hall to... Well, the girl's locker room is down that way and I...*" His voice went up an octave. "Oh... Oh, no... *Oh, shit! It's Mom and Dad. I forgot they were coming. Get rid of them. Pretend you're the janitor.*"

He skittered into the shadow under my desk as I plopped down on my office chair. This time, the captivating smell of the leather did nothing to calm my nerves.

Norman Loveless began talking in a slow and deliberate voice. "Mr. Bertarelli, our son, Arland, disappeared the day all those strange people came to Western. It seemed they came from out of nowhere—so many of them they filled the streets, alleyways, and every yard in town." His demeanor was shaky, his hands trembled. "We were wondering.... Would it be possible...?" He looked over at my mother and then back at me. It sounded as if he were chewing his words—unsure of what to say. "I mean, we heard you helped the officials to relocate them and we were wondering— "

Irene Loveless interrupted, "Norman, stop beating around the bush." She gave him a dismissive wave and addressed me. "What my husband is trying to say is, we think one of those weirdo, boxcar riding street jockeys, may have abducted him." As harsh as her words were, there was a pain in her eyes I never dreamt would be there; not from the woman who said she wished I'd never been born.

My first inclination was to try to make her understand that those lost souls were not hobos, but when Norman bit his trembling lower lip and a tear rolled down his cheek, my words refused to make their way out of my mouth, my palms started sweating, and my heart skipped a beat.

He gave his wife an arguable glance before saying, "Irene, I can speak for myself." He paused. "Mr. Bertarelli, we've talked to his friends, but they were no help. Not knowing what else to do, we turned it over to the police, and as of yet, they haven't been able to find him. We've exhausted every channel... We're desperate for any help." He paused before running his hand through his hair, a habit I seemed to have inherited. "Mr. Bertarelli, Arland was in your class. You knew him. Did you see him, at any time, when you were working with those strange homeless people? It's possible one of them... Well, might be some kind of...of freaky degenerate and has kidnapped him."

My mom broke down and wept. I pulled a couple of tissues from the Kleenex box I kept on my desk and handed them to her. "That's what happened! Don't ask me how I know... but I know it. Some pervert has taken our boy, and he's lying in some gutter—dead by now!"

I felt my vocal cords tighten up and my eyes watered. I pulled a tissue for myself.

"Oh no, not you too." Mr. Dark sounded more frightened than aggravated. *"Buck up and say the right words—deal with this! Man, if it's going to turn into a mushy pity party, I'm leaving."*

I forced my silent words back at him. "That's right. Run when the going gets rough. Do me a favor, shut up and go take a short hike off a tall cliff." What Norman and Irene heard me say was, "Mr. and Mrs. Loveless. Arland has run away before. If I remember correctly, he ran away last summer a year ago, and if I'm not mistaken, you found him in Kansas."

"On second thought, I better stay and keep you on track. There's no telling what you might confess." Mr. Dark's chatter clouded my mind.

Sorting my thoughts, I tented my fingers in a controlling pose. "It's possible he simply ran away from home again. Arland is a clever and resourceful young man, and I think it's far more likely he doesn't want to be found."

It was my turn to clear my throat. I casually ran my fingers through my dishwater blond hair. "Is there any reason he would want to run away from home...again? You don't fight or argue much, do you?" It was a question to which I knew the answer all too well, but I let my eyebrow quizzically rise a bit.

Norman looked over at his wife and gave her a grimaced smile. "Every couple fights now and then." He dropped his head. "Maybe not as much as we do."

Irene sobbed. "You were right, Norman. He left because of my complaining." She held her hand out for more tissue. I took the hint and put several more between her outstretched fingers. "I might have fussed a little, but there's nothing wrong with wanting him to be the best person he can be. That's why I stayed on his case so much. It seemed he slacked off on purpose. It was like he always wanted to make me angry. Things would have been different if he hadn't made me yell."

"So, from what you're telling me, you think all the fighting in your home is Arland's fault." By all rights, I should have been furious with her for blaming me for all their problems, but I wasn't. The only emotion I could muster was pity.

Despite her failings and her struggle to evade my question, a bigger truth remained. She was a mother who lost her son and my heart went out to her. My emotions had to stay in check. One slip and I would find myself making an irreversible mistake. It didn't matter how much I wanted to make her understand that her son sat right there before her—I wasn't that boy anymore. Sadly, I could never go back to that point in my life.

Hearing Irene use me as a scapegoat while grieving over my disappearance touched a raw place I thought was healed. My tears dried up, and I pressed my lips in anger. This was nothing more than another opportunity for her to take complaining to a new level. She was using me for one last narcissistic meltdown.

Time had reframed my view of childhood with a softer, kinder version, but the memory of every morning waking up to my parents yelling at each other overcame whatever empathy I felt.

Mother's screeching screams about Norman's failings and my uselessness was burned deep into my consciousness. So deep that no matter how she blubbered and tried to shift blame onto me, and regardless of her present regret, I believed her remorse was oddly deserved. The mere echoes of her past shrieking in my face; screaming irrational accusations at me; and cursing the day I was born still blistered my ears. With this realization, my attitude changed.

"*She treated you like shit,*" Mr. Dark said. "*Don't even think of forgiving them for turning every morning into a living hell. Tell them their son is dead and get them out of here!*"

My parents couldn't hear me when I turned my silent thoughts to my dark friend, so with closed lips I focused on the part of my mind his voice came from. "Mr. Dark, forgiveness is a virtue you need to acquire. By holding a grudge, I'm the one it will harm. You realize what she is talking about now, for us, happened over a century ago. I'm afraid it's too late to help Mom. She has forged her bed in iron, and sadly, no matter how cold, hard, and unyielding, it's hers to lie on."

"That's a bunch of psychological mumbo jumbo. I've enjoyed seeing her cry a bucket of tears. Give her another tissue and send her home."

I ignored his blustering, and said, "Mrs. Loveless, I sense there is a lot you haven't come to terms with about why Arland would want to run away. And I can't promise he will ever return, but in his absence I suggest you start doing what you can to make things better in case he were to come home." I gave her a sincere smile and said, "If I know anything about Arland, I would say he has forgiven you for the things you are still holding against yourself."

"Oh, Principal Bertarelli, you must've misunderstood. I'm not the reason Arland disappeared. Someone has kidnapped him. I just know it."

I shook my head in disbelief. "Oh, I see." She was never going to admit to her guilt.

"That's right, play right into her pity, pity me game. That cow said things to us that no mother should say to her son. This is a once in a lifetime opportunity you're letting slip through your fingers." Mr. Dark had a point and I suppose he was due to his opinion, but it wasn't mine.

My silent thoughts made my point clear. "Mr. Dark, even if they don't deserve it, I'm forgiving them to clear my own conscious. If they can't find it in their heart to forgive me for disappearing and themselves for the abuse, they dumped on me. I can't do anything about that."

"I kind of feel sorry for Dad. Truth be told, he wasn't so bad. At least, he never yelled like a wounded harpy. He got dumped on almost as bad as you and I did."

I doubt she knew why I was nodding, but Irene met my eyes and said, "Do you really think he ran away? And he will come home?" The look on her face made me think that might not be the happy ending she wanted.

"Honestly, I can't promise he will. Of course, how would I know? But from what you two have told me, no doubt, he had reasons to leave. I must confess, I've stayed abreast of this case and was aware you called in law enforcement. What you may not realize is that according to state law, he is no longer listed as a runaway."

Irene's face went pale. "They gave up on finding him?" For a moment, I thought she was going to go into another crying meltdown.

"If those records were correct, then as of this past September, he turned seventeen. At seventeen, he is no longer considered a runaway. Do what you can to make things better while he is gone. There is always hope he will return...someday." Her face contorted. I thought it might be from grief...but more likely, it was horror. She looked terrified just thinking that I actually might return.

"*Arland, I apologize for thinking you're a marshmallow, a wimp! You hit the jackpot. That expression on her face is worth a whole bucket of tears.*"

I stood and held out my hand to help Mrs. Loveless to her feet. "I promise, if I hear anything about Arland, I'll let you know."

"*Liar! You said you wouldn't lie anymore.*"

I gave her hand a pat before letting it drop. "Irene, what I want is for you to find a way to move on with your life, whether your son returns or not."

Hearing the focus of the conversation return to her, an uncommon smile graced her face. "I don't know what there is about it, but talking to you has made me feel so much better. If I get depressed and want to talk about my feelings, may I make an appointment with Miss Wilson to counsel with you again?"

I walked them to the office door. "That will be fine, but I think Norman needs to be a part of those appointments. He may not tell you how he feels, but this was his only son. He's hurting, too." I paused, holding the door handle.

She gave Norman a hard glare and slightly lifted her nose.

"Yes, of course, anytime," I agreed. "All I ask is that you please make an appointment with my secretary."

Silent, dry-eyed nods passed between us, and I shut the door.

Returning to my comfortable leather chair, I sat and swiveled it around so I could look out the window directly behind my desk. I watched as they both climbed into Norman's old pickup truck and drove away.

"*Good riddance, I say.*" Mr. Dark's attitude remained sullen.

"I wish I could tell them what happened," I replied.

"*Yeah, why don't you do that and they'll take you straight to the funny farm.*" For a moment, silence filled the place in my mind where his voice came from...then his clamoring continued, "*She will never change, and I'm guessing he likes being bullied.*"

"Don't act like you know everything about them. She might change. Only time will tell."

"*Yeah? And Hell might freeze over.*" He laughed. "*Only in your dreams, Arland, only in your dreams.*"

"In fact, my dreams have been troubled as of late." The Loveless' pickup slowed at the corner and turned east toward their house. "I may go roller skating tonight, for old time's sake."

"I don't think so! You haven't been on a pair of skates in years. You'll break your neck and I care too much to let you hurt yourself."

"Ha, the reason you don't want me to go is because between the two of us, we only have one neck—mine."

CHAPTER TEN

Lady Gewalt, The Red Rider

A plastic cover draped across Miss Wilson's typewriter. She must have left for the day while I was counseling with the Lovelesses.

Pacing my office floor, I reminisced about past events. Nothing about my life had been easy, so why should I think it would get better just because it was the twentieth century? I grabbed up some paperwork, which must be completed by tomorrow, and stuffed it in my briefcase. Made one last check to see if I had all I needed for the evening, before pausing and giving thanks for not having to listen to Irene Loveless, day in and day out.

Locking my door behind me, I stepped out into the hall and found myself in a whirling kaleidoscope of vivid colors. Like a vacuous tunnel, a force sucked me down into the battleship tiles under my feet. I fell for what seemed an eternity before I landed on a soft layer; some kind of firmament. With the wind knocked out of my chest, I lay there confused and disoriented, for there was no way to separate reality from illusion. Gasping, I inhaled, only to choke on the odious stench of decaying flesh and cankerous pus. The foul air caught in the back of my throat and made me vomit.

At length, I managed to tolerate the vaporous corruption without heaving, and sat upright. Trying to make sense of what had happened, I glanced about. Above, barely piercing the endless shadow in which I sat, were smoldering stalactites, casting a subtle illumination. The mournful wails of cursed souls echoed in the distance. It all seemed very familiar, near darkness, sweltering heat, and an unbearable stench.

"No!" The word escaped my lips as a whisper, but reverberated from every corner of my mind. This was impossible.

I felt for the briefcase, which I had clutched to my chest as I fell. Finding it, I withdrew some invoices and a list of student grades. Using *the Prophet's Voice,* I commanded, "Paper, catch fire and burn slowly."

A tiny blaze erupted at the edge of the rolled bundle.

"*Where are we?*"

"Mr. Dark, is that you?"

"*Is there anyone else who talks to you in your thoughts? Of course, it's me. Where the devil are we?*"

Not confessing my suspicion, I answered, "I'm not sure."

"*You better get sure, fast. I don't like it here.*"

"Okay, but let me think."

Kneeling, I took a closer look at what I landed on. I ran my hand over the surface. In the light of my makeshift torch, I could see this was no floor, but a mass of gigantic worms, some sticky and others slimy. I knew this place.

"If I didn't know better, I'd say we were in Hell. You know, the place where the worm never dies."

"*Oh, shit.*"

"Yep. From the smell of it, I'd say there's some of that close by too."

"*Do something. Command us out of here.*"

"It doesn't work like that and you know it. My gift gives me power over the elements, animals, and some half-witted people, but I can't teleport us home."

"*Then, we're doomed!*"

"Hang in there. Don't lose hope."

"*Arland—*"

"I said let me think."

"*Do something, Arland. If I were you, I'd be—*"

"I can't think with you chattering in my brain. I'm not even sure this is real."

"*Have it your way. Just don't get us killed!*"

Everything I could see in the light of my slow burning wad of bills and official grades made me believe I stood in Lucifer's pit, but could I trust my senses? I ran my hand over the worm ridden floor and plucked a small one from the tangled mass. It crawled upon my hand. Unlike common worms, it bared a mouthful of teeth and bit into my wrist. The sensation of a thousand needles shot up my arm.

Dropping the makeshift torch, I gripped the thing with my free hand and ripped it off—tearing skin with it. A single drop of blood dripped from my wrist, inciting the smallest of the hell-worms to churn into a frenzy...rising up out of the floor and gnawing on one another for a taste of that droplet. The commotion moved under my feet and I all but fell. This wasn't a hallucination.

"*I tried to warn you about those worms. They aren't ordinary.*"

"Really? Was it the size of the big ones or their teeth that brought you to such a remarkable conclusion?"

"*Smartass! You're not being careful.*"

I reached for my makeshift torch. Unlike my blood, the burning papers I dropped had no effect on the worms. But paper burns fast even when enchanted. Moments later, it burned to ash, and I again sat in near darkness.

"*Arland, get it together! If you're going to find your way out, you need to see where you're going. I vote to burn a few of these nasty worms. I bet they will make a good bonfire.*"

"You're kidding, right? If this is Hell, then those worms are fireproof. You saw my torch fall on them, and they didn't react at all."

"*Might as well try. What harm can it do?*"

I pointed my finger at a high point near me, and commanded, "Worms, catch on fire and blaze." A spark glittered and died away.

"I think it almost worked. Try it again."

This time I mustering all my will into the words, "Worms, obey! Catch on fire and blaze." Sparks flew from the place I pointed. Flashes similar to fireworks spewed up from the tangled vermin...then nothing. The worms didn't react at all. "See! Like I said, fireproof."

"*Well, the light show was entertaining.*"

"Entertainment is the last thing we need at the moment. If you can't be more helpful, be quiet and let me come up with a plan." Keeping my wits about me could save my life, and as Mr. Dark kept reminding me, his life too.

"*Listen to me, Arland! You need to give that worm bite some attention. It's worse than you think.*" I detected an urgency in his words.

"That's odd. It doesn't hurt."

"*There was some kind of venom in those tiny fangs that numbed your wrist. Your hand may go numb too...I can't be sure.*"

To my surprise, Mr. Dark was right. The wound was seeping blood. Without a proper bandage, I did the next best thing. I pulled my silk handkerchief from the lapel pocket of my tweed jacket and wrapped it around my wrist, tying it off like a fabric bracelet. Without success, I searched my briefcase for more papers. For the time being, the dim overhead light would have to suffice. Anyway, by then my eyes were adjusting.

"*What to do? What to do? Hum, should we head off into the unknown, or do we sit here and contemplate our fate? Oh, yes...I vote to start walking. Go somewhere...anywhere. And while you're strolling through Beelzebub's garden district, maybe you could answer a few questions? Like, how did we get here?*"

"If you want me to say it, I will... I'm clueless. I don't know how we landed smack in the middle of *The Fallen's*

Kingdom. As far as I know, Western High doesn't have a Hell's gate—not anymore." I stood, scratching my head. A worse problem occurred to me. If this was Hell, then how in the name of all the archangels was I going to get out? It baffled me, but I thought it best to keep moving—to where I didn't know.

I turned to get a lay of the land...or at least as much as I could see, when a monstrous fist flew out of the darkness, blindsiding me. A pain shot through my jaw, and I heard my bones crackle. The impact sent me sailing a good ten feet.

Rubbing my chin to insure it still clung to my face, I picked myself up. Despite the cracking, it all felt intact. I couldn't take another one of those pile-drivers.

"*Now you've done it. All that sparking drew the enemy right to us.*"

"Shut up and let me alone, or we're demon food."

"*Certainly not the devil's food I like.*"

"Shut up! I'm serious."

With one fist bigger than the other, this hell-spawn was built for war. Strategically equipped with two eyes in front of his bald head and two behind, I couldn't escape his sight. Long, forward arching horns protruded from the trapezoids beside his neck, and its hinder parts were that of an upright goat. Attached to its backside, a grizzly rat-like tail lashed from side to side, preventing me from approaching from the rear.

In his smaller hand, he carried a metallic mace. I dodged behind him. To my surprise, he swung his weapon and landed a glancing blow to my chest.

I yelled, "Hell-born, listen to my voice! I am now your master. You will stop your assault."

The demon stopped, shook his head, and snorted, blowing his noxious breath out through his flat nostrils. Like a dog shaking a residue of water off its back, the demon shuddered and shook off my command.

"*Well, that didn't work.*"

"Shut up."

"*The mace. The mace.*"

"What?"

"*It's metal. It's an element.*"

Lifting my hand toward the mace, I screamed out, "Weapon, I command you to turn on the hell-born and pummel him."

Making a great effort to obey, the mace shook and jittered in the demon's fist. Still, he held it tight enough to remain in control. I covered my face with my hands, preparing to get pummeled again by his huge fist.

"*The Sword of Gabriel, use the sword!*"

"No time," I cried. "Worms, draw this giant hell-born down into your mass."

The instant the words left my lips, the worms began to writhe. They wound themselves around the demon's hairy goat legs and pulled him into the thatch.

His free hand, balled into a fist, slammed into the slithering vermin, only to get sucked farther into the parasitic thrall. Flailing the mace, he viciously attacked the worms, splattering them one way and the other. The demon fought until the hell-worms wound their way around both his arm and the weapon. Encased in a squirming cocoon, it too became part of the unearthly landscape. At length, only his fanged head and the tips of his protruding horns stuck out above the worms. The demon let out a mournful cry, as inhuman as it was dreadful.

"*Now, what are you going to do with him? He'll bring all of Hell down on us.*"

"It's time to let the worms have him." I commanded with all the intensity I could muster, "Worms, eat the demon!"

In a frenzy, not unlike that of a mass of piranha, he was nothing but a green, bloody mess spread over the thatch. The gore sent the worms into an insane hysteria—chewing, biting, and gnashing upon anything the demon's blood touched, even other worms.

"*Well, wasn't that a pretty sight?*"

"Now who's being a smartass? The demon's toast. Isn't that what you wanted?"

"*Sure, but you didn't have to be so messy.*"

"Keep quiet and let me find our way out of here."

"*You don't have to be rude about it...geez.*"

CHAPTER ELEVEN

The Flaming Sword

Time in Hell is an abstract thing. I had no way of knowing how long I meandered around before noticing a bright glow flaring from over a nearby rise. The muddled sound of mingled voices echoed through the cavernous void. I climbed the worm ridden mound to see a shocking sight. hellish creatures, both demons and hell-beast alike, had gathered at what reminded me of a student pep rally; a bonfire included. Except, this blazing light emanated from a fiery red horse and its rider, a she-devil in red amour.

There was no doubt in my mind, this had to be the horseman called Gewalt. Around the blazing equine, the multitude of wretched creatures waved their arms and cried out, cheering for their champion. Careful to stand in the darkness beyond the reach of the flickering glow, I stopped.

"Mighty minions, you who were created by the power of the Fallen, we are about to seize the day," the rider yelled. **"Your indomitable numbers and my might will overpower**

the mortals. The stupid creatures find comfort in their misguided wisdom. More than ever, the deluded children of Adam no longer believe in God or the Devil. Trusting only in what they can see, they say we no longer exist, and this will give us a great advantage. The element of surprise is on our side. Follow me to the world of men and fill your bellies with human flesh."

The demons cheered in gleeful shrieks. Claws clanked together, and hooves stomped the worm-ridden ground.

"First, we kill those who dare challenge us, the marked prophet and his companions, then we feast. Yes, my hungry horde of specters, incubi, succubi, and wraiths; my starving hell-born abominations, an entire world of sweet human flesh, will be your reward. A bounty to feast upon, and more, you will also savor the red blood of the Favored's chosen ones. I can smell the aroma of a prophet's blood even now." She paused, sniffing the air. "**I do smell human blood, but from where**?"

The thought of this demon being able to smell a drop of blood over the sickening funk emanating from everywhere around me seemed impossible.

"**The master has given us a morsel to bolster our strength**," the rider yelled. "**Find the human**!"

The demons and hell-beasts scattered, going one way and the next. They didn't appear to possess the acute senses of the rider. Using the *Prophet's Voice*, I commanded, "Worms protect me."

A rumbling underfoot followed an eruption of enormous, savage worms. They wound themselves around the demons and bit into them, ripping them to pieces. Disembodied arms flopped and severed legs jittered on the writhing thatch, before the hell-worms swallowed their gory parts.

Like sentinels on guard, three very large demons placed themselves around the rider. They stayed by their master's side as the worms, the foundation of hell, attacked the horde. A deafening scream akin to a banshee's howl followed the fleeing few. Fending off the worms, those hulking sentinels surrounding the rider maneuvered her to safer ground.

The she-devil's minions amidst the frenzy became worm fodder, and the few who survived fled into the darkness. Only the rider's hulking guards remained by her side.

"Prophet, where are you? Step into my glorious light. I know it is you, for none other could command the immortal worms."

I stayed where I was, hidden in the darkness.

"No matter. You are wounded, dearest Prophet. I smell your blood even from here." She waved her hand through the air and closed her fist as if she were collecting my scent. She brought it to her face and inhaled. **"Everywhere humans go, you leave a trail behind—an odious stink only we demons can smell. I have your scent now, and it will lead me to you. You cannot hide from my magnificent power."**

She had distracted me. From out of the darkness, two of the sentinels grabbed me from behind. One gripped my right arm, a green three-eyed monster, his nine-inch claws cold as ice even through my sports coat. The other wrapped its tentacles, which sprouted from where arms should have been, around my left wrist. Together they drug me over to the rider.

"**There you are Prophet...oh, delicious Prophet**." She dismounted the blazing steed. When she stepped aside, no fire followed her. Only the horse remained engulfed in a crimson inferno. "**You made this far too easy**." She drew her sword and held it above her head. It burst into flames.

I screamed out, "Worms come to my aid!"

The entire cavern shook. The demons holding my arms let go. They screamed in pain as worms chewed their way up their legs. Without warning, the writhing thatch underfoot parted, pulling the gory demons down into their mass. The struggling hell-born creatures slid in between the slithering worms and vanished, followed by the distinctive sound of bones cracking.

Under the rider, the worms untangled themselves. She fell into their mangled mass, and with both hands, tried to pull free. Her flaming sword landed inches from my foot. The slithering vermin writhed and wrapped themselves around the blade. With her weapon anchored in the firmament, she struggled, slowly pulling herself free. "**Good effort, Prophet, but you failed**."

"*Take Gabriel's sword out and finish her while she's trapped.*"

I pulled the card from my jacket pocket and attempted to reach into the picture and extract the sword—then stopped. "Here, I'm outnumbered. If I take it out and these devils overpower me, they will get the sword, but if I leave it hidden, then they can't get to it. I can't take that chance."

"Chicken! Arland, if you're not going to use it, then take hers! She'll be on you in seconds."

"It's still burning. I can't touch it." The moment the words left my lips, the fire engulfing the sword died away.

I felt a cool breeze blow over me, and my perception of time changed. It seemed the Rider went into slow motion. Although I couldn't see my guardian angel, Reuwel must have been close by. I hurriedly stuffed the crest card into my back pocket and thumbed the button loop down to lock it in. Ripping off my jacket, I wrapped it around my hand and grabbed up the rider's sword. I heard a tinkling sound, like wind chimes, and time reverted to normal. In a state of frenzy, I ran. The direction didn't matter as long as it was away from her.

I had gained the few moments I needed to put some distance between me and that red she-demon called Gewalt. She pulled herself to her feet and screamed, **"This cannot be! That is mine!"** She called for her mount and glided up to sit astride the saddle.

From her bosom, she took a tiny flaming coal. She held it in her hand, high up, letting the glow it created encircle both her and the horse.

Even though I wasn't directly in the ember's illumination, I felt its mystic prowess. The voices of every person I ever failed throughout my lifetime filled my ears. Guilt overwhelmed me. Hope abandoned me. I stopped in my tracks, drowning in despair. Louder and louder, they screamed. Echoes followed...each voice resonated in my brain. Petrified, I stood there, utterly impotent.

My mouth wide open, I gasped for air. I watched as the glowing circle of light came toward me, and I wasn't sure what I feared most—Gewalt or the flaming coal she carried.

At that point, I could only guess why the rider put the flaming coal away. Perhaps she felt my defeat was inevitable. Or, she wanted to take her sword back, and with both hands make a lethal swing to decapitate me. Whichever it was, the voices in my head silenced. Fear's icy grip released me, but the trauma my emotions had experienced froze me in place.

She dismounted. In the distance, I heard haunting voices chanting her name, "Gewalt... Gewalt... Gewalt... Gewalt..."

Holding the reins of her steed in one hand, she reached down toward me with the other. **"Now, give me my sword."**

Involuntarily, I lifted it over my head.

"*Arland run!*" Mr. Dark's voice broke through the rider's hypnotic charm. "*Run! Run! Now!*"

Turning on my heels, I fled. Still holding her sword, I wagged it over my head as I ran, and the red she-devil racing only steps behind me. Closer she came. No matter how fast I ran, she gained on me. I yelled, "Red demon, trip and fall!"

Nothing happened. She barreled on after me.

Trying desperately to summon the voice of the prophet, I screamed out, "Red witch, stumble!"

The demon quickened its pace without hindrance.

She ran up beside me.

I slapped her helmet with the flat of the blade and dug my heels into the worm laden firmament—sliding to a stop.

Half dozen cadaverous arms reached up through the worm laden firmament and grabbed my ankles and legs, preventing me from escaping. In that moment, fear gripped my heart. Hell's terrain surrounded me. Where was I to go that she couldn't follow? Revelation pained my chest with icy, stabbing jabs. There was nowhere to run. I swayed. Barely able to stand, a dizzy bout of vertigo rushed over me.

Around me, the cavern moved. It twisted underneath, and a vortex spun, inhaling me into a cyclonic void. With only empty space to grab onto, it caught me up in the rotating gale.

I closed my eyes, expecting the worst. Nothing happened. The smell of rotted flesh faded from my nostrils and the floor stopped moving. I gasped. My eyes were still closed tightly, but there was no doubt I had returned to the school. Never once had I predicted what a joy it would be to inhale the lingering odor of hundreds of sweaty teenagers, but it sure smelled sweet compared to Hell's nasty funk. Before me, Jimmy Dugan stood beside Tuck. She held Sarah's drawing. Rebecca came around the corner.

Rebecca's voice carried over the roaring in my ears. "There it is. Wait... Jimmy, Tuck, stop! Stay right there..." She turned and yelled down the hall. "Nurse Cumberland, I found it!" She tried to take it from Tuck, who pulled it out of her reach. "That's not yours. Where did you find it?" She stomped her foot to emphasize her demand.

I caught my breath and took in my surroundings again. "Where? How? What's going on here?" Confusion consumed me and my delicate nerves sent more pains through my chest.

Tuck explained, "This greenhorn in a bowler hat cornered me, called me by name, and said that he'd left me a gift in front of the school office."

Jimmy took the drawing from Tuck and held it out to me. I stepped back, away from it. "Is it yours, Mr. Bertarelli? All I did was pick it up." He waved it at me again. I dodged so the paper wouldn't touch me.

"Mr. B., when Tuck picked it up, you came out of nowhere." His eyes grew large at the sight of the red sword. "Hey dude, you're carrying one wicked looking saber, there."

Tuck snatched the drawing back from Jimmy, and she held it out toward me. "Is this yours?"

My face must have expressed the horror I felt inside. If I were sixteen, I'd say my nerves had exceeded all the DEFCON levels. The missiles had launched and exploded...but then I wasn't sixteen anymore.

"Mr. B., What's wrong?"

Tuck's voice reflected her confusion. "Hey Doc, Ya don't want it?" Turning the picture upside down and back again, she finally gave a low whistle. "It's...it's a picture of...Hell. I don't blame you for not wanting it." Holding it at arm's length, she took another look at it. "Yeah, I get it. No matter how good a drawing it is, a girl would be dumber than Sam Addams' cow to wanna ever look at that place again. I sure don't, not even in a picture." She scratched her head.

"Don't know how anybody could draw Hell so accurately?" She paused. "On second thought, it's too good to be done from imagination. Who drew this?"

"Cowgirl, it doesn't matter right now. You haven't noticed, but Mr. B. don't look so good."

Tuck turned to me. "Doc, Jimbo's right. You look a bit green. Would it have anything to do with how you pulled off that appearing from out of nowhere trick?"

"Thank you, friend Tuck. Thank you for the rescue." It was all I could get out of my mouth.

"Rescue?" Tuck wrinkled her forehead and sounded even more confused.

"Yeah, well, I don't get it." Jimmy looked concerned. "Mr. B., you just suddenly appeared from thin air."

Tuck straightened up and tilted her head to the side. "Hold everythin', my gun's talkin' ta me." The silence in the room felt thick...until Tuck spoke again. "The pistol said this gosh-awful picture was lying like a doormat in front of your office, and it's to blame."

Still holding the sword with my wadded up coat, I teetered; my wavering balance was still uncertain. Tipping the saber down, I leaned on its hilt. "Yes, without a doubt, the drawing is awful."

Jimmy pushed it toward me again.

I put up the flat of my hand and declared, "I'm not touching that dastardly thing."

"Well, Doc, where ever you got that big red pig sticker, you can't leave it sticking out of the floor," Tuck said.

I blinked and looked down. The tip of the sword was so sharp, my weight had forced the blade to pierce through the linoleum and into the concrete below.

"Every kid in school will be grabbing it, trying to pull it loose," Jimmy added. "Like in that story, we had to read in English class. What was that guy's name? Oh, yeah, it was about a king named Arthur and a magic sword."

Ignoring Jimmy, I addressed Tuck. "You say that drawing was lying like a doormat when I stepped out of the school office?" Gazing at my shoe, I sighed. "That's what happened. It all makes sense now." Staggering, I caught hold of the upright sword to steady myself. "Iggarest must have left it for me to step on. He sent me to Hell." With a hard jerk, I pulled the red sword free from the flooring and unintentionally waved it at Jimmy, who dodged backward.

Flower came from the direction Rebecca had called to. Her voice interrupted our discussion. "I've been looking for that drawing." She marched toward Jimmy. "Sarah left it in my care and it disappeared from off my desk."

Giving Tuck and Jimmy an authoritative glower, Flower said, "Jimmy, Tuck, come into my office." Her tone was more of a command than a request. "I have a lot to catch you up on." Ignoring my pale pallor, she turned to me. "Arland, I could use your help to explain what this drawing is." She blinked, suddenly realizing my stressed condition. "Are you all right? You don't look well. Get in my office—right now."

CHAPTER TWELVE

Unsolicited Help

After Flower explained to Jimmy about the drawing, I sat with a thermometer in my mouth and a blood pressure cuff on my arm, while Flower listened for the heart pounding thumps with her stethoscope. Although a wave of disorientation came and went, I was feeling better. She read the mercury through the glass and declared me to have a slight fever, but nothing to worry about. Finally, uncuffed from that air engorged tourniquet, I examined my wrist where the worm bit me. The wound was still fresh. That had not been an illusion. It happened.

"Wait, a minute." Jimmy glared at Flower. "You're telling me Sarah has a supernatural gift?" He thought for a moment, pressed his lips together and sighed. "Okay, I get that. She isn't the first one the angels dropped a supernatural bomb on. What I don't get is why Mr. B. went off by himself, all the way to Hell, and confronted the red rider without the team to back him up?"

"Trust me when I say it wasn't my idea. I barely escaped with my life." A deep breath helped me regain my composure. Silently, I again thanked God for fresh air. "I must have stepped on that drawing Sarah made and it transported me there."

"Well, that's a doozy of an angelic gift!" Rebecca exclaimed. "Wait, Jimmy touched that drawing and he didn't fly through space and time."

"No," Flower explained, "for some reason Sarah's gift is linked with Arland's prophetic power. Her drawings only become supernatural at *his* touch."

Rebecca stood behind Tuck and leaned back against one of Nurse Cumberland's medicine chests. I thought of asking her to hand me the bottle of aspirin. Even though my head was pounding like a bass drum, surely it would stop soon.

Tuck stated, "Well, I'll be hog wallered, and that's why you didn't take it from me when I offered it to you. Sorry, Doc. I didn't mean to put you in danger again."

The door opened, and Iggarest stuck his head into the room. "**Tell me you killed Red with Gabriel's pretty pointy.**"

"Iggarest, you ignorant Elohim! What were you thinking? You put that drawing where I would step on it!" I fumed with anger. "You almost got me killed!"

"**That wasn't the idea, but once in the camp of the enemy, so to speak, you could have wielded old Gabe's sharpie and taken out dozens of those worthless hell-**

dwellers...including Red herself." He huffed. **"What went wrong?"**

"I should use Gabriel's sword to cut your wings off and have the earth imprison you for a millennium." I meant for the accusation to sting, but my rant may have gone too far because if that blade ever broke the skin, the essence of death would rush into his body and vanquish him instantly. "You didn't tell me about the plan before I hurdled through the cosmos. That's what went wrong. The red rider would have killed me, if not for Tuck. When she picked up the drawing, it pulled me back through to where I started."

"Calm down, Prophet. You survived. Admit it, the trip was worth it."

I crossed my arms and glared at him in disgust.

"You are such fun. I'm so glad we are on the same side in this." He laughed. **"Buck up, old bean, you're made of tougher stuff than that."** He raised his eyebrow and stared at me skeptically. **"At least I thought so. Although I admit, I wish you had chopped all of Madame Gewalt's minions into mush."**

With his eyebrow still raised above the rim of his sunglasses, he spied the handle of the cooling red sword lying on Nurse Cumberland's desk. It was sticking out from where the blade had been wrapped in a wet towel. We didn't know exactly what else to do with it. After all, there was no way it would fit in my desk drawer with my relics, so as soon as the demon blade cooled enough to touch, Jimmy laid it on Flower's desk.

"I see your trip truly wasn't in vain." An insidious laughter filled Iggarest's words. **"I bet you had a time getting that away from Red. And more...I'd wager you learned something you didn't know."**

Jimmy stood and stepped toward Iggarest. "You wanna know what I learned? I learned that a smart mouthed fallen angel is getting into our business." He waved his massive fist in Iggarest's face. "We don't need any help from the Fallen. Got it?"

Iggarest replied, **"My, what big muscles you have. I bet those aren't original parts. You remind me of this guy I once knew. He got really mad and yanked the gates of a city right off their hinges and carried them up a hill. That poor gate never did anything to him, but like a bully will, he proceeded to break them into little pieces. His name was Samson."** Index finger extended, Iggarest poked Jimmy in the bicep. **"His muscles didn't come as standard equipment either."**

Jimmy growled, and drew back to clobber Iggarest, but the angel shrugged and vanished, leaving a wisp of smoke and the faint odor of brimstone behind.

"Mr. Bertarelli, you know, that angel is right," Rebecca said. "We did learn something."

Scowling, I leaned over to Rebecca. "And what did we learn? That stinking fallen angels can get me killed? I didn't need an object lesson from him to teach me something I already knew."

Rebecca's smile went dim. Her gaze dropped to the floor and sat back in her chair. She whispered, "Whatever you say, Principal Bertarelli."

"Arland, that is quite enough." Flower scolded. "I think you're still overwrought from your experience. Settle down and think about what happened." She tapped her fingernails on her desk like she had done on my conference table. "You learned that Sarah's drawing doesn't only open a *window* for you to look through. This one, and possibly all of them, will transport you by means of some astral phenomenon. While you are there, on the other side of death's veil, you can physically interact with others, but they can also hurt you."

I took some deep breaths. "Dear Miss Rebecca, I apologize. Perhaps adrenalin was flooding my brain. At any rate, I snapped at you and it was uncalled for. If you had a valid point...I'd like to hear it."

Rebecca's bright smile returned. "In the rider's speech to her minions, you told us she pointedly stated all the riders are going after you first, but that's not all... it won't stop there. They want all of us—they want to kill the Champions."

"Oh..." I groaned while tilting my face down and locking my fingers together behind my neck. "...just the good news I was waiting to hear." For the moment, at least, my head had stopped hurting.

Tuck added, "We also learned how to fetch you back to this side of the great beyond. One of us has to pick up the dad-gum drawing, and—"

Rebecca interrupted, "Or maybe simply touching the paper might be enough to bring you back. We don't know for sure. Not yet."

Unlike before, the wound on my wrist was aching. "Lovely Flower,"...that didn't sound like I had meant it too... "You're right about getting hurt." I swallowed hard. My throat felt fry as the dunes of North Africa, and I broke out in a sweat. "Remember the mass of worms we encountered, the ones that form the structure of Hell's firmament?"

Had I said something strange? I wasn't sure why she gave me a quizzical look. My words felt thick and mushy in my mouth. A trickle of perspiration ran down the side of my face. Maybe I wasn't making myself understood. Why was it taking her so long to reply?

At length, she answered me. "Yes, I remember." Her hands were busy putting away her blood pressure cuff, the stethoscope, and dropping the mercury thermometer in a receptacle marked alcohol. "We saw them when we made that rescue mission to Purgatory."

I nodded. "Well, one of those vermin bit me."

Taking my hand, Flower said, "Let me see it. I'll heal the wound for you."

She closed her eyes, and nothing happened. A strained expression crossed her face, and the wound healed over. When she took her hand away, a dark gray spot appeared on my wrist where the bite had been. Again, she put her hand on mine and concentrated. This time, the gray spot vanished. Flower staggered and grabbed for her desk. She caught herself before she fell out of her chair.

"My dearest Flower, what happened?" I asked. "You don't have trouble healing our wounds, even when we're injured from battling hell-beasts and fallen angels. This one took a lot out of you."

Again, that look returned to her face, and she put a hand on my forehead. "This bite carried some kind of hell-born bacteria. I vanquished it, I think. But the strain is very visceral."

Ever since my return from Hell, Mr. Dark had scurried off into some shadow. He chose this moment to speak his mind. "*See, I told you it had venom in it.*"

"She said visceral, not venom." No one realized I was virtually talking to myself—my less cheerful, more pessimistic, self-centered, cynical self. Minced up, muddled words stirred inside my mind. I wanted to say more but found it hard to talk. "Visceral vermin carrying a vicious plague to verify the downfall of virtually all vindicators of victory." My words didn't sound like my own. Something was wrong. "Violate me not. I refuse to be the vandalized in such a vulgar act of villainy." Bewildered by my own statement, I clasped a hand over my mouth.

"Very what?" Jimmy asked.

"Jimmy, he's delirious. You know, taking out of his head." I mused at the concern in Flower's voice. Was it for me?

I blinked, pressing my eyes hard before opening them again and forced myself to speak more coherently. "Verily I say, an idea has taken root...Dear Jimmy of Western. There is a very great possibly a part of Hell itself lingers inside me."

"That's what I've been trying to make you understand," Flower insisted. "This bacteria...it isn't exactly normal. It's a breed of demonic bacteria. You might as well call them micro-demons."

"Oh, is that all?" Rebecca remarked. "Sounds horrible, if you ask me."

"Micro?" Tuck pulled her eyebrows together. "Like very tiny critters?"

"Yes, very, very tiny," Flower added.

"You're correct, my dear Rebecca," I remarked. "Sounds quite horrible to me, too." I inspected my hand. Tiny scars from the worm's teeth still marred my skin. "And to think, those tiny beasties were running rampant inside me for a time." I shuddered.

Flower softly replied, "Yes. I'm afraid they are still in there...for now. My apologies for not finding the source of the infection the first time I laid hands on you. Arland, the micro-demons are extremely elusive. No doubt I missed some. From what I can tell, ever since you were infected, a multitude of them ran carte blanche throughout your circulatory system, and I have no idea what damage they did. I vanquished all of them I could. But like I said, some remain." She breathed a heavy sigh. "It's those little escapees I'm worried about. They could manifest into a greater problem."

"Fear not, milady. Your deed is greatly appreciated. I feel fine, absolutely smashing. Don't worry about this old dogfish. When is the devil not on my heels?" I cast my eyes down to my hand. "'Oh, worm's horrid bite, art thou a plague sore, a carbuncle to corrupt my blood?'"

"Things must be going from bad to worse," Flower said. "Either his delirium has turned into classic prose or he's misquoting Shakespeare. I can't tell which."

"Don't despair, fair one, I'm fine. 'Tempt not! I forbid you to hate mine spirit, for I am...'" Tunnel vision narrowed my peripheral sight, and darkness closed in around me. It was like seeing the world through the bottom of a dirty glass. I couldn't keep my balance. Flower and Rebecca grabbed my arms to prevent me from tumbling over. "I am sick, indeed." My eyes rolled back into my head. Blackness enveloped me, and my body sank to the floor.

"Arland, Arland! Talk to me! Where did you go? I'm here, inside your head, but for the first time, ever...I'm alone."

CHAPTER THIRTEEN

Micro-demons

Behind my closed eyelids, ink-like clouds swirled—a sticky black mist clung to my skin, adhering me to the darkness. I found it hard to breathe for this fog and I became one. All my senses screamed out for reality, and only this nightmare replied. A sensation of weightlessness overwhelmed me. Unbelievable as it seemed to me, my corporeal body floated as light as a cumulus cloud.

I dared to open my eyes. Far down, I beheld a mass of roads: the interstate, rural pathways, and lonely highways all connecting and interconnecting the town of Western. While it unfolded beneath me, a fleeting thought ran across my mind. Perhaps I'm not a man at all, but a tiny spider viewing the world from a high vantage point. And these thin black lines are my webbing. Each mark, stroke, and line all part of my domain.

I closed my eyes again; denying what they told me. If I were to believe what I saw, my grasp on sanity would undoubtedly slip away. I held on...but to what was I holding? I opened my eyes to behold—darkness.

An oddly familiar voice came from out of nowhere. "*Who are you?*"

Why couldn't I identify that voice? The thought weighed on me. "I am a man of letters." My emotions all but muted my reply. "At Harvard, I earned them one by one."

"*What separates us from this? Nothing?*"

I spouted off textbook answers. Even though I felt there was more to be said, it was the best I could do. "Intellect, the single difference between men and beasts."

"*And what is intellect's tool?*"

"Memory, the ability to retain and accumulate knowledge.

"*What, then, is intellect?*"

"The ability to rationalize memory...."

"*Are you merely a speck of cosmic dust collected in some vacuous nexus, or are you flesh, bone, blood, intellect, and memory?*"

"I am," I said. The declaration ignited a light somewhere far overhead. Out of the darkness, a flood of words came rushing through my mind—words in endless repetition. The disjointed phrases clung together into a myriad of lines, sentences; all oddly familiar. Words I recognized. Quotations I remembered. I quoted bits of speeches, uttered snippets of scriptures, and recited a smattering of scripts from a plethora of tragic plays. In a strange fashion, I could see the words. Chain-like, the verbal became substance. Syllables took form before me and twisted themselves into a strand, linking and binding each letter into a sturdy rope. I caught hold of the line and hoisted myself upward through the darkness and into the light.

"*Arland! That's enough. We are here. You have arrived.*" I knew that voice. It was Mr. Dark. Whatever it was that Flower missed in my blood evidently caused my malady.

"What's going on?" Panic edged my voice. The voice only Mr. Dark could hear. "Where are we?"

"*Welcome back, old friend. For a minute there, I thought we were toast.*"

"Thank God, I never liked toast."

"*Funny. Very funny...you must be feeling better.*"

"At least I'm not hallucinating." I took in my surroundings. I stood on nothing and yet I didn't float. My existence appeared to be normal except for this brilliantly illuminated void surrounding me, and for the moment, my thoughts were my own again. Confusion assaulted my calm emotions: a fearful sensation akin to the panic of a lost child...I felt disembodied. Here, once more, my rational facilities obeyed my commands...or so it seemed. "Where are we? Am I hallucinating?"

"*No...and yes. Kind of.*"

"What is that supposed to mean?"

"*We passed out. Or, to be more accurate, you passed out. I think your physical form is lying in Nurse Cumberland's examination room. What you're seeing is a dream state conjured up by your consciousness, a place you created somewhere between life and death. All I ask is that you don't cross the point of no return.*"

"Are those hell-born germs still in me?"

"*You mean micro-demons. Yeah, they went straight to the brain and started chowing down. They hid in the folds between the gray-matter, and, like parasitic worms, ate away at its host, burrowed and feasting. I can't chase them out by myself. For a moment there, I thought we were done for. Then I figured out how to scoop them up, not to brag, mind you. But I chased all those little buggers out to a localized part of your body.*"

Deciphering the consequences of his actions, I recoiled at his words. "You left the little buggers in me? You pushed them together and let them stay? Why didn't you build them little homes and put out the welcome mats too? You useless blob; why didn't you annihilate them?"

"*The bigger ones are stronger. I couldn't...but on the bright side, they can't break loose either; at least not yet.*"

His words haunted me. As far as I could tell, after twisting my hands and flexing my feet, my limbs reacted to my commands. The sensation was normal. Perhaps my physical body moved too, but since I remained comatose, I obviously had no way of knowing.

"*What you call a hell-born germ is exactly what Flower called a micro-demon. Like I said, there's a bunch of them chewing away...they did some damage...and caused your brain to turn against you.*" Mr. Dark made a kind of huffing noise. "*You might show some gratitude. After all, if not for me, those parasitic little nasties would have completely taken over. I saved your life.*"

"No. You saved your life. You don't fool me at all. Wait!" I sighed and shoved my hands into my pants pockets. "Wait one minute. You chased them to one part inside me. What part? Where are they now?"

"*What about me scooping them up didn't you understand?*" I know Mr. Dark can't exhale, but I'd swear I heard an aggravated sigh. "*Yes. For the moment, I have encapsulated them in a section of your spinal column under the medulla oblongata. It's like they have a layer of cybernetic grease coating their wormy little carcasses. Rounding up those little suckers took longer than making the trap. I didn't have time to warn you. I mean, what would I have said?*"

"Oh, I don't know. How about...Arland, your being invaded by rampant brain eating cooties!"

"*In the middle of my crisis, I didn't have time to waste on pleasantries. Every time I thought I had one, it slipped out of my grasp...then another, and another.*" He went silent for a moment. "*Compare it to trying to catch goldfish with your bare hands.*"

"Ok, so they are still in my head. What does that mean, exactly?

"*For an educator, you don't listen very well. Like I said, I pushed them out of your brain, down into your spinal column. There, they stopped eating; I guess because they ran out of gray matter, but now you're incapacitated. The invaders are blocking the sensory output to the rest of your body.*"

"Incapacitated? Meaning I can't move?"

"*Well, maybe a bit worse. As long as they are in your system, you'll probably stay in a coma.*"

"Great, how am I supposed to lead my friends to victory when I can't even communicate with them?"

"*Don't ask me. I just work here.*"

"Smartass!"

"*And I thought you would be more concerned with how much of your brain those beasties gobbled up.*"

"Okay. You're right. I should be. How much did they get?"

"*You'll be glad to know how good I did. Because of my quick thinking and rapid reflexes, I got to them before any major memory disappeared. However, you may have a hard time remembering some of your childhood. Like, do you remember your parents fighting a lot?*"

"My parents used to fight? Really? Oh, whatever...I don't see that as important as your incorrect sentence structure. You didn't do good, no, you did well."

"*Arland, shut up...hear me, shut up.*"

"I assure you, I have no idea what you're talking about."

CHAPTER FOURTEEN

My Enemy's Enemy

I suppose anyone who has ever experienced lying in a coma would compare it to being submerged in a tank of cold water. I wouldn't say it was outright painful, only extremely uncomfortable. Time had very little meaning in my state of oblivion. Still, my senses told me days were passing by, each minute dragging on in a lugubrious march to nowhere. I would occasionally feel the knee-jerk sensation of a twitching muscle, but couldn't tell if my body responded or not.

Mr. Dark told me to make myself at home because he thought we would most likely spend eternity there in the recesses of my atrophying brain. A light, brighter than the milky haze surrounding me, appeared in the distance. I gazed at it in awe. It grew brighter still, drawing me to it. Instinctively, one foot stepped out in front of the other until I found myself striding through the murky void toward it. The brighter the glow, the faster I walked; until, despite the viscous atmosphere, my gait became a dead run. Without slowing, I slammed into the glare. It engulfed me. The brilliance subsided, fading into nonexistence.

In that instant, every failure...every mistake in my long life flashed before me. And I wished for a quick death to relieve my guilt-ridden past.

One hand broke through the glaring barrier, then the other. Finally, I burst forth to the other side, and at my feet, an inky blob followed.

***

My eyes flew open, and I sat up; the white haze that had surrounded me, completely gone.

"*You did it. You brought us back.*" I don't think I've ever heard Mr. Dark so excited. Without another word, he dripped off my shoulder, down my arm, and scurried off, anxious to get under the cot on which I laid.

I took in my surroundings. A medicine cabinet, three chairs, three cots, and three nightstands, one by each makeshift bed—this was Nurse Cumberland's examination room. I pulled my feet up and out of the stark white bedding, swinging them onto the cold linoleum floor. "You're right, my old friend. We made it back, but not because I did anything spectacular to instigate the passage. Not as far as I know."

Taking inventory of my person, I realized, except for my missing jacket and my stocking feet, the clothes I wore were the same ones I had on the day I fell ill. Jerking my head toward the calendar hanging across from my bed, I gasped. With an *X*, every day had been marked out down to December twenty-third; one day after I had stepped out of my office and into the pit of Hell. My eyes hunted down the wall clock—6:20, and since sunlight flooded straight in from the west, I supposed it had to be in the evening. What felt like weeks had only been a matter of twenty hours or so.

I tilted my head and waited for my gift to kick in. Most times, it would at least inform me of any immediate danger. All I got was a kind of static; the kind I'd get on my TV after the last late night broadcasts. I guess my gift was off the air.

Trying to stand, I fell back onto the cot, pushing the bedside table and making a clatter. Flower burst into the room. "You're awake. Thank God, you're awake." She rushed to my side. "I didn't know if I had gotten them all, but looks like I did it. Inexplicably, those hellish germs huddled together and I could eradicate them, at last." She laid a hand on my forehead before announcing, "Arland, they're out of your system for good; I promise."

At her touch, a warm sensation rolled up my arm and into my chest. For a moment, I saw her like I did the first time we met. I was a doe-eyed boy just arriving at the Happy Hollow commune in Kansas. She came toward me through a field of wildflowers, wearing love beads, a long, blue jean maxi-skirt, and a fringed leather halter top. She touched me and my head filled with peaceful thoughts and the fragrance of fresh cut grass. Right then, I knew right then...I knew she was like me—gifted.

No doubt I was on the mend, but I had fallen back onto the cot. Again, I pushed up. Perhaps it was the memory or something tugging on my emotional heartstrings, but the desire to sit beside her overcame me. I smiled and took her hand. It was the best I could do, and the most I had to give.

"Dearest Felisha." It wasn't as difficult to form words and sentences as before. Tragically, the words I wanted to say wouldn't come to my lips. What I did say sounded more like a confession. "The moment before I awoke, the memory of every failure flooded over me. Including the time when I failed you most." My words froze in my throat. How could I tell her? Would she even understand that if not for the life giving hilt-blade on Gabriel's sword, she would be dead? She deserved better than me. I let go of her hand, and with quite an effort, stood. My wobbling sense of balance held me upright.

She ran her hand through my hair. "Arland, you look so much better. Color has returned to your cheeks and you're up walking. Don't overdo it right away. Sit back down on the bed and I'll get Jimmy. Don't try to stand until I return." She stepped to the door. "I won't be but a moment. Down the hall she went."

There it was again. That strange doe-eyed expression I remembered wearing when I was fifteen. The warmth of her smile reached all the way across the room before she hurried out the door.

Moments later, she returned alone. "Jimmy's not in the hall anymore. He must have gone home." She sat by me on the cot. This time, her demeanor felt distant—less spontaneous. I wondered if she had run into Roger out in the hall and what he had said to her to make such a change in her attitude, but decided to not ask. At the time, the team was barely on my side, anyway.

The fog in my brain cleared enough for me to remember. I had been carrying the charmed crest picture in my inner left jacket pocket. Callously pushing her hand away, I stood. "Where is my jacket?" I demanded.

With her usual calm demeanor, and without a word, she leaned over to the side table and pulled open the drawer. Inside lay my jacket, folded neatly. I grabbed it up and searched the inside pockets. The crest picture hiding Gabriel's sword wasn't there. A pain shot through my chest, all but stopping my heart. "It's gone!" I exclaimed.

Panic made my blood run cold. I rubbed my temples. My head hurt like never before. This time, the pressure behind my eyes was all but unbearable.

"Arland," Flower asked, "What are you talking about?"

"The crest is gone!" I'm sure she heard the urgency in my voice.

"What? Could you have dropped it when you went on your excursion to Hell? Did you ever take it out of your pocket?"

"Yes, I took it out and put it..." Like a light coming on in a dark room, I remembered. "My back pants pocket. Reaching around to the button fastening my back right trousers' pocket, I struggled to open it. The thing argued with my fingers until it stubbornly released, and I pulled the magic crest out. Gabriel's sword was still there in the picture.

I exhaled a sigh. "Whew. It's still safe."

Flower calmly smiled and nodded. "I knew it wasn't in your jacket anymore. I looked when I folded it and put it away." She touched the edge of the picture. "Oh, the magic tingles under my fingertips!"

"Have you seen any more of Iggarest? He's nothing but a devil in sheep's clothing." Despite the scorched marks, I put my sports jacket back on. "There's more he isn't telling us. I feel it in my bones." Flower pulled my shoes out from under the cot. I hurriedly put them on. "If he thought he had a snowball's chance in Hell of beating Lucifer alone, he would double-cross us in a twinkle from his green eyes."

"My past dealings with the fallen have proved one thing," Flower said. "It doesn't matter, even if they mean well. They say one thing and mean another. They can't keep themselves from misrepresenting the truth."

"You mean they lie?" I laughed. "Of course they do."

"Yes, I guess some people would call it lying. Still, there is a grain of truth in everything they say." She tilted her head in an understanding gesture.

"Trust me. Any time the fallen are moving their lips, they are lying," I said. "He has an agenda of his own. I'm sure of it, and I think I have him figured out."

"Really? So what do you think he's up to? Is he on our side or not? He sounds pretty sincere."

I tilted my head and listened for my gift. It never before told me lies and if it spoke to me, I knew it would be the truth. Sure enough, it confirmed what I already expected.

"It's the sword. He wants it." I leaned back and let my arms hold me upright. "He calls it Gabriel's *pretty pointy*. The story he told me when he came to see me...that was a half-truth. He laid it on thick, and I fell for it. I missed the one question in all his elaborate bunk that meant something. It came to me when I realized I didn't know where my coat was. He only came to my office to ask one question—how did I vanquish one of the five called the devil's favorites?"

"If he simply wants to foul up Ishtar's plans, why would he care what happened to any of them? Don't you think every fallen angel is an egocentric maniac? No matter how many we vanquish, the rest won't shed a tear for their dead. But, I don't know, Iggarest seemed different."

"Don't be fooled. Iggarest is smarter than his kind gives him credit for. I think he's mounting a coup, and, at least for the moment, we are a part of his plan. He wants to kill his master, and he needs Gabriel's sword to do it."

Flower reached for my arm and leaned close, her whisper almost unintelligible. Either she was getting more forward than usual, or did Flower not want anyone to eavesdrop? Maybe she felt the presence of one particular smartass fallen angel, who might be lurking close by, listening?

"That sword in the hands of a Fallen..." She shook her head. "Well, he would be invincible. I don't think he'd stop at pulling a Brutus on his archangel. The power the sword wields is too great. After getting rid of his master, it would be very tempting to rid himself of us all."

My head pounded with pain. I found it hard to concentrate on my answer. "If his takeover is successful, then he'll have his army of demons and he won't have any use for humans ever again. And without the Champions to stop him, it would be Iggarest who'd bring on the end of days and annihilate mankind."

"*I don't like the sound of this.*" Mr. Dark's silent voice broke into our conversation. "*I told you to vanquish him on the spot. If he gets the sword, it will be your fault.*"

I directed my thoughts back to him through the pain pounding at my temples. "Sometimes I wish others could hear your mewling. They have no idea what a pest you are. If you can't help, keep quiet. You're making my head hurt."

"*But Arland.*"

"No buts, I said keep quiet."

"*Okay, then. Have it your way.*"

CHAPTER FIFTEEN

Odd Behavior

During my mental conversation with Mr. Dark, a strange expression must have crossed my face. Flower remarked, “I almost forget you have that famous split personality. Is it saying something important?”

Because it was Flower who helped me understand what Mr. Dark was back when I first discovered my abilities, her words struck me as being a bit strange. However, I must have still been dazed from my harrowing experience because I found it to be quite funny.

My lips were helpless against the crooked smile my wit conjured upon my face. “That old ink blob is as clueless as we are.”

“So, what’s the plan?” Flower asked, acting as if my smirk was normal.

“Protect the sword and keep it away from Iggarest.” I knew quite well there was nothing humorous about our topic of conversation, nor about our situation, and yet, I all but laughed out loud at her question.

"I know the sword hides in the picture in your pocket, but how? The sword is long, and that card is tiny."

"Here, let me show you." I took the card out of my pocket and showed Flower the crest with the crossed swords.

"Oh. That one looks like Gabriel's." She tilted her head and paused. "But how do you get it out of the picture?"

"Like this." I gave my hand a shake before pressing it into the flat surface and pulling the sword out.

"Wow, that is amazing!" she exclaimed. "Can I hold it?"

I nodded and handed her the sword. In the next instant, Jimmy walked through the door.

"Hey, Mr. B., I ran into Nurse Cumberland, outside, and she gave you a clean bill of health. Said, you're awake." Seeing Flower sitting by me, his eyes widened. "How did you get in here so fast?"

I gazed incredulously at the woman sitting beside me. "Iggarest? Is that you?"

A manly voice came from Flower's lips. "**What a clever fellow you are, Arland Bertarelli. Even in your debilitated state, you have seen right through my disguise.**"

"What did you do with Flower?" I called out in concern.

The face of the person sitting beside me blurred. I watched as her whole body transform into a fallen angel wearing a cravat and a British long coat. "Iggarest! Answer me!"

"**Thanks for the pretty pointy.**"

"Get the sword!" I yelled.

Jimmy lunged forward and barely missed being skewered before the fallen angel vanished.

"That's what I was trying to tell you...but no, you wouldn't listen. All I got for my effort was a SHUT UP!"

From out of nowhere, the disembodied voice of the fallen angel reverberated through the room. "**Thank you, my dear old prophet. While you slept, I tried to remove the sword from Gabriel's hiding place, but I failed. It wouldn't respond to my touch. Oh, Gabe, you old dog, you did well when you made this pretty.**"

Without warning, his head appeared, floating above the door. As he spoke, his visage became more translucent until it completely faded from sight. "**I told you, I am on your side in this muddled mayhem—at least at the moment, I am. With this, I could have ended the lot of you. And perhaps I should have, but if not for the slight chance, you might still be useful. Trust me...I would.**"

He sighed. I could barely make out his arm, waving a hand at his face as if he was overwrought. "**When I return, it will be me wearing *The Crown of Power*.**"

CHAPTER SIXTEEN

The Designated Driver

Tuck rushed in a little late to witness the action, and stopped short. Wide eyed, she took in Jimmy's face. It mirrored my shock. "Doc, what's happenin'? You and Jimbo look like you spilled the milk in the cistern."

The narrow eyed, pressed lipped expression Jimmy returned to Tuck in response didn't need words.

"Iggarest stole Gabriel's sword," I said. "Like a dope, I handed it to him."

"You what?" Tuck's eyes went as big as saucers.

"In my defense, all I can say is that I didn't know it was him at the time."

"He fooled Mr. B.," Jimmy said. "Heck, I thought it was Flower, too! I mean, he looked exactly like her, and sounded like her, too,"

"We're doomed." Unable to come to terms with the fact, I had failed once more; I buried my face in my hands.

Jimmy said, "Mr. B., it's not like you've started that Armageddon war already." He looked down at his shoes. "And not all by yourself. We've got time to fix this."

Lifting my head, I gazed over everyone's head. I couldn't look them in the eyes. "No? My actions just doomed millions of people. This can't be fixed." I lowered my head and locked my fingers across the back of my neck. "What I did has cursed all mankind."

"I can see the headlines now. Principal Bertarelli is responsible for starting World War III. Not a demon...not an angel...but the hero of Heaven, the great marked prophet—Arland, the fool." Mr. Dark's ridicule did nothing to improve my despair.

I didn't have the fortitude to tell him to shut his mouth, mostly because he was right. Not even prophets have power over life and death like the sword did, but as I saw it, the enemy's greatest weapon...was me.

Listening for my gift, I hoped it had turned on again. Faintly, there was something. It told me I wasn't well. Self-loathing flared in my soul, and I shook my head. What good is a prophet that only gets whispers and flashes about things everyone already knew?

"Well, Doc, at least you're back in the land of the livin'. You're not talkin' out of your head, not like you was for a moment there." She gave me a squirrelly smile. "I hates puttin' on funerals." She took off her western hat and leaned against the wall, one foot propped up on the sheetrock like James Dean. "I knew somethin' was wrong when we found ya in the hall holdin' the red saber, and moments later, ya keeled over. I thought ya passed out because of a bad case of heatstroke or dehydration." She chuckled. "You had just come back from Hell, and it's pretty darn hot there. But I been chewin' the fat with Jimbo, and he told me ya got bit by some cursed critter and that's why ya passed out."

In retrospect, I know Tuck meant well, but I took her words to be more condemnation. "I don't know." Grabbing at my head, I twisted from side to side. It had stopped pounding as badly, but that wasn't saying much. "I just don't know why you guys don't choose a new leader. I'm such a screw-up. If you ask me, it would be better for me to be still stuck somewhere in my imagination with that loudmouthed ink blot than being awake and have given the enemy our most formidable weapon."

"Oh really? An ink blot, am I?" Mr. Dark's voice roared in my mind.

"Heavens to my Aunt Betsie's pet pig! You're throwin' a Texas sized pity party for yourself! Sniff, sniff—I'm all a cryin' over spilled milk. Well, blubberin' ain't gonna fix nothin'." Tuck slapped my face...twice. Not like a hard whack, but it stung. "Now, git up and stop throwin' a conniption fit. Always took you to be a more ornery cuss than this."

"Hit him again for me. He called me an inkblot." Of course, no one could hear Mr. Dark speak...no one but me.

Jimmy pushed her backward onto the cot. "Nobody hits Mr. B. while I'm around." Fist waving in the air, he poised, ready to retaliate.

"Jimbo... I mean. Jimmy, use your brain for once instead of your muscles. It's time this *gaucho* dusts off what's left of his self-respect and buck up."

I yelled, "Wait! Stop!" They both turned and stared at me. My mind wasn't on their bickering at all. The emotional trauma must have triggered a secondary response. "Jimmy, you're too reckless. You must keep away from that sword's blade. It will kill you instantly. Confronting Iggarest head on while he held Gabriel's sword was foolhardy, and I can't see you get killed again."

"What?" Jimmy turned toward me with disbelief written on his face. "You can't see me...what?" His conflict with Tuck instantly vanished.

"Stay away from that sword. You don't understand. It's like the blade is poisoned. Even a single prick is lethal. The Archangel Gabriel forged the spirit of death into the metal's edge." Unintentionally, my eyes welled up with tears. My emotions were running unchecked, and it certainly wasn't from my headache. Miraculously, my head stopped hurting after Iggarest left.

Mumbling the words, I looked up, teary-eyed. "I can't go through that *again*." Gazing up at him, my breath caught in my throat, making me sharply inhale. "Ignore me. I didn't mean to say that. I...I meant to say... There is no way I could bear to see you die."

Tuck sat up straight. "I ain't buyin' it. You definitely said *again*. I heard it." She grinned. "Come clean. Out with it. Tell me how this city slicker died."

"No." I slammed the palm of my hand down on the cot. "No, means no!"

"Mr. B., you're a lot of things, but you've never been a good liar. You saw me die, didn't you? I need to know," Jimmy pleaded.

"I want to hear this too." Tuck poked Jimmy on the arm with her index finger. "I like doin' that. It's like tapping a steel plate." She eyed Jimmy with what I took to be admiration. "I'm guessin' he's different than regular folks in more ways than one."

Jimmy gritted his teeth. "Don't poke me, cowgirl. You understand English?" He shifted his gaze back to me—waiting for my next words.

Tuck kept on, "If you died, then I bet your gift saved you somehow. Who knows, there's a slim chance the angels fixed it so you can't die."

"No, he can—I mean...he...." I started to explain, but stammered, and drew back my words. They waited in silence. I finally spoke, "Jimmy, the sword cut you."

"Mr. B., you change subjects worse than my old man does when he's on a drunken binge." He checked his hands and shirt for blood. "No," Jimmy replied. "It didn't cut me. I'm sure."

"Yes, Jimmy, it did. The *hilt blade* cut you."

"No." He sounded emphatic. "Iggarest was swinging the other end at me. I'm sure, it—"

Tuck interrupted. "Hold up, big Jim. Somethin' tells me he's talkin' some serious turkey." She focused on me. "Ya mean, he's been cut by the thing before?"

"Yes. It was last year, Jimmy, and all the team died, and they had to be pricked by the hilt blade—the life blade."

"I don't remember that," Jimmy said, "and I think that's something I'd definitely remember."

"Well..." I hesitated. "I've made it clear the sword's long-blade has been imbued, with the essence of death. That is why it can kill an immortal like a fallen angel, and why Iggarest wants it...but on the hilt, the butt end of the handle, it also has a sharp protrusion, a second blade. Within that small blade, Gabriel forged the essence of life...and without it, my friend, you would have died at the hand of Abaddon; correction, you did die, and I was powerless to stop it."

I paused. Jimmy, mouth agape, sat in silence, waiting for my next words. "And hence, the reason I had to prick you with the tiny life giving part of the sword." I swallowed hard and ran a hand through my dishwater blond hair. "It's true."

Jimmy's vinegar faced expression clearly contained disbelief. "Let me get this right...I was dead?" He put the palms of his hands on his temples. "You stabbed me. Now I'm alive...Why didn't you tell me about this before now?"

"I don't know. *How do* you tell a friend that you let them down? How could I tell you...you died because I failed?"

"We all knew the risk when we took on those devils. The fact you saved me...that's what matters." He tilted his head and asked, "Do the others know about this? Did they see it happen?"

"No...and you can't tell them about it, either. They must never know. I didn't want you to know." In my pleading, a half-smile crossed over my lips.

"Ha. Look there. Arland cracked a smile. Jimbo, he's pullin' your leg." She slapped the side of her jeans. "Old man, that's one heck of a yarn." She guffawed. "Ya sure can tell big ones. Ya almost had me belivin' ya...this time."

"Cowpoke, he ain't kidding. I can tell."

"Jimmy, Tuck, you have to promise me that this will remain our secret. You can't tell the others because I didn't only prick Jimmy with the hilt blade, but Flower, Rose, Rebecca, and Roger, too," I confessed.

"What are you talking about?" The skepticism in Jimmy's eyes turned from disbelief into shock. "We were *all* dead?"

"It happened. I can't change the past. God knows I would if I could, but I can't." With pleading eyes, I said, "Don't tell them. Not yet. I'm not ready for any of them, especially Roger, to know what happened. For now...don't say anything about it."

CHAPTER SEVENTEEN

A Traitor in the Camp

"Okay, city slicker." Tuck stood facing me. I read a strange expression on her face, some odd blend of trust mixed with disbelief, knitted her brow. "You don't ask for much, do ya?" Sounding similar to a leaky steam valve, she expelled a low whistle. "Ya know how hard it's gonna be to let this go when Roger starts his *I don't wanna be a Champion anymore* routine. I'd like to see his face when he finds out you brought him back from the dead."

"Not a word. Promise me," I pleaded.

Jimmy and Tuck nodded their agreement, but I could tell they didn't like it.

It felt as if the room tilted, and my perception shifted. "Stoney! Stoney!"

Flower rushed in carrying her Rolodex full of student phone numbers. Stoney was right behind her. She said, "Sorry about not returning right away. Rose stopped me. She was calling her parents from the hallway payphone, trying to convince them to extend her curfew. But they said no." She laid her Rolodex on the medicine cabinet. "If you call them, they might change..." Her cheerful tone abruptly changed.

My emotional crisis must've made me look like a scarecrow...a really sad one...maybe, a scarecrow attending a funeral.

Nurse Cumberland's scowling gaze moved from one to another. "I suppose it...it's probably for the best, since they still don't know about her gift." Flower's words slowed. Her speech became erratic. "She had to...get home right away, so...I gave...her...a...ride." Flower stopped talking.

Tuck cracked a smile. My heart sank thinking my secret was going to be outed. "Miss Flower, you missed all the excitement. The Doc here— "

Jimmy interrupted her. "Better to let Mr. B. explain about Iggarest." He gave Tuck a warning glance.

"Why? What's wrong?" she asked.

I held up the charmed crest, missing the sword.

Flower gasped. "Where is it?"

"Gone! I thought...I thought I was giving it to you." My words faded in midair.

Flower hurried over to my cot and felt of my forehead. "Me. Why?" She shook her head. "What's done is done." Her fingers slipped between mine. "Old friend, you looked better before I left." Closing her eyes, she went into a meditation.

"I wouldn't be up and around if they were still inside me." My statement had nothing to do with my emotional feelings because my outlook was as dark as a moonless midnight. I checked on my gift to see if it whispered any foreboding. It answered. Much like an old car with a weak battery starting on a cold day, it gave me an impression—a flash, like a tiny piece of a larger puzzle. All I heard it say was *the rider's sword*. That could have meant anything.

"I think you're alright—for now. It's good to see you up and coherent." Flower sounded more cheerful. "At any rate, I don't sense any more micro-demons in your system."

"I need Stoney." My words sounded feeble, even to my own ears.

"Here I am, Arland." Stoney replied.

"The sword I took from the red rider... take care of it. Keep it safe." Trying to stand, I fell back down onto the cot.

Tuck's smile did little to ease my emotional trauma. "Don't worry about it, Doc. We've got you covered." No doubt, Tuck was doing her best to console me, but nothing short of finding the *Sword of Life and Death* would help my mood.

Flower shook a finger in my face. "Enough of that. You need rest. Jimmy..." She motioned for him to come close. "...see that Mr. Bertarelli gets home. You might stay with him a while to be sure he's alright."

"You buckaroos not goin' without me. This's been more entertainment than I've had in over a century." Following Flower, Tuck headed for the door. "I can't wait to see what y'all do for an encore."

Jimmy didn't even look her way. "Okay, Mr. B., come on. Let's get you home."

"Stoney," Flower commanded, "Arland keeps a number of important relics in his office, and we don't need any more angelic artifacts falling into enemy hands. Take Gewalt's sword from my desk and put it with the artifacts he already has. For now, you're on guard duty there. At least until we know what our next step will be."

He nodded, wordlessly heading through the door and into the hall. A haze filled my mind and for a moment, I thought I was standing on the veranda of an opulent white, Greek Revival-styled mansion overlooking a freshly plowed field. The thought came to me—this could be Heaven.

"Mr. B.... Mr. B.... Are you still with us? You passed out." Panic...maybe it was concern...energized Jimmy's voice, but he was correct. I had lost consciousness for a moment.

Jimmy's eyes widened when I gave him the key to my car. "Mr. B., you must be really bad off, if you want me to drive your Jag." He tossed the keys up over his head and caught them. "You never let anyone drive the Jag."

I weakly smiled up at him. "You'll be fine."

Tuck held out her hand. "Jimbo, I'll follow in your Mustang."

Jimmy hesitated. "You even know how to drive?"

"Of course I do," Tuck replied. "It's nothin' compared to wranglin' the reins of a six-horse coach."

"No! You'd wreck it for sure," Jimmy flatly stated.

Waving at Flower to get her attention, Jimmy tossed her his car key. "Nurse Cumberland, please, follow in my car, so I'll have a way back." He cleared his throat, and added, "You wreck it. You bought it."

Flower smiled back. "Sure thing, just don't hot rod the Jag and leave me in the dust."

"Nobody's ever left my Mustang in the dust—nobody!"

Jimmy offered to help me out to the car, but arrogant pride overwhelmed me. I didn't have the willpower to control myself. My exact words were, "I don't need any help from anyone...ever...not today, tomorrow...never. Got that? Never!"

I knew there was no reason for my outburst, and hopefully Jimmy did, too. Immediately, regret replaced impudence. "I apologize, my friend. You mean well."

Barely lifting my feet, I traversed the empty school hallway with unsteady steps. The corridor looked eerily forlorn. In a moment of disoriented perception, I could imagine the old building telling me how sorry it was to see me leave. Was it my imagination or some prophetic intervention? I couldn't tell.

Outside, Flower revved up the Mustang and pulled behind the MK2. I reminded Jimmy that my house wasn't in Western. In fact, it was located in a sparsely populated rural community, almost to Lubbock.

Tuck yelled, "Shotgun," and hopped in the front seat of my car.

"Jimmy, if you don't go home soon, your dad will get worried." The words left my lips, and I remembered Jimmy's dad was his secret shame. Again, I felt regret because some things should never be said.

Jimmy whispered, "Don't worry about it, Mr. B. My dad won't notice me gone. All he cares about is how much liquor's left in his bottle. That is until he passes out."

I nodded my understanding. Not everyone was privileged as I to know about Jimmy's home life. The fact he was becoming a star under the Friday night lights surely lessened his personal drama. Or perhaps the word I looked for was *trauma*? It fit his situation better. God willing, he will graduate in May, and he has made plans to move out on his own. In silence, we headed off toward the interstate. I think my mind was wandering. I found it hard to focus on what was happening at the present.

Jimmy's situation was surely something he stressed over, but it was nothing new. My emotions must have been on edge because I felt so sorry for him?

An attack of dizziness made the interior of the car spin around me. The bucket seat felt like the Tilt-a-Whirl ride at the South Plains Panhandle Fair. Or maybe it was all in my imagination. For the life of me, I couldn't understand why the edges of my vision blurred. Dizzy again, everything tilted, shifted, and irrationally moved. I thought I was going to faint.

"Stay with us, Mr. B." Jimmy shook me awake. "Don't drop off to sleep or nothing more serious like..." He stopped before he got to the end of his request.

"Maybe we should keep him a talkin'. Bet that would help them brain cells ta wake up," Tuck suggested.

Jimmy gave her a grimaced look. "Okay. If you think so." Shaking me again, he asked, "Why don't you live in Western? Doesn't the long drive every day get old?"

Looking up, I smiled. Except for a sign advertising a Quick Mart's convenience store, I could see nothing but empty cotton fields on either side of the road. "I'm used to the drive. In about twenty-five miles, take Exit 16. It heads off toward the east well before you get to Lubbock. I'll show you where, but for now, drive south."

He nodded. "Hey, Mr. B. Don't go to sleep on us. We need you to stay awake to tell us how to get to your house."

He paused. "Do you have any hobbies? Mr. B., can you hear me?"

I knew he was right. I should stay awake, and yet, sleep's charm whispered, enticing me into her peaceful slumber. There was nothing I wanted more, but for Jimmy's annoying insistence to stop.

"Yes, I slay demons. That's my hobby." My statement sounded haughty, arrogant even. Surely, there must've been some problem with the neurons firing in my brain. My social filter had broken. Normally, I'd never call demon hunting a hobby.

"We are coming upon Exit 16, Mr. B." At that moment, Jimmy's voice could have come from another planet, and I would not have known the difference. It seemed so far away.

"*Wake up, Arland. I let you sleep, but I need to tell you that I'm....*" Even Mr. Dark's usually loud, clear voice didn't resonate in my head like before. It softened as he spoke until completely fading out of my mind. I sat up and stretched. "For once, you shut up on your own. After all these years, I guess you're learning some manners."

I shrugged off my weariness. "Take the exit and head east four miles. You'll see a group of houses off to your left. The two-story one, that's mine. Here, it's a small community where most keep to themselves. But when supernatural weirdness pops up out of nowhere..." I was finding it oddly hard to express myself. "Jimmy, of all people, you should understand. I'll just say the near isolation makes life easier."

I blinked and realized Jimmy was driving my Jag. Confusion filled my mind. I lashed out. "What are you doing? Stop the car and give me those keys!"

He glanced up at me in the rearview mirror. "Mr. B., we are almost at your house."

The unmistakable look of pity filled his eyes, and he tried to placate me by speaking in a soft voice.

I didn't need to calm down. He needed to be more respectful.

"I'll pull over when I get you home." There was a kindness in his voice that touched something inside me. I opened my mouth to protest, but fatigue weighed on me, pushing me back onto the Jag's comfortable back seat.

I didn't fight them. Tuck on one side and Jimmy on the other, they brought me into the house. Flower stood back and let them do the lifting.

"You're a good man, Jimmy Dugan. What would I do without you?"

CHAPTER EIGHTEEN

Eavesdropping

Jimmy tried to return my house key, but I motioned for him to hang it on my key rack by the front door. My head hurt and my emotions were screwed up. My thoughts were distracted, a bit abstract, and certainly distant. It was getting harder to focus on anything for very long. I looked up at Jimmy hanging the key fob on my old rack. Every morning, before removing that key and taking it with me, I touched the simple carved cross cut into the top of the wooden plaque made by Rev Loveless, my ancestor. I suppose few would understand how uniquely comforting it was for me to know that old piece of wood with wrought-iron hooks waited there on the wall, but it never failed to offer its assistance.

Originally, the hooks held gun belts, horse tack, and such. Things Rev didn't allow in his church. I kept it to remind myself of a man who would face every day with conviction and thankfulness.

My friends cautiously stood by as I traversed the stairs to my bedroom. Even in my dazed state, I remember Jimmy's kind offer to help me get ready for bed, but I told him I could manage. More accurately, I demanded he leave my house. I didn't need his, or anyone's, help. Thankfully, neither he nor Tuck argued with me, but rather, ignored my unreasonable protests. More from necessity than choice, I fell fully clothed across my bed, shoes and all.

I took one look at Tuck and remember how I sent her to Hell by accident. "I should have been more careful. This whole mess is my fault. You don't belong in this time. You were happy living in the old west. What have I done, bringing you into the Twentieth Century?" In an uncharacteristic response, tears filled my eyes, and I wept.

"Tuck, Flower, wait in the hall. I'll get him ready for bed." I knew it was Jimmy's voice, and I was thankful for his help, but an indignation arose in me.

"Help me? What do you think I am, an old man who can't do for himself? I'll have you know I am as strong as I ever was." My outburst drained me of my remaining strength and I resigned myself to accept his assistance. Once more, my tone came out calm and collected. "Jimmy, thank you for the kind offer, but I think I can manage."

I decided to change into my pajamas before climbing into bed. It was a struggle, but I finally pulled them up onto my round frame. Out in the upstairs hallway, I heard Tuck, Flower, and Jimmy talking.

"He is far too sick for us to leave him without supervision," Flower said. "He's pale, and his pulse is hardly perceptible."

"Jimbo, Flower's right, he don't look good, and he's not making a bushel of sense either. I don't think leaving him alone is a good idea. If one of those green demons showed up, he would be too far out of it to defend himself."

I stumbled into the hall. "Let me at those devils. I'll give them something to..." I lost my words. My train of thought left me, and to catch my balance, I grabbed for the wall.

"Don't fret, Mr. B. One demon sticks his head in this house and I'll make green goo out of him," Jimmy said.

Tuck's tone sounded very sure. "Yep. They pop in for one reason—to attack. Best to get a drop on 'em."

"They don't always show up to attack." After making such an outlandish claim, I realized that was exactly what most fallen angels do. "Well, sometimes they do, but they haven't always." I paused, trying to make sense of my words. "Okay...they attack, but if they are looking for something they sometimes..." My fingers went straight to my temples... Rubbing them helped. I leaned against Jimmy, who easily supported my weight. "You know, that red demon rider sure doesn't like me. I took her sword." My feet slipped out from under me.

"Jimmy, catch him before he hits the ground," Flower cried out.

Jimmy scooped me up and dropped me onto the bed, where I lay covering my eyes and pressing my thumbs into the sides of my head.

"I don't think I should be talking." My memory fluctuated between my horrific encounter with the Gewalt; when Iggarest came to my office to offer his help; and those amazing west Texas cotton fields.

Flower waited in the hall while Jimmy and Tuck threw a cover over me, closed the door, and left me to my thoughts. Through the silence, a thin, small voice kept mumbling. I thought it must have been Mr. Dark... that was until I realized I could hear my guests through the door. I lay there listening to the conversation in the hall.

"You heard Doc's story. There is a red horse riding demon who's got it in for him. She even told her minions to take him out first, and then gobble up the rest of humanity." Tuck paused, and I heard a soft thud. A smile crossed my face as I imagined her slapping the back of her hand into the middle of Jimmy's chest. Tuck always dared to go where the angels feared to tread.

"What was he doing in Hell, anyway?" Flower asked. Jimmy replied, "Don't know. That's no place to just stop off at, like it's a tourist town."

"Your guess is as good as mine," Tuck replied. "What I want to know is *how* our fearless leader stole Madam Red War's sword." I heard the jingle of Tuck's spurs as she sauntered down the hall toward the stairs. "Frankly, you're nuttier than my Aunt Betty's Christmas fruitcake if you *don't* think she's gonna come huntin' for it, and him, too."

"Good point, cowgirl." Jimmy paused. In my quasi-slumber, I imagined him rubbing his stubbly chin. "I'll take the first watch and you get some sleep. If demon-red shows up looking for her sword, we'll be ready for her...and I'm only telling you one more time, stop calling me Jimbo!"

Their voices faded off as they got to the top of the stairs and I drifted into the peaceful solitude of slumber.

CHAPTER NINTEEN

Cotton Fields of Home

At the edges of my thoughts, I knew this to be a dream. Yet in every way, it appeared real. I found myself in the midst of the most pleasant day I can ever recall. The wind blew a light warmth across me as I lay back on the bank of a lazy river. A familiar herbal odor wafted with the breeze. Cool grass filled the spaces between my toes, and between my teeth, I held a twig broken from the wooded stalk of a cotton plant. I sat upright, pressing the soft grass flat under my hands. Over the knoll, rising up beside of the water, I could see an ocean of white. Fluffy cotton plants were lined in rows, like soldiers awaiting orders to drop their weighted packs. That was what I smelled. Of course, it was familiar, West Texas and cotton farming went hand in hand. I had no sooner laid back and closed my eyes, letting the sun warm my face, when a bone chilling breeze snapped out from nowhere.

When I opened my eyes, I lay covered with a layer of white—not cotton, but frigid ice and snow.

Nearby, at the top of the rise, a boy of ten or eleven, who I took to be of Middle Eastern descent, stood looking down at me. On his right side sat a lion, its mane gracefully moving in the gentle breeze. On his left lay a lamb, meek and spotless white.

Dressed in a simple white tee-shirt, knee-length shorts, and saddle oxfords complete with knee-high socks, he appeared common. There wasn't one remarkable thing about him—and yet the lion showed no aggressive behavior, nor did the lamb tremble with fear.

I gazed at him in awe. Hands on his hips and a stern look in his eye, he spoke with a thick Texas accent. "Some folk ain't got the sense God gave a goose. Better get your bones up from there and follow me up to the house lest you freeze to death."

Shivering, I jumped up and hurried to walk with him, choosing the lamb's side, not the lion's.

"So this is where you live," he said. At the end of the path stood Norman and Irene Loveless' house, my childhood home.

Truthfully, I hadn't lived there in years, but the words came flowing out of my mouth, "Yes. Yes, I do."

I took a look around. In the distance, Western High School stood in the middle of the field, and directly across from it was my two-story prairie style house. Why had I not said that was home? "This is all so familiar, and, yet, bizarrely abstract," I said.

"Lots of fluffy white cotton out here. Yep, so much to love about this flat land. You can see someone coming from a long way off."

"Yes," I replied. "West Texas is mostly flat, with miles of farmland. Between each little town, there's nothing but cotton and more cotton."

"You do love it here, don't you? I mean, both the land and the people."

"Yes. I suppose I do."

"No matter where you've been," the boy said, "you call this place home."

I gazed down the path to the waiting house. "This will always be home...to me."

"Home is precious, isn't it?"

"Among other things," I said.

"Arland, what do you think is the most precious thing in this world?"

I shrugged my reply. All the while wondering how he had called me by name. I didn't recognize him, but then, this was a dream. Dreams don't always make sense...or was this something more? A tingle at the base of my neck made me think it might be a premonition brought on by my supernatural gift.

"I don't know," I answered. "Is it more time...time to keep on living?"

"Being that you have never had to worry about more time to live, I thought you might choose that answer." He kicked through the snow, leaving earth-brown footprints in his wake. "You know, for some folks, it's gold they think is most precious. And, then, for some it's like you say, but, my friend, that's not what I see in the eyes of most folks at the end of their days."

"How would you know such things?" more sarcasm filtered into my words than I intended.

I shivered, and he put a little arm around my waist. Warmth rushed over me, and I felt content. Glancing behind, I marveled at the sprigs of grass sprouting up from wherever he'd stepped.

"When it's all about to be said and done," he said. "Some folk are tired and ready to move on. Without fail, these saints realize they already possess the secret ingredient that proves their lifetime to be worthwhile—and for the last few moments, they revel in it. By now you know I'm talking about memories, treasured memories. They see their lives flash before their eyes." He laughed, giving me an innocent smile. "My dear friend James said it best in the first chapter of his book. 'Blessed are the ones who persevere under trials because, having stood the test, that person will receive the crown of life....' Oh, there's more, but that's for another day."

"As a student of the human condition, I must say, this surprises me. Perhaps one is ignorant of what one might say in such a circumstance until—"

"Oh, for heaven's sake...what big words you use. Life is much simpler than you make it." He lifted his head toward me and winked. He quickened his pace, and I hurried to keep up. "Arland, what is faith made of?"

This time, I gave his question some thought and realized that for all my experiences, I couldn't answer.

"Yep, it's not something people think about, and yet, it's right there in the scriptures."

"It is?"

"Yep, the good book says that a measure of faith is given to every man, woman, and child." He giggled. "I put it there. It's the part of your mind that allows you to reach beyond what you see, hear, and touch. It helps you to believe in something more." He paused. His eyebrows pulled together in a worried expression. "If this part of you is damaged, then you'll no longer be capable of..." He looked away from me. "Let's just say you'll lose faith. I'm talking about faith in others, faith in yourself, and worse, hope will have no meaning."

I looked toward the house. It stood so small at the end of the path. "Are we going to get to the house today? It's so far away."

"No, dear Arland. Not today."

"Then why are we having this conversation? Why am I walking with you?"

The lion yawned, flashing his powerful teeth.

I flinched and moved to the edge of the path.

"You walk with me because you want to...and as for why we had this conversation. Have you not guessed by now?" He stopped.

I stopped.

He cleared his throat and said, "In the light of your recent misfortune, I thought you needed a little guidance—from my heart to yours."

I tilted my head, not sure if I should believe anything he said.

"Oh, Arland. If you insist, I'll make it plain. Your faith center...that part of your brain that allows you to reach beyond what you know to be true...the part that helps you trust, it's injured. Your friend, Mr. Dark, is yet unaware of the extensive damage the micro-demons have caused. When it seems you cannot trust, remember that you can't meet this challenge alone. You need the other Champions to stand with you if you are to succeed."

"I need them?"

"Yes, Arland, you do." The path narrowed, and we stopped. He reached up and gently touched my cheek. "Your redemption will come when martyrs shed tears for you, but for now, rest, dear friend. Rest. Rest and heal as well as you can."

I closed my eyes. A warm blanket of darkness covered me, and I slept.

CHAPTER TWENTY

Send Me Your Champion

I awoke to more voices filtering through the door. "He isn't acting like our old Mr. B." It was Jimmy's voice.

Flower's voice replied, "He isn't even acting like our old Arland. Something has happened to him."

"Ya think?" Tuck said. "He's flip floppin' between trusting completely and not trustin' anyone."

"One minute he's giving me his keys and the next he wants to know why I'm driving his car," Jimmy added.

"That's because ya drive like a half blind, near-sighted hound dog chasin' down a squirrel."

"Funny, cowpoke. That's nothing compared to the pity party your face sent him into." He made a low whistle. "Your mug is ugly enough to make a grown man cry, and I have the proof."

They got quiet and what Jimmy said next made me remember what the boy in my dream told me. He wanted me to remember that I need them... No matter how I felt... I need them.

"Seriously, I'm worried about Mr. B. This is something new; I've never seen him like this." Could that have been a tear I heard in Jimmy's voice?

Of course, he was right. I knew it, they knew it, and even my gift had told me so. Without a doubt, something was definitely wrong in my head. Perhaps my dream was a premonition, or maybe it was a supernatural visitation. Whatever it was, the child's warning reverberated in my thoughts. He said the micro demons had damaged my brain. If that were true, then I couldn't depend on anything I felt or how I perceived others. From this moment on, I had to trust my friends and take their advice.

I opened my bedroom door. To my surprise, Sarah and Rebecca stood there with Jimmy, Tuck, and Flower. "Well, my friends, I have come to the conclusion, I am not myself. If you can find it in your hearts to bear with this old man, I would appreciate your guidance in what is to come."

My words drew smiles from most everyone but Tuck.

"You plan on goin' off on us like you did last night?" Bitterness colored her words. "For a minute there, I couldn't tell the difference between you and a diamondback."

"Frankly, friend Tuck, I can make no promises. My recommendation is for you to help me focus my hostility toward our enemies." I looked down the stairs to where light filtered through my thin curtains into my living room. "Is it day? How long have I slept?"

Jimmy checked his watch and replied, "It's only 5:30 in the morning. Sun isn't up yet."

"Then what's the..." Before I finished my statement, a tree branch came crashing through the window.

A clatter out in the yard drew everyone to the front door. They all packed together—each stretching to see, while I stood behind them. Moments later, I knew what they were seeing.

"**Prophet, come face me. I challenge you like days of old. Two champions on the field of battle decide the fate of the entire army. This time, the victor keeps the flaming sword.**" I would recognize her voice anywhere. It was the red demon rider.

CHAPTER TWENTY-ONE

Staggering into the Light

My team of Champions huddled at the door and on my porch, gawking at the red rider called Gewalt. "We can't let him face her...not in his condition," Sarah said.

"Certainly not!" Flower agreed.

"No half loaded firecracker is going to do my dirty work." Tuck patted her gun holstered under her coat. "Jimbo, step aside and see what Saint Michel's enchantment does against that red hussy. My gun will make fast work of her braggin'."

Jimmy stood his ground. "No! What this horseman needs is a reality check. I'll pound that demon right off that hell-beast and belt her hard enough to keep her out of our hair for a hundred years."

With everyone disagreeing, the room broke out into a heated argument.

Flower managed to be heard over the commotion. "Stop! Stop it, right now! Not one of us can take her alone and she knows it. That's why she made this challenge." She gave me a tender glance. "Between us all, Arland stands the best chance of victory, and he's *not* going out there."

"And why not?" I bellowed. "No one's going to tell me what I can and can't do. I'm not decrepit...not yet."

Rebecca put her hand on my shoulder. "Mr. B., that's not you talking. That's your condition making you feel this way." She smiled. "Like you said...let us guide you."

I took a deep breath. Every molecule of my being wanted to rebel. I held my breath and counted backward from ten. When I finished, I relaxed.

"I haven't seen you do that in a long time." Flower's encouraging tone helped my mood.

"It's a trick I learned when I was young. Back then, I was kind of nervous."

"Kind of? You were definitely on the high-strung spectrum," Jimmy said.

"**Prophet, did you hear my challenge? What say you? Do we have an agreement**?"

Tuck yelled out, "No, he don't agree, you surrogate of Satan."

I gave Rebecca a push, and she fell against Jimmy's back. He tumbled toward the doorframe. Pushing again, this time I plowed my way through. Tuck only had time to pull her pistol before stumbling out onto the porch with me. Her free arm grabbed onto the door to keep from falling. I screamed, "Here I am." Nothing had prepared me for what awaited.

In my yard, the rider sat astride her blazing mount. The beast's nostrils flared, shooting fire with every snort. In her hand, she carried a sword; not the fiery sword I stole from the red rider. I stepped back. Staggering, I fell to my knees for I recognized the sword. I took another look. A pain crossed my chest and my lungs refused to inhale. In her hand she didn't hold the flaming sword, but Saint Gabriel's. I stood and gathered my courage, then stepped forward, prepared to do battle against the most powerful weapon ever forged by the angels.

The rider dismounted and stepped toward us. She stopped twenty yards from my porch. "**Prophet, come to me and let us battle. Let the victor choose the fate of those who follow us.**"

CHAPTER TWENTY-TWO

The Relic of Saint Sebastian

From the roadside, I heard the popping backfire of a tiny engine. In the edge of the horse's firelight, George rode his Vespa into my yard. He hopped off and stood, holding a sword. The one I took from Gewalt. "**I am the prophet's Champion. I will fight in his name**." His voice resonated like that of an angel. My gift kicked in and I saw translucent wings, six of them, on George's back.

Flower rushed up to my side and steadied me. I took another step and almost fell, but her touch fed strength into my body and soul. I whispered, "Where did you put the rider's sword?"

"When I left, it was locked in my office, and Stoney was standing guard on it." She gazed up at the rider. "At least it was there."

"Obviously it's not there anymore," I replied. "I just hope Stoney is alright."

"As far as I can tell, this is one of the favored angels who's aiding George," she said. "They would never harm Stoney."

"I wish I could say the same about this red devil," I said. "She looks angry enough to grind anyone in her way to dust."

"**Reuwel, I recognize you,**" the rider said. "**Why do you persist in your quest to protect the mortals? They are not worthy of your devotion.**"

"**I stand in the prophet's stead.**" George's mouth moved, but the words were not his. "**Accept or flee back to the depths where you belong.**"

"**Fight me as yourself, not as a puny mortal.**" The rider cackled and continued. "**Hiding in mortal guise will only make your demise the quicker.**"

George didn't even blink. "**Again, I say, I fight in the name of the marked prophet. Face me in battle.**"

"**Do you see the weapon I carry? It is Gabriel's sword. No Elohim can stand against it, for it is death, and the one who carries it, the master of death!**"

George said nothing. He just stepped closer to the rider.

"**It makes no difference. You will die this night, and heaven will have one less bothersome guardian to watch over the human scum.**"

George stepped closer, still.

"**Come at me then, and I will make worm food of you.**" The red rider bellowed.

My instinct, the years of demon fighting, and my wounded pride made me want to go fight at Reuwel's side, but when I tried to move, my muscles refused to cooperate.

"Can anyone move?" I asked—my words louder than necessary.

"No!" Tuck yelled. "What's wrong with my legs?"

"It's Reuwel's charm. He has us immobilized!" Flower answered. "He's done this before, but never to us."

"All I can move is my head," said Jimmy.

Unable to help; we watched and waited for the eventual horror.

With the flaming sword held over his head, George closed in. One step forward and then two to the side; he circled his foe.

The rider leveled Saint Gabriel's sword, ready to thrust it into George's heart. "**Why hesitate? The faster you charge me, the quicker your immortality will be stripped off your bones. Your spiked carcass will hang as a warning to all who challenge the Fallen.**" She opened her mouth and from the yawning cavity came a horde of cockroaches, belching out into the space between the opponents. They scurried through the dried grass and up George's legs.

The vermin reached his knees before he waved over them. They floated out and away—straight toward the rider—each one popping like firecrackers in her face. He took advantage of the distraction, swinging his sword and cutting a slash across her red robe. She drew back, avoiding his slicing backswing.

"Favored angel, you have drawn first blood, but all I need do is scratch your wretched hide to bring certain death." She wailed with cackling laughter.

In silence, George whirled his blade overhead and brought it down hard.

The rider made an upward swing. The clash of charmed steel erupted into blazing sparks and a thunderous clatter. Another swing of the rider's sword swooshed like a mighty wind, but the only thing the blade cut was air. George had dodged with superhuman speed and leaped into the air, hovering above the rider's head.

"Reuwel, taking to the air will not save you. Pitiful Elohim, for the valiant way you have fought, I bestow one mercy on you. This is your last chance. Flee while you may."

George stabbed his flaming sword down at the rider, who sidestepped the jab.

"You think you are out of my reach? Fool, flight will not save you from my soul stealing clutches."

The rider's shoulders contorted. Claw tipped bones sprouted out from her shoulder blades. A leathery mass followed, all emerging through red tinted skin. Tiny chunks of unholy flesh flew in every direction from the open sockets around the embryonic wings. The protrusions twisted into unnatural positions. Scaly leather like veils, formed between each claw tipped growth—until bat-like wings flexed across her back. Flapping them, she roared, flexed the new outstretched appendages, and like a dog finding comfort in its own skin, shook off a residue of demon blood.

Loose pieces of cursed skin flew like shrapnel; some landed inches from the porch. Everywhere they touched the ground, it turned black, vapors sizzled, and a foul odor, reminiscent of rotting fish, assaulted my nose.

Rebecca called to me, "Do something, Mr. B. You can talk. Use the prophet's voice to help George!"

I tried to speak, but the muscles in my jaw had seized, preventing me. All I could do was mumble. Before me unfolded the most terrible fight I'd ever witnessed.

Claws scratched, metal bit into metal, and the sound of battle raged. The demonized sorceress struck out with her taloned wings while Reuwel, in the form of George, countered her repeated blows. Hacking at him as if he were a piece of raw meat, still he came at her.

Again she opened her mouth and this time spat something like venom at him. The vile green goo slid off his skin, leaving open sores wherever it touched. She extended her jaw wider, contorting her mouth into a grotesque, gorge-like yawn. Scorpions, the size of rats, hurdled out from her throat, through the air, and covered him with their spiny stings. He waved his hand, and they fell to the earth in piles, where they swarmed one another in a frenzy—stabbing and chewing.

She flexed open her wings, blowing a brimstone laden gale in his face. He didn't even blink. In fact, he hadn't blinked since he arrived. It seemed that no mortal could possibly have withstood the punishment, but George kept advancing his attack despite the pounding.

Then it happened. George moved close, leading with the flaming sword. Gewalt slammed Gabriel's sword down onto George's blade. There was a terrible flash of light and a clap of thunder. The percussive wave made me close my eyes and when I opened them, I couldn't believe it. George's blade had shattered and dissolved into glittering dust.

Before he could retreat, Gewalt drew her blade across George's chest—deep enough to draw blood. I expected him to fall dead, but instead he flew forward. His right hand grabbed her by the throat, and his left gripped the demon's wrist, preventing her from striking with Gabriel's weapon.

Perhaps it was my theatrical imagination, but I believe fear dripped off the only word she spoke. "How?" Its intensity made me shudder. Then the realization hit me—I could move again.

George yanked the blade down between them. She engulfed him in her wings and pulled him close. They fell to earth and George landed on the red horseman. The blade sandwiched between them. My sense of time froze; it was like the universe stood still and the two fighters were in control...in control of everything. When her wings relaxed, it was George who stood over Gewalt's unmoving body.

CHAPTER TWENTY-THREE

Bitter-Sweet Victory

Standing in my yard, watching George battle the red rider of war, made me feel utterly useless. My head hurt and my pulse boomed in my ears. Every time I took a step, the ground moved, and I would all but fall to my knees in a dizzy fit of vertigo. Rebecca and Flower hurried to my aid. With one on my left and the other on my right, I managed to stay vertical. Like seeing a surreal painting by Salvador Dali, I watched as the red horseman lay defeated at George's feet.

She moved her gnarled hands to her bosom, where a gash had been cut across her torso from shoulder to waist.

Over Gewalt, stood George…The *death blade* embedded in his chest. The wound mirrored the one on the fallen demon.

He reached up and pulled it free. Then he turned the hilt blade, *the life blade* affixed to the sword's pommel, toward himself. Unblinking, he plunged it into his stomach. Finally, he fell to his knees and let the sword drop to the ground. The supernaturally sharp blade sliced into the earth and buried itself halfway to the guard.

The rest of the team rushed toward George, only to stop in their tracks when Gewalt moved. She screamed out, **"Ichabod be your name and all of Beelzebub's curses be on your head. Gehort mir Das schwert!"**

To our horror, the sword sank into the earth. For the briefest moment, I'd swear the blade tried to pull itself free…but failed.

Tuck ran for it at the same time as Jimmy. Awkwardly, they tripped over each other, both reaching for the sword. It sank through the dirt and out of sight before either one of them could retrieve it.

"I curse you, mortals. Dominikus, the destroyer, once crowned to be the bride of Abaddon, is now the harbinger of death. She is vengeance incarnate, and will stake your hearts before the altars of men for all to see."

"Adora, it is I, Reuwel, who vanquished you. Your curse is pointless."

The rider of war shuddered and died. Her twisted corpse decayed—the hellish, red tinted, scaly hide grew translucent, the muscles thinned and withered. Pulling away from the bone, tendons snapped and sinew stretched. Her skeleton changed from gory red to black before completely turning to dust.

Rebecca stayed with me while the others hurried over to George's side. The ugly wound across his chest gaped open, but to my surprise, it bled very little.

"**Healer, lay your hands on this vessel before I leave it,**" Reuwel said. "**My time draws nigh.**"

Flower grabbed George by the arm. In my prophet's vision, I saw Reuwel separate from George as The Kid screamed in pain and fainted.

"**As long as this vessel wore the relic of Saint Sebastian, we would not die. The impregnated blade was no more dangerous than another. I regret that he *now* feels the wounds Adora inflicted upon him.**" The angel put his hand on George's limp body. "**Be blessed, brave one. After the healer restores you to health, you will be well.**"

"I'll be a half pint horned toad," Tuck said. "The Arkansas Kid might be more important than we thought." Eyeing me, she added, "Do we need to get him to a doctor?"

Like a silhouette, Reuwel appeared at the edge of the street. The overhead lamplight cast a shadow across his features. "**This is the one and only time I have permission to physically interfere in mankind's matters. The Creator says the Champions must fight their own battles.**" He raised his hand and clinched his fist. A thunderous rumble emanated from the sky and the faint image of Reuwel faded from sight.

Flower moved her hands up and down George's legs and arms. His bruises and lacerations disappeared under her healing fingertips. "I suppose this makes George an official part of the team? Reuwel threw him straight into the fight!"

"The poor boy deserves a medal for what he did this morning," Sarah replied.

Looking down at George's unconscious body, Jimmy added, "I hope and pray he doesn't remember being in that fight."

"He'd be better off if he can't," Rebecca stated. "It's my guess, Reuwel just kidnapped him."

I mumbled, "Reuwel doesn't kidnap people. Shanghai them...maybe. Kidnap—never. The real issue here is that we lost the sword again!" No one was paying me any attention. Everyone's focus was on George.

"Maybe that's all for the best," Jimmy said. "If he remembers any of it, he may not want to help us."

Rebecca added. "I still don't think it was fair for Reuwel to use him like this."

"Really," Tuck said, "I'm glad he did, or else we'd all be dead as my Aunt Gussie's Sunday goose." She made a low whistle. "I've never seen a tussle like that. Gewalt was one tough devil-mama."

"Reuwel knew what he was doing when he gave George Saint Sebastian's relic." I sighed and pointed to the gold laced rope looped around George's waist. "That relic was the only way to defeat a foe carrying Saint Gabriel's sword. It kept George alive even though his wounds were fatal." My words sounded familiar. Then I recalled, Reuwel had told them the exact same thing. My mind was slowly healing or else I wouldn't have remembered.

"I still think the angels should respect us enough to ask what we want..." Rebecca glanced over at Tuck, who gave her a hard stare. "...well, from time to time at least," she added.

"This could be a short-lived victory. You know there are three more just as wicked and perhaps even more dangerous headed this way," I stated. Still, no one paid my words any attention, despite the fact, I was feeling much more focused.

Jimmy lifted George and carried him into my house. I asked Flower to usher everyone inside. Standing on wobbly legs, I took a last look out into the yard. In the twilight of dawn, I could make out a crowd forming in the street and alongside the house. My neighbors must have heard the racket and come out to see the fight, but no, there were too many bystanders for that to be true. I squinted to get a better look.

I called to Jimmy, "We have a problem out here. Come see for yourself."

When he came to the door, he spat on the porch in disgust, and said, "And we thought the worst was over."

Rebecca peered over his shoulder. "Are those people all lined up shoulder to shoulder? What are they doing?"

"Yes, and no...that depends on if your definition of people means they have to be alive." I answered. "To most, they look like normal mortals, but because I'm a prophet, I see through their disguises. These poor creatures are demon possessed corpses." Putting a hand on her shoulder, I forced my vison into her mind.

"Oh, Heaven help us!" Rebecca blurted. "It is. It's a horde of demons disguised as mortals. They're all in twisted forms with glowing eyes." She ducked inside and stood by the window. "Why are they gathering at the edge of your property?" She dared another look. "And they are saying something. I hear them mumbling."

Bowing my head, I tapped into my prophetic gift. I, too, needed the answer to that question. In a moment, I knew. "They are encircling us and chanting in angel tongue to trap us. They intend to imprison us here."

Flower spoke, her tone sounded harsh and cynical. "Can they do that?"

"Yeah, they can," I said. "You know how Phoenix trapped your dad's carnival and put it outside of time."

"But he was a powerful fallen angel." Flower got louder with each word. "These are minions. They don't have that kind of angel magic."

"True," I said. "Individually, they aren't very magical, but look how many there are." My vertigo was gone, and I was acting a lot like my old self.

From where I stood, I could only see some of them, but there had to be a lot more. I stuck my head out to estimate. The lawn next to mine had filled up with them, and after scanning the rest of the neighborhood, it was more frightening than ever. The living dead had already surrounded us, every one of them chanting—eyes red as burning coals. "I wish Roger were here. He could send them packing by reciting one charm from the book of Uriel."

"Doc!" Tuck bellowed. "When is it going to get through your thick skull? Roger don't give a flying flip no more." She huffed and went inside to help Jimmy and Flower with George. When she returned to the porch, she blurted, "Hell's bells, how many of those zombies are there?"

"Don't use the word *zombies!* It creeps me out," Sarah insisted.

"What would you call them? They're walking, and they're dead. To me, that equals a zombie," Jimmy said. "They move around because there's a demon inside that dead hide. I can't think of much worse."

Flower looked out of the living room window. "I can't see them like Arland can, but they don't walk with the grace people do. Even an awkward person doesn't lumber like a zombie." She shuddered. "Demons are relentless."

A disturbance among the living dead rumbled directly at the edge of my driveway. Some lost soul pushed through the circle and headed up the walk. As he approached, I recognized him. It was our reluctant ally, Iggarest.

CHAPTER TWENTY-FOUR

Chanting Zombies

"Iggarest! What did you do?" I yelled. "You gave the red rider Gabriel's sword!"

Jimmy pushed past me and ran out into the yard.

As he passed through the crowd of walking dead abominations, Iggarest's humanity faded, and his beautiful, majestic form appeared. The fallen angel passed between the ranks of the walking dead and not one demon turned on him.

Jimmy charged like a linebacker. Upon impact, I expected the fallen angel to tumble to the ground, but instead he dematerialized and allowed Jimmy to pass straight through him.

Staggering, Jimmy fell and rolled sideways, as if expecting Iggarest to attack. I knew Jimmy was exceedingly angry. I have always been the only one who could see his invisible armor, and to me, it was glowing a bright blue as he bounced upright and quickly crouched on one knee.

"Brains of a buffoon and the brawn of ten armies, the creator never fails to entertain." Iggarest scowled.

"Did you give that red demon-witch on the fiery horse Gabriel's sword?" I demanded an answer.

He gazed back at me from over his shoulder. **"No. Why would I do that? I took the blasted thing to kill Lucifer. Not many weapons can kill an immortal."**

Jimmy stood, dusting off his pants. "And how did that go?"

"Before I had a chance to use it, old pig face had one of his lackeys ambush me. It was Dominikus. The lord of Hell has made her indomitable. She took the sword by force!" Iggarest's mortal appearance returned. **"Even I am stumped. It seems he knows what's said in your midst."** He straightened his cravat and coat. **"You have a traitor on your team."**

Tuck yelled from the door. "The only traitor here is a big fat lyin' goober by the name of Iggarest."

"Lady Teresa Ann, I assure you, this humble Fallen has not betrayed any of the Champions. My motives are pure."

She pulled her charmed gun from its holster and leveled it at Iggarest. "Call me Teresa Ann one more time and I'll put a devil piercing shell right between your nasty green eyes."

"Aside from providing you with personal satisfaction, it would only prove to be an annoyance; save your ammunition for some unsuspecting demon. It will have a more grave effect." Iggarest shook his head at her. **"No one**

listens these days. I just told you, we Fallen are not so easily vanquished."

"I'm gonna count to three and you either tell the truth or I'll perforate your noggin." She cocked the hammer on the charmed 45 police special. "One... Two..."

Iggarest blurted, **"Wait... No, not now!"** He bowed his head and clinched his fists. **"Stay away from me, you hell-bent harpy!"** His visage blurred as a violet mist oozed its way up his body and covered him.

When the purple fog cleared, the air was filled with the fragrance of cinnamon and Lilacs...and in Iggarest's stead, Miss Wilson stood on my walk. **"At last, I am free of that hideous parasite."** Her voice resonated with more authority than I remembered.

"It don't matter to me if you grow two heads and one looks like Richard Milhous Nixon. I told you I'd shoot, and I meant it." Tuck stepped closer. "I've been hankerin' to know if fallen angels bleed."

The angel flipped back her fluffy hair. **"You wouldn't shoot a woman, now would you, gunslinger**?"

Tuck made a sideways smile, "Woman to woman, yeah, I would."

My hand went up in front of the gun. "Iggarest, disguising yourself as my secretary won't save you. Tuck means business."

"Unlike when Iggarest took on Nurse Cumberland's appearance, this is no disguise. At the present, you may think of it as my alternative-self." Miss Wilson patted herself on the chest. **"Arland, I've typed hundreds of pages**

for you and made your coffee. I even reminded you of that dreadful appointment you had with the grieving Loveless family. By now, we've known each other long enough. You can call me by my real name, my angel name—Amethyst."

Tuck lowered her weapon. "What? Naw, you can't do that."

"I thought your name was Iggarest." Sarah's accusing tone was unmistakable. "You can't change...everything...just because you want to."

Standing there in the form of Amethyst, she revealed her angelic persona to be completely different than that of Iggarest. Undeniably beautiful, she sparkled, every muscle a sapphire, ruby, or emerald. Her hair, thin strands of spun gold, slowly moved as she tilted her head. Clothed in folds of light, she stood adorned in a gown cut from a glimmering rainbow. She was radiant. "**Why Not? An eon ago, I found that I could transcend into Amethyst, but alas, the persona of Iggarest haunts me. That sniveling sneak found a way to inhabit my psyche.**"

"Oh, Hell's bells," Tuck blurted. "He's...I mean, she's a schizophrenic angel. There's two of them in there."

"**Mortal woman, you scorn me. We are sisters, you and I.**"

"I ain't your sister, you schizo-lohim!" Tuck exclaimed.

"**Iggarest and I often disagree; however, we both have one goal. Kill the lord of Hell and take his throne. The problem is that I'm the superior angel. I could have done it by now if not for his bungling.**"

My head pounded like the whole WHS drum core was using my forehead for practice. Amethyst's angelic form was so gorgeous it was hard to concentrate. "Hold it. Stop right there. What are you saying? You're both Iggarest and Amethyst?"

Sarah stepped behind me, and Rebecca moved behind Tuck. Sarah peeked around and asked, "Who exactly gave me my gift...you or Iggarest?"

"That was all Iggarest's doing. I warned him about gifting a mortal. It never turns out like one expects. Blame him for any misfortune it has caused."

"And you can just change personalities at will?" I asked.

"I usually get *my* way. As you have seen, my magnificence is hard to deny." Her mortal appearance returned. **"I think of myself as a superlative Elohim, for I have risen above them all. I possess something they could never attain, not even Morning Star, and he is jealous of my abilities."**

The mere idea of Miss Wilson and Iggarest being one and the same made my head hurt all the worse. I stepped over by the house and rubbed my temples.

"**When I appear in my lower form, I am Iggarest. When I choose to reveal my true self, I grace the world with Amethyst's awesome magnificence.**" She flipped her hair.

"That's a bunch of junk," Sarah blurted out from behind me. "You consider yourself superior, and yet, you chose to spend your days at our high school, typing and making coffee for our principal?" Sarcasm dripped from her words. "That's sad...really sad."

My head hurt worse. "Sarah, isn't it obvious? She spent all that time hoping to find out how we vanquished a fallen angel. All angels are immortal. Iggarest... I mean...her... Aargh!" I held my head. It throbbed, pounding against my skull. I turned toward the angel and pointed. "You have one goal and you've botched it. Now, our enemy has the greatest weapon ever forged."

"How dare you!" Rebecca yelled. "You're accusing one of us of telling Lucifer our plans, and you heard every word of all the conversations going on in Mr. B.'s office. I think you're a two-faced rat! You've been snitching to the Fallen."

Rebecca's words appeared to hurt Amethyst's feelings. Or so it seemed.

CHAPTER TWENTY-FIVE

The Green Line

Flower and George stepped out onto the porch. Both of them looked tired, but well. All his injuries appeared to be healed. He sounded like a true gladiator, a Champion of the Favored. "Too bad that sword broke. I liked the feel of it."

Looking up, they both went pale and gasped for air. I thought it must have been because Amethyst had made such a jaw-dropping disclosure, but Flower pointed past us to the edge of the yard and yelled. "Fight that Fallen later! We have a more pressing problem. Those circling demons are chanting some kind of occultic spell, and the yard is catching on fire."

Indeed, a green fire kindled from the edge of the circle of cursed souls. Another group of demons emitted more green sparks, and another—and another. Moments later, the flames merged into a substantial blaze. They flickered and flashed upward along the edge of a green circle. Those tiny blazes ignited like on a trail of gasoline. The flames followed the green line and encircled the entire house. Everything on my side of the line didn't spontaneously incinerate, but behind that line the grass and lawn burned with a fury, towering up into the sky. Then, like Poe's swinging pendulum, the line moved closer toward me. The green circle was shrinking, and with it, certain death.

Angry, I leveled an accusing finger at Amethyst. "Fallen, is this your doing?"

"These are corpses, not mortals, who have sinned. I promise you have not been lied to. Iggarest's minions are the living who wallow in their iniquity." A disgusted look came over her. **"These creatures are abominations. Even in my eyes, they reek of Hell's breath. Do not insult me with your accusations, mortal!"**

I watched as the approaching green curse climbed over the fence between the houses. It, too, burst into flames. Wherever the glowing green circle passed, it ignited. Next came the dried grass on the road verge. It caught on fire. The flames outside the green ring set the cedar fencing that lined the backyard alight and eventually engulfed the neighbor's yard. With slow persistence, the green blaze moved to their house. Behind the circle's edge, the fire grew out of control. Inside the circle, nothing burned, and no smoke blew back onto us. There, we were trapped, awaiting the unavoidable shrinking green ring to consume us.

"What happens when it gets so small only the house remains inside that circle?" Rebecca asked.

"Duh, we get in the house," Tuck replied.

"And when it burns the house down, what then?" Rebecca pressed for a better answer.

Tuck shuddered. "D...Don't think about it."

My irrational monotone was calmer than my emotional state. "I guess we die." My words sounded terrifying, even to me. But, for the moment, we were safe inside the shrinking circle.

With the fence, the walk, the drive, and the neighbor's yard all engulfed in flames, the people who lived next door, Janet and Roy Fitzgerald, ran out of their house screaming. "Fire! Fire!" They ran over to another neighbor's door. Banging until someone roused, they pleaded for help.

Still, the cursed line moved steadily toward my house, and we watched, unable to escape or assist the innocent inhabitants of my rural village.

The fire spread across the dried lawns to other yards. More neighbors came out of their houses as a siren wailed in the distance.

Usually, I had to be in contact with someone to read or cast thoughts, but in this situation, it was worth a try. Putting my fingers to my temples, I concentrated on Janet's friendship and sought my prophetic gift. A jarring sensation pushed her thoughts into my mind.

She saw the people standing around as just creepy spectators drawn by the fire. It seemed impossible for them to overlook the zombies standing directly in the flames and not burning, but that's how angel magic works.

When spirit creatures are involved, mortals...unless they have some spiritual gift...rarely see what's actually happening.

The raging fire ignited the fuel in my Jag. Like a scene from some sad movie, it blew the car apart. The flying pieces injured a dozen of the zombies. They turned to a black rocklike substance before dissolving into ash.

Next the Vespa caught fire. It, too, blew shrapnel around. Last to catch fire was Jimmy's Mustang. It must have had exactly the right amount of fuel in the tank, because it made the biggest mess when it exploded.

CHAPTER TWENTY-SIX

The Fallen's Gift

Like a dazed fool, I stood speechless. Then something inside me felt like it too exploded—just like the cars did. I screamed out, "No! No, not my Jag. Oh, heaven help me, please! Not my poor car. You sorry, hell-cursed zombies, you're all going to pay for that!"

Jimmy pulled on my arm. "Someone bigger than these minions is pulling the strings here..." He met Amethyst's gaze with a snide stare, "...and I have my suspicions as to who it is."

Disdain coated the transformed angel's speech. **"In opposition to what this muscle-monkey here might think,"** the angel pointed and tilted her nose to the sky. **"I didn't come to argue or fight. My purpose was one of angelic benevolence."**

Amethyst spoke, but the voice was not hers. It was Iggarest's distinctive baritone. **"Do not despair. I've already**

provided your escape from this unfortunate situation." She put a hand on her mouth, like a child who spoke out of turn.

"Stay down, you worm. I am in control now." She shuddered from exerting the effort to restrain Iggarest's persona. She sighed and regained control. **"That Cretan doesn't know what he's talking about. Ignore his outburst."** She put a hand on her hip and flipped her hair back over her shoulder. "**You can thank me later for the advice."** Without another sound, Amethyst faded from sight.

"What does he...I, uh...she mean by that?" Rebecca stammered, awkwardly spitting out her words. "Iggarest didn't give us anything."

"Never trust a Fallen," Flower said. "They lie even when their mouths are closed."

Sarah hurried to my side. "I hate to say it, but Iggarest gave me something." She cleared her throat. "It's my gift, and I'd bet that sorry excuse for an angel had a plan all along!"

I thought for a moment. "Do you think Iggarest really made a way for us to escape? He gave you a Champion's gift...is that what he was talking about?"

"It's not likely," Tuck said. "You have the gift of drawin'. I don't know how that can get us out."

"Even if it could," I added. "When someone touches the drawing, I pop right back, like a Yoyo, to where I started."

"Yeah, maybe...just maybe, Mr. B. could escape certain death," Jimmy pointed out, "but what about the rest of us? We'll be trapped in here."

Too bad Rose isn't here. If she had Mr. B.'s angel feather, she could transfigure a pair of wings and fly us out one at a time.

Tuck shook her head. "That would only dump us from the frying pan into the fire. With those zombies out there, we'd be in for the fight of our lives. I can hold my own with nine or ten...twenty, maybe, but look at 'em. There must be five hundred or more, and they look like they's ready to tear us limb from limb right now."

Jimmy looked up at Tuck and grimaced. "I'm glad Rose isn't here."

"Come on... We've got to do something," Rebecca said. "Standing around talking is going to get us killed."

Sarah popped a hip outward and tapped her black patented Prada. "But what if I draw a picture of the school, and we all hold on to Mr. B. when he touches the drawing? Maybe my gift can save us all from being burned alive."

Pointing her finger at us like a gun, Tuck said, "And, pow, no one will be here to touch the drawing. It will simply burn up." She rubbed the back of her neck. "It's worth a try."

Since Amethyst disappeared, my head was finally getting back to being somewhat normal. I scrambled through the house for some kind of drawing tools for Sarah. Typing paper and graphite pencils were all I could find. She went to work drawing, and in the next twelve minutes, had a reasonable rendition of the school. Twelve precious minutes that brought us closer to being burned alive as the blazes danced, taking tall leaps and bounding across the roof of the house. Creaking timbers; the stifling smell of burning tar paper; and the crackling of the fire set my nerves on edge.

The green line had ignited the doorway and set the living room ablaze. It burned up the back porch and ravaged through the kitchen. We huddled in the hallway next to the dining room; all around us, the house went up in flames.

Outside, Firemen labored with no success. Like true unsung heroes, those first responders hosed no less than three tanker trucks of water on the blaze, and that was only the ones I counted. A thick, black pillar rose into the air, forming a monstrous cloud. All the while, we huddled in the hallway behind the glowing green line. Only minutes remained before the entire house was engulfed in the inferno.

Sarah sheepishly handed Flower her picture. "It's not as good as the horse, but I hurried."

She took it and announced, "It's now or never. Grab ahold of Arland and don't let go."

They all got a handful of my tweed jacket, and I hesitantly touched the picture. My stomach took a leap into my mouth, and the room spun, turning into a churning mix of colors. A falling sensation overcame me. Nausea bubbled up inside and I closed my eyes, trying not to vomit. I landed with a hard thud and dared to look around. We were on the winter-brown front lawn of the school.

Everyone lay on the grass beside me, holding either their mouth or stomach. Tuck leaned on one elbow and hurled up a sizable portion of whatever she had last eaten.

"What's wrong, cowgirl?" Jimmy scoffed. "I thought you were made of tougher stuff." Then he, too, leaned over and retched.

"Speak for yourself, Jimbo. At least we're alive." She took a bandana from the inside pocket of her western styled leisure suit and wiped her mouth clean.

Sarah had fared far better than the rest and stood first. She tugged on her miniskirt and smoothed the wrinkles before dusting off the clingy bits of dried grass. Tossing her hair back, she dug through her handbag for a tube of lipstick and a silver compact. Flipping it open, she complained, "My hair is standing on ends, and my eyeshadow is smudged."

Tuck fluttered a hand at her own face. "Oh, the world will end if anyone sees me like this!" and laughed. "Girl, I keep mine short, so three passes of a brush and I'm ready to do some demon huntin'."

"Some of us have higher expectations," Sarah replied. "If you ask me, a little lipstick wouldn't hurt you."

"Naw. My mama told me I had natural cherry red lips. It would be a shame to cover up such beauty."

Sarah stared at her, tapped her foot on the sparse, crispy grass, and dropped her lipstick back into her purse. "I don't know what's worse, the fact you believed her then or you still believe her, even now."

Like a sexy movie star, Tuck put her hand on the back of her short cropped hair. "Hey, what you see is what you get."

Rebecca rolled her eyes. "I hope you two are through sharing beauty tips. You're making me ill."

"Pretty danged sure it's not us making you feel queasy," Tuck replied. "Everyone but Mr. B. barfed after that...whatever it was."

"Astral-teleportation..." Flower interjected, "...that's what I've decided to call it."

I chuckled. "You made that up. There is no such thing."

"There is now." Flower dusted the dried grass off of her white nurse's slacks. "We are proof it works."

"You think the house and the picture have burned up by now?" Jimmy asked.

"Probably, we barely got out alive," Rebecca answered. "I've no doubt everything behind that green line turned to ash."

Flower added, "I wonder what happened to your poor neighbors? Their houses were burning, too."

"Don't take this wrong, but who cares? We can't be responsible for everyone in the world. I mean, really, man, no one can save everybody, right?" Jimmy said as he rubbed his hands on the cool brown grass. "Anyway, looked like they were all out of their homes by the time the horde's fiery charm forced us into Mr. B.'s house."

George, who landed between Tuck and Flower, lay in silence, prostrated on the school lawn. Not that he talked much, anyway. Perhaps the sudden landing had knocked the wind out of him. Without warning, he jerked upright, his eyes went wide, and he looked around. He sighed and sat cross-legged on the grass. A relieved expression replaced the wild fear in his face.

Stoney ran out of the main doors to where we were. "How? What...Are you guys okay?"

"Same old story; demons, possessed corpses, and an ass-kicking Champion. This time it was Sarah who saved us, or else we'd be French fried heroes," Jimmy said.

"Sarah introduced us all to something called astral teleportation," Rebecca added.

"Alright. Don't tell me, but don't act like I'm dumb," Stoney complained.

"No. It's the truth. Angel magic at its best. Even..." I reached for a name, but it wouldn't come to mind. "Yes, my friend..." I paused, trying to remember. "The name I'm wanting still eludes me. But take it from me, no one could do better." I thought I had all my facilities back, but I suppose a few of my marbles were still lost.

"Are you talking about Roger?" Stoney asked.

"Yeah, that's the fellow," I said. "Forsooth, he would be proud, indeed." His stare betrayed his concern.

"A flash of light and here we are," Sarah said.

"Thankfully, there are no classes today. However, the school's free meal program is going on in the cafeteria," Stoney said. "Those kids come in through the back cafeteria door. I'm pretty sure no one saw your magical arrival."

"Do not worry, my dear friend." It was hard to complete my statement with normal speech. "If they did, they would simply assume a logical reason for the mystical occurrence. That is what people do."

Stoney took my hand and helped me up. "None the less, we need to get inside," he said.

CHAPTER TWENTY-SEVEN

Parting Words

"We have to be expedient. If another of the horsemen shows up, the early bird students arriving for the free breakfast program will be endangered." To my perception, the lawn around me moved, and I stayed still. An indication I was not completely well, yet. I staggered, but not enough to fall. Leaning on Stoney for balance made the vertigo affected world stop moving.

I asked, "Did you think to unlock the door before bursting out to help us? If not, the panic bars are set to lock."

A contrite expression wrinkled Stoney's forehead. "No, I didn't. We're locked out."

I rummaged through my pockets for the school keys. Thankfully, I found them and hurriedly ushered everyone down the hall and into my office. George and Tuck chose to sit on the ebony chairs while Rebecca, Sarah, Jimmy, and

Flower sat around the conference table. I asked Stoney to sit by me, for I still didn't have a competent sense of balance.

"Hey, *Kid*," Tuck put her hand on George's shoulder. "Do you remember anythin' of your scrap with the red she-devil?"

George broke his silence. "Yes. I remember all of it, but the weird thing is, it's like someone else was doing all those heroic things and I was watching from the sidelines." He looked down at his chest, and the huge holes sliced in his tee-shirt. "I know I got cut really bad, but I didn't feel anything until the angel's presence left me." He paused and took a deep breath. "Then it hurt like nothing's ever hurt before."

"That's simply wrong. What a terrible thing to have happen to you," Rebecca said. "I didn't even know angels could merge with a person."

George looked up with a sheepish expression. "I didn't either, but I don't know much about angels."

"So what does it feel like to be possessed by an Elohim?" Stoney asked.

"Numb," George answered. "I felt totally numb."

Flower tapped on the tabletop. "This isn't getting us anywhere. There are three hyper-charged demons out there."

Tuck turned her chair around to straddle the seat and rest her arms across the back, and asked, "Okay, boss, what's the plan? What do we do next?"

I caught my breath and sighed. "I go it alone. This has become too dangerous for anyone but me."

"What you really mean is..." Stoney said, "...you don't trust any of us to vanquish one of these fallen angels."

"Has any one of you ever actually killed an immortal?" I asked.

George raised his hand.

"Well, other than George, and technically, it was Reuwel who did it."

The room fell silent.

"I have, and that makes me more qualified than any of you. I think my fears are well founded."

"Stoney's right. You don't mean fear...you mean mistrust," Jimmy said. "You think your mistrust is well founded, but that's a bunch of crap."

I stood at my chair, holding on to the table for balance. Even closing my eyes didn't help; I wished the room would stop inching back and forth. Stiffening my legs and arms helped anchor myself into one place. "Call it what you will. I'm still the leader of this team and I'm making this call."

"That's the affliction talking, Mr. B." Compassion filled Jimmy's eyes. "You know you'll need help with three demon riders."

"I can't put you at risk." The words didn't even come close to describing the determined feeling I had. "I'll take on the horsemen alone."

Flower hurried over to my side. "Think about what you're saying. This is exactly what you told us would happen. You're losing faith in us."

"Am I not a prophet? After all, I see what no one else can. I have a discernment no one else has."

"Ask Mr. Dark if this is the best plan?" Flower suggested. "He knows your situation."

"Mr. Dark?" I struggled to make sense of her request. "Who?"

"The shadowy entity that haunts you night and day," she replied. "You know, your dark side...it talks to you."

I thought before answering. "Mr. Dark?" I hesitate. "Of course, I remember Mr. Dark."

"Do you?" Her reply sounded oddly worried.

"Oh, yes. I remember that fellow. He is usually very vocal, but I haven't heard anything from him in a while now." I sighed. "Just as well. He doesn't always give the best advice—too self-centered and egotistic for me to trust him."

Shock spread across Flower's face. "Mr. Dark has gone silent." She put a hand on my shoulder. "I fear his condition has progressed. He's getting worse."

"I am not. The fact is, I'm much better. I can focus and use my gift now. Before all I got was static."

"Static?" Her eyebrows went up and her eyes widened.

She put her hand on my arm. I could feel her trying to use her gift on me, but instead of giving in to the inviting warmth of her touch, I pushed her hand away. "How dare you use your hocus-pocus on me? I don't need it. What we need is to get Gabriel's sword back."

George raised his hand, asking for permission to speak.

"Don't do that," Jimmy said as he pulled on George's arm. "You're not in class."

George nodded, and said, "Don't fret, Mr. B. I have something to share."

"George." My tone came out less than complimentary. "I know you mean well, but, really, I can do this on my own."

"Trust me. You're going to want to hear this." He shifted his weight before shoving his left hand deep into his pocket. "Reuwel told me something interesting." His other hand went to the top of his pants, where he looped his thumb under the charmed rope.

"Spit it out. Don't swallow if you know what's good for ya," Tuck said.

George pulled his brow tight and gave her a confused look. "Uh, b...before he left me...de-possessed... Uh, before he went away... Uh, whatever... He—"

I stepped over to where *The Kid* sat. "We already know why he possessed you. It's because you have the relic of Saint Sebastian, but what did Reuwel actually say?"

"He said that there is another relic...a weapon...more powerful than the sword of Gabriel."

Stoney's mouth fell open. "Not more powerful than Gabriel's sword?"

"That's impossible. You're lying." The words fell out of my mouth before I knew what I was saying.

"No. I don't lie. That's what the angel said before he split and left me hurting."

Sarah shook back her bouffant hair and huffed. "If you don't lie, then you're the only one in the world who doesn't. It's enough proof for me if Arland says so."

George raised his hand again.

"Stop that!" Jimmy commanded. "You're among friends. Not a bunch of stogy teachers." He looked my way. "Present company excluded, Mr. B."

I took out the picture where the Sword of Gabriel once hid. "This is where it should be." I held it up for all to see. I shook my head in despair. "It was safe, protected in this charmed crest." The image was clearly missing a sword from the pattern. "I'm the only one who can..." I stammered. "Correction, I'm the only one who could have reached in and taken it out." My headache returned with a vengeance. "Like a bumbling idiot, I put it in the hands of the enemy. I was a fool. And now, thanks to Gewalt's last enchantment, the rest of the horsemen have the most powerful angelic weapon ever made."

CHAPTER TWENTY-EIGHT

It Doesn't Like Us

Maybe it was my condition or maybe it was simply my insecurities coming to the surface, but I couldn't find it in me to take George at his word. After pushing the crest in everyone's face, I slammed the card down on the conference table and took another look at the design. It was as it had always been, right down to the spire and the inscription on the second sword. The inscription read: *Victoria Domini est.*

"Let me see that picture." Urgency edged Tuck's words.

I picked it up and passed the charmed card over, and Jimmy placed it in her hand.

"Arland, my old buckaroo, I know you believe every word you're saying," Tuck remarked, "but George is right!"

"No! George doesn't know what he's saying. Gabriel's blade is imbued with the essence of death. One prick and you're a goner." I looked up into Jimmy's face. "Trust me, I know."

"That's right, cowgirl," Jimmy chimed in. "Mr. B.'s been around a long time and he knows about these things. And by the way, you call me Jimbo again and I'll clobber you so hard, you'll be picking yourself up in Montana."

Tuck leaned close to Jimmy and laughed. "Sure you will, big boy...and don't think Arland knows everything about everything." She held the picture in Jimmy's face. "There's still one sword in this picture." Tuck pointed. "That is *Saint Michael's Sword.* I should know. He's my guardian angel and I've seen it lots of times."

"Wait, I thought Saint Michael used a lance," Rebecca interjected. "Doesn't he have a lance in all those sculptures and paintings?"

"That's right," Sarah added. "Two summers ago, Daddy took me to Rome, Italy. I remember seeing a sculpture of Saint Michael on a building, and he had a lance."

"Michael appeared to me once," I said, "and when he did, he had a lance." I glanced at Tuck. She met my eyes with a dark, scary stare. "But that doesn't mean he couldn't have a sword, too."

Tuck waved a dismissing gesture at them. "You guys are as stubborn as Granny's old fat sow. Don't you know that's only what an artist thought might be true? I'm telling you I've seen it, and this is the genuine article. The sword in this picture is Saint Michael's."

"Okay, Tuck," I said. "I'm willing to put your story to a test. If it's an enchanted weapon, I will be able to bring it out."

Bracing my hand, I pressed against the picture. As if the surface were only water, my fingers broke through. When I gripped the handle of the sword, something unexpected happened. A sensation ran up my arm. It tingled—the same feeling my gift made when I stood in the presence of the seraphim, Reuwel. This had never happened with a mere weapon, no matter how powerful the charm. I pulled. It didn't come out. I pulled harder. It didn't turn loose of the picture. Letting go of the weapon, I withdrew my hand.

I hesitated. The sensation was so intense I didn't know how to explain it. Closing my eyes, I inhaled sharply before beginning. "Tuck is correct. The sword in the crest is indeed of angelic origin. Not only that, but it's a powerful one."

"Great!" Jimmy exclaimed. "Get it out here so we can use it."

"It won't come out."

"What do you mean, it won't come out?" Sarah asked.

"I don't know why it won't come out, it just won't. I pulled hard, but...this is going to sound crazy...It's possible the weapon is consciously refusing to respond to my touch."

Slack-jawed, Flower stood up and spoke, "What do you mean *consciously*? Is it alive?"

"Indubitably," I replied.

"Them be some pert big words, Doc," Tuck said. "If I heard you right, you said the sword don't like ya."

"That's one way to explain it..." I thought about her explanation, "...and I believe you've summed up our situation fairly well."

Sarah popped one hand up onto her hip and flipped her hair out of her face with the other. "I guess it means we don't have any real defense against Gabriel's angel killer blade," she grimaced, "except for George and his relic."

"We all saw the beating he took at the hand of the red horseman!" Rebecca exclaimed. "If it weren't for Reuwel numbing his whole body, he could have never endured the pain." She gave George an admiring glance. I recognized it because that was how she had once looked at me.

Sarah stood behind George's chair. "We can't ask him to do that again."

A red bloom flashed over George's cheeks before he bowed his head in silence.

I tapped on the table. "I think this conversation is unfairly presumptuous. George should speak for himself." I redirected my attention to him. "How do you feel about being the tip of our spear in the coming battle?"

George stood, pushing back his chair with the calves of his legs. "I...I...I'm certainly not looking forward to it. I'd gladly give Saint Sebastian's relic to one of you."

He pulled at the knot, fastening the rope to his pants. It didn't budge. He twisted it, trying to loosen the loops. If possible, it tightened.

"Tuck, see if you can get this thing off of me."

She fiddled with the bundle of tightly looped ends, without success.

"When I pull an end free, it tightens back before I can untie it," she said.

George stepped back. "Is it alive, too?"

Tuck nodded. "I thought it was only my gun that acted on its own. It talks to me, you know."

I confessed, "I've heard the gun's voice. It does talk." Briskly, I rubbed the stubble growing on my bristly chin. "Imagine how many other relics might also have a will of their own."

"I get it, and you're right," Sarah said. "Thinking about it, the Crowns of Abaddon only worked when they wanted to." She paused. "I blamed you for all those screw ups when it was the crowns that were...rebelling."

"So," Tuck said, "it was the relic that sent me to Hell for a century, not you." She looked at me with more confidence than I ever remembered before, but considering my failing memory, that wasn't anything to brag about. "So, where does that leave us? Do we get the sword, or not? If— "

Flower interrupted, "It only means there is something about Arland that the sword doesn't like."

"You actually think a sword can choose who it likes and doesn't like?" Stoney asked.

"Indeed! In the light of this information, I concur. There seems to be no doubt that at least some of the relics are sentient," I said. "As Tuck so articulately put it...The sword doesn't like me. It wants another to wield it."

"Well, what are we waiting for?" Tuck's tone sounded more like a demand than a question. "Line up and see who the thing likes."

CHAPTER TWENTY-NINE

Amethyst

Leaving the crest lying on the table, I stepped away and watched as Tuck tried to get her hand past the shiny top layer of the picture. Fingertips held stiff, she jabbed at the surface, but the charm never allowed her to reach inside. She blew an exasperated huff. "I should be the one to carry the archangel's sword, since he's my guardian." I never before saw her so determined. She doubled up her fist and hit the picture with a downward punch. My table vibrated with a thud, and Tuck yelped, pampering her injured hand.

Stoney tried next, without success; Rebecca and Sarah, too. Jimmy boasted about what he would do with the sword, but he didn't get any closer to it than anyone else.

George hesitantly stepped up and gave it a try. The charm rejected his efforts, as well.

"That's everyone!" Jimmy exclaimed. "It doesn't like any of us.

"I haven't tried," Flower said.

She closed her eyes and reached out her hand. It passed through the upper surface of the paper and allowed her to grasp the handle of the weapon. She gritted her teeth, struggling to pull the sword free. It refused her, just as it did the rest of us. She took her hand out of the crest, and with wide eyes, looked at her empty hand.

"Like I said, it doesn't like any of us." My headache came back. Rubbing my temples, I said, "I don't know what to say. I felt sure it would have chosen one of us." My throbbing head shot daggers into my brain with every heartbeat. I rubbed my forehead and sat down at my desk.

Tuck scratched her head. "Me too, Doc. Makes no sense to have a powerful relic like that at our fingertips and we can't use it."

A voice, somehow familiar and yet more melodic, more powerful than I remembered, came from the direction of the door. **"Mind if I give it a try."**

There, standing halfway in my office, was the woman I knew as Miss Wilson. "Iggarest, what are you doing here?" I demanded.

"Mortals are always so full of mistrust." With an indignant glare, she tilted her head. **"Don't call me by that miscreant's wretched name. I'm not Iggarest, the name's Amethyst."** Her expression changed to a comforting smile. The difference in her countenance drastically affected my perception of her. It gave me a warm feeling, and more, I suddenly wanted to trust her. **"Fear not...I'm here to help."**

Shaking off the inclination to believe her every word, I laid the charmed crest on the table and stood guard over it.

"Isn't that just like the Creator to put the means of our triumph so close at hand and yet it's far away? What a terrible shame!" She shook her head.

"You heard," I said. "Then you know we can't remove the sword from the card. If we can't get to it, then certainly a Fallen can't either."

"Yep," Tuck's tone was contemptuous, "just knowing it's safely out of your reach made a warm fuzzy snuggle up to my sacroiliac."

"I think I've been insulted." Amethyst put a hand to her breast. **"Oh, no... what will I do? A mortal insulted me. I might as well go eat worms."** She put a finger to her lips. **"As tasty as that would be, I don't think it would solve our dilemma."**

Flower stepped toward the door. "If you truly want to be helpful, tell us what you can about Saint Michael's Sword."

"That sword was forged to accomplish one task. Although it may be used against any foe, its purpose is to conquer the Morning Star, and if prophecy holds true, it will be Archangel Michael who does the dirty deed." She paused. **"That is, if I don't kill him first."**

Sarah took a seat beside George. Her eyes spoke volumes as she soaked in every detail of Amethyst's story. At length, she asked, "Conquer a star! How can anyone conquer a star?"

"Angels never say exactly what they mean," Rebecca complained. "Morning Star is what God called Lucifer."

"Well, bless my Aunt Bessie's hog pen. You mean it's destined to kill old pig face himself?" Tuck's questions always sounded a bit like statements.

"I said conquer, not kill." Amethyst put a hand on her hip. **"Mortals, you all hear what you want too, not what is said."** She raised an eyebrow along with her index finger. **"I suppose it could be wishful thinking."** A smile spread across her lips, distorting them into a ghoulish grin. "**If only**." She paused. **"Yes, what a divine thought."**

"It's useless! We can't get it out," Sarah said.

"Let me try," Amethyst demanded. **"We've got nothin' to lose."**

"I don't want a Fallen to touch the card," I said, scooping up the picture from the table.

"Why?" Amethyst asked. **"Afraid I might aid you in your quest?"**

"No, I— "

Jimmy interrupted me. "You psycho angel, You're not going to get a chance to try!"

The Fallen reached out toward Jimmy and chanted, "***Gadewch i mi fynd i mewn i'r wyneb wedi'i gerfio.***" She took a deep breath. **"Alright, muscles for brains, now you try it."**

Jimmy snatched the crest from me and pushed his hand against the picture. Nothing happened.

"The magical language of the angels didn't make a difference," I said.

Jimmy asked, "You don't think it's chicken or something?"

"It doesn't matter what we think of it," Sarah said. "The fact is, as long as the sword is stuck in the card, it's useless."

"Oh, too bad. Looks like I'm the only ace you have up your sleeve. It's team Champions and little old Amethyst against the most evil and mighty strongholds in Lucifer's army." In a nonchalant manner, she rubbed her fingertips against her periwinkle sweater and the color of her nail polish changed from pink to the same periwinkle hue as her wrap. Holding them out to admire the pastel blue-violet shade, her focus changed, and she gazed up into my eyes. **"I fear for you mortals. There isn't any hope of victory without that weapon trapped in your card. Or my help."**

My head felt as if would split open. "Amethyst, stop trying to be helpful...you're not," I bellowed. "All you've done so far is to make my life misera—" I couldn't continue. Sharp pains shot through my head.

As if she were talking to the air, the Fallen bellowed, "**Leave me. Iggarest, you worm of Hell, go back into the aether where I banished you. No, you can't return now. I deserve to live. What are you doing?"**

Amethyst's image faded, and Iggarest stood where she had been. **"Finally! Thought she would never shut up and leave."**

"Iggarest, you are not welcome here," Flower yelled.

"Fear not, Lady Felisha. Even if you don't appreciate my participation, there is yet some assistance I may provide.

There is a secret only the most elite Elohim are privy to." He beamed with pride. **"You see, I know something neither Amethyst nor Lucifer himself knows."** He gave a wink and his eyes twinkled. **"There is another relic of power—one that may be useful to you."**

CHAPTER THIRTY

Iggarest's Secret Shame

Sarah was quick to reply to Iggarest's news. "If you are talking about Abaddon's crowns, we don't know where they are."

Iggarest adjusted his vest. **"Oh, how uncouth! Amethyst always leaves me so disheveled."** He dusted his cravat with his fingertips. **"No. No. Those particular pretties have merged into one crown and Ishtar now wears it."**

"Forget that! What are you talking about?" Jimmy demanded.

Iggarest held out his hand, and a gold-tipped Victorian cane appeared in it. **"I'm glad you asked that. Once she found the crowns sh—"**

"No! I don't care about the crowns," Jimmy yelled. "What weapon?"

"Oh that. Well, I shouldn't have mentioned it. You can't find it. No one can. It's been lost for almost two millennia."

Tuck raised her gun again. "That forked tongue of yours better start spillin' everythin' ya know about this all mighty weapon before I count to four. One... Two...."

"So persistent, and so dark, are you sure you're on the side of the Favored?"

Tuck continued, "Three...."

He waved his hand in Tuck's direction. **"Okay,"** he took a breath, **"There was this guy who the Morning Star had the Romans kill."**

"What guy?" Tuck pulled back the hammer on the gun. "What was his name?"

"Nope, you're not goading me into saying it." Iggarest shook his head. **"We Fallen don't say that name, no matter the language it's spoken in. Anyway, he had a crown, too, and that is the relic you want. It's not a weapon per-say, but it is very powerful and would be very effective against the remaining horsemen."**

Rebecca pulled her eyebrows down and said, "I don't get it. Who had a crown?"

Flower spoke up, "I think he's talking about a crown of thorns." Our eyes met. "There is only one name that the Fallen won't speak."

"I get it," I said. "The crown worn by the Son of God would be more powerful than any made by angel folk." At that moment, I understood what this relic was, and a dreadful doubt crossed my mind. "But there are two problems. One, it must be far from here in the land of Israel; and the second is, if we could get there, no one knows where to even start looking."

"I might be helpful on that second count." Iggarest fidgeted with his cane. **"But I can only relate a small bit of knowledge, for it is all I know. One of the duty guards on that fateful day had orders to return to Rome. I saw this particular Roman pick it up. I think he took it with him."**

"Italy or Israel, it doesn't make much difference, it is too far away," I said.

"Maybe Amethyst knows more than you do. May we speak with her?" George asked.

"What? You want to talk to her? No. Nothing this side of the veil can make me let her back in. After all, I just arrived?" Iggarest huffed and gave me a quizzical look. **"You think her interaction is benevolent, don't you? How wrong you are."** He sighed. **"It's not like that, you know. She'll be back. No matter how I try to keep her out, she finds her way back."**

"So you don't have any control over when Amethyst appears?" Tuck asked.

"Who told you I have no control? I have control." Iggarest's chuckle sounded belligerent. "I love control. In fact, I crave control."

I blinked and wondered if Amethyst was psychotic or some kind of usurping power hungry parasite. Their voices faded into the background and the feather under the bell jar caught my attention.

I moved the glass from around the feather and picked it up. Why did it look familiar? Where had I seen it before? If I kept it on my desk under glass, then it must have some significance. It certainly was a pretty thing, all trimmed with gold. I wondered if, maybe, that's why I have it. Dissatisfied with my reasoning, I laid it on my desk. Reuwel's voice resonated from the direction of the feather. It came to me in my mind like I used to hear Mr. Dark, and I was sure no one but me heard it. **"Parasite,"** it said.

My eyes went wide, and I returned the feather to the glass encasement.

Stoney's yelling snapped me out of my momentary distraction. "Wait, wait... This is weird. Are there two of them, or does this Fallen have a dual personality?" Confusion furrowed his brow. "That's too freaky for words."

George said, "Her manifestation at the exact time Tuck aimed her gun between your eyes sure seemed purposeful."

"Her entrances are serendipitous at best, but if I lose focus, she can suppress my presence."

Tuck gave him a skeptical glare. "Serendipitous? You want me to believe Amethyst's appearing and disappearing is as random as my Aunt Fanny's farts. Ha! I should have guessed when she first called you a parasite. I'm from the country, but I'm not dumb." She waved an index finger in Iggarest's face. "You're two separate beings, but only one of you can exist in this reality at a time? You can't completely block her out. What I want to know is which one of you is the original, and which one is the supernatural tapeworm?"

"Tuck, you make her sound like an infestation—a parasite." My comment stemmed from my personal experience with Mr. Dark. "Does it matter who came first, Iggarest or Amethyst? Maybe they inhabit the life force equally."

"Equals? She is not my equal. No, no! You misunderstand." Iggarest cleared his throat. **"Alas! You have seen through my charade."** He perched upon the conference table, swinging his dangling legs. **"I must keep a certain focus to ward off her persistence. When your lady in black there threatened me with Michael's popgun, I slipped up and Amethyst crawled out from under the rock where I keep her hidden."** He ran his hand over the inlay at the center of the table. **"The important thing is, I'm back and I plan on staying."**

George waved his fist at Iggarest and sounded disgusted. "You didn't transcend into Amethyst, in a way, she possessed you!" George and Tuck's revelation made so much sense I didn't see why I hadn't thought of it.

"No! No spirit can possess a Fallen. She does not share my most elegant form, and she is not my equal. If you must know, Amethyst is a Necrothyst—the homeless spirit of a vanquished angel. From out of the aether, I heard her voice, and she convinced me that we are stronger together than alone. With my consent, she attached herself to my life force. And, for a millennium, we were in the Morning Star's favor." He bowed his head and spoke softly. **"It is regretful how demanding she has become. If I gave into her will, she would banish *me* to the aether."** He raised his head. **"My**

only hope is to vanquish the Morning Star before she does, then it will be *me* who takes his throne. I alone will rule over the demons, not that husk of a thing she has become. I will—."

Before he could finish his thought, a thunderous crash shook the building. Cracks broke open between sections of bricks, mortar dust filled the air, and I grabbed my desk for support. Stoney reacted first, running out into the hall. Iggarest vanished. Sarah and Flower quickly followed Stoney. George ran to catch up, leaving Rebecca and me to follow.

Gazing through the dusty fog, we stared at the end of the hall to what should have been the outside door. It was torn away leaving a ghostly portal to the darkness beyond. From the edges of the gaping hole, broken electrical wires dangled. Sparks flared, dancing across the void. Loose bricks fell, crashing to the concrete floor and breaking the silence with staccato applause for the entrance of a ghostly white horse, extremely gaunt—ribs protruding and belly sucked up to its spine. A mist wafted off of its mane and fell to the ground where it settled into a vaporous cloud. I could barely see its glowing eyes through the haze. Then an unexpected huff of flames billowed out from its muzzle, turning the surrounding mist into a radiant spectacle, illuminating the rider in detail.

Astride the mysterious mount sat what appeared to be a grotesque female phantasm. A leprous white figure wrapped in filthy strips of linen marked with angel runes. In its face, deep black sockets recessed tiny eyes and stitches sewn across a wicked mouth made me shudder with cold chills.

Scruffy tufts of tangled, soot-gray hair escaped from between the ill-placed wrappings. Chains crossed her bosom and bound her odious wrappings to her willowy form. Spreading across her back were the translucent wings of an enormous albino bat. In her left hand, she held a glowing arrow. Terrified, I wanted to turn away, but couldn't.

CHAPTER THIRTY-ONE

Pestilence

We all stood outside the school office as the white horse slowly came toward us. In an unnatural silence, it strode atop the wispy mist. I'm sure the others were as struck with fear as I was, for no one said a word. Beads of sweat broke out on my brow as I watched the apparition advance.

The ceiling over the void collapsed when Pestilence reached the intersecting halls leading to either the lunchroom or the gym. Debris filled the far end of the hallway, cutting off the exit. My horror-struck trance broke when Tuck fired on the rider.

Her chin dropped in disbelief when the shells passed through the spirit and blasted into the fallen rubble without turning and wounding the angel. By then, Jimmy had run halfway down the hall. He skidded to a stop beside the hellish horse. He reached up to pull the rider off her mount, but his hands clutched nothing, passing through the apparition.

The Fallen stabbed downward with the arrow. It went into Jimmy's shoulder without leaving a wound or tearing his clothing. From all appearances, the arrow was as noncorporeal as the phantasm itself. Then Jimmy fell to the ground, screaming in pain. Boils erupted on his face and arms. He rolled to the side, perhaps more by instinct than planning, and huddled next to the wall a few feet this side of the intersection.

The rider pulled up hard and brought the horse to an abrupt halt. She dismounted and aimed the arrow at Jimmy's head.

Running at the phantom rider, Stoney leaped into the air, levelling a well-placed foot between Pestilence's eyes. As he passed through the vaporous figure, her image tore into wisps. We watched as the pieces of her face pulled back together and reformed.

Stoney's attack completely failed. He fell a few feet to the far side of the horse.

She threw the arrow like a dart. When it hit its mark, a leprous plague covered Stoney's dark skin. In the quiet hall, the echo of his scream amplified the horror. His skin withered. Deep set lines ran through his face and his eyes sank into their sockets. His limbs atrophied into mere sticks covered with crinkly flesh. They quivered as if some unnamed disease infected them.

The reoccurring headache came back with a vengeance and hampered my focus. Using the Prophet's Voice, I managed to call out, "Linoleum, cover the Fallen and block her approach."

The moment I spoke, squares of battleship tile unattached from the concrete floor and flew up at the Rider. Clapping together, making the sound of a heavy rainfall, the airborne pieces of linoleum sandwiched empty air. After they slammed together, like a deck of playing cards, the obedient tiles tumbled to the ground.

Through my brain fog, I yelled, "Rubble and broken bricks attack the Rider." Pieces from the mound of debris, blocking the end of the hall, flew toward the Phantasm. More followed. Flying dust prevented me from seeing exactly what happened next. I tried not to inhale the trash, filling the air.

When my vision cleared, each chunk had flown straight through the rider without causing injury. The pieces torn from the building were piled up in the middle of the hallway and lay littered on the floor, but the apparition remained unharmed.

The beast cantered forward toward me.

I lunged for it, only to be attacked with the dagger she pulled from her belt. Fear and despair broke into my psyche and flooded me with a tangible darkness—a despair so real I could taste its bitterness. Helpless, I gasped like a drowning man.

Again, the rider struck. This time, she hammered down with her arrow. My chest pained to the point of heart failure as I watched the rust laden shaft hit my face. No pain instantly followed...then came a rush of unspeakable agony as my skin erupted with hundreds of cankered lesions. My flesh withered just as Stoney's did until I lay, a heap of useless flesh.

Flower rushed past Pestilence to reach me. As she ran, the apparition turned on her, slicing the air and jabbing. Passing through her, the ghostly blade looked like it had dipped down into water and when pulled up, something dripped off the edge, falling back into Flower herself. The rider let out a piercing, high-pitched scream. Almost In reply, Flower tumbled head-over-heels to land near me.

At breakneck speed, the white horse ran at the others. I could barely keep my eyes open enough to see them try to clear out of its path. The colorless hooves came crashing down on George first. Inexplicably, the attack didn't appear to harm him, but the same drippy substance fell back onto his body. He stepped away and screamed before toppling to the ground. On his skin, boils erupted.

Rebecca and Tuck pushed back as far as possible, flattening themselves against the lockers lining the wall outside the school offices. One swipe of the arrow and they tumbled to the ground. A gasp must have caught in Tuck's throat, for it sounded like she screamed underwater.

The rider pulled hard on the reins, aiming her mount at Sarah. Holding the handles of the hall lockers in a death grip, the horrified young woman cried out in terror, closed her eyes, and turned away from the beast. It reared up on two legs and came down on all fours, directly in front of Sarah. The rider pulled in hard on the reins and stopped only feet from the terrified student. Again it reared, this time it blew fire from its nostrils roasting a place on the Celotex ceiling. The horseman appeared puzzled as she tilted her head to the side, snorted, and huffed her odious breath between the crusty stitches pinning her mouth shut. The horse also settled down and sniffed.

Pestilence leaned forward, toward Sarah, grunted, and turned the hell-horse toward the gaping opening. Again, the Phantasm pulled back on the reins, making the horse rear up and flail its hooves against the ceiling, kicking down tiles. Seconds later, the ghostly rider vanished, leaving Sarah totally out of control. Eyes closed, Sarah still clutched the handles of the lockers. She screamed, and screamed again, unable to stop. The hysterical sound grated on my nerves. I pushed up to face her. Pity gripped me even through my suffering, for she trembled like a wounded animal.

Flower sat up, shook herself, and ran a hand over her own arms and legs. The diseased skin cleared. With a half-cocked smile, an expression of resolute determination came over her. She put her hands on me and the plague affecting me vanished. Too bad it didn't have the same effect on my failing memory.

"As unpleasant as that was, it appears my gift makes me somewhat resistant to her powers," Flower said. "Whatever pestilence infected me with was only temporary."

I examined my clear skin where moments before painful boils had been. "I assure you, my experience was far different—painfully different. Nor did the gift of prophecy prevent any long-lasting effects."

After running her hand along my limb, she said, "I've done what I can for you. Now help me with the others. They are in dire need of assistance."

One by one, we revived them. Lastly, and while the others recovered, Flower and I approached Sarah. Her screams had turned into whimpers, but her fists were still locked onto the locker handles.

Eyes yet closed, she crumbled to the floor. "What happened?" Sarah asked. "Did we win?"

"You don't remember?" Skepticism filled my words with an icy coldness. "How could you not remember?"

Flower put a hand on my arm to calm me. "It's a natural response to a traumatic event. The mind can't cope with what happened, so it deletes the memory."

"I suppose you're right," I said. "Still, I saw everything, and that demon didn't attack her." I paused to think. "Maybe it was all the screaming that drove Pestilence away before attacking Sarah?"

With Flower's hands clasped against Sarah's temples, the hysteria subsided. Still wearing her cheerleading uniform, she sat on the floor, eyes wide open and her breathing more normal. She reached up and held Flower's hands. "Nurse Cumberland, don't let go!" she pleaded. Soon the trembling stopped and a calm demeanor came over her.

Sirens blared out in the night beyond the hole broken in the front of the school. I glanced over my shoulder. Flashing lights threw red, yellow, and blue beams through the dusty air. Ten police officers ran in. leaping over the rubble littering the hall.

I had sat down next to Sarah in hopes she would feel safer, and, in some way, it might have helped to calm her. I asked, "Stoney, if you will, please, help me up and then go into the..." The police officer interrupted me.

"Did anyone get the plate number off the truck that ran into the school?" he asked. "It sure did leave a mess."

Dumbfounded by the absurd assumption the policeman made, my words caught in my throat. "What truck?"

"The semi that crashed into the front entrance of the school, of course." The officer answered.

Stoney whispered, "He is obviously convinced this was an accident and not a supernatural event."

Flower leaned nearer to me. "Let them think what they will."

CHAPTER THIRTY-TWO

Sarah's Immunity

"No...no, it happened so fast." I yelled back to the officer. "The truck took out the end of the hall and drove away." There was no reason to explain what actually happened, and they had already chosen a viable explanation they could live with.

Sarah put a hand on my arm and asked, "Really? Is that what happened?" She looked dazed. "Then why are we all sitting here covered in dirt?" Mine wasn't the only brain suffering from a power outage. After a scare like that, it appeared she was worse off than I was.

Flower held up her index finger and called out. "Everyone, let's go into my office while the police inspect the scene of the hit and run." The way she said it, even a child could have known something was up.

We all stood and made our way down the hall toward the nurse's office. Flower softly asked, "Arland, why didn't the rider attack Sarah? It took that harpy less than ten minutes to take down our entire crew—except her?"

A sense of distrust flooded over me. "Not now. Let's get behind closed doors," I said.

We filed into Nurse Cumberland's office, and Tuck perched on the corner of her desk.

"I can't believe it. Not one onlooker saw the horseman?" A tone of stark disbelief gave her question a sarcastic ring; but I'd come to expect that from Tuck. "They think the damage was caused by some natural calamity. If you can call a car wreck natural."

"So much for defeating the rider called Pestilence," Jimmy said. "We all just got kicked in the teeth by one single demon."

"That was no demon," I said. "That was a full-fledged devil! These riders are more like angels than demons." After a moment's thought, I tapped on her desk for attention. "Flower has brought up a question," I said. "Why didn't Pestilence attack Sarah before it left?"

"Maybe she scared that she-phantom away," Stoney suggested. "Her screaming sounded like an African Egbere."

"I don't think it has anything to do with her lung power," I said. "I think it's because Sarah is different from the rest of us."

"You all are talking about me like I'm not here," Sarah said. "I don't appreciate it! If you're gonna talk about me, do it to my face." She poked me in the arm. "And what do you mean, I'm different?"

"We got our gift from the Favored. Yours came from the Fallen. I think the rider could somehow tell the difference," I said.

"The red rider targeted us before it would unleash its corruption on mankind. It's possible this horseman is doing the same thing," Rebecca said. "Sarah, it may even go after you, too, but for now, it's us Champions she wants to kill."

"Do you think another angel will possess someone to help?" George asked.

"That may never happen again." I ran a hand through my dishwater blond hair. "What's important is that with the help of the angel Reuwel, George vanquished one of the four horsemen, and I think they fear us. These riders are like champions of the Fallen. There's another certainty. They won't stop with us because their whole purpose, the reason they exist, is to bring on the apocalypse. If we fail...the entire world will fall under their devilish powers."

"And by *us*, you mean the Favored's Champions. I was never chosen by the Favored, so I'm not first on the hit list," Sarah said.

"No, and that's why the rider didn't attack you." I took a deep breath before continuing. "But there is someone else who is on that list, and I fear he is in grave danger."

Flower jerked her head up. "Roger... We didn't think about the riders going after him, too."

Rebecca tossed her hair back and put her hand on her hips. "He made it perfectly clear that he's not a Champion anymore."

"He doesn't want to have anything to do with demon hunting, angels, and especially us!" Tuck's words were hot with indignation.

"It's not us he's mad at," Sarah interjected. "It's Arland."

I pounded a fist on Flower's desk. "Hell, nor the horde of demons it harbors, could give a fig about what Roger wants or thinks. The favored angels chose him as a Champion. That's what he is and nothing Roger arrogantly decides can change it...and the riders are targeting the Champions first."

"We better get to him, fast," George said.

CHAPTER THIRTY-THREE

Police Chief Martin Langster

"I agree. We've got to find Roger, but we don't know for sure where he is," Jimmy said.

"Remember," Sarah replied, "he told us all where he would be. He went on a date with Dee Dee last. So I expect they had a late night, and he is at home in bed. Except for spending time with Dee Dee, he doesn't care about anything anymore. He's more than likely sleeping in."

A startling knock on the door interrupted our focus. Police chief Martin Langster pushed it open. "Principal Bertarelli, we've blocked the hole with crime scene tape and I'm leaving two officers there and one has been stationed at each of the remaining entrances. Since the foundation has been smashed with a semi-truck, we don't know how stable the rest of this old building is. There is a chance some part might collapse on a student, or worse, a whole classroom. Thank goodness, the students are on Christmas Break.

Classes will resume after the first of the year. By then we'll know if we need to tear this old building down and combine WHS with the new high school built across the Interstate. But for now, this structure is off limits."

"What about the students who come for the free breakfast program?" I glanced over at Flower. "If I remember correctly, today was this year's last day for serving free eggs and toast."

"The kids who qualify for that service always congregate in the cafeteria in the mornings," Flower said. "I'm sure there are at least a few kids there."

"Oh, my, that could have been unfortunate." The police chief turned to the nearest policeman. "Officer Grimes, walk the halls and usher everybody out—even the ones in the cafeteria."

Officer Grimes didn't question his orders. He immediately headed off toward the cafeteria.

"When we make our final sweep of the building, Ya'll will be the last here. As of right now, by the power invested in me by the city of Western, I'm declaring this building quarantined. I want everyone." He caught my eyes. "...and I mean everyone out as soon as possible. I'm posting an officer at every entrance and two at the crash site to keep the curious and the mischievous out. If vandals get in here, it's a guarantee the school board will vote to demolish this old place."

My mind went straight to the artifacts in my desk drawer. "I...I need some time to empty out my office."

Leaning close to Flower, I barely whispered. "There are some relics in there I don't want to fall into unwitting hands."

Flower nodded her reply. "Of course, you're right."

"Too bad, none are powerful enough to use against a horseman," Stoney said. "Still, I agree. We can't leave them completely unprotected." Turning back to the Chief, I loudly replied, "It won't take me but a few minutes."

Tuck stepped to the door and said, "Hey, Doc. While you box-up those things from your office, we'll take care of *that problem* we've been chewin' on. You can meet up with us later."

Flower interrupted, "I don't think that's a good idea. Arland is not at himself enough to accomplish anything important." She gave me that look again. A look I should recognize, but its meaning faded from my mind.

I fought a rush of temper. Her words caused an indignant attitude to well up inside of me. I opened my mouth to scold her, but the chief called out, "Do what you got ta do. I have paperwork ta fill out on this accident. Principal Bertarelli, I leave this in your capable hands. Just don't stay too long, here? It could be dangerous." Then he turned and made his way over the debris and toward the police tape.

"He ain't got no idea how right he is," Tuck said.

As soon as the chief left, out through the gaping hole, Rose came running down the hall toward us.

She called out, "There you are. The police said that a group of students accompanied by the school nurse and the principal had witnessed the truck crashing into the school. I knew it must be you all." She stopped when she reached me.

"I came in the back door to the cafeteria with a bunch of other kids who got free breakfasts, and then the cops tried to send us all home. They said the school was *off limits*. That's when I snuck out to the girl's gym and hid there until the coast was clear."

An all too familiar pang of guilt pricked at my conscience. I leaned on the door to the school office, hesitating. "Rose, if you had been here, you would have been injured, too."

"Don't give Arland's words too much credit. He is putting all the responsibility on his own shoulders," Stoney said. "And yet, if not for Flower, we would all be at that devil's mercy."

"So it wasn't a semi-truck that crashed into the school. I didn't think so." She turned to Flower. "What exactly happened here?"

"It was the horseman called Pestilence. You can guess the rest." Flower sighed, "This time, we didn't win."

"How can I help?" Rose asked.

"You can't," Jimmy retorted. "Honey, I don't want you anywhere around that white washed she-devil. Pestilence is too powerful."

"We've defeated all kinds of demons," Rose said. "This one can't be that different."

"It's different, alright!" Tuck exclaimed with a sigh. "Be thankful. You just managed to escape her wicked touch."

"Don't you get it? Rose can't escape!" I blurted the words with uncontrolled emotion. "The horsemen consider all the Champions too powerful, and so, they're targeting us first. After we are defeated...and I mean completely done for, humanity will be wiped out."

It wasn't the first time I had made an emergency announcement to this team. Rose didn't bat an eye, only accepted me at my word. No wails of terror, and sobs of frightful, jaw dropping expletives. Not her. She hesitated for a moment and asked the most important question she could. "So? What are we going to do about it?"

"Mr. B. has a number of angelic icons and relics in his office." Stoney said.

Rebecca added, "Stuff we might be able to use against the horsemen, but the police have quarantined the school until they can determine if it is safe or not."

"We're going to gather up what angel stuff Mr. Bertarelli's collected and take it with us before heading over to check on Roger." George opened the door to the school office. "He has a bad feeling about Roger, and since Mr. B. is a prophet. I guess it's not a good thing for him to get a premonition about somebody."

It was true. My premonition about Roger's wellbeing was becoming more intense by the minute. Finally, I couldn't justify saving the few relics I'd kept in lieu of the impending danger I felt coming Roger's way. Anyway, none of those mystical empowered objects were going to help us in this fight—not against any of the *Horseman of the Apocalypse*. What was I thinking? Yes, Roger was more important than a relic. A tingle ran up my spine and chilled the back of my neck. I knew with a certainty; he was in terrible danger.

"No," I called after them. "These things will still be here later. Let's go." I turned, prepared to run down the hall toward the gaping hole protected by the two officers.

Flower put a hand on my chest. "Every relic in our possession is important. We are responsible for them and need to make sure they're safe. Anyway, at this point, I have my doubts about you fighting any of the horsemen."

"We are Champions. They fear us for a reason," I said.

"Maybe it's your injured memory," Jimmy said, "but have you forgotten how helpless we all were against Pestilence? Every one of us got our butts handed to us on a silver platter." He faced Flower. "If not for your resistance to sickness and your gift of healing, we would be diseased and frightened wads of mush."

I replied, "I'm going to help Roger, and I'm going now!"

"Yes, you're both right," Sarah said. "That's why I'll stay and empty your desk, relics and all, into boxes. My Camaro is in the school parking lot. I'll bring them with me when I get through. I'll meet you at McDonalds." Sarah shifted her model's pose to the other foot and focused on Rose. "You want to help me?"

"Yes, I need to feel like I'm contributing something to this fight," Rose said. "Mr. B., we'll get everything out of your office, we can stuff the Camaro's trunk."

"I'll stay, too," Rebecca said. "Three people will get things done faster than two. Anyway, I'm in no hurry to see you and Roger go at each other again."

"I've never gone *at* Roger—not once. However, I'm sure he will have a few choice words for me," I insisted.

"Stoney, if the police see students taking things out of the school office, they're sure to stop them. As a member of the faculty, you could make it all look official," Flower said.

"I had already thought of that possibility," Stoney said. "It would be advantageous for me to stay and help the girls."

"If you would, please." Flower smiled at him. "I said please."

"Yes, of course," Stoney replied. "I get it. A teacher should be seen overseeing the students."

"Oh, one more thing..." Flower said in a mournful tone, "...Arland's Jag was destroyed. We don't have a ride."

Stoney sighed, "And when was he going to realize he didn't have a way to get to Roger's house?"

"Right now, our dear principal is not exactly with it, you know," Flower said.

"Yeah. He's not running on all cylinders," Jimmy added. "...not batting a thousand; you know."

Rebecca put her hands over her ears. "Argh! I don't know what's worse...another sports metaphor...or the trite automotive analogy."

"I may not be at my best, but I'm still standing here." I shook my head. The headache wasn't throbbing like before, and I was feeling some better. It seemed to get worse in the presence of a demon or fallen angel. Facing Stoney, I said, "Old friend, don't harken to gossip and foul words concerning me. A great man once said, 'A man who moves a mountain begins by purchasing a wheelbarrow.' As always, I will prevail."

"He made that up, didn't he?" Jimmy asked.

"Either he made it up or Confucius worked at a hardware store," Flower replied.

"Normally, he could quote Confucius with elegant wit." Stoney sighed, and this time, he nodded. "Don't let him challenge a demon in his condition. Like this, he doesn't have a chance." He paused. "What are you waiting for?"

"The Jag and my Mustang got burned up by some spell casting zombies," Jimmy replied. "I don't have wheels."

"Here." Stoney handed Jimmy his keys. "Take my van. It's in the parking lot."

"Come on Doc, let's get on down the road." Tuck pulled on my sleeve.

"Yeah, we're wasting time," George said. "If what you said about the horsemen targeting us is true, then Roger may need our help."

CHAPTER THIRTY-FOUR

Roger Reynolds

George, Tuck, Jimmy, Flower, and I went out to the parking lot to where a brightly painted hippy van was parked.

"I remember this old thing," Jimmy said. "Looks like you got the roof fixed."

She gave him an incredulous look. "Neither Stoney nor I couldn't drive around with rips in the top, now could we?"

George asked, "What does she mean, rips? Was she in a wreck or something?"

"No. It's a long story involving a little girl and a particularly angry demon," Flower replied. "I'll explain later."

We piled into the van and Flower drove to 2616 Willow Drive, Roger's house. When we arrived, I glanced at my wristwatch. It was nearing 8:30 a.m. For a moment, I imagined how the police would be turning the students away from the school and sending them home. My thoughts were interrupted when Jimmy and Tuck volunteered to do a check of the property before we roused Mr. and Mrs. Reynolds.

"There's no sign of any demon-like varmint anywhere here-a-bouts," Tuck said.

I stepped up onto the porch. "Okay. I guess we better knock."

To my surprise, Roger's brother Michael answered the door. In a momentary lapse, I blurted out, "What are you doing home? Playing hooky from school?" He stood in the entry, hair disheveled and pajamas askew.

He yawned and rubbed his eyes. "No, Mr. B., The Christmas break started when school was dismissed yesterday. Don't you remember?" Then, as if he suddenly realized who I was, his eyes grew wide and his mouth flew open. "Principal Bertarelli, what are you doing here?"

"Is Roger here?" I asked. "We need to speak to him, please."

"Oh? What has he done now? I bet it was something terrible to get the school principal out to our house, and on a holiday, too," He said. "You gonna yell at him? Can I watch?"

"Young man, are your parents home?" I asked.

"Naw, they left about seven-thirty, gone out of town to visit my granny in the nursing home. They'll be back Christmas Day," Michael said. "It's just Roger and me."

Jimmy stepped up to the door.

"Hell no!" Michael bellowed. "Jimmy Dugan's not coming in my house!"

Jimmy leaned closer. "Michael, can't you tell? I'm not like that any—"

"Principal Bertarelli, keep him away from me!"

Jimmy's reputation as a bully was well deserved. That all changed when he was chosen by the angels. Still, guys like Michael, who Jimmy terrorized since grade school, had reasons to not trust him.

Jimmy said, "Michael, give me a break."

I didn't have time to waste even on well-founded phobias. Besides, since in my guise as Mr. Bertarelli, I had never been to their house before, it would seem odd if I marched in and went straight to Roger's room. So, to make life easier, I summoned up my Prophet's Voice. "Michael, take us to Roger and go back to bed."

Miraculously, he calmed down and led us to a closed door at the back of the house. "This is his room."

Again I spoke, using my gift, "You're tired. It's time you go to bed."

He yawned. This time it lingered in his wide open mouth. "I'm awful tired. I think I'll leave you guys and go back to bed."

When we opened the door, we found Roger clad in his pajama bottoms, huddling on the floor, and incoherently mumbling. His chest and face were covered with quarter size pox sores. A scary white-crust also caked his tongue. He reached his hand toward us with fingers the size of sausages. Through swollen lips, he mouthed the words, *help me.*

"Looks like Pestilence got here before us," Jimmy said.

Flower rushed to him and began rubbing his arms and face. Everywhere she touched returned to normal. She held a hand on the center of his chest and his entire torso was healed. He tolerated her touch a bit longer before pushing her hand away.

Roger muttered, "Flower, the book's gone. An albino demon took *The Book of Uriel*. The enemy will be more powerful than ever." The sound of panic filled his words. "From out of nowhere, a crazy-looking she-demon on a white horse burst into my room and, with one touch, sent me into rigors of pain. Much more of that and I'd be in the funny farm playing patty cake with the loonies."

"It wasn't my idea to come looking for you—it was Arland's," she replied.

"Don't fret about it." I consoled him. "The book is not a true relic without the talisman we removed from the cover. I have that in my desk. Don't despair, it's safely under Stoney's protection."

Roger sighed. Possibly, my statement put him more at ease, but he didn't directly acknowledge me as Jimmy helped him to sit on the side of his unmade bed.

"I'm sure you have the entire volume memorized by now." Even though he didn't look me in the eye, I still leaned down to him. "I've seen you work miracles without it. You don't need it to cast angel magic...not anymore."

Shaking like a man with legionaries' disease, he pulled on me, needing help to stand.

Flower rubbed her hands up and down his arms again to make the trembling stop.

"Thank God, you guys came." There was a whimper in Roger's voice I had never heard before. "I thought I could take on any demon Hell threw my way, but this one was tough—super tough. I cast every defensive charm in the book at her and everything passed straight through. Almost like she wasn't really there, but she was because when she touched me... She touched me and...." Roger's eyes welled up, and a tear fell down his cheek.

"It's my guess the demon is made of vapor or something?" George said. "Nothing we did affected it, either."

"Yep, she's one tough devil-mama," Tuck added.

"Tough is an understatement. She's the Horseman of the Apocalypse called Pestilence," I said.

"Whatever..." Roger rolled his eyes and closed them before speaking. "But if you guys hadn't got here soon, I'd be a goner for sure—a dead duck, dead as a doornail, a dead dodo, a—"

Tuck interrupted. "Did you hear right? It was the Doc here who saved your sorry ass." She kept her words quiet, but the incessant tone was impossible to mistake.

"I heard," he said.

"What do ya have to say about that?" Tuck pressed him.

Roger put his lips together into a grim line. "I say...how are we going to win against demons this powerful?"

Jimmy whispered from behind me. "So it's we again. You rejoining the team, are ya?"

Roger pulled open a drawer, took out a tee-shirt, and stretched it over his thin frame. "You got a problem with that?" A quick moment of silence, and he continued. "Even with all us heavy hitters, how are we going to win against demons we can't touch?"

Tuck sat on the end of the bed. "Yeah. That's a good question. Pretty clear, we're no match for any of these horsemen. Especially, Pestilence."

"What's clear is that we need to talk to Reuwel," I replied. "Iggarest said that there was one possible way to beat the horsemen. We have to get hold of a crown of thorns, and if anyone knows where it is...Reuwel will know."

CHAPTER THIRTY-FIVE

Reuwel, the Guardian

Tuck crossed her legs, mounting a boot on her knee. “How do we summon an angel?”

“You don’t, but, as a prophet, I can.”

Roger huffed. “If I had the book, I could do it, too. It adds an extra boost to my charms.”

“Yeah, but you don’t have it,” Tuck retorted.

Roger took a fresh pair of jeans out of his bureau. “Well, get to it. I want to see you pull an angel out of your hat.” He grabbed the elastic band at the top of his pajama pants. “If ya’ll have a sensitive disposition, look away.” In the next moment, he pulled his pajama bottoms down and changed into his jeans.

Flower spun around, setting her eyes on the blank wall over his bed. “Oh, dear,” she gasped.

“Roger, what the hell?” Tuck blurted out. “Next time, give more warning before you strip!”

"Don't get your boot scooting britches in a knot." Roger scoffed. "I'm wearing undies more decent than Arland's old, Frankie Avalon style swimsuit." His judging scowl probed across my portly frame. "Tell me you don't wear it anymore."

"Fear not," I said. "When I became a man, I put away childish things. That swimsuit is ancient history."

"Maybe, to you...not me," he replied under his breath. "Since when did ancient history happen last school year?"

Everyone else, standing further away, could not have heard his contentious whispers.

Ignoring Roger's bitter attitude, I faced the closet door and closed my eyes. "Reuwel, guardian angel, servant to the Most High, and keeper of holy knowledge, we need your wisdom." Even though the windows were closed, a cool breeze blew thru the room. From behind, I felt a hand on my shoulder, but when I looked back—no one was there.

"What a surprise." Roger's sarcastic tone felt like a sharp poke. "Doesn't look like you got what it takes, again."

"Maybe he needs some more time," Flower said.

Jimmy pulled Tuck by the sleeve. "Let Mr. B. have the room. Maybe he can get it together enough to make a toll call to Heaven."

"I can walk by myself." Tuck jerked back. "I may be older than Arland, but I ain't no antique."

"Did you say you're older than Arland?" Roger's eyebrows flew upward. "But he is over a hundred—"

Michael called out from the hall, "What ya'll doing in there?"

Jimmy stepped to the door. "Don't worry about it, bro. We'll be done in a few minutes." With an open hand, he reached toward Michael and Roger's little brother almost lost it.

"Jimmy, don't. I didn't mean it." Michael's arms jerked up to cover his face. Sweat beaded up on his cheeks, and he turned his head to the side. "It's okay. Take all the time you want, just don't hit me."

"Are all the Reynolds dingbats? Get out of the way!" Jimmy blurted.

Michael hurried back into his room and slammed the door.

Everyone filed into the living room, everyone except me. Roger gave me one last scowl before closing the bedroom door behind him. "Don't screw this up."

Alone, I looked around at the room where Roger and I had played as children. The place where we made plans to date all the cheerleaders and become rock stars like Mick Jagger and Keith Richards; but I hardly recognized it. While standing by Roger's bed, those plans faded out of my mind. It was like I'd never been there before. The damage to my brain had taken most all my childhood away from me, and I could feel these memories slipping away. All I had left was the battle ahead. I inhaled a deep breath and closed my eyes.

"Reuwel, guardian angel, servant to the Most High, and keeper of holy knowledge, we need your wisdom."

The room temperature severely dropped, and a cold wind rushed over me. Exhaling, I opened my eyes. My breath froze in midair, and an icy frost lay on the windowpanes. A crack of thunder and a flash of light welcomed Reuwel into the room. He stood next to me. This time, unlike all others before, he didn't appear as a giant, but as a normal man—no glowing robes, nor did his hair shine like radiant moonbeams. He wore a common plaid tie with a blue pinstriped suit. His short hair looked just as pedestrian.

"Reuwel?" I questioned, trying to fit the being before me together with who I knew him to be. "Is that you?"

"It is I." The angel's voice resonated with the same power as I remembered.

"You look so different. Why have you come in mortal form?"

"Before, I came to you at the command of the Creator. This time, you have demanded my presence."

"We have just cause. The enemy's horsemen have proven more powerful than the gifts we possess." I sighed in frustration. "If it weren't expedient, I would not have called out to you."

Reuwel put his arm around my shoulder. **"Fear not,"** he said. **"The Lord of Hosts has not brought you here to be destroyed so easily."**

"The white horseman has pressed through all our defenses. She marched over us with ease, and left us afflicted, completely helpless, in the wake of her power." I sighed in frustration. "This battle was lost before it had begun."

"**Say what you desire, for I have come with blessings**."

"It would be easier to accept your help if you looked like an angel instead of a banker."

"Each step in your journey has required faith. By now, you know that you can't depend on your sight to bolster faith. It comes from a far deeper place. But I've not come to lecture you. Make your request."

"We seek a particular relic—a holy article described as a crown of thorns. We need your help to find it."

"You seek *the Crown of Sorrows?* Why is it that you chose to seek this relic? Who told you the crown could aid you against the horseman?"

"A Fallen who plots against his master told us. I don't know for sure if his name is Iggarest or if her name is Amethyst. She is a confusing individual. Frankly, I'm not even sure she is an angel. What was it Iggarest called her...? Oh yes, he called her a Necrothyst."

"Do not put your trust in a Fallen. The relic you seek is not a weapon. Indeed, it is powerful, but there is a reason both mortals and angels alike call it the Crown of Sorrows." He reached above his head and brought his fist down in front of me. In it he held a circle of intertwined vines, each branch lined with twisted thorns. He said, **"I cannot give you this relic. Your desire to defeat the enemy would tempt you to wear it, but your victory would pale compared to the following devastation."**

"Reuwel," I bellowed in anger, "you show it to me, and yet you withhold its power from me? Why put it within my reach only to take it away and dash my hopes of victory?"

The edges of the angel's lips tilted upward as he snapped off three of the thorns and laid them in my hand. **"These thorns are infused with the Blood of the Redeemer;**

such power is beyond mortal understanding. Three thorns are all I may provide of this relic. Each may be used once, so use them wisely, marked prophet."

When he dropped them into my hand, I felt a sensation, a surge of untapped strength. I called it strength because I didn't have a better word to describe it. Without a secure place to keep them, I tucked the thorns into my shirt pocket.

He again lifted the crown over his head, and when he brought it down, this time in his fist was a sealed horn filled with liquid. **"Do you know what I now hold?"**

"How can I know unless you tell me?"

He broke the seal and lifted the horn over my head, and said, **"I anoint you with martyrs' tears."** Tipping the horn, something akin to fragrant oil dripped onto my hair. It ran over my head, down my shirt and through my pants—saturating my clothes. It made a puddle where I stood. **"Each drop is empowered to make right unimaginable wrongs."**

Totally soaked, I stood on soggy carpet. Gazing around me, nothing looked different or more familiar than before. I still couldn't remember my childhood, and I still had no idea how to use the thorns. I sputtered, "Thank you...I think."

Opening my mouth to speak again, a familiar voice spoke from a distant part of my mind. "*About time you brought me back. I've been stuck in here and couldn't even get a message out.*"

"What's going on? Who's talking?" I struggled to remember. "Mr. Dark? Is that you?"

"*Well, it sure isn't George Burns.*"

"I see your restoration has already begun."

I rubbed the fluid out of my eyes and looked up. He had vanished.

"*How much of this are you going to tell the others?*"

"You always did have a way of beating around the bush before getting to the point. You want to know if I'm going to tell Flower I can hear you again?"

"*Okay, well, are you? Are you going to let them know I'm back?*"

"I didn't tell them you went away." I paused with my hand on the doorknob. "As always, I'll tell them what they need to know."

"*Right...sure you will.*"

"What's that supposed to mean? I think I liked it better with you gone. At least my thoughts were my own."

"*You know Reuwel left that bottle...I mean, the horn...in your pocket.*"

"He what?" I checked my left pants pocket. There, I found a small version of the same sealed horn.

"*Did he explain what these tears can do?*"

"He's an angel. What do you think?" I shivered in the room's chill.

"*By the way...I'm thankful we're one again.*"

I reached for the door handle and smiled. "Yes, old friend, me too." When I opened the door, cold air flooded out into the rest of the house.

CHAPTER THIRTY-SIX

The Secret Weapon

"Good grief! What did you do...? Open the windows and turn the air conditioner to high?" Roger stuck his head in the room. "And there's a big dark place on the carpet—it's wet. The carpet's wet. Oh hell, tell me you didn't take a leak in the middle of my floor?"

"*Funny guy, this one. I guess things haven't changed. Roger is still acting like a butt.*" As usual, Mr. Dark's voice spoke to me alone.

"Shut up already!" I yelled. "Stop making stupid comments!"

Roger's mouth dropped open, and he stepped back. Never, since my return as an adult, had I spoken to him in anger, and although I hadn't intended my outburst to be directed at him, it was well deserved.

This time I only spoke sternly, "It's your choice to be part of this team or not. If you want, we'll leave and you can fend for yourself. Just know, next time a demon knocks you off that pedestal you live on, no one's going to be there to pick up your arrogant behind. If you're back, then act like it and stop being an ass! Believe it or not, we have more important things to do than save you from these horsemen. The future of the world is at stake. So, my dear Roger, grow up and shut up."

Needless to say, my demonstrative outburst was unexpected. Flower looked as if I'd stepped on her sore toe, and Jimmy's eyebrows shot up in surprise. As for Tuck, she slapped her knee and guffawed.

George punched Roger in the arm and said, "Man, I don't know what happened to you, but something did. You sure haven't been acting like the same guy I met last year in Mr. Bertarelli's classroom. I liked him."

"If not for Mr. B., you'd still be sitting by your bed; hurting," Jimmy said. "He figured out where that white devil would strike next."

"What do you want me to say?" Roger retorted. "Yeah, I never should've left the team. I know that now."

Flower said, "We've more important things to focus on than bickering about who made what mistake. Roger's back, and we need him. Even without his relic, he's a force to be reckoned with."

"Yeah, we do. We've got to find that crown," Jimmy said. "Did Reuwel tell you where it is?"

I bowed my head. "No. He didn't."

It was Roger's turn to yell. "What?" He shook his index finger in my face. "If Reuwel doesn't know where it is, then how are we going to find it? Arland, did you screw up again?"

George shot him a harsh look.

"No, Reuwel knows where it is. In fact, he showed it to me."

Tuck gasped. "He showed you the crown but didn't give it to you?"

"Reuwel said that the Fallen who told us to use the crown was deceiving us." I put a hand on Tuck's shoulder. "He called it *the Crown of Sorrows* and if we use it as a weapon, we'll wish we hadn't."

"Oh, Arland... Where does that leave us? What are we to do?" Flower asked.

I didn't answer. Evidently, my mind still needed time to heal because I got distracted by the color of Flower's beautiful eyes. George's voice brought me back to our dilemma.

"We still have our relics," George pulled at his belt. "I have the *Rope of Saint Sebastian.*"

"And Rebecca has a splinter from *The Ladder of Ascension,*" Flower replied.

"Yes, and Arland has knives blessed by the Leper King of Jerusalem," Jimmy added. "Those suckers will sever immortal flesh from bone. Take that, you horsemen!"

"Even though I lost T*he Book of Uriel,*" Roger said, "it will do them no good without *The Talisman.*"

"True, but even with all these things together, they won't give us enough of an advantage..." I pulled the thorns out of my pocket. "...but Reuwel said that these will help."

Three long, sharp thorns lay in my hand. "These are from the Crown of Sorrows."

Tuck asked, "Looks like stickers from a bramble bush. How do we use them? Do we scratch the Devils, forcing them back to Hell?"

"Don't be absurd!" Roger blurted. "That would be stupid."

Flower huffed. "Not necessarily. I've heard of things just as odd."

George reached for the thorns, but I closed my hand and dropped them back in my shirt pocket. "Truthfully, I have no idea how they work or what advantage they are supposed to provide. Reuwel didn't exactly leave instruction for us. All he said was that they are infused with the *Blood of the Redeemer*."

"No way!" Roger exclaimed. "That means they have been saturated with the *Blood of Christ*, and I can't even begin to imagine how powerful that is."

"No matter how much high-octane spirit juice them supercharged goat-heads have, they're useless if we don't know how to tap into their supernatural dynamo. A cattle-prod would be more effective," Tuck stated.

"Then we learn," I said. "The more we know, the better off we are in the battle to come."

"And how do we do that? Do you think the angels left some clues or something?" Jimmy asked.

"Yeah I do," I said. "There must be some way to figure this out...else Reuwel would have said more."

“Angels never make things plain,” Jimmy said. “With them, it’s always a puzzle.”

“Well, I guess it wasn’t a complete bust,” Roger said. “But, if he had given you the whole crown, then you would have lots of thorns...but no, you couldn’t get that.”

Jimmy shook his head. “Think about it, Numbnuts. There had to be a reason he called it the Crown of Sorrows.”

“Well excuse me,” Roger blurted. “That’s why I left. It’s impossible to work with idiots.”

“That’s enough!” I said. “Roger is not responsible for his actions. I see that now.” Iggarest laughed when he told me about Solomon’s curse, and I didn’t realize it was an actual affliction.

A tingle ran up my spine and made the hairs on the back of my neck stand on end. It was my supernatural gift. I bowed my head and got a word of knowledge. It was only a flash of a bigger picture, but it was enough. Pulling the horn from my pocket, I broke the seal and poured it out onto Roger’s head. “I anoint you with the tears of martyrs. Come to our aid and make right every wrong.” The small horn didn’t have enough in it to wet down his clothes, but it made a mess of his hair.

The others stared, mouths a gape. Tuck dared to speak first. “Did you just dump oil on Roger’s head?”

I didn’t answer. I waited for Roger to say something. He looked up at me and grinned. “Was that revenge for me accusing you of taking a leak on the floor?” he asked.

“Revenge?” My tone sounded more humorous than my mood. “Perhaps.” Only time would tell if it made a difference.

"Enough fun and games," Tuck said. "We've got to get down to serious business."

Roger took a towel from the linen closet and wiped up the residual liquid from his hair.

Holding the horn, I pushed my hand in my pocket and smiled as I felt the mystical container disappear from under my fingers. Like many supernatural objects, the horn had a onetime usage limit.

Flower led the way to the front door. "It never fails to amuse me how men can act so much like children." She opened the door and held it for us to exit. "It's my guess that the crown might win the day for us, but it would also take something in return—something precious. Most relics, that have anything to do with sorrow or grief, exacts a price for their miracle."

"And who decides what is to be taken or sacrificed?" Roger asked.

"The object, of course. It decided," Flower said.

"That goes back to what Arland said about the remaining sword in the crest." George stepped through the doorway. "He said it has a will of its own—like it can think."

"The more we learn about the relics, the more convinced I am that they all are sentient, at least up to a point," I faced Roger. "Come along. We are going to rally the troops. Everyone is meeting up at McDonald's, our old hang out, and there's room in Stoney's van for you, too."

"What? That old hippy van? I've ridden sandwiched in there before; no thank you. I'll take my own wheels."

Since my Jag had been destroyed as well as George's Vespa, we had to make do with what vehicles remained at our disposal. With Roger's parents out of town, he had the use of his mom's tiny, eleven-year-old, unreliable Rambler, or his dad's two-year-old Chevy truck. Roger turned and yelled. "Mikey, I'm taking Dad's truck."

Before I could step out onto the porch, the phone rang and Michael called out, "Mr. Bertarelli, there's a lady on the phone asking for you."

He stretched the cord through the doorway to the hall and handed it to me. It was Rose. "Mr. B., we found a few empty boxes in the school supply room. They were the perfect size to fit into Sarah's trunk. Anyway, we got everything out of your desk and the few books from your bookcases, and if Rebecca's Volkswagen hadn't been destroyed in that fire at your house, we could have rescued all your books."

"Great. We're finished here. Meet us as planned." I handed the phone back to Michael.

"Who was that?" Michael asked. "Her voice sounded familiar."

"That was Rose McFarlane," I replied.

Michael spoke loud enough to be heard outside. "Oh, I almost forgot, dumb-head Dugan is here, and she's his chick. Somebody needs to teach that bully a lesson."

"I heard that, Michael," Jimmy shouted back from where he stood on the porch. "You gonna teach me a lesson? Are ya?"

"Oh, shit!" Michael exclaimed as he ran for his room.

CHAPTER THIRTY-SEVEN

Transfiguration

By noon, Rebecca, Sarah, Rose and Stoney were supposed to meet us at the McDonald's located off the interstate. Our brightly painted hippy van pulled onto the blacktop in time to see Rebecca lying on the pavement trembling from some plague that Pestilence afflicted her with. Sarah stood to the side. However, Rose was standing in front of the phantasm, hands extended and mouthing words we couldn't hear.

We stepped out onto the restaurant's parking lot just in time to be bewildered, for it was the ghostly demon who was shrieking out louder than a banshee—obviously in pain.

"Rose! Babe, I'm coming!" Jimmy yelled.

I pulled him back, only to have him jerk away from my grip. "Jimmy! No!" My voice was lost in the rider's cries.

Before he could dash to her side, the horseman shook loose from her grip and headed off, *hobbling* down the street.

The steed leaped into the air as if to fly away into the clouds, but failed to take flight. Instead, it tumbled to the ground. Both horse and rider staggered to their feet, shook themselves, and limped away toward the school.

"Should we chase them?" George asked.

"I don't know," I called out as we raced toward the girls.

Flower got to Rebecca first and laid hands on her, healing the plague the rider inflicted.

Jimmy reached Rose before I did and put his big arms around her.

Gazing down the street at the fleeing demon, I asked, "Rose, what did you do to Pestilence?"

"I used my gift of transfiguration and turned her into a human. The effect never lasts long after I break contact, but at this moment, she and that scary horse are as powerless as any normal person. Looks like the experience scared her bad enough to make her run away."

"I'd say it surprised her. Look there on the pavement, it's the Book of Uriel. The rider had it with her when she attacked you," Flower said.

"That she-devil must have dropped it in the ruckus," Tuck added.

"My book! Oh, thank Heaven." Big tears welled up in Roger's eyes. "Thank you...Thank you, Rose. You're beautiful. You're gorgeous. You got my book back for me." Roger grabbed up the Book of Uriel and hugged it up to his chest.

"Your book?" Tuck blurted. "I thought it was the angel's book."

"Tuck, right now, I can't even be angry with you." Roger joyously jumped and literally skipped in a circle.

"Earlier," I said, "you wanted to know what weapon we have that could beat a phantom like Pestilence. I think we found one."

"What? Are you talkin' about that book?" Tuck asked.

"No!" I replied. "I'm talking about Rose."

"She did it!" Roger exclaimed. "She scrambled Pestilence's molecules and now...she's got my book back."

"I don't get it," George said. "Did the book do this? At the school, when the white rider attacked, we all tried our relics and gifts, but nothing worked on that phantasm. If Rose did it, then what makes her gift so special?"

"The angels gave Rose a unique supernatural ability," I said. "She can transfigure anything into its perfect form. As far as I know, she can't turn one thing into something else, but she can make something broken whole again. The change is limited to how long she has touched it."

"Okay. So how did she turn the rider into a mortal?" George asked.

"It's because all the riders but one were at one time mortals," I said. "By returning Pestilence to her human form, Rose stripped the hellion of her supernatural powers."

"Rose, you rock. Come on guys, team hug." Roger put his arms around both Jimmy and Rose, but got pushed in the face by Jimmy's big mitt.

"Back off, Numbnuts!" Jimmy demanded.

"*What's up with Roger?*" Mr. Dark's silent voice whispered in my mind. "*Last time I saw him, he was rude and crude. Now, he's all buddy-buddy.*"

I silently sent a mental message to his part of my mind. "As always, your timing is terrible. I'll explain later."

George gave Rose a look of awe; well, maybe it was fascination. "Transfiguration, huh?" *The Kid,* who was usually timid, had been more vocal after his ordeal with Gewalt, the red rider. "I bet that's really handy in a pinch."

"Yep," Jimmy added, "it's just what you need to climb out of Hell, or turn a demon rider into a mortal." He hugged her closer.

"Let's take a gander at those relics you guys took from Doc's desk," Tuck remarked.

Sarah opened the top box, which was still lying inside the trunk of her car. One at a time, she held up the relics I'd collected over the last century; The Talisman of the angel Uriel and the charmed knives belonging to the Leper King of Jerusalem. Rebecca had put in the sliver of the Ladder of Ascension, and Rose included her ruby crested dagger that once belonged to God's friend, Abraham. The last things she pulled out of the box was the spike Jael hammered into Sisera's head in order to save the Hebrew nation, and a silver diviner's cup once belonging to Zaphnath-Paaneah, also known as Joseph, son of Israel.

"*Too bad that cup never talked to you.*" Mr. Dark spoke in my mind. "*It might give us an idea about what's fixing to happen next.*"

I focused my thoughts on him and replied, "It's not from my lack of trying. Perhaps it doesn't like me." I reached in my pocket for the Horn filled with martyrs' tears and stopped. I forgot. It had vanished right out of my pocket after I used it on Roger.

"Goes to show you're not back to a hundred percent yet." Mr. Dark said.

I slapped the side of my head as I would a seized up engine, refusing to start, and scolded myself for not remembering. "Arland, old boy, you have to try to do better."

"You're not going to tell them everything that happened between you and Reuwel, are you?" Mr. Dark asked in his silent way.

"Maybe...in time." I whispered back. "Not now."

Sarah dropped the silver cup back into the box. "Do you really think these will be enough to fend off the attack of the horsemen?" she asked.

"Probably not." Roger spoke up. "None of us have been able to stand up to a horseman except for Rose."

"Not true," George replied. "With the help of a giant angel, I vanquished the one called War."

"She called herself Gewalt," Stoney corrected. "The direct translation is violence."

"Wait... back up a minute." Roger turned to George. "You did what?" Roger's question sounded more like a sarcastic exclamation. "*The Arkansas Kid* took out one of the Horsemen of the Apocalypse all by himself?"

"The details are pretty hazy, especially about the fight—but I remember the pain," George said.

"I may have to stop calling you *The Kid* and find a new name for you...one that fits a true Champion," Roger replied.

"I'm all for nicknames that fit the person." Tuck popped Roger on the arm. "I wanna know why Jimmy calls you *Numbnuts.* There's got to be a story behind it."

Roger cleared his throat and gave Tuck a poisonous stare. "Nobody but Dugan gets away with that. We go way back, Jimmy and I."

Tuck slapped her knee and guffawed. "When you get ready to share, I'm listening. That's got to be a doozy of a tale."

They finally got quiet, allowing me to speak. "We've never won a battle when one-person shows off...and tries to be a superstar. We have to work together as a team." I was wasting my breath. Talking just didn't work with these guys.

Maybe we would never be a real team, but with every demon encounter, it gave us another chance to learn a bit more about how to depend on each other. Or maybe I was looking through rose-colored glasses, hoping they would finally figure it out.

What I needed was a ray of hope, and Rose gave me that. Yes, thanks to her, we've even found one of the horsemen's weaknesses, and there were bound to be others.

"Right now, we must find out everything we can about these thorns," Flower said. "Reuwel gave them to us for a reason. I'm betting he knows something we don't."

"My dear Flower, that is an oversimplification. At this time, I have to agree with Roger. All we get from the angels are puzzles and more questions. However, Flower also has made a good point. This quandary is all about unlocking the supernatural power from three thorns soaked in the Blood of Christ. So, my friends, how do we do it?"

She shot me an admiring glance. I remembered something about that look in her eyes. What was it? Surely it would come back to me now that the tears were overhauling my brain.

No one spoke up with brilliant ideas, so I made an executive decision. "Roger, settle in with the Book of Uriel. Go through everything that's written in it about the Crown of Sorrows, and especially the thorns."

"Come on, book, let's get started." Holding the book tight to his chest, Roger went inside the restaurant to read.

"Rose, as for you and Sarah, since our previous librarian was a demon harpy from Hell, there may be some arcane writings hidden by Miss Crouch in the library. The police have posted officers at the school entrances to keep out prospective looters. To do what I ask, you'll need to sneak back in."

"Don't worry, Mr. B.," Rose replied. "I got this. If she had any information stashed there, I'll find it."

"Take Jimmy with you. He's good at providing a distraction, and that's just what you'll need to gain entrance."

"Flower, you and Stoney, check with the council of angelic elders to see if they can provide any guidance for us."

Flower didn't speak, only gave me a nod, before she and Stoney loaded up in his hippy van and headed off.

"George, you're a science geek. I'm guessing that means you can speed-read technical journals and such."

"Well, I do like to read..." George nodded, "...and I go through at least two books a night."

I handed him a stack of books Stoney and the ladies had taken from my office. "Read over these old and arcane volumes to see if you can find anything pertaining to holy relics touched by Christ. Be careful with them. I've had some of these books for over fifty years, and their bindings are showing their age." Like Roger, he too took the books inside.

"Tuck, when we're through here, put the box with the rest of the relics in the back of Roger's truck."

Tuck replied, "You mean his father's truck?"

My gaze was short-tempered. "Ok, then...Roger's father's truck."

"Just saying...huffy boy here ain't all that, like he thinks he is," Tuck said.

Rebecca glanced at Tuck. "Let's stay focused, please!" She looked through the box at the various relics I had collected before asking, "What is it you want us to do?"

I handed her the blessed knives from the box. "Take these and use them if necessary. Keep in mind, they won't vanquish an immortal, but they can cause a lot of pain." As I spoke, she eyed the daggers with what I took to be intrepid awe. "Tuck, if there's anything you want from here, take it. I trust you still have that charmed gun loaded and ready."

"Ha!" she said. "You know it's loaded, and I'm always ready to take on a demon or two."

"I'm going to attempt to summon Iggarest. I think he's holding out on us. He may get testy with us. And more importantly, it may depend on if Amethyst has taken over his form or not. In short, I don't know how this is going down," I added. "Reuwel reminded me of something I knew all too well; a Fallen can't be trusted. Stay alert and bear with me. We are going to pay Iggarest a visit."

CHAPTER THIRTY-EIGHT

A Wheel within a Wheel

After assigning everyone a task, they headed off. Roger and George went inside the restaurant. Flower and Stoney took off in the van, while Rose and Jimmy tagged along with Sarah in her Camaro.

"You planning on summoning a fallen angel right out here? ...in the open? ...in plain daylight?" Rebecca asked.

"Of course not," I said. "That's why we're going around back to the alley. I'll summon him back there."

Tuck craned her neck, looking around at the open cotton field behind the restaurant. "Not sure that's a bunch better, but ok."

She had a point. There wasn't much of a secluded place anywhere nearby. At least, this McDonald's was built at the edge of what most people called *town,* with the field almost butting up to the back of the building. The drive thru came down from the front and made a U-turn without going around the building. The customers getting their French fries and sodas could exit back onto Main Street, unaware of anything taking place in the tiny alley.

As for curious onlookers, who might be driving down the interstate a mile and a half away, a line of tall juniper trees obscured their view. Not that they would understand anything going on here.

Across the highway was the new Bentwood High School. The city fathers situated it about two miles farther to the north, where a westward housing development had begun. I felt relatively sure there would be no prying eyes watching—even at a distance.

"Stay vigilant!" I demanded. "If I'm right, we're going to have more company than an introverted fallen angel."

Rebecca, with daggers at the ready, took watch on my left and Tuck, pistol drawn, covered my right. I drew a deep breath and called out in the Prophet's Voice. "Iggarest, fallen one, despised of angels and man, I call unto you. Hear me and obey my words." The breeze died away and an unnatural warmth surrounded us. We waited. Nothing happened. Again I tried. I screamed at the top of my voice. "Iggarest, peon among Elohim, worm of Hell's dung, I call to you. Show yourself, the Marked Prophet commands."

The air temperature became as warm as a tropical breeze. A small, swirling wind filled with dust broke the surrounding stillness. It danced around us, throwing sand, rock chips, and dirt in every direction. From it came a voice. **"Why do you call me despicable names? I have done you no wrong. Marked one, has your brain cankered? Me thinks,**

you've forgotten I am on your side? But then, you have been sorely handicapped by those rot infested microbes from Hell!" The mild wind picked up speed, whirling and whipping around us.

From out of nowhere, thunderclouds blew in and the little dirt devil roared with the sound of a diesel locomotive. Unexpectedly, the dirt devil grew into a twister. One large enough to tower overhead and spin with gale force wind. We pressed up against the building and hunkered down in hopes of protecting ourselves from flying garbage.

Squinting to see through the grit infested air, I peered into the tornadic vortex to witness something strange—totally supernatural. There, at the heart of the tempest, was Amethyst. I cast my eyes to the left, and for a brief moment, I saw Tuck as a lion rearing up and pawing at the fallen angel. The sound of a flying soda bottle shattering against the brick wall drew my attention behind me, and there, Rebecca's visage overlapped with a faint image of a lamb, kicking at the wind. My fear ceased, but a creepy sense of déjà vu made me quiver.

The angel's voice changed. It became thinner and higher pitched. **"Your affliction should have crippled your prophetic powers by now. The demons had plenty of time to chew enough gray matter away to turn you into a babbling husk. Reality, as you know it, should be spinning away from you...and yet, here you stand, sure-footed and upright. The healer is not gifted enough to do this. What brought on your miracle?"**

"Trickster, stand before me. Amethyst, face your judge and confess your cowardice." My words blew back in my face as I yelled.

"I sent you on an endless quest to find the Crown of Thorns. For I know the Creator considers it too powerful for mortal kind to even come in contact with it. He keeps it hidden."

"Amidst all your boasting you yet do not understand the heart of the Father," I cried.

"If He has entrusted it to you, put it on and see what power it possesses."

I closed my eyes, and a startling revelation flashed through my mind. "The Crown of Sorrows has been saturated with all the sins from each and every man, woman, and child who has, or ever will, live. This was the sorrow the Redeemer had to bear. That is why no mortal can bear its weight. The thorns that line the branches hold the power of the blood." I waved my fist at the wind. "This much I know. The Father of all has revealed it to me. Fallen one, your plan to send us on a quest in hopes we would find our doom has failed!"

The tornadic wind speed subsided, and the voice became deeper. Even though I still couldn't see who spoke, it sounded like Iggarest again. **"I...I don't know why I told you about it. The legend of the crown is one of the great mysteries told among the Fallen. It is said to hold the greatest power known to the Elohim. I knew of the twisted vine, I knew of the great pain and sorrow it contains, but since I also knew that the Creator himself protects the crown, you have no chance of finding it... Or should I say,**

you have a slim chance of finding it. Still, if you did, just think of what a mortal could do with so much power."

The wind blew harder. I felt almost weightless in the whirling vortex. "What else does your legend say? Tell me all about the legend of this relic."

"It represents the day of our derisional disgrace. It is a day we do not speak of, for on that day *the keys of life and death* were taken from our Lord and Master." Iggarest's voice changed again. The melodic baritone ringing that characterized his voice wasn't the same. Something wicked, a harmonic timbre I'd heard from Amethyst, replaced it.

"Prophet, I refuse to let Iggarest, the worm, lower than the refuse on Satan's hoofs, stand before you. He is lower than a dung beetle and knows nothing. In my presence, he is powerless. Marked prophet, I do not fear your meager power. I am the supreme form of Elohim, nothing less than the pinnacle of mystical mastery, and soon all the Fallen will fear my name. Hear it and despair for I am Amethyst."

Through the flying dirt, I could barely make out the form of an angel, nine feet tall, with lightning flashing from her fingertips. When the wind subsided, I wiped the grit from my eyes. Before me, she stood baring six arms and six wings. Around her rotated a ring like a wheel, and upon the edge of it, a multitude of eyes watched from every direction. Before I could rein Tuck in, she fired on the giant.

The rings whirled, spinning at a violently turbulent speed and undulating in a wavelike arc, creating a crackling sphere of power around Amethyst. The charmed bullets ricocheted off those cyclonically charged rings and struck the building behind me.

"You dare strike out at me. I am the master of all mortal-kind, the mistress of human thoughts, and the perpetrator of men's darkest desires. Witness my dominance and fear me."

The tornado warning system sirens went off, bellowing a sonic blast at a screeching pitch.

The inside spinning edge of the wheel exuded a violet mist filling the sphere's interior and hiding her from view.

"**Prophet, you won't always have your puny minions with you. I'll be watching. You will yet provide my means of victory; just as I planned all along.**"

Before she finished speaking, a rushing wind descended, stirring up the dust from the field. When it cleared, Amethyst was gone and in her place stood two demon possessed corpses.

One was green, and exceptionally ugly, wearing what looked like a disturbingly bare human skin sewn awkwardly around the devil inside. Lumps protruded from different parts of its unstitched body, and above a mouth full of jagged teeth, solid white orbs for eyes stared at me with an unmistakable hatred. The other was small and impish, wearing an oversized skin. Folds of flesh pulled up and pinned with something akin to safety pins held it on the devil's tiny frame. At the left side of its head, a pointy ear escaped the miss-mashed seams.

The big zombie lumbered towards me.

Rebecca bravely met his attack with three slashes of the blessed daggers. The first cut into its midsection, the second lacerated the thing's arm, and the third perforated a large part of its hulking right leg.

Staggering backward, it appeared confused by the pain the daggers inflicted. Another jab and the demon blew up like a balloon.

"Rebecca, watch out, it's going to...."

She jumped back, pressing against the building moments before it exploded. The shock waves threw chunks of demon gore in every direction.

Tuck leveled her charmed gun on the other zombie. She fired three times in rapid succession. The squirrelly little devil bounced from side-to-side, quick and agile enough to evade each shell. Again, it rapidly bounced back and forth, inching forward.

Tuck lowered her weapon and smiled as if awaiting his attack. Just as before, the green devil leaped into the air, throwing itself into the air, fangs bared and claws extended. The charmed shells turned around in midair and fixed themselves onto their target. A dull expression blasted across the demon's face...that and three smoking holes in its forehead.

A sizzling sound vibrated from inside the small green monster, and the demon ignited into a ball of fire, leaving nothing but ashes on the pavement.

Then there was silence. Amethyst was gone, and so were her demon possessed corpses.

From inside the building, Roger and George came running to aid in the fight. "We heard gunfire and figured it wasn't farmer Jones taking potshots at coyotes," Roger said.

"Who are we fighting this time? Is it another rider? Famine, maybe?" George asked.

"It's Amethyst and her cronies." Rebecca waved the daggers at Roger as she talked. Demon juices flew in his direction. "She finally showed her true colors. She evidently has more than a few perverted humans at her disposal. After that, there's no doubt in my mind, she's *Queen of the Zombies*."

"Even if she doesn't have a herd of monstrous green and blue devils at her command, she's got two less corpses to boss around now." Tuck gave Rebecca a sideways glance. "Remind me to never get on that filly's bad side. Rebecca's got lots of spunk...and a lethal, back fisted jab."

Rebecca wiped her blades off on a white lacey handkerchief and continued to inspect the hilts and handles. "That'll show Amethyst just who's a minion and who's not."

Roger blinked and lifted his head a bit higher. "Zombies? Minion?" Grit entered his voice when he said, "Did I hear right? Did that winged she-devil called me a minion or a zombie?" Roger fumed. "I've never been anyone's minion, and I'm certainly not a freaking zombie." He stopped and his brows furrowed. "Who's Amethyst?"

"That devil chick, we were a fightin'. That's who she is." Tuck wave a hand in the direction Amethyst had appeared. "Ignore her. It's not worth gettin' all riled up over what she says." Tuck rubbed the barrel of her gun on the sleeve of her leisure suit.

That tingle ran up my spine again. My gift was trying to give me some kind of warning. I tilted my head to listen, and sure enough, what I got was a confirmation of my suspicions.

"Evidently, causing discord is Amethyst's bag. And she's good at it. I think she's been working us for some time now, maybe even at my country house," I couldn't help but add a modern colloquialism. "Dig, Babe?"

"Doc, you spoutin' hippy talk makes as much sense as my grandpa did when he called in the pigs. Nobody understood him either." Tuck grimaced at my words. "I don't think I could take another change in your personality, not today. And I ain't anyone's babe."

"Yeah, Mr. B., no more jive slang, please." Jimmy sided with Tuck. "But you make a good point about Amethyst and those zombies that burned down your house. They were all demon possessed corpses."

"Iggarest swore those zombies weren't his. The question is...was he lyin'?" Tuck's worried brow set me on edge.

"Do you know what the word of a Fallen is worth? Nada! Not a thing," Rebecca added.

Roger caught my eyes. "They burned your house down?"

"It was an old house," I said. "But I'll miss my Jag."

"They got the Jag, too?" Roger sounded incensed. "I liked that car."

"Rebecca is correct. Just because they didn't call Iggarest master doesn't mean the zombies couldn't have belonged to Amethyst." I ran my hand through my hair.

Wide-eyed puzzlement crossed Roger's face. "Zombies? I think I missed something. Flower told me there's no such thing as zombies." His voice took on a strained tone. "I hate zombies!"

"What? That was over a year ago...no wonder you don't remember so good." Rebecca sounded definite. "Aww! Forget it. That was then. This is now. Get over it!"

"Roger, old buddy, you just stick close to me and let me take care of those zombies." Tuck popped Roger's arm with a friendly thump. "Got it, Roger, I got you covered like a sharpshooter on the westbound Santa Fe stage."

Roger's focus went from Tuck to me and back. "Arland, I don't like zombies. They eat your brain." He closed his eyes. "I hate zombies."

"*Wow, he's brave as the cowardly lion! Tell me again why you wanted to be his friend.*" No doubt Mr. Dark's scathing remark was meant to condemn me for all the times I fretted over Roger's asinine attitude. And yet, in those immature and fearful words, I recognized my old friend again.

"Focus! Roger, focus!" Rebecca snapped her fingers to get his attention. "I'll explain later about the zombies, and yes, you missed a bunch.

CHAPTER THIRTY-NINE

The Hypothesis

"Your telling me there's a schizoid-fallen angel named Amethyst, and she's been playing us for fools." Roger had listened to our tale with earnestness. Thankfully, his temper was aimed at someone other than me. Letting him loose on Amethyst might be exactly what we needed.

He roared, "Why didn't someone tell me? I didn't know there was a Fallen named Amethyst until today."

"Well, you must admit you've been..." I chose my words carefully, "...distracted, as of late."

"If she's anybody important, she'll be in here," Roger said as he flipped page after page in the Book of Uriel looking for something, anything, about an angel named Amethyst.

"So, is she mentioned in the angel's book of wisdom?" George asked.

Roger shook his head and closed the book. "No mention of her. If she's playing us, then she's doing a bang-up job of it. I doubt she could have fooled Uriel, though. From what you told me, Iggarest and Amethyst may both be formidable nemeses. They each seem capable of formulating this elaborate fabrication." Over the course of the past year, I noticed Roger's vocabulary had improved. That usually happened when his gift kicked in. What else should be expected from someone empowered with the Wisdom of Solomon.

I nodded and straightened my sports jacket. "Iggarest accuses Amethyst of betraying us, and she blames him for about everything she doesn't like." With my fingertips, I dusted a fine layer of grit off of my sleeves.

Tuck took off her Stetson hat and waved it at us. "You may never hear me admit this again, but I agree with Roger. There's something about that she-devil I never trusted. The look out of her eyes is too much like a rattler's gaze charmin' a prairie dog... And now, for her to sic her demon lapdogs on us, she's proved it."

"If by all that countrified jibber jabber you mean she's been setting us up, then I totally agree." Rebecca chuckled at Tuck's round-about way of stating the obvious. "And maybe she told Iggarest to get it for her, too." She grabbed a dangling piece of George's torn tee-shirt and pulled hard, ripping a strip off, into a rag. Using it to finish cleaning and polish the daggers before she put them away. "But that's all conjecture."

"Hey, stop. That's my shirt you're ripping." George complained. "Don't you have a hanky?"

"Yes, but it has demon juice on it. Can't clean by spreading more demon juice on top of other demon juice. Besides, that thing you're wearing used to be a shirt. After your battle it's..." Rebecca took another look at George's tee. "I don't really know what it is now. There's not much shirt there."

"If you'll stop butchering my clothes, maybe we can stay on track here. Think about this rationally. Amethyst and Iggarest's actions don't make sense. It's like he has his plan and she has hers...and they don't talk. The craziest part is why a Fallen gave Sarah a supernatural power, a Champion's gift." George scratched his head. "Was that a blessing or a curse?"

"Don't ask me. I don't know. As handy as her gift has been, I can't get over how it almost killed me." I explained. "Perhaps that was what Amethyst hoped for all along?" I was feeling tremendously better, but I paused to gather my thoughts. "Frankly, I'm tired of Iggarest deceptively using me."

That tingle returned to my spine. My gifting was working at full power again. Closing my eyes, I bowed my head. Flashes of truth illuminated the back of my closed eyelids like a wall to wall movie screen, and I nodded as I received a word of knowledge. "My gift has revealed to me that Amethyst realized she couldn't completely manipulate us when I returned with Gewalt's sword. Amethyst became frightened because she couldn't predict our moves and motives, so she gave Iggarest a burning desire to get the relic he called Gabriel's pretty pointy. How much of this Iggarest is aware of is questionable. He could be a dupe. Anyway, that's what the spirit just told me."

"This Fallen is slicker than a two-bit riverboat gambler," Tuck said. "But that doesn't explain how the sword showed up in the hand of a rider."

"I suspect Amethyst gave it to her in hopes a powerful principality like that would take out one or more of us," Roger said. "I'm going with that version. As for Iggarest being straight with us... Well, the Fallen rarely tell the truth."

"Exactly!" I exclaimed. "I think there is one thing we can count on. Amethyst plans on using the sword to kill the Morning Star and take his throne."

"I doubt she's very happy about how her plan is working out so far," George said. "She probably doesn't like you very much, Mr. B."

"Probably not," I agreed. "Enough about Amethyst. What did you find out about the thorns?"

"Nothing," Roger said. "I mean, I found nothing directly mentioning the thorns. However, I did find several references to *the blood of redemption*. It has countless supernatural properties. There is even a reference about blood being the only sacrifice for sin, which isn't surprising because, after all, it is the blood of the Holy One we're talking about."

"Interesting, but frankly, not much new information; Reuwel said as much." I bent down and dusted off a couple of tiny demon gore chunks from my pant leg. It struck me as odd how, when I was sixteen, gore on my pants would have freaked me out; at a hundred and sixteen, not so much. I stood up straight, my expression—deadpan serious. "Reuwel insisted, neither the crown nor the thorns are weapons."

"True enough, I think." Roger agreed with me—not a hint of an argument. "I didn't only look through the Book of Uriel for references, but my gift lit up like a beacon when I meditated about the Blood of the Redeemer. That stuff is super spiritually potent and has infused six items with supernatural power; the wood of the cross, the crown of thorns, three spikes, a death shroud, and a lance. That last one is something worth exploring."

"Considering it's the only weapon on the list, I'd say it's the only option we have."

"If we have three of the thorns, why would we need anything more?" George asked.

"Because we need a weapon!" Roger blurted. "And the thorns aren't weapons. Have you been listening?"

"That was dramatic." I put a hand on his shoulder. "Tell me what your gift has revealed to you about this spear." I actually expected him to recoil from my touch, but instead he calmed down and sighed.

"It sounds totally stupid," He replied.

"No, old friend, to the contrary. I dare say, the angels may be cryptic, but they are far from stupid. What revelation did they entrust to you?"

"Every time I meditate on a spear anointed with the Blood of the Redeemer..." he hesitated, looking down at his shoes, "...all I got was that it is within our grasp."

Rebecca looked as if Roger had recited the funniest joke she ever heard. "Ha, Ha...have you totally lost it? That's not stupid. It's absolutely absurd. We don't have the spear." She plopped down on the asphalt by where I stood. "If we had that spear, I wouldn't be slicing and dicing with these charmed butcher knives."

"Maybe the angels placed it somewhere around the school," George said. "If they are as smart as you say, then they may have guessed we would need it and secretly stashed it where we would find it."

"Then we're really in a fix," Rebecca said. "The police are guarding the school."

"By now, I'm hoping Jimmy and Rose have solved that problem, and are in the school library," I said.

Roger's sideways glance reeked of skepticism. "You didn't really think Miss Crouch had left some scrap of paper describing how the Fallen could be defeated...did you?"

"I am a prophet, you know. Sometimes I get a feeling...that's all, just a feeling."

"If you can hear your gift whisperin' things again, then you must be recoverin' from..." Tuck hesitated before continuing, "...your ailment."

"In the groovy language of the young...*right on*, my dear Tuck; right on."

Roger put his hands on his ears. "I think I liked it better when you acted like my old history teacher. After hearing you spout out that hippy talk, I realize how wrong I was to demand you to stop using Shakespearean styled Berti-speech and quoting everybody from the Beaver to the Bard."

"Thinking of giving me a second chance to rush in where angels dare to tread?" I asked.

"You never needed my permission to rush in willy-nilly, usually dragging us into the fray with you," Roger added.

"*Oh, he knows you all too well.*" Mr. Dark's voice cried out from his corner of my mind. "*You risk your life and mine too without consulting me for anything. If Roger could hear me, I'm sure he would only add to my—*"

"That's enough!" I shouted at Mr. Dark.

"Sure as my spurs jingle, that's enough!" Tuck shouted.

"But you don't know," Roger complained. "He never asks us if it's okay for him to walk straight into—"

"Oh, for heaven's sake. This is too sentimental for me. If you keep this up, I'll pack my saddle bags and head off into the sunset," Tuck said.

"Hold up, my dear Tuck. In the near future, I fear that we'll need every man, woman, and relic."

Mr. Dark's voice echoed through my mind. "*Arland, stop this sappy crap. Roger's back. You're as near friends as you're going to get, and we have three Mega-demons on horseback to stop.*"

CHAPTER FOURTY

The Library

Lacking air-conditioning and other luxuries my Jag provided, Roger's dad's truck was our only transportation. We climbed in it and headed down Main Street, Tuck and I rode back in the truck bed, and Rebecca and Roger rode inside the cab. The chill in the air cut through my sports jacket like a hot knife through butter.

I thought things were looking up. That was until I spotted Dee Dee staring at us through Woolworth's picture window. With hands on her hips, she stood eyeing Rebecca in the seat beside Roger. For once, I was glad I wasn't a teenager. In fact, I should have been happy about Roger's return to the team. Instead, I had reservations. Perhaps I had been hasty in the first place when revealing my true identity to my teenage friends. Things might have been better if I'd remained plain old Mr. Bertarelli. Then Roger would have taken leadership of the team, and I could have anonymously helped from the sidelines.

"You don't really believe all that junk...do you?" Mr. Dark sounded upset. *"If you're not carrying on about how your friends aren't accepting you, then you're moping like a dopy diva because they're pushing you to take the lead. Get over yourself."*

I focused my thoughts on his corner of my mind. "How dare you accuse me—" I stopped mid-sentence. He was right. I had let the years of longing and uncertainties affect my ego and damage my identity. Roger's anger had fed into my funk. Fretting over my self-esteem had become an obsession.

With calm determination, I sent him my thoughts. "You are absolutely correct. You keep reminding me, I may need it." For the first time, I could remember, Mr. Dark fell silent without my yelling at him.

The neighborhood around the school parking lot looked eerily deserted. No one was outside, and no cars were moving along the street. I told Roger to park in the principal's parking space because it was close to the school's back door.

Even as we piled out of the truck, clearly something was wrong. "Where is the police guard? Do you think Chief Langster sent them home?" Rebecca asked.

"No," Tuck replied. "He was as boisterous as a banty rooster about puttin' those guards here."

"I'll lead the way, but stay alert," I said. "I bet we see some action before we get to the library."

George grabbed my arm. "I appreciate the gesture, but because my relic will protect me and your gift won't...well, it makes more sense if I take the lead."

Roger added, "He means we're being more offensive than defensive if you don't go first."

"You and Jimmy..." she shook her head. "...do guys always put everything in sports terms?" Rebecca asked.

"Yes...maybe," Roger replied. "I guess."

No demon showed its face in the cafeteria, or down the hall. We carefully traversed the empty corridors and found the double doors of the library uncharacteristically open. A woman's scream came from inside. We threw caution to the wind and rushed in.

To my complete surprise, the screaming woman wasn't Rose or Sarah; it was the rider called Pestilence. She was struggling to free herself from Rose's grasp.

"I've transfigured her back into a human!" Rose shouted. "But I can't hold her much longer!"

"Roger," Tuck asked, "what's going to happen when she lets go and the rider gets loose?"

"We have a short window of time to vanquish her while she's in her mortal form," Jimmy said. "When she transfigures back to her demonic state, we won't be able to stop her."

Putting my hand forward, I used the Prophet's Voice, "Mortar and rock, wood and plaster crush this emissary of evil."

The ceiling above the rider cracked, chunks of plaster and wood fell loose.

"Rose, run!" Rebecca yelled.

Bricks from both sides of the room broke free and slammed into the rider. Splinters of wood tumbled down onto both her and the horse. A piece of glazed brick tore away from the wall by the door. As if thrown by a baseball pro, it crashed into her head, knocking her off her mount. Another dozen flew at her from the walls, pelting the hell-beast she rode. It reared up on two legs, spewed fire out of its muzzle, and with a sizzle, it disappeared amidst the spray of stone.

A series of tiles peeled off the industrial crown molding, and like deadhead missiles, targeted Pestilence. In that moment, her physical form faded, followed by a hiss from the devil's lips. A cloud of vile, green stench billowed out of her mouth and she dissolved piece by piece until nothing remained. My gift made my hair stand on end and a tingle ran along the back of my neck.

"Whew! Arland, you stank up the room," Roger said with a chuckle. "Give us a warning next time you fart."

"Me? Stink? That odious wretch was the cause of such an offensive assault on our noses, not me." I stopped. His humor had caught me off guard. All I could do in return was smile and blush. Then a revelation hit me. We had a missing team member.

"Sarah! Where is Sarah?" My question was more of an urgent request. "Didn't she bring you to the school?"

"She dropped us off and left," Rose replied. "Said she would catch us on the flip side."

"She probably went home to change clothes and fix her make-up." Tuck's tone was scathing. "What good is the supernatural gift of drawing? Can't gut punch a demon with that!"

"Sarah's gifting has already saved us once. Don't discount one gift as inferior and another as superior." I faced Roger. "Right old buddy?"

"Uh...right," Roger said.

"Did we just vanquish an immortal without Gabriel's sword?" Jimmy asked.

"What does he mean we? You and Rose did that. He had nothing to do with it."

I ignored Mr. Dark. There was no sense scolding him for his snide remarks. "Yes. I think that's exactly what happened...thanks to Rose's extraordinary gift." I picked up one of the scattered books littering the floor of the library. It appeared to be a brand new edition, "Helter Skelter, The True Story of the Manson Murders." by a guy named Vincent Bugliosi.

"Do you think he knows about how Manson really was a prophet of the devil?"

"Mr. Dark, I don't know...maybe. We are not the only ones who know about the end of days."

"Excuse me! I doubt he's encountered any angels—ever. It's a ten-to-one bet he doesn't know about the Fallen's hand in all that."

A cold chill went up my spine. I dropped it back onto the horse trodden volumes, and commented to Rebecca, who stood closest to me. "Look at this place. The horsemen sure make a mess everywhere they show up."

"Not to mention those holes in the walls you made flinging pieces of the room at her," Roger added.

I wasn't sure if his remark was some cynical jab or if he was serious.

Roger gave me a knowing grin. "We won't tell the insurance adjustor what actually happened here. Let him come up with something on his own."

"Is that rider coming back again?" Rebecca asked. "Is she gone for good?"

"No, she's not coming back this time," I replied.

Jimmy slapped me on the back...a little harder than I would have liked. "Looks like you're back to your old self, Mr. B."

"This morning you couldn't focus enough to walk a straight line, and now you're commanding the elements like a real prophet. What happened?" Rose asked.

"Reuwel anointed me with some sort of virtuous liquid." I started to pull the horn from my pocket and remember that it had vanished after I used the contents on Roger. I shrugged. "Yeah, well, he called the ointment *Martyrs' Tears*."

Roger's eyebrows perked up. "Did you say Martyrs' Tears? Is that what you poured on me?"

I nodded. "I don't know what all it does, but it didn't hurt me, so I thought... Well, it might help."

I winced, expecting him to fly into one of his rants, condemning me as usual...but he didn't. He let it go and sheepishly said, "We have work to do, and we're wasting time standing here."

"You don't think it was those martyrs' tears that made a change in Roger...do ya?" Mr. Dark commented.

"What else could have made such a change in him?" I mentally whispered back. "He's actually being civil."

"I might like this version of Roger as well as the one we knew as kids." Whether he meant for his words to stir up long forgotten pieces of my childhood or not, a flipbook of photographic events which I thought lost forever flashed through my mind.

"He's the same Roger, only he's not forging headlong into anger, and I'm glad of it," I replied.

Jimmy overheard my whisper and whispered back, "Me too. It's good to have old Numbnuts back."

To make our way out of the library, we pushed some of the fallen debris away from the door. The school hallway was as quiet as death.

CHAPTER FORTY-ONE

Famine and Dominikus

"*Arland, there are demons here!*" Mr. Dark's voice all but screamed in my head.

I whispered back to him, "You mean other than Iggarest?"

"*Wherever he went, I can't feel him anymore. But there is a strong presence of evil nearby.*"

I made the corner leading to the cafeteria, and a shadowy figure stood in my path.

I reached for my sides; pain shot through my chest as fear swallowed my courage.

"Arland, you scared me! I all but had heart failure," Flower said.

"What are you doing here?" Jimmy asked.

"More to the point. Is it really you, Flower? Or are you one of the fallen in disguise? My questions had merit.

She didn't answer, only put her hand on my shoulder. A familiar warmth flooded over me. No one could mimic her supernatural gift.

"It's really her," I said.

"Where is everyone? Did you relieve the guards of their duty?" Flower asked.

"I haven't seen any humans since we arrived." Rebecca sighed. "I'd trade an angry cop for that demon, Pestilence, any day."

"Does that mean you haven't seen any people here either?" I asked before giving her a sideways glance. "I thought you were with Stoney?"

"Arland, I have a car, you know. Stoney dropped me off at my apartment. I talked to Miss Tabitha, at the Kansas Commune, on the phone and hurriedly drove here to find the school has been turned into some dank supernatural cave."

She looked around at the dark hallway. "And, as far as I can tell, every room is completely vacant."

"Maybe not completely," I said. "I'd be surprised if there wasn't someone...or something here." I gave Flower a grin that said more than words. "Mr. Dark tells me there are demons close by."

"Would you like to know what Miss Tabitha said?" Flower asked.

"Well? What's the verdict? Are they sending an angel army to help us, or what? Tuck asked.

"No...They don't have an army." Flower sighed. "Miss Tabitha told me to tell Arland something. The message must be for him because I sure didn't understand it." Flower faced me. "Her exact words were, 'Look for the blue light.' Do you know what that means?"

"Not a clue," I replied.

Looking down the dark, school hallway toward my office, the backlit silhouette outlined a man wearing a hat shaped like that of a policeman. "It's just me, officer. It's Principal Bertarelli."

The man didn't make any acknowledgement of our being in a restricted zone, so we hurried on to the back door.

Jimmy leaned over toward me and asked, "That cop wasn't very friendly, Mr. B. You think he'll make trouble?"

"No, he wasn't friendly and to answer your next question, I say let's get out of here—and quick. It's likely more police will make their presence known, or perhaps a demon or two may cross our path before reaching the parking lot. Either way, we are not welcome here," I replied.

Tuck quickened her pace and took the lead. "Somethin' feels wrong, and I can't put my finger on it—my stomach feels like it did when Ma first told me what chitlins really were. I liked 'em till then."

The seven of us: George, Jimmy, Tuck, Rose, Rebecca, Roger and I strode back through the halls of Western High School. With the library wrecked and the entire front entrance nothing but a gaping hole, it hardly resembled my school.

"Is it me, or do you think it's weird that we haven't seen but one guard since we arrived?" Mr. Dark asked.

It was a question I had been pondering. I shrugged. We made our way out the back door. Cold air from the outside rushed in, chilling me to the bone. Although a Texas' winter's day may be warm, the nights aren't. The change in temperature encouraged our hurried passage over to the parking lot.

Few pedestrians were out, but those who were stood still, looking our way—watching. Their stares made a chill creep up my spine. Scattered foot traffic, which should have been hurrying down the sidewalk, stood gawking in our direction.

Tuck hesitated at the curb outlining the parking lot and looked around. "Arland said it. This ain't right. People don't stand still and stare for nothin'. I don't even have a country anecdote for this. It's too creepy for words."

Ahead, parked by Roger's truck, was Flower's Chevy Corvair. I started that direction and stopped, turned, and saw it. Standing about fifteen feet from the back door, a night time shadow fell across three police guards, and they were also standing still as statues. I whirled around to look beyond the glow of the overhead parking lot security lights and there, in a neighboring yard, was a dog in a running position, frozen and suspended in midair.

"*See, I told you!*" Mr. Dark exclaimed. "*There are demons here—nasty ones.*"

"Demons can't do that..." I silently replied. "...only angels can." I yelled to my team, "They're here! The Fallen have taken us outside of time, into an altered reality."

"Arland, I don't have a holy relic to fight with," Flower said.

"Stay close to me," I replied.

The air lost its chill as a hot wind blew over the asphalt, leaving us standing in a hellish heatwave.

"**Here in this realm, you can't escape our combined power.**" The raspy voice of a woman came from behind. We jerked around to see what appeared to be a wraith on a pale gray horse. I don't know how, but I knew it had to be Dominikus.

A different voice came from across the lot—a man's voice. **"It was foolhardy for Gewalt and Pestilence to underestimate your abilities. Their bolstered ego has brought them down. Their names have been removed from the fateful, for they are no more—vanquished into the aether. Now you face *me*. I am Famine, and your fate is in my hands, for I see everything which is to come."**

His voice spoke from behind a lipless sneer, exposing a row of inch long teeth, razor tipped and misaligned. His thin, all-be-it near skeletal figure straddled a black horse. A filthy scarf wound around his head, covering his eyes. The dome of his head was hairless, likewise his chin and bare, emaciated torso. Long, hideously gaunt arms were eerily bone-like, his legs as well. Nearly naked, he wore a tattered Asian style wrestler's kaupinam wrapped around his loins. Thick, hardened fingernails grew from his boney fingers. In his grip, he held a golden scale. Weights and measures moved about it in an inexplicably mysterious manner.

"***This is the Scales of Condemnation. It*** **weighs your worthiness, and it finds you wanting. My judgement is death!"** The voice echoed strong and virile.

Tuck snarled up her nose. "Oh great, another she-devil and he-devil to boot."

I tried to sound self-assured when I called out loudly to the angel. "You can't stop us. We are *the Champions of the Favored*—we will be victorious." He probably knew my words were nothing but more blustering, hot air in the hot wind. I made a fearless show, even though my insides were quivering like a scared rabbit.

The woman's raspy voice called out. **"I am Dominikus, the angel who was known as Ishtar. Tremble in my presence, for I am now the reaper of death. Despair, you who stand against the fallen are marked for gleaning."** Her mount stomped and reared, flailing its hooves in my direction. **"It is not possible for humans to kill immortals."** She tilted her head quizzically. **"What you have done to the devil's favorites is not possible. Pestilence and Gewalt's spirits dwell without form in the aether. For now, we await others to prove themselves worthy and take their place in our ranks."** There were no visible hints that this Fallen was female except for the tone of her voice.

A wispy garment made of what looked like spider webs—each rag with tattered edges—hung out from under the armored plates she wore. A helmet like mask resembling a Japanese demon covered her face. Between the armored plates, those wispy spider webs covered her limbs and anything not protected by the dull metallic shell. Scaly nubs, where once wings might have been, protruded from her back. In one hand she held a black sword, and in the other, the reins of her pale gray horse—a terrible beast with glowing red eyes.

From the pale horse's muzzle, the creature snorted out brimstone, and where it stomped, sparks flared up, melting the asphalt under its hooves. She nodded toward Famine, who lifted his weight and measure higher. It began to glow.

"Hey, old bean, I think you missed something there. What does old Ishtar...uh, Dominikus mean, they are waiting for another to—"

Before Mr. Dark could finish speaking, Jimmy gave a crude battle cry and charged at Famine. When he rushed in close, the horsemen held the *scales of conscious* out toward him and a flickering light illuminated a circle around both rider and Champion. The shape grew brighter and shimmered.

Jimmy stumbled and fell, sliding on his belly. The sound he made resembled the cry of a wounded animal. Instead of bouncing back to his feet, he lay there. "Stay out of this light. I can't... it's crushing me."

Flower pushed past me, disregarding Jimmy's warning. "He's in pain. I can help him," she said.

She didn't get as far into the illuminated circle as Jimmy before falling face first onto the asphalt. Her cries were muffled sobs.

"Ah, an ancient one dares to face condemnation's bitter power. Your long life provides a wealth of sins to cripple your soul." Famine's voice was thin, hauntingly shrill, and weak. In his fragility, I couldn't see how he could have stayed atop his steed, much less controlled a supernatural light powerful enough to stop Jimmy in his tracks.

"Release me, you deformed monster," Flower yelled.

My first instinct was to stand between this demon and my friends to protect them, but I'd have to enter that light. I especially wanted to help Flower. Hearing her cries for help and doing nothing severely hurt me. If it overpowered me like it did them... Well, I didn't think that would be advisable, and yet, necessity forced me onward. As I said before, a lack of knowledge is dangerous; I needed to find his weakness. I approached him and stopped just outside of the scale's circle of light.

I'd seen a lot of creepy things in my long life, but the sight of a blind demon seriously freaked me out.

"These mystic scales reveal all. You pretend to wear virtuous garments of the worthy, but you are covered with rags of self-righteousness. In ignorance, you flaunt your sins in the face of mankind." Famine pulled back his thin lips, exposing black gums, plaque, and rotten teeth.

He continued, **"In the light of condemnation, it matters not your professed allegiance to righteousness. This relic illuminates your most devious and dark sins, proving them both abominable and apostate."**

Famine tilted his blindfolded head and sniffed the air. **"Man-child, you're the Champion called Jimmy Dugan."** A gruesome grin spread across his face. **"To me, your young sins are delightfully delicious. I know the secret of mortal kind. It has been hidden for eons. Mortal, do you want to know what it is?"**

CHAPTER FORTY-TWO

The Scales of Condemnation

Both Flower and Jimmy had bravely faced the devil's horseman called Famine, and failed to get close to him. The temptation of knowing the great secret of all mortals didn't faze Jimmy. Roger would surely have been asking to know more, but not Jimmy. He gritted his teeth and didn't answer.

"It is a fact, every human heart is filled with self-loathing because it desires sin. Give in, Jimmy Dugan, succumb to the light of condemnation. Die and join me. Together we will celebrate the wicked nature of man."

"Just wait," Jimmy yelled. "When I get my hands on you, I'll rip you limb from limb."

"Fool, you fight against the pricks and press against the thorns, when all the time you are guilty of hypocrisy. Your sins have found you out. The scorching light will rip your iniquities from where you've buried them and burn each misdeed upon your consciousness; let it consume you.

Man child, fear me, the harbinger of your destruction, for condemnation feeds on fear."

Dugan's next cry didn't sound human. It could have been the howl of some crazed animal caught in the biting jaws of a steel trap.

George had been holding Rose back, preventing her from rushing to Jimmy's side. "Rose, stay back. Don't get close to him. Didn't you see what happened to Flower when she ran into the light?"

Rose pushed George away, but he still held her arm.

"Think about this. Running headlong into danger won't help. Let's work together," I said.

Twisting and jerking away from George, Rose broke free of his grasp and dashed into the shimmering light.

"Jimmy! I'm coming," Rose called out. "If I can just touch that devil, he'll regret ever hurting you." She ran at the demon, only to be trapped in the focused glow shining from the unholy scales, just as Flower and Jimmy were. With a muffled whimper, she too fell to the ground. Remarkably, she had made it as far as Jimmy before succumbing to the curse, for she lay at his feet.

"Jimmy, honey," Rose said. "I can't make it far enough to touch him and transfigure him into a mortal. Push yourself free of the curse. You can do it."

"I can't. It's like a huge weight is crushing me," Jimmy yelled. "Every time I push away, this overpowering heaviness pushes back."

"Woman…" Famine's shrill, sinister voice could barely be heard over their groaning, **"…condemnation conquers**

even the strongest of Champions. Feel the weight of your own iniquity."

Rose screamed, "Stop... No... Don't, it hurts!"

Famine grinned and with his thin crackling voice he whispered, **"Die, wench! Die under the weight of your sins."** The echo of that soft whisper boomed louder than the spoken words. The air filled with the repeating sound—*DIE...DIE...DIE...DIE.*

George had followed too close to Rose as she threw caution to the wind and ran to help. Caught in the glimmer of the glowing circle, he awkwardly stayed on his feet, staggering this way and that.

"Give up!" Famine demanded. **"...For no one is righteous enough to overcome their own sins. All I need do is hold the Scales of Condemnation until you drown under the weight of Adam's curse."**

"This is not logical. It's only light. It doesn't have perceptible weight," George replied before he stumbled forward. Like an ungainly dancer. He caught his balance, only to stagger and fall a few feet away from Famine.

"*He got farther than any of the others did,*" Mr. Dark said. "*I told you that kid was made of good stuff.*"

"You said we should get rid of him," I replied.

"*Oh, you remember that, do you?*"

I didn't answer.

"What you fight against is your own devilish will. You cannot be victorious for you battle against yourself. The only release from this pain is to give in and die." An insidious grin spread across his face. **"Oh, how I revel in your darkest**

desires. The weight of your wickedness will be your end, for when a Champion dies by condemnation, you may take the place of one of the fallen horsemen. Join us and be victorious."

"See...see! That's what's been bugging me. There are five of the favored. From what Amethyst said, another demon just takes the place of a vanquished."

"Shut up, and let me think," I whispered. "These horsemen must have a weakness."

I focused on the strained expression scrunching up Jimmy's face. He clearly couldn't get closer. That light had easily overpowered him; made him groan and made him sweat. His limbs trembled, exerting a great effort to press up to his knees, only to fall back to the ground.

"Never!" Jimmy yelled.

"George is the closest thing to a scientist we have on the team. He had said that light couldn't do this, and I believed him. This is the effect of evil. Is there a way to turn off that light?"

"I don't know of one. You have any suggestions?" I replied. Of course, as always, Mr. Dark made great observations but didn't come through with a solution. I had to come up with something, but at the moment, all I could do was watch.

As Jimmy strained, his tendons flexed and his muscles bulged. Each time he pressed upward, he fell harder than before until he flattened against the ground, looking like a helpless, prostrated penitent.

A blue glow emanated from around Jimmy's arms and shoulders. I took it to be his supernatural armor, invisible to everyone but me. He lifted his torso upward. Famine gasped as Jimmy resisted his curse. He pushed up to his knees before falling headfirst onto the blacktopped pavement.

Flower was crawling on her belly toward Jimmy. She would manage an inch or two before stopping and moaning.

I turned to look around at the rest of the Champions and I had to blink again when Tuck came in my view. There it was again. A blue glow, but this time, it was around Tuck like some radiant aura. It shouldn't be there. She didn't have supernatural armor. A commotion drew my attention behind me.

Rebecca had withdrawn one of her blessed daggers and amidst the confusion surrounding Famine, she'd plunged it into Dominikus' leg. The rider made no reaction…no sign of pain…no surprise. She only reached down, and with one hand grabbed Rebecca by the hair. With the other, she took the dagger from her leg. Effortlessly, the horseman tossed both girl and dagger into the light, toward Famine. When the glow from his unholy scales fell on her, she, too, cried out in agony, writhing to-and-fro before lying flat.

"Looks like it's up to us," Roger said. Raising his hands toward the black horse and its rider, Roger spoke in angel tongue, "*Defend nos in proelio. Uriel, succurrat…esto praesidium nobis. Salvatorie, Angelus redemptionis proferet in vapores scandere viridem colorem, et venerunt ad nostram presistant opus.*"

Before his voice died away, stout vines broke through the blacktop. They grew upward, wrapping around the black horse and winding up the legs of its rider. He called out again, "*Circa hunc daemonem oriuntur spinae et vepres.*"

The vines tightened and became thicker. They grew fatter, spreading over Famine's body and across that of the horse. In moments, he appeared to be a solid leafy mass...a morbid topiary in the shape of a horse and rider. Only the scales, shining brightly and casting its light on my friends, remained untouched by the angel magic Roger cast.

Roger approached Famine. From what I could tell, the rider appeared to be defeated, encased in a layer of wood and sprouting limbs with leaves. When Roger entered into the circle of light, shining from the scales, he dropped his book, fell to his knees, and screamed. Upon the branches, leaves withered...the limbs cracked and dropped off...the casket of wood encapsulating the horseman broke open...the horse shook its head and reared up on its hind legs.

The last bits of bark fell away, and still holding the scales, he dismounted the steed, and walked over to where the Champions were lying helpless on the ground.

I stood aghast at how easily my comrades had been defeated. My hesitation proved foolish, for Dominikus grabbed me by my collar and lifted me off my feet. **"Feeble and weak, I expected better."** Without breathing hard, she tossed me ten yards to land at Famine's feet. The trauma of the landing caused me to huff out a cry. Underneath my chest, my crossed arms were unintentionally pinned by an enormous weight holding me down. There I lay face down in condemnation's light.

Suddenly, every failure in my life paraded before my eyes. A cold chill ran over me, head to toe. My nervous disposition shot up through every DEFCON warning level and barreled past emotional missile launchings, straight to nuclear holocaust. I felt as if the actual weight of the entire world had crashed down on me. Amidst my emotional meltdown, unimaginable guilt pushed me to the ground—crushing me.

"Amber eyed Champion, my master knows your name and curses it. He has pronounced your fate," Famine declared. **"You are to die before me and I am to send your spirit into the aether."** He paused. **"That is, unless you agree to become one of the favored five—join us."**

"Not in your wildest nightmares, demon. Do your worst."

From where I lay, I could see Mr. Dark scurrying back and forth outside the lighted circle. "*What are you saying? Don't make him madder than he is.*"

"Say your last prayer, Prophet," Famine crowed.

The light grew bright and every failure, every wrong, and every hypocrisy I committed in my entire life projected in my memory. I felt as if each ancient event happened only moments ago. The knife of guilt's sharp remorse pained me. My heart would explode at any moment. For once, I wished those micro-demons had made me forget those terrible betrayals.

"Pain," I screamed, but this was not because of anything Famine had done. "Oh, Heaven help me!" I exclaimed. My hand lay under me only centimeters from my shirt pocket. In all my writhing and twisting, I must have shoved it into that pocket where I kept the thorns from the Crown of Sorrows. A sharp jab had sliced one into my finger, and it felt like fire shot through my veins.

Instantly, my eyes bulged open, I think, wider than ever before. A supernatural virtue, way beyond my understanding, flooded over me. All at once, my many faults, my sins, receded into my mind. I knew I had trespassed against my friends, my family, and even myself, but the knowledge of these sins didn't sting my conscious...the weight of guilt no longer forced me to the ground.

I stood.

"Impossible," He shouted. Famine's voice no longer sounded feeble.

Gazing up at the shimmering light, realization struck me. The blood on the thorn had made me worthy to stand in the scrutiny of the scale's condemnation. I was liberated from Famine's curse. Not only could I stand, but I was free to attack.

CHAPTER FORTY-THREE

The Blood of the Redeemer

The demon stepped back and lowered the glowing scales. It looked as though confusion overtook him. **"What have you done? No man can stand in the light of condemnation**."

Looking around to find something I could command and bend to my will, I spied the power cable hanging over head. It supplied electricity to the school. I yelled. "Power lines break free and let your current run through this horseman called Famine."

In the next instant, the overhead cable snapped and fastened itself to Famine's back. Untold volts of crackling electricity ran through the gaunt devil. He jerked this way and that, but in the end he pulled the cable loose and shook the electrical residue off like a dog shedding water. Thankfully, he dropped the weighted scales.

They fell to the ground, and no longer glowed.

Breathless, the Champions struggled to push up to their knees; all but Rose, who apparently hadn't recovered from the scale's condemnation.

George leaned back toward Jimmy. "Before Famine regains his wits, grab Rose by the arm. Let's make a sling-shot."

Jimmy gave Rose a pull, swinging her up beside George, who pulled her closer to Famine.

Rose stretched out, her fingertips touching the demon rider's foot.

A change came over the blind horseman and his cadaverous complexion took on a tanned tone. He fell, feet splayed out forward.

Rose latched onto his knee and continued to transfigure him back into a human. He reached up and ripped off the bandages covering black empty craters where eyes should be. Brown centered orbs formed in the sockets. In patches across his bald head, dark auburn hair grew.

Rose lost her grip. Her hands dropped to the ground.

Jimmy scrambled to his feet and put Famine in a headlock, preventing his escape.

Rebecca stumbled and fell, but while stretching forward, her remaining dagger pierced the transformed demon's foot. To my surprise, it had a devastating effect.

The man-demon shivered. A vaporous stench exuded from his mouth, and what looked like sand poured out from the wound on his foot. What once was a rider from Hell became an empty sack of skin. I reached down and poked at it with my finger. It didn't dent, but rather, like a delicate piece of ash, it dissolved before our eyes.

"No...not possible! Satan's favored five are immortals. We cannot be defeated," Dominikus screamed.

Energized by the power in the thorn, I faced Dominikus, and her pale horse. I cried out, "Worms of Hell, I command you to come to my aid! Appear and devour this champion of the Fallen." Before me, a section of the pavement gave way and fell into a bottomless chasm. From its depths, a mass of carnivorous hell-worms, like those living in the outer ring of purgatory, spewed forth from the pit and towered over the demon-rider astride her evil horse.

Dominikus drew the black *Sword of Retribution* and stood her ground. Every time a worm thrust down upon her, she pierced the carnivorous invertebrate with the tip of the sword, and it turned to ash and crumbled into the wind.

More worms belched out of the pit. They came at her all at once. Biting into her armor and entangling themselves around her limbs. The demon-rider screamed, swinging her sword back and forth. Great gobs of worm flesh splattered onto the pavement before turning to ash.

The ground shook and the gaping gorge I created closed.

Flower sat next to Rose. She was using her gift to pour strength back into Rose's spent limbs.

Tuck turned her attention to Dominikus. She pulled her charmed gun and shot three shells into the Fallen angel's chest armor. The bullets sizzled and dissolved, leaving no dent or damage.

It wasn't the gun or the sizzling that drew my attention. I became distracted by a blue glow emanating from around Tuck's hands, and wondered if anyone else could see it. A query crossed my mind; what was the gunslinger doing to make the glow appear?

Getting to her feet, Rose said, "I'll transfigure her like I did the other horsemen."

"It won't work on her," Flower replied. "She was never human. Before she transcended into one of the devil's horseman, this creature was Ishtar, one of the Fallen."

Roger grabbed up his book and yelled in angel tongue, "*Ewch yn ôl i'r isfyd lle rydych chi'n perthyn.*"

A silver mist arose from the blacktopped parking lot. It clung to Dominikus like a second skin and hardened into an opaque shell, making a weird cocoon. The Earth trembled under our feet and the shell broke open. The slivers of silver flew like shards of glass. One sharp piece came right for Roger's head.

Tuck pulled him to the side and caught him before he completely stumbled over his feet and crashed to the ground.

"Why did you do that? I had it under control!" Roger fussed.

"Oh, is that how you say thanks for saving your life? That sharp stuff would have permanently changed your hairline." Tuck huffed. "Next time, good buddy, you're on your own."

Raising my hand toward the exploding cocoon-like capsule, I prepared to attack the emerging rider.

Inside the shell, it was empty.

"There, that'll show her who's boss," Roger boasted.

Before he finished his statement, a violet mist spewed out of the ground...and when it cleared, Dominikus, and her mount, stood exactly where she had been before.

"Nice try, Numbnuts. Too bad it didn't work," Jimmy said.

"Metal from the truck, hear me," I yelled, but before I finished the command, Jimmy jumped in front of me.

"It's my turn, now. I'll pummel her into dust." He ran at the demon-rider, grabbed her leg, and pulled her from atop her mount. The horse went wild, flailing its hooves and blowing fire out of its nostrils into the air. When Dominikus stood, she pushed Jimmy away with one hand. He went flying back ten feet and landed on his butt.

The rider of the pale horse took her rearing mount by the reins and whispered in its ear. The hell-beast stretched its mouth unnaturally open, and from the yawn, rancid smelling brimstone shot out and rolled toward us across the parking lot.

"Concrete, stone, and pavement, build into a wall, shielding us from this assault," I yelled in the Prophet's Voice. The spray of molten rock splattered harmlessly on a mound of asphalt and rock that sprang up between us and the horse.

Jimmy stood. Anger flared in his eyes. "I'm better than all of you. I can stop her all by myself."

Rose stepped in front of Jimmy. "Honey, that's not you talking. The rider's touch has infected you with some kind of curse. Fight it."

"Get out of my way. I'm the strongest Champion here. Let me at her. In fact, I bet I'm the greatest Champion the angels ever had."

"He sounds a lot like Roger," Rebecca said.

"I never sounded...well, maybe...just a little," Roger replied.

"Arland, stop him. Do something!" Flower demanded.

Jimmy grabbed Rose and pushed her aside. She tumbled to the ground.

Dominikus watched, laughing. **"I don't have to fight you to be victorious. Mortals are so predictable."**

"Exactly what are you going to do?" Mr. Dark asked. *"He's a raging idiot with the strength of fifty men. On second thought...let him alone. He would probably cause you severe bodily harm and grievous pain. That Hawaiian sabbatical is looking better all the time."*

"If Jimmy gets close to Dominikus, she'll touch him again and his condition will worsen," George said.

I reached into my pocket where there had been three thorns—only two remained. Taking out one of the thorns, I gave my best football charge and tackled Jimmy.

His rage exploded. "I'll break every bone in your body. How dare you—"

Before he could say another word, I pierced his arm with the thorn. I could tell from his face that he felt the same virtue running through his veins I had felt. He calmed down, and asked, "What did you do to me...give me a supernatural vitamin shot? Wow! I feel...I feel...different."

"That's because of the thorns Reuwel gave me. They are soaked in the Redeemer's Blood. Now that blood is mingling in your veins. It changed me. That's how I resisted Famine's cursed light. Now, you've been changed, and I dare say, both of us will never be the same."

Jimmy put his hand on my shoulder. "Let's take down that demon-rider together."

While we were talking, Tuck had picked up one of the blessed daggers from where Rebecca had dropped it. The gunslinger ran at Dominikus with it. She faked a downward thrust and stabbed the rider with an upward jab. The Jerusalem steel buried deep in the rider's chest.

Dominikus didn't flinch. She didn't make a move to remove the knife... while impaled into the devil's chest, the Damascus steel sizzled and vaporized into thin air. Before Tuck could retreat, the rider grabbed her arm and tossed her to the side. She slid on the pavement, tearing holes in her black polyester leisure suit slacks.

Fury blazed in Tuck's eyes as she stood. The same affliction Jimmy had just experienced obviously had infected her. "Let me at that bucktoothed sidewinder. I'll skewer her with my Heaven made blade." She pulled her knife from her boot.

I raced over to Tuck with all intentions of pricking her with the third thorn. However, in an extremely agile move, she sidestepped me and headed straight for Dominikus.

"Grab her," I yelled at Jimmy.

He lunged at her and caught her in a forward tackle. Jimmy had her by both an ankle and a wrist.

"Let me go!" She wailed. "That Demon-Lady is mine." Hatred and anger flared in Tuck's eyes. The mouthy cowgirl had turned into a frenzied hate monster. She gritted her teeth and clawed at Jimmy with her fingernails.

"Mr. B., do something before she hurts herself, and me, too."

She laid into Jimmy's leg with a series of impressive spiral punches, giving me enough time to approach her from the back. Using the last thorn, I scratched her neck, leaving a thin red line on her skin.

The rage left her face as she exclaimed, "Oh! What a rush."

The pale horse blew fire out of its nostrils, setting the asphalt ablaze.

As the fire got close, I took off my jacket and used it to beat the flames back, all the while commanding them to extinguish. Moments later, the fire went out. I must have looked a sight, sitting on the pavement huffing and puffing, with smoke and soot all over me. Jimmy lifted me to my feet by my arm.

He reached down and picked up my tweed sports jacket and my Prophet's Vision took over. I saw Jimmy wearing his glowing blue armor. The way I used to see him a long time ago. He looked like a knight of the round table, shielded in translucent blue light.

Then I caught a glimpse of something else glowing from inside my coat. It was in the breast pocket. Jimmy courteously helped me into my tweed jacket, and I immediately reached in to see what caused the blue light. It was the crest. I hadn't thought anymore about it. After all, the weapon we could have used was no longer in it and the other sword refused to come out.

Jimmy's hand still glowed like he was wearing a supernatural gauntlet. "Jimmy, try to reach in and remove Saint Michael's sword."

"Hey. It won't work. I've already tried it, Mr. B." Jimmy stepped back, away from the crest I held out to him. "You've had a hard couple of days and your memory has been on the fritz. But try to remember. We all made an effort to get it out, and the thing wouldn't let any of us have it."

"Humor me, please. Try again," I pleaded.

Jimmy reached into the card. His hand entered the surface of the paper as easily as if he were breaking the surface of water. He grabbed the sword and pulled.

It moved.

He pulled again; it moved a bit more.

"Give it another tug," I encouraged.

Again, he yanked at the sword. This time, he removed it from the card.

"Mr. B., I don't get it. What changed?" Jimmy asked.

"Haven't you felt different...more powerful...since the thorn scratched you?" I asked.

"Sure, but..." Jimmy held the sword up and blue sparks flew off the blade's edge.

"No, really...?" Tuck grabbed the paper crest. "How did this hunk of muscle remove the sword when he couldn't do it before?"

As she held the crest, my Prophet's Vision revealed something else to me. Tuck, too, appeared to be wearing a glowing blue gauntlet identical to the one I saw on Jimmy's hand. As she held the picture, I examined it. The spire in the picture glowed with the same vibrant blue.

Dominikus reached up above her helmet and closed her fist. Pulling down, she opened her hand and in it was a hangman's noose. She held it out toward the Champions and something else strange happened. Again, only Tuck, Jimmy, and I were not affected. Everyone else, all the team members, just sat down and acted totally bored.

"What's the use? I'd rather be eating pizza and playing Pac-Man," Rebecca said.

Rose yelled at Jimmy. "Honey, stop fussing with that angel and get over here. I want you to snuggle with me."

"Who cares about what the horsemen do?" George cried out. "Let's treat all these people to a picnic. I'm dying of hunger."

"Yeah," Rose said. "It's no skin off our nose. Jimmy, if we can't get pizza, let's go to your house and watch TV. I'm missing my soap operas."

Flower called out to me. "Arland, come sit with me. Leave that poor angel alone and come sit."

Tuck holstered her gun and said, "Roger, what's going on? Why did you just plop down on the ground? ...and, why are you using your book under your head like a pillow?"

Roger yelled back, "Hey Tuck-a-rooney, I feel like blowing off some steam. You wanna drive my dad's truck? It's not much to look at, but it's good enough to get us back to McDonald's." A lackadaisical expression filled his eyes. "At least it's groovier than sticking around here."

Tuck gave me a sideways glance. "Doc, this is crazier than watchin' a bluetick hound tryin' ta tree a bobcat." She blinked...and blinked again. "Have they lost their citified, horse swappin' marbles?"

"It's the noose," I said. "It's possessed by a spirit called Apathy."

CHAPTER FORTY-FOUR

The Spirit of Apathy

Everyone lazed around. Some wanted to leave, and others found the simplest things to play with and occupy their time.

"What happened to them?" Jimmy asked. "They just gave up."

"I never thought I'd see this happen." Tuck's mouth flew open in astonishment.

"It's the noose. That artifact has a horrific effect on people. It makes them not care about anything...anything at all!" I cried out. "We have to hurry. There's no telling if that artifact has power enough to work on us, but it's best not to take the chance."

"Really?" Tuck asked. "If so, then why *are* we not affected?"

"I suppose it's because the Blood of the Redeemer was grafted into our bloodstreams. Remember the sensation you got when I scratched you with the thorn?" I yanked at their sleeves and pulled them close. "We have to hurry!" Facing

Tuck, I demanded, "The rider is coming this way. Quick! Reach into the crest and grab the spire."

"What are you talking about?" Questions filled her eyes.

"Just do it!" The sound of urgency raised my voice an octave.

She pressed her hand against the paper, and like Jimmy's had done, hers went into the crest. She pulled on the spire and it moved under her hand. She pulled again, and it came out. What we could see in the picture was only the tip of a lance—the Lance of Destiny—the only weapon ever to be touched by the Redeemer's blood.

"Now it's time to fight!" Jimmy exclaimed.

Dominikus had been slowly walking toward us, all her defenses down. Probably thinking we were under her spell.

From the shadows, I heard mumblings. Something was chanting her name. Dominikus...Dominikus...Dominikus.

People—normal people that should have been outside the time freeze were lining the parking lot. They were all under her spell, lackadaisically leaning on each other, laughing and chanting Dominikus' name.

The rider of the pale horse stood laughing at us. "I don't need to kill you. Either anger or rage will cause you to kill each other... Or the spirit of apathy will turn you all into sitting ducks, awaiting execution by my demons."

I casually walked toward her, wanting her to see she had no control over anything I did. Jimmy and Tuck nonchalantly sauntered up to her, as if they were taking a stroll on a spring day.

"Harlot demon, hear me. This is the Sword of Michael, forged to imprison the Morning Star," Jimmy yelled.

"And I hold the Lance of Destiny empowered by the Blood of the Redeemer." Tuck cried out. "Fear this, Fallen. I don't come at you alone, but with the power of the Creator."

The fourth horseman placed her hand on her hips in defiance. **"You do not possess weapons powerful enough to harm me. Every time you come in contact with my armor, you will find yourself more enraged by hate than before. Touch me, and see."** She cackled a harsh laugh. **"After a brutal skirmish, Champion against Champion, I will take the one left standing and make them one of the devil's favorites, one of the five."**

"It's like she's in a world of her own. Can she even hear us?" Tuck asked.

"I don't think she believes us. In her mind, she's invincible." My whisper was loud enough for her to hear. "Attack now."

Jimmy went for the noose with Michael's sword and sliced it away from her hand. When the charmed blade cut into the cursed relic, the rope turned to ash.

Tuck went for the fallen angel.

Seeing the Champion's approach, Dominikus reacted by unsheathing the black sword and swinging the deadly weapon from side to side.

Using the pole end of the lance, Tuck vaulted into the air. The trajectory positioned her above the rider's lateral swing. It looked to me like she focused her flying arc to land, lance blade first, squarely in the fallen angel's face.

The rider pulled the black sword up hard against the spearhead.

Tuck's downward stroke didn't waver as the Lance of Destiny's blade sliced the black sword in half. The rider might have reacted if not for Tuck's second attack. She whirled the lance over her head and brought the spearhead down hard, forcefully piercing the rider's helmet.

I expected devil-blood and demon-green, gray matter to explode in every direction. That didn't happen. The moment the lance-head sliced into the Fallen's helm, the entire suit of armor fell apart, clanging to the pavement—empty.

I rushed over and reached out, throwing my arms around both her and Jimmy. A voice came from out of nowhere. **"What have you done to me? My magnificent form destroyed by a power I don't recognize, for only the Creator can... Mortals, what power is in your hands that you can do this thing?"**

"We have become overcomers by the Blood of the Redeemer," I yelled back. "Show yourself, devil, and be vanquished." When I said the word *vanquished*, sparks emitted from my fingertips.

Roger stepped forward and opened his book. He read, "It is written, light and dark cannot coexist, for if they try, they become something neither light nor dark. Neither warm nor cold and is cast into outer..."

"Mindless mortals, I do not need a corporal body to kill you." Barely visible under the incandescent lights placed across the parking lot. A shadow appeared before us.

I called out to Jimmy and Tuck, "Both of you, point your weapons at the rider and say what I say."

Tuck faced me with a puzzled expression.

"Just do it!" I demanded. Then I lifted my hand toward Dominikus and said, "By the virtuous Blood of the Redeemer, I vanquish you."

The Rider screamed, "No! ...Not...that! ...Not...the aether...."

Leveling their weapons at Dominikus, Flower and Jimmy yelled the words. "By the virtuous Blood of the Redeemer, I vanquish you."

A blaze of white light flared out of the tips of their weapons and illuminated Dominikus.

"Again!" I yelled. "Grip your weapons good and hard."

Tuck and Jimmy repeated my words.

From the tips of their blades, white light, together with bright flashing strobes of lightning, clattered toward the fallen angel. The rider's shadow disintegrated. It was hard to tell, but I believe shock and raw fear crossed her shadowy face before she staggered backward, falling to one knee.

Reaching down together, *we touched her*, and said, "We, who were made righteous by the Blood of the Redeemer, vanquish you." Light, brilliant white light, outlined our hands.

I expected the shadow entity simply to disappear in the flash emanating from our fingers, but no. She withered. Her strong and healthy limbs shriveled. Wrinkles formed in her dark face and our handprints left scars, much like I'd seen on the rump of cattle after they had been branded. A hideous stink fumed from her dark form. What had been a gigantic shadowy version of the rider shrank to the size of a ten-year-old child—a very wrinkled and smelly child.

We stepped back to avoid the rank odor. The hell-beast on which she road lifted its hooves to the sky and raked them at the clouds, but with its master gone, the evil horse she rode vanished, too.

Free from the rider's curses, an exhausted Rose walked over to Jimmy and joyously threw her arms around his neck. George put Rebecca in a bear hug. Roger timidly walked over to where I stood. "Don't take this the wrong way. I mean, this was a glorious victory. I get it. The horsemen are vanquished and all, but something is worrying me," He said.

I laughed out loud. "What could possibly be wrong? Look around. All the horsemen have been vanquished. The danger is over. It's time to celebrate."

"Didn't you hear those riders? They were promising us a place in the devil's favored five. They wanted us to replace Pestilence and Gewalt. That means before this set of demons are all kaput, vaporized, down for the count, out of the playing field, off of the..."

"Okay, Roger, I get it. What's your point?"

Roger pushed his brows together in concern. "There could be one more devil out there—Abaddon's replacement."

CHAPTER FORTY-FIVE

The Puppet Master

Roger's words dampened the joyous spirit surrounding our victory, at least mine, because he was right. He usually was.

The presence of the demons had raised the temp on the asphalt to equal a warm summer day. Without them, the cold air of a Texas winter's night blew in and chilled the air.

That's when I remembered... This was Christmas Eve and at midnight, Christmas Day would arrive.

Stoney drove up in the hippy van and hurriedly stepped out.

"Did you talk to Master Paul, head of the angelic Council of Angels?" Flower asked.

"Indeed, I did, but don't expect much help from them," Stoney replied. "Master Paul said they were aware of our dilemma, but the archangels, Michael, Gabriel, and Raphael, have all forbid giving us aid in this fight. They said those angels have each supplied us with a weapon already."

"Don't worry about it, Mr. Abara," George boasted. "We kicked butt, vanquished all the horsemen, and now it's time to celebrate."

"Yep, the darkness has been pushed back for another generation," Jimmy added. "But I don't think it happened exactly like George remembers it." He slapped the Kid on the back. "I don't remember you doing a lot of vanquishing. It was mostly me, Tuck, and Mr. B."

"It's true. Mr. Abara, Tuck, Jimmy, and Mr. B. were amazing." Rebecca's joy sounded euphoric. "We don't need help from the council anymore," she added. "You should have seen me. I was jumping and kicking. Is there a gift of martial arts? If so, I think I've got it."

"Uh, no." Flower looked puzzled. "There's not a gift of martial arts. Not that I've ever heard of."

"Flower," Stoney said, "I leave for a few minutes and our crew has turned into a bunch of prideful reprobates."

In a rare moment of humility, Roger spoke, "Ok, gang. Take it from me. I've been there." The redhead shoved his hands deep in his pockets and looked at his shoes as he spoke. "You all need to suck it up and get over yourselves."

A hesitate sigh followed Roger's pause. "If Flower has never heard of a martial arts gift, then it doesn't exist. And as for you, Jimmy Dugan, you should know better than to start bragging and carrying on about how wonderful you are...and what got vanquished—or not."

Roger raised his head and made eye contact with any who would look at him. "Did any one of us accomplish anything without a supernatural gift? Did anyone give credit to the spirit? No! It was the supernatural power gifted to us that won the day."

"*Oh, yeah. I do like this version of Roger...can I keep him?*" Mr. Dark's dumb quips were usually untimely, and this was no exception.

"Actually, it was the Blood of the Redeemer on the thorns that turned the tide," I said.

Stoney's eyes widened. "You figured out how to use the artifacts? And they worked?"

"I didn't exactly figure it out on purpose. It happened mostly by accident," I said. "But there's no denying the power those thorns have. Too bad they dissolved after using them."

George raised his hand.

"I told you to stop that," Jimmy fussed. "That's not groovy."

"But I have a question."

"*Did I say George is a keeper? I may have jumped the gun.*" Thank goodness no one but me could hear Mr. Dark's snide remark.

"Speak your mind. George," I said. "Ask away."

"Why did the angel only give you three thorns? Wasn't there enough on the crown for each of us to get one?"

The question stopped me. I had no idea why. "Yes, there were lots of thorns on the crown. I guess the answer to your question is...I don't know."

George raised his hand again.

Jimmy rolled his eyes. "Man, you gotta stop that. Really! Man, I mean it."

"Don't worry about Mr. Dugan. He's lacking in the manners department." I smiled as I said it. "What is your next question, George?"

"Mr. Abara said that this council had heard from three archangels, and these same angels gave us one thing each." He paused as if to gather his thoughts. "Well, what are those things?"

I shook my head. "Well, young man." I suppose one is Saint Michael's sword, and the other is the lance. As for the third, I don't know. I walked over to him and put a hand on his shoulder. "There are things even a prophet isn't privileged too."

"*You got that right.*" Mr. Dark didn't even try to hide the cynicism in his voice. "*Most times they are useless... and I do mean useless with a capital U.*"

Why Mr. Dark would say things like this when he knew only I could hear him? I wondered.

Rebecca put a hand on George's arm. "Maybe one of those things is the rope you wear as a belt."

"No, Reuwel gave him that. It wasn't one of the archangels," Stoney remarked.

"Michael gave me my gun," Tuck replied. "Maybe it's one of those three weapons."

Stoney shook his head. "I don't think so. You had that way before you joined up with us."

"There were three thorns. What else is there except the thorns?" Tuck asked. "It must have been the thorns."

"It may no longer be of importance," Rose insisted.

"Yeah, true...at least, I hope so," Roger lightheartedly pointed out. "After all, the four horsemen have been vanquished, sliced and diced, retired, sent out to pasture, kaput, vaporized..."

"Enough of the crap, Roger," Tuck bellowed as she twirled her gun like a western sharpshooter before holstering it under her arm. "See this...don't make me use it on you, squirt."

"We get it, Numbnuts. And if I were you, I wouldn't make cowgirl mad. She's a tough cookie. She might really shoot you and then skewer you like a roast on a spit with that fancy lance." Jimmy couldn't help but laugh at his own joke.

Roger's eyes cut over to see if Tuck's lance was visible. When it was nowhere in sight, he exhaled and his shoulders dropped two inches.

"All kidding aside." I cleared my throat. "I think George's question has merit. He's a young man who thinks logically and so do the angels. They plan things out and make strategies that fit inside of larger plans." I ran my hand through my blond hair. "There is a definite reason we were given three thorns." My eyes met Tuck's and Jimmy's. "I hope I used them wisely."

Behind us, a familiar voice called out.

"Prophet, I have little time. I have found that I have been used, a pawn in a momentous and wicked game." It was Iggarest.

He looked uncharacteristically disheveled. His waist coat was tattered and torn at the sleeve. His cravat was missing and even his shoes had a layer of soot on them. **"I**

assure you my motives were true, and I held no animosity except my hatred for the Morning Star. It was he who I intended to undermine, not you. Amethyst has made a deal with our wretched archangel. Unbeknownst to me, he put powers and principalities under her domain. I rule over the heretical few living among mortals. She traded my allegiance for the corpses of those mortals who Abaddon stole their life force. She has amassed an army of zombies, the living dead."

"I encountered Abaddon years ago when he was collecting souls by having the men sign their names in blood," I said. "These signatures were kept in a book which I destroyed." I paused, gathering my thoughts. "Was she siding with that devil prince back then?

"Then, and longer still. She has been plotting this attack for millennia." Iggarest shuddered as if he struggled to keep his composure. "**What you say is true. And although she kept me in ignorance, the result will be the same. I have brought disaster upon myself when I made a pact with that harpy."**

"Why should we believe you? Your father is the king of lies." Tuck yelled. "On top of that, you tried to get the Doc killed."

"It is as I said before. You should not trust me. It is dangerous to trust anyone but yourself." He sighed and wiped his face with a dirty handkerchief. **"But times are changing...and dangerous times call for dangerous measures. I lived in ignorance, but no more. Now I'm aware**

of the multitudes who fell under Abaddon's control and were traded off to Amethyst before he was vanquished."

"She's not all that," Rose said. "I mean, we can take her easily. She may talk like a bigshot, but we got her number."

"Can you really? The time for her deception is over. She has revealed her true power, the anointing laid upon her by the Morning Star. It is mighty and awesome. It came from the lower depths of Hell. And she rides it like a beast. I came to warn you...she has taken Abaddon's place among those in Morning Star's inner circle."

"You stood by, letting this happen, and have the gall to come to us and feign innocence?" I yelled.

Tuck drew her gun and leveled it at Iggarest. "You old polecat. To think...you allowed a multitude of souls to be harvested by the Fallen? You're as sorry as the maggots in the bottom of my Aunt Bessy's grain bin. You're just as bad as Amethyst because you stood by and did nothing to stop her."

"Even as we speak, her power is growing," Iggarest said. **"Soon I will not be able to contain her and I will fade into the aether, just as the vanquished horsemen have. Ages ago she had a Fallen by the name of Phoenix do her bidding. He cursed a carnival to reap souls for her to give to Abaddon. We were going to rule the underworld together, but she betrayed me."**

Flower gasped. "Amethyst was responsible for the curse on the Cumberland Carnival?" Her expression made my blood run cold.

"I have hence excused her treachery as foolishness, a folly never to come to fruition. Now, I say folly no more, for she's the one who convinced Ishtar to release the horsemen, and soon, I'll have no minions of my own."

"Arland!" Flower interjected. "Wasn't it a Fallen who told us Ishtar was behind this? He could have been lying." She huffed. "They all do."

"That's right. They lie and tell lies upon those lies. It becomes a web so tangled, they lose what shred of truth was behind the original falsehood." Scrutinizing Iggarest, I weighed what he told us. "Fallen, you deserve whatever misfortune ensues." I called over to Roger. "My wise friend, what do you think?"

Roger closed his eyes like he used to do when he first consulted the Wisdom of Solomon. "No doubt, Iggarest is afraid. As for whether he is telling the truth? Only time will tell." He nodded at me. "After hearing about Amethyst, I suspected she has some kind of supernatural manipulation power. How else could she have turned the horsemen into her puppets? Behind the scenes, she used their powers, and bent their will, giving her the advantage. She has probably been syphoning off their strength."

"She was causing trouble last year?" Rebecca drew her brows down. I could see in her eyes how she mused over her question. The narrowness of her eyes widened with sudden realization. "That means Amethyst could have instigated my kidnapping at the commune."

"It appears we all have been deceived, my friends. Perhaps even the angelic council, too. If Iggarest is to be believed, then Ishtar and all the horsemen have been her lackeys," I said.

"Don't feel bad Mr. B.," Jimmy replied. "The Fallen are masters of deception, and Amethyst... Well, she's the worst of the worst. Maybe the worst we've faced."

"Why should we believe anything this Fallen says?" Stoney asked. "What makes his lies...truth?"

"I didn't betray you...not on purpose. I can no longer control her—at least for any length of ti..time."

A strained expression crossed his face. **"I must leave you before she... I must hurry."** Like a vapor, he disappeared.

CHAPTER FORTY-SIX

The Cherry Red Dodge D

Talking about Iggarest, Rebecca asked, "Think we'll ever see him again?"

"Not if'n I have anythin' ta do with it," Tuck replied.

"Well, what's our next step?" Jimmy asked. "Like always, we need a plan."

"I'm exhausted." Rose laid her head over on Jimmy's shoulder. "I think it's time to get some sleep without having to look over my shoulder, wondering if one of the horsemen is going to be there."

Sarah's Camaro roared up onto the parking lot. She stepped out, obviously freshly showered and wearing a pleated black miniskirt and a mohair sweater with Merry Christmas emblazoned on the front in gold lame' embroidery. Walking over to Rebecca, she said, "What happened here?"

"Hey, prom Queen, you missed it," Tuck called to Sarah. "The last of the horsemen got their upends. You should've been here."

"No, thank you. I've had my fill of demon fighting for today," Sarah replied.

Rose said, "I'm dirty, exhausted...and I'm starving, too."

"My car got kayoed in the fire at Mr. B.'s place," Jimmy said. "I can't just run to the store for sandwiches."

"But Jimmy," Rose added, "I haven't eaten a bite, and last night, I couldn't sleep, afraid that Mr. B. would croak on us."

Flower insisted, "We all need some nourishment and rest. Soon we'll be zombies and it will have nothing to do with Amethyst's minions."

"I would normally invite you all to my house, but it seems I am homeless," I said.

"And mine is the size of a matchbox." Flower put her hand on her mouth, realizing I most likely was still sensitive about losing my home in a fire. "Sorry Arland. I didn't mean to insinuate—"

"Don't worry about that. I stopped putting an emotional value on property decades ago." Our eyes met. "I'm fine, really."

She quickly looked away from me and cast her eyes down on her shoes. "Anyway, now that Sarah's here, there's ten of us, and my little apartment isn't big enough to seat everyone."

"My place is," Stoney volunteered. "I got this great pad about a mile and a half north of the new high school. It's in that new housing development. There's way more room there than I need. Providing a safe house may be exactly what the angels had in mind when the council set me up in such a large place."

He paused, an expression I would describe as thoughtfulness, wrinkled his brow. "In fact, they mentioned something about consecrating my property. They must have done all that before I arrived. Between two windows, on the front side of the place, there is a wrought-iron cross affixed to the brick. For some reason, all council properties, including the commune in Kansas, had to be consecrated."

"The council bought you a house? Here in Western? And you live there scot-free?" I wasn't quite sure if I heard skepticism in Rebecca's questions or if she was being incredulous. "Must be nice. My aunt has a hard time making her rent, and you have a mansion?"

"I didn't say it was a mansion." Stoney corrected her.

"Dang." Rebecca's word had spikes on it.

"Well, has your aunt ever asked the council for help to pay her rent?" Rebecca shook her head and I paused to make my point. "I'm guessing it would draw attention to both you and your aunt if she suddenly had the money to move into a big house."

She sighed. "You're right. But that's only part of it. My aunt doesn't know I help the team fight demons." Rebecca rubbed her face with the heels of her palms. "It's just so hard making up excuses for being out late and coming in with bruises after a night of vanquishing demons." She crossed her arms and gave me a stern look. "I have no idea how I'm going to get away with it this time. I took off before my aunt got up yesterday morning and I haven't been home since."

"I wouldn't worry too much," Stoney said. "The council usually fixes things for us. Have a little faith, girl. I don't think they bought me a big house for the property value. They purchased it because they knew we'd need it. I don't know how, but they knew!"

A quizzical expression bloomed on George's face. "You're telling me that this council can see into the future?"

"I don't know, seems like it, or they have a wholesale deal on coincidences," Stoney said.

The team hadn't eaten in a while, so Flower took orders and collected money. It was Sarah's choice to take Rose, George, and Flower to get burgers. The plan was to bring them over to Stoney's house. He specifically instructed Sarah on how to get there.

After the Camaro pulled out, we got down to the job of sorting out who was riding with whom. Tuck offered to take her pickup. Come to find out she had a vehicle all along. She just hadn't mentioned it. Sitting at the far end of the parking lot was a cherry red pickup truck.

"What? This is yours?" Jimmy asked. "You said you didn't have a ride."

"No. When you drove the Doc home last night, you assumed I didn't. You're the one who tossed Flower your car keys."

Jimmy huffed. "You didn't make any noises to the contrary."

"Good thing too, or else my pickup would be melted sludge, just like your Mustang." Tuck pointed to the vehicle at the far end of the parking lot. "Her name is Bessie."

We got closer to Tuck's pickup. To me, one truck looks like another. I didn't think anything about it, but when Roger saw it, he went gaga and ran over to see it.

"This...this is your pickup?" I didn't know Roger could open his eyes so wide. "You drive a cherry red '64 Dodge D?"

Tuck shrugged and nonchalantly nodded.

Jimmy ran a hand along the chrome trim before he hurried to pop open the pinstriped hood. "What? A Mopar, 375 horsepower, 426 wedge V8! What do you have on the tach? It's gotta be at least 6,000 rpm before the red line."

"Yep." Her eyebrows pulled closer together when she said, "I had trouble finding someone to do the specialty modifications on the Hurst shifter. Bessie has a performance transmission, ya know. But it was worth it. She shifts smoother than goose grease, and as quick as one of Nolan Ryan's fastballs." She made a throwing motion.

"Sports again? Not you, too." Rebecca languished.

"You know who Nolan Ryan is?" Roger asked.

"Get real, bucko. Doesn't everybody? Yep, he's a hometown hero in Alvin, Texas." She closed the hood of the truck. "Bet he don't got a Dodge D truck, though."

Roger stuck his head in the cab. "Ha! Not only that, I'd bet he doesn't keep a lasso in the cab of his truck, either." He held up the end of Tuck's lariat.

"Cowgirl," Jimmy shook his head, "just when I thought there was hope for you. What's next? You planning on having steer horns mounted on the front of the grill? Or maybe painting Bessie's name on the side along with black and white Herford spots?" He laughed.

"Well, who knows?" She popped her fist into Jimmy's biceps. "Can't take all the country out of the girl, so don't even try."

Rebecca had stood patiently for as long as she could. Tapping her foot, she complained, "If you three are through playing shade tree mechanics, can we get going? Sarah will have the burgers delivered before we get over to Stoney's house."

She was right, of course. Roger left his dad's truck parked by Flower's Corvair and opted to ride in Tuck's hotrod pickup. Roger wanted to drive, but no...Tuck didn't give in. All-the-while she dangled her keys at him like some kind of bait. I opted to ride with Stoney. I figured it would be a smoother ride. After all, Tuck and the boys acted like they wanted to peel rubber all the way. However, since only Stoney knew how to get to his house, they had to follow us in the hippy van and keep their speed under control—with only short bursts of pavement tattooing screeches.

It was late when we approached the new housing district. I felt a tingle run across the base of my spine and up my neck. Along the way, we had passed an unusual number of people walking along the sidewalks. Night time pedestrians might not have been strange for a town the size of Lubbock, but this was little Western. People here drove everywhere. They didn't walk—even when they were only going down the block.

Even weirder, the ramblers and strollers were all going north—the same as us. From out of nowhere, a flash like a photographer's strobe faded my vision, and my prophetic gift kicked in. I could see through the disguises hiding the hellish creatures walking on the sidewalk. These had to be the zombies that Iggarest warned us about—Amethyst's horde. We pulled up into the driveway and parked in the two-car garage. Tuck's truck rolled up alongside the van and stopped on the other side of a supporting pole affixed dead center of the garage.

We all disembarked and walked out onto the drive, watching the motley crowd gather around.

"Looks like we're going to have unwelcome guests for supper," Tuck said. "My gun started talkin' to me on the way over. All those flat-footed jaywalkers headin' this way aren't what they seem. I'm a thinkin' those yahoos are zombies just like the ones that burned down Arland's spread."

Jimmy poked Roger and said, "Ya know, for a cowgirl, she's got a lot on the ball. I might have misjudged her at face value. Drives a hot truck; talks to her gun; and she keeps a lasso wrapped around her Hurst shifter...she's not so bad."

"Yeah...I guess. She's not *so* bad." Roger's expression suddenly changed. "Not that she's my type. Dee Dee is my type. Blonde, frilly, and legs for miles...yeah, that's my type. I didn't mean—" Then it was like Tuck's words had finally soaked into his head. "Zombies? No...no...no. We are not fighting any brain eating zombies." He stared out at the night walking pedestrians. "I hate zombies. I hate—"

"I got it, Roger." Jimmy grumbled the words out in a gruff growl. "Enough already."

"Friend Tuck, you are correct." With a casual gesture, I addressed the assembling crowd of lumbering spectators. "My *Prophet's Vision* has already enlightened me to their true ugliness. No doubt this masquerading mass of unfortunate humanity is, in fact, zombies."

"Stop saying zombies! Can't we call them something else?" Roger's voice sounded an octave higher than normal.

"Down Roger. It's going to be okay," Jimmy said. "I'm sure Mr. B. has a plan."

Roger grabbed my arm. "Arland, tell me you have a plan to keep those crazies from eating our brains."

I smiled. "Not yet. Not exactly."

The zombies arrived a little at a time. Unlike when they had arrived at my country home, these cursed souls didn't huddle and chant. Each one continuously tried to step onto Stoney's consecrated property, but failed. The concentrated barrier the council placed around the house held strong, even though these demon-possessed souls were more like savage beasts after its prey.

"Look there." Stoney pointed down the street toward the sound of a car roaring into third gear. It was Sarah's

Camaro, and hanging on the top was a green demon. Its claws dug into the metal roof.

When it got closer, we could see more holes in the top, hood, and side windows. The demon raised an arm to claw the car again. Instead, the hellion was knocked about like a rag doll. The centrifugal force of the high-powered vehicle sliding around a corner threw it off balance and caused it to lose its grip. The hellion fell off and hit the pavement, splattering like a juicy green slime balloon.

Sarah didn't slow down. Tires screeching, the Camaro careened toward us, knocking a dozen zombies out of the way before breaching the invisible barrier, darting over the sidewalk, and with a deafening howl, vroomed up into Stoney's yard. The fallen zombies simply got to their feet again and resumed their trek.

George and the girls exited the car in haste. Sarah stood close to me, pointing at the crowd heading this way. "They are doing it again. They are going to burn down Stoney's house. What are we going to do?"

Stoney put a reassuring hand on Sarah's trembling arm and said, "You are safe here. They aren't going to touch this house. Neither them nor their sorcery can cross onto the property. It's been consecrated, you know, like a church. This is a sanctuary of sorts."

Sarah loosened her grip on the steering wheel and nodded her head—beads of sweat and tears running through her mascara.

Flower helped her out of the car and calmed her nerves.

Stoney's neighborhood was much like mine had been before the fire. The difference here was to our advantage. Fewer homes littered the development area, and even fewer roads were cut between the houses. It was the perfect place for a showdown.

CHAPTER FORTY-SEVEN

The Necrothyst

The gathering zombies beat their fists against the invisible barrier protecting our safe house. They chanted and cast curses, but to no avail. Green, scaly demons were interspersed in the crowd. Some with three eyes and some with only one; they all clawed at the invisible wall of protection.

Sarah had calmed down, or at the very least, she didn't scream and cry in the face of the approaching danger. As for me, I felt safe, and I assume the others did, too. If only for that, this small respite provided a bit of peace in the midst of this storm. The horde couldn't harm us as long as we stayed inside the barrier the council put around the property. I took off my tweed sports jacket and laid it on the steps of the porch beside where I sat.

There was no sense everyone standing around outside watching the crowd of both green demons and the living dead surrounding the house grow larger by the minute. I had volunteered to take the first watch and let the others get some rest. Sarah brought a burger and a glass of iced tea to me and stayed a while. She, too, sat on the porch, and we talked...just talked...like we used to do.

"They are repulsive, aren't they? The demons, I mean. I guess the zombies are gross in their own way, too." Sarah's initial question sounded more like a remark.

"Yes, very gross." I agreed. "Worse, if you could see them the way I do." I took a bite of burger, swallowed, and said, "The sad thing is, these people didn't choose to be demon skins. After they left their body, an evil spirit moved in before their heart stopped and it's that spirit keeping them alive in a perpetual state of near death."

"Sounds horrible."

"I suppose so. The only upside is that the people, I mean their spirits or who they really were, moved on. They aren't trapped in those husks." I took a bite of the burger. "They have transcended. Whether they went to Heaven or to Hell—don't know."

"There's that word again. Roger said that Amethyst called herself a transcended form of angel. What does she mean by that?"

"Iggarest told me that Amethyst is power hungry."

Sarah tilted her head and shrugged. "Imagine that...a pushy, conspiring, megalomaniac with wings. Sounds a lot like Abaddon."

"Exactly." I nodded and gave a chuckle. "Well, angels are given gifts much like we Champions are. You know that each supernatural gift is unique, and so, it is with angels, too.

Evidently, there's more to Amethyst than we assumed. In other words, she is no simple angel. Amethyst has a specific supernatural ability that makes her useful to Satan." I cut my eyes toward Sarah and chuckled at the irony of my statement. "That is, if you can call angels simple."

Sarah smiled back, but her eyes didn't say she was happy with what she heard.

"It seems that Amethyst is capable of robbing other angels and supernatural entities of their powers. It's like she absorbs the part of them that makes them special." I looked away and my words felt alien. "Like a vampire bat or, even worse, a gigantic tape worm she feeds on supernatural energy. Evidently, that's how she escaped the aether when no other angel could. She sucked up all the residual spiritual energy from every creature there until she had enough to power her way into our existence. At that time she was probably more wraith like than angelic."

I took another bite of the burger and continued. "It's my guess that over time, she realized Iggarest could hear her, meaning he can identify meager amounts of supernatural energy, like the kind in mortals—his minions."

"I get it. Iggarest's minions are all mortal and he's attuned to them...us...uh, people. You know what I mean, right?"

"That's exactly what I think." I paused, gathering my thoughts. "But, according to Iggarest, he was an archangel at one time. Somewhere under that quirky bowler hat, Lucifer locked away a lot of power, and Amethyst found it. And true to her nature, she's been feeding on it. Eventually, she was able to take over Iggarest's life force and return to this existence in angel form, but only at Iggarest's expense. Mind you, I don't know for sure, but I think that's how it happened. So as Amethyst changes and becomes more powerful, well, she calls this *transcending.*"

"What if she consumes all of Iggarest's life force?"

"I don't think there's any question about it; if she hasn't already, she will soon." I looked out at the barrier protecting us from the unspeakable evil stalking us—leering at us with an insatiable hunger. "I think she's consumed most all his locked away power—the might of an archangel. Once she gets it all, there will be no more Iggarest, only Amethyst will exist."

"Then she will have the power of an archangel?"

I nodded and chewed more burger. "Add that to whatever power she has already accumulated and you have quite a dynamo."

"Do you think she will be able to breach the barrier the council set up around this house?"

It was my turn to look at my shoes. Again, I nodded.

She sighed. "We faced down Abaddon, you and I." Her subtle laughter sounded soft, maybe gentle. "When I returned from...let's call it our adventure. Being *Miss Popularity* didn't mean as much as it did before. In some ways, Dee Dee has taken over my posse of fashion crazed girls. When I graduate..." she looked up at the walking dead, ready to tear into our flesh, "...if I graduate. We may not get out of this alive." She didn't finish her thought.

After a few minutes, Sarah stood up and turned toward the door. "One way or another," she said, "it will be Dee Dee's time to shine. I'm not sure what I'm going to do then. I had it all planned out last year before you and Jimmy decided to become...." She stopped talking.

"We didn't exactly choose to be the tip of the spear in this war. But if we hadn't accepted the responsibility, people would have died. You know that."

"I know. Maybe...just maybe, it's our turn to die." She walked back into the house.

Alone, I stood on the porch steps and gazed out at the incredible mass of zombies pressing against the invisible wall protecting us. The idea of them breaking through made a shiver run up my spine. Or was that a warning from my supernatural gift?

Mr. Dark's inky blob skittered across the newly laid grass, under the Camaro, and up beside the porch. *"I have news. Maybe bad, maybe not. I don't know."*

I silently directed my thoughts to him. "Where have you been? I thought you had gotten lost, or worse. You know Amethyst can feed on you just like she can any supernatural creature."

"Bite your tongue! Oh, what a horrible thought. Now, if you're through trying to scare the bejeebers out of me, you might want to know what I found out."

"Okay, what is it?"

"Miss Angelethyst—"

I interrupted him. "If you mean Amethyst, she's a Necrothyst."

"*Tomato—tomatoe. Potato—Potatoe,*" Mr. Dark huffed.

"Don't get mad at me. That's not my word...it came straight from an angel."

"You call her what you want, and I'll call her what I want."

In an involuntary reflex, I think I rolled my eyes. "Tell me."

"Back there behind the restaurant. Where you guys took out those demon-ombies."

"There's no such thing as a demon-ombie."

"If you keep interrupting me, I'll never get this said."

"Sorry...go on."

"Well, Amethyst and Iggarest were doing something freaky. One second, it was Iggarest standing by the Jones' cotton field, and the next second Amethyst was there, the next it was Iggarest, and then Amethyst. They changed places over and over again. Repeatedly, this kept going on. Each time Amethyst appeared, she got a little bigger, and every time Iggarest appeared, he got smaller."

"Are they still at it?"

"How should I know? I left. It freaked me out."

"Iggarest is stronger than she gives him credit for."

"But what happens when she syphons off all his strength?"

"I'm afraid...it's only a matter of time now."

Roger stepped out onto the porch.

"Oh, great. Do we have to listen to his insults? I'm not doing it! You stay here if you want. I'm going inside."

"Talking to Mr. Dark again?" Roger asked.

I nodded.

"Every time I catch you talking to yourself, I figure he's talking back...even though *I* can't hear him."

"He doesn't like you very much."

"That's okay. Sometimes I don't like me either." He paused to sigh deeply. "Do you ever regret how all this turned out?"

"Yeah. Sometimes," I admitted.

"Yeah. Me too." He gazed out at the ghoulish creatures pawing the barrier. "Would you have done anything differently?"

"No, probably not. The consequences were too great." It was my turn to pause. "How about you?"

"Yeah. There are a few things I'd change." Roger confessed. "But getting with Dee Dee's isn't one of them. Ya know, I really... I really... I...." He didn't finish.

"Yeah? That serious?"

He nodded.

"Good for you," I said.

Roger physically shivered as he gazed out at the mob of hellions, each one ready and waiting to break the barrier. "Do you think they really eat brains?"

"Most likely, yes...and other body parts, too."

"Oh, shit," Roger replied.

CHAPTER FORTY-EIGHT

The Electromagnetic Induction Principle

George and Jimmy joined Roger and me on the porch. Jimmy had a toothpick between his teeth, and George was wiping sauce off of his tee-shirt, or rather, what fabric remained of his tee after his battle with the red rider. A lot of his lean chest showed through the gaping holes; in fact, there was as much brown skin exposed as there was fabric hanging on his teenaged frame.

"George, if you ask Stoney for a tee, I bet he has one you can wear," I said.

"After Nurse Cumberland laid hands on me and healed my wounds, all the scars left." George puffed out his chest. "This shirt is the only reminder that I won that battle."

Jimmy made a sour face. "That's not a reminder. That's a souvenir."

"Just the same," George replied. "I don't feel the need to change."

Tuck, coffee cup in hand, joined us on the porch. She sipped and listened.

"Look there." Roger pointed at the barrier directly at the entrance of the driveway. "Did you see what I saw?"

I kept watching, and beside a particularly large zombie stood a scaly-green, little devil with long sharp fingernails protruding from boney fingers. Every time it clawed at the invisible wall, the barrier glowed, emitting a bright orange outline around those hideous fingernails.

"Does that mean the barrier is weakening?" Roger asked.

"That's exactly what I think," I replied.

"Did I mention how much I hate zombies?" His voice quivered halfway through his statement.

Tuck tossed the rest of her coffee in the grass and set the cup by the door. "What's the deal with you and zombies. Man, get over it!"

I shot Tuck a look that quieted her mouthy remarks. "Roger," I laid a hand on his shoulder, "try to put that fear out of your mind for now. I want you to work on another puzzle. I'm afraid our lives depend on getting this one right."

He turned his back to the zombies and said, "Shoot. What's the puzzle?"

"Tap into your gift of wisdom and answer my question. Why did the archangels tell the council that they had each given us a weapon to use against the enemy when we only have two?"

He thought for a long moment. "I'm getting nothing. No, wait...three blades. Yes, three blades."

"I had that much figured out... I was hoping you'd come up with a bit more." Contemplating his answer, I scratched my head. "Maybe two will be enough," I replied.

He whipped around and gave me a hard stare. "And what do you mean by that? Do you think my gift isn't as good as yours? I'll tell you a thing or two about your quirky gift. It's failed us on more than—"

"No...for goodness' sakes, no." I could tell he was winding up for a full-fledged rant. I put a hand on his shoulder. "I'd never think that. Don't get wisdom and knowledge confused. It's easy to do." I sighed. "I mean, wisdom isn't going to help because we don't have enough knowledge—not yet. What my gift is telling me is that the two weapons alone will not win the day. We need knowledge. Yes, I fear my ignorance may be the end of us."

His mouth dropped open. "You're talking about when we face Amethyst?"

I gave him a concerned nod. Gazing out toward the street, I again checked out that little devil with the long claws. This time, the orange glow outlined its whole hand. "I'm afraid we don't have much time left to figure this out."

Overhead, rolling thunder shook the house. Rebecca, Stoney, Sarah, Rose, and Flower filed out and into the yard to see what was happening. We all stood gawking as lightning flashed across the sky revealing a fast moving wall cloud forming overhead.

"Looks like we're in for some bad weather, Mr. B.," Jimmy said. "Let me help you put your jacket back on." This time I didn't get a psychic flash of him wearing blue armor.

All I saw was just plain Jimmy as he helped with one sleeve, then the other.

"I don't see Saint Michael's sword. What did you do with it?" I asked.

"Wait! You gotta see this." Jimmy held out his hand and commanded, "Sword of Saint Michael, come to me." From out of nowhere, it appeared. "And you know what Tuck said about her gun talking to her?"

I nodded and listened to him.

"I get it now. This sword talks to me. That's how I knew it would do this."

"Just don't let anyone other than a Champion know you're hearing a voice coming from a miracle sword." I advised. "They don't understand things like that."

"Well, Tuck gets it. The lance and her had a long conversation." He stopped and appeared to be in deep thought. "Now that you mention it, she did look kinda looney, like she was out of her head." He cracked a smile. "Just normal for her."

"Out of her head? In a way, that's exactly what she was doing—talking out of her head." I couldn't restrain an understanding smile. "Anyway, like I said. Don't let anyone outside of the team know about this."

A thunderous commotion in the sky alerted everyone who had wandered back into the house of approaching danger, and they all rushed back outside. From directly above us, a whirling wind descended. It whipped around with hurricane force, pushing everyone to the ground except

Jimmy, Tuck and me—they all lay flat against the earth. Miraculously, we three were the only ones able to resist the mighty windstorm pounding down on us.

I figured the reason Jimmy could withstand the onslaught was because he carried the angelic blade of Saint Michael. Of course, I guessed Tuck was protected by the Lance of Destiny. Amazingly, I didn't get forced down, like all the others.

At the center of the wind, Amethyst descended from the cloud. Three rings of power encircled her. Like a wheel in the middle of a wheel, they whirled. The mystic gears moved in synchronization. One ring would stop. The eyes on the surface would open and close before it resumed whirling around. Moments later, the next ring would stop and the eyes did the same thing. After the third ring restarted its vigorous motion, they repeated the sequence. In the center of the whirling rings, Amethyst stood on empty air; her hair barely moved despite the gale rushing around her.

"Mr. B.," Rebecca called to me. "I can't push myself up off of the ground. I'm stuck."

Spitting out a mouth full of dirt and grass, Roger yelled, "What's causing this gosh-awful wind? I'm trapped, too!"

"I don't know if you can see her, but it's Amethyst. She has these things...these rings...no, they are more like wheels. Maybe...? Anyway, they're spinning around her. They're producing this gale."

I could hardly hear George scream out, "Mr. B., I can't see the enemy. I can't lift my head that high. Does the combination of wheels look kind of like rings on a gyroscope only they're spinning around her?"

"Yes, exactly," I cried out. My words all but got lost in the unrelenting and debilitating gale.

"If this were a science project," George yelled, "I'd say it sounds like a generator. She's generating some kind of power. In physics, it's called *the electromagnetic induction principle*."

Jimmy yelled back, "George, I don't speak geek. Talk in English."

George tried to push up, only to be pelted back to the ground by the mighty wind. "You understand cars, right? It's like a generator in a car. Every car generator uses magnets sliding over a charged surface to create electrical energy. She's making the rings slide against each other to generate some kind of power. But I don't know what kind or why."

"Got it," I said. "The power hungry Necrothyst wants more power." That sounded more sarcastic than I intended. "If she's going to kill us, then she'll need significantly more power than any of the horsemen to do it."

Roger looked up at us, standing on the porch. "How are you three resisting the wind and we can't?" He sounded totally confused.

"We have some kind of protection," Jimmy yelled back. "Really don't know."

Amethyst's descent came to a stop. Those wheeling rings, spinning around, dug a crater, flinging dirt and grass in every direction. And yet, still, they whirled.

Jimmy had answered Roger, and his response was as good as any I could have come up with. Upon opening my mouth, a face full of dirt and grass pummeled me. Actually, the angel never touched the sanctified ground, but floated in the middle—between the parts of the spinning apparatus. In her hand, she held Gabriel's Sword of Life and Death.

CHAPTER FORTY-NINE

Made Worthy by the Redeemer

There we stood, our friends unable to stand in the gale force wind and the three of us, Jimmy, Tuck, and me, facing Amethyst together.

With her free hand, Amethyst reached up to the sky...and like I had seen Reuwel and Michael do before, she pulled it down into a fist. The wind stopped blowing. Even the cars on the highway stopped moving. Frozen between moments of time, my friends on the ground stopped struggling. Only Jimmy, Tuck, and I were mobile. We had not been affected by the angel's charm.

"Sword of Michael, come to me!" Jimmy exclaimed...and the sword appeared in his hand.

"Lance of Destiny, come to my aid," Tuck cried out, and the lance materialized in her hands.

Amethyst scowled at the three of us from her lofty height. **"Why are you not frozen in time? How dare you defy**

my angelic enchantment?" From the sides of her head, ram's horns grew out and coiled around. Her radiant, crystalline body form darkened and her fair face hideously twisted into an indescribable repugnance. **"I know not where you obtained the might to defy my Penitence's Wind, but you are still mortal and I rule over your kind. Like it or not, you are my minions."** She scowled, and a smirk crossed her lips. **"What impudence you three mortals possess, or is it ignorance that makes you stand in my presence and defy my magnificence?"** Like turning off a light switch, the scathing, scolding tone changed. Amethyst's radiance returned and her voice became tender and sweet; so kind and gentle that it made her allure hard to resist. **"My little ones, I am now the ultimate Elohim. This form you see before you is the highest evolutionary pinnacle of all angelic kind. Nay, I am more than an angel..."** Gone was the sweetness. Her voice abruptly took on the roar of the mighty wind, and her repulsive visage returned. **"...I am a god. Bow before me!"**

"Is she so schizoid she can't control her own personality?" Tuck said. "That's more messed up than handlin' copperheads at a Rattler Roundup."

Amethyst pointed the sword toward the porch where we stood. Red lightning shot out of the blade. A split second later, the bolt bent and crackled in midair. With a booming explosion, it landed a few feet in front of us.

"Amethyst, looks like you need better aim," I yelled. "You missed!"

"I am far superior to the likes of you, Prophet." Her eyes glowed so brightly I could hardly look her in the face. In my imagination, I saw those eyes as twin cosmic explosions radiating from some novae star. Or perhaps that was my prophetic gift talking to me.

"I have syphoned the power of demons and succubi, archangels and principalities, powers and thrones. Look at me and despair. Not even he who sits on the throne of the Fallen can match my might, and soon old Morning Star will be but a memory and I shall become the Queen of Hell."

"You best watch your words," I yelled to be heard above the grinding sound of the whirling rings. "The Morning Star just might put you in your place. From what I hear, he doesn't share well."

She aimed the blade directly at me. **"Prophet, what makes you think you can stand between me and the glory I deserve? Neither you nor the mortals standing at your side can stop me."**

Another lightning bolt crackled out of the blade, danced about in midair and hit the ground. It, too, had fallen short of its target and exploded several feet in front of us.

"She couldn't have missed us that time," Tuck said. "What's wrong with her?"

Both Jimmy's armor and Michael's sword glowed a bright blue. The Lance of Destiny, and the invisible gauntlets I had seen before on Tuck's hands, shone with a brilliant blue as well. The words the council sent to me rang in my ears...*look for the blue glow.*

"Do we attack now?" Tuck asked. "Why are we waiting?"

"Hold on," I said. "Something else is happening here. Don't attack. You'll get your chance, but for now...wait. Listen to your relics. You'll find they are agreeing with me."

Tuck looked up at Amethyst. "You're right. There's something funny about that sword. As crazy as her aim is, this can't be a fluke."

Tuck was right. This was no coincidence. I found it hard to believe a force, as undeniably powerful as Amethyst, had missed even once, and certainly not twice. I tapped into my Prophet's Vision, and between the three of us on the porch and this angry Necrothyst was a luminous red shield of protection.

"The barrier the council put up is protecting us. It's preventing her from blasting us to atoms," I said.

"No mere mortal, not even thee, can wield power enough to thwart my will. This is not angel charm, it comes from the Creator. How do you have such power?"

In a rage, both she and the wheeling rings ascended to a height of about thirty feet. She raised a hand toward her minions. In my special vision, I witnessed their life forces leaving their bodies and joining with that of Amethyst. Her horde of zombies caught fire. Blazing, each one fell onto the ground, sizzled, and exuded a vaporous stench before crumbling. The wind from her spinning rings blew their ashes into the air.

"Oh, great!" Mr. Dark's silent voice spoke in my mind. His comments were correct, mocking, but correct. *"Now, the air is filled with zombie ash. Hold your breath. There's no telling what inhaling the remains of zombies will do to you...er, us."* After

a couple of seconds of silence, he blurted, *"On the bright side, I guess that solves the zombie problem for Roger."*

The combined life force of her entire horde made Amethyst grow. Before our eyes, she became no less than 20 feet tall. The spinning rings expanded, whirling with a diameter of thirty feet. And in an appropriate ratio, the sword also expanded. In her hand, Gabriel's sword took on a brilliant blue aura.

The wretched giant Necrothyst held the sword straight up in the air. Lightning from the roiling storm clouds overhead struck the blade and ran, crackling down her form. She extended a hand toward us; electricity danced down and circled her arm. A power bolt flew from her fingertips. It zigged and zagged until it struck the steps of the porch. With a boom, chunks of concrete blew apart and the three of us tumbled to the ground. Tuck and I landed on one side, and Jimmy on the other.

"We've stepped in it now! Your gift has never been effective against angels. You might have had a chance if you stuck a talisman or a relic in your pocket, but no, you let her catch you unaware," Mr. Dark said.

I ignored his complaining. All I could do was try. Standing, I held both hands out in Amethyst's direction. "The prophet commands broken chunks of concrete fly up and pelt this Fallen one."

Like bullets from a machinegun, the pieces of man-made stone strewn throughout the grass instantly hurled themselves at Amethyst.

The concrete projectiles crashed into the whirling rings. Some of the stones shattered into dust and others bounced off. None hit their mark.

She lifted a hand toward us and sent another blast of lightning down at me. This time, I expected to be fried to a crisp.

Moving faster than I ever thought possible, Jimmy leaped directly into the bolt's path. With the sound of a car crash, the electricity hit the sword. He lifted his blade, high up, over his head, and the path of the bolt veered across his body and blasted upward. The chattering blue lightning ran up the metal shaft and shot straight back into the clouds, leaving Jimmy unharmed.

"How did you know to do that?" I shouted.

Jimmy grinned as he faced me. "Well, I saw her use Gabriel's sword to direct the lightning, so I figured it was worth a try."

The ground under Jimmy's feet exploded as another bolt of lightning barely missed him. He went flying over my head and landed between the house and where I had stood.

Amethyst raised her sword again, and with both arms, drew more electrical energy out of the clouds. Then she aimed the tip downward—pointing directly at us.

"The prophet commands the red glow, set in place by the council, to surround us and protect us from Amethyst's assault." As I had no idea what I should have said, my words surprised even me. It was like my gift had taken possession of my body and it knew more about what to do than I did.

Around each individual person, an aura of red encapsulated us.

In the next half second, a miracle happened as the blast hit us. We went flying this way and that, but we were unharmed by the high powered electrical charge. Surely, being tossed like a rag doll was an insignificant price to pay for survival.

Without me purposefully saying them, my words again left my mouth, "Rings of power, mighty wheels within wheels, hear me! The prophet commands you to open your eyes."

Instantly, the rings slowed, and every eye on them opened at once, bringing the whirling action to a complete stop.

Amethyst screamed in anger, **"No! You are not powerful enough to command a wheel of power. A mortal has no right to make demands of a god!"**

I caught a glimpse of my shadow as the lightning flashed overhead. It had wings...six of them. "Mr. Dark, was that you who helped me?"

The voice that answered sounded more like Reuwel than the gravelly Mr. Dark. *"Of course, you weren't expecting help from Santa Claus, were you?"* The assistance may have been heavenly, but the asinine humor was definitely Mr. Dark's, though I could only guess where those inky wings came from unless Reuwel had a hand in the fight.

My gift, by then, was constantly talking to me. In the recesses of my mind, the answer came. I smiled because although the Creator banned my guardian angel from helping me or any mortal on the Champion's team; my blob-like alter ego wasn't exactly human.

CHAPTER FIFTY

Blasphemy

"Nice trick, Mr. B., You got any more up your sleeve," Jimmy said.

"Don't know, maybe." My reply may not have been as encouraging as he liked, but it worked for me. Thanks to Reuwel, I wasn't standing alone at the crux of the problem. I had an ally—a powerful Seraphim.

Jimmy slashed one way and another, trying to draw devil blood.

Amethyst stepped back away from the wheel-like rings, and for reasons unknown, shrank. She lost five feet of her gigantic stature before she grabbed the inner ring and gave it an electrical charge. The eyes blinked, and the ring started moving again.

Whispering, I said, "Thanks for supercharging my gift."

The smooth melodic voice came to me just as Mr. Dark's voice usually did. *"Son of Norman, I only coached the words out of you. That kind of power is not mine to give. Only one made worthy can command the mysteries ordained by the Creator."*

"Made worthy?" there were those words again. I knew instinctively that it had to do with the thorns from the Crown of Sorrows being saturated with the blood of the Redeemer. But I never dreamed the difference it would make in the level of power I wielded. A thought crossed my mind. It seemed impossible, but then, so did the idea of me being strong enough to bring Amethyst's power generator to a halt.

Tuck and Jimmy ran to my side.

Amethyst had been holding Gabriel's Sword of Life and Death up and gathering electrical energy from the clouds. She laughed as she held out her hand toward us, shooting another bolt from her fingertips. This time, the crackling electricity traveled straight into the metal of Michael's sword and the Spear of Destiny. Like a battery, they absorbed the power, vibrated, and glowed a brilliant red. Even from where I stood, I felt the charge building to an exploding vertex.

"Before they overload, return fire..." I nearly screamed to be heard above the rolling thunder booming overhead. "...aim your weapons at the angel!"

Jimmy and Tuck pointed the sword and lance at Amethyst moments before the tips emitted a potent blast that resounded like a sonic boom. It hit Amethyst, and she shrank another five feet.

Still twenty feet tall, Amethyst was yet a force to be reckoned with. The wheels of power crackled with electricity. They were generating more power for Amethyst's attack.

She pointed her sword at me, and the metal shaft quivered. Before it emitted another blot. The blue aura around the weapon returned, but just for a moment. The blast went awry, missing its mark completely. It was like the sword was on our side, even though Amethyst held it.

That's when I felt it. The sword wanted to escape the grip of the Necrothyst. It was being forced to do something it disliked. Indeed, the sword had a will of its own, and I could feel its desire.

I reached toward Gabriel's weapon and called to it. "*Sword of Life and Death*, if it is your will, come to me, for the blood of the Redeemer has made me worthy."

Bewilderment shot across Amethyst's face when the angel forged weapon jerked out of her hand, shrank back to its original size, and flew toward me. Terrified, my eyes grew wide, watching the sword's missile-like trajectory. I wasn't sure if it would skewer me or what.

At the last second, the sword veered downward and buried its tip into the ground. I breathed a sigh of relief. Unconsciously, I had been holding my breath. I reached forward and pulled the blade out of the ground. Energized, every molecule of my body vibrated. It didn't surprise me when I saw the grass around where the sword landed had instantly died and turned yellow. The blade was still infused with the essence of death, something I doubted Iggarest had told Amethyst, or else she would have used it for more than a lightning rod.

"Did that sword just leap over here all of its own accord?" Tuck asked.

"It certainly did," I replied. I held it up and listened for any other emotion coming from the angelically forged steel.

"You do not have the ability to take the Sword." Amethyst waved her fist at the lightning flashing through the heavens. **"Angels leave this battle to the Champions. Stop helping them."**

I tilted my head, listening to my gift as it whispered to me. "We are supposed to put the three blades together," I instructed.

Jimmy didn't do as I asked. "Do you think it's the blood on the thorns that made it respond to you?"

"Yes, I do." My words were charged with emotion. "I think you have already figured that out for yourself. It's why you could withdraw Michael's sword, and Tuck could withdraw *the Lance of Destiny*. We were all three pricked with a thorn from the Crown of Sorrows, and the blood of the Redeemer which was in those thorns, now mingles with ours. In other words, it has made us worthy." I held the sword out toward Amethyst. "We must hurry. Lay your blades on mine."

Jimmy did as I asked, and placed Michael's sword across mine.

I softly said, "Now for the lance."

Tuck laid the spearhead of the lance atop Jimmy's sword.

I nodded and cried out, "And these three are one."

The three together resonated and hummed like the Hoover Dam Power-plant. Blue sparks ran the length of the blades and shot one way and another. They vibrated in our hands and when the shaking stopped, the three had become one swordstaff. A unique weapon with a short pole attached to the blade of a sword. We three each held it by the sturdy shaft.

The necrothyst faced us. **"Feel my wrath. Mortal swine,"** Amethyst bellowed.

From her fingertips, lightning flashed toward us. It danced across the space between her and where we stood. The tip of the swordstaff's blade erupted in a magnificently brilliant and blinding light; an illuminated ray aimed directly at the Necrothyst's face. In midair, it collided with her lightning bolt and ripped it into tiny sparks.

The ray of light grew in intensity and engulfed the fallen one. Amethyst went into spasms. Spasms of pain, I'm sure, and curled up into a fetal position.

From out of nowhere, a red glow surrounded her.

I gazed upward and my gift kicked in again. I realized that this creature was neither truly an angel nor a vanquished spirit. It was an abomination that needed to be eradicated. Like a vermin infestation, she had invaded this reality.

CHAPTER FIFTY-ONE

The Morning Star

Before the Necrothyst disintegrated, a voice boomed from out of the clouds. **"Stop! Amethyst's demise is in my hands. Her blasphemy has come full circle, for she has claimed to be more powerful than I, the Morning Star. Hear me, Amethyst, you vile creature who came from nothingness full of spite and jealousy. From your lips, the haughty words of the fool have reached through the cosmos to my ears...words that have brought down my wrath upon your head. Your demise is mine, not the Favored one's champions. I claim your life force, and that of every creature you have syphoned."**

"No! Don't let him!" I screamed. The illumination blazing out from our combined weaponry grew brighter.

Amethyst's body uncoiled from the fetal position. She stood and shook her fist at the heavens. Despite being held prisoner in the light of our combined weapon, she cried up to the sky. **"I am a god. Do you not know, I have drawn life**

giving power from demon and Elohim alike? Multitudes of souls, life forces innumerable as the stars which were supposed to be yours, are now mine. These lost souls fuel my power. I challenge you! Morning Star, meet me in combat and die."

"You speak blasphemy! It is I who sits upon the dark throne." The clouds grew black and roiled with internal lightning. The sound of distant thunder echoed in my ears.

Lucifer, the Morning Star, proclaimed, **"I am Prince of the Air, your master...and you are nothing but a parasite. You must pay for your arrogance. I will reclaim the souls you have taken by consuming you."**

"Stop him. Destroy Amethyst before he can take all that power—all those souls."

She made fists, and clapped them together overhead, throwing a bolt into the clouds. **"You cannot harm me. I am a god."**

A shadowy finger reached down from out of the clouds toward the Necrothyst.

"Hurry," I demanded. "Hit her again with the combined power of our weapons." Each one of us held onto the shaft of this unique weapon.

Together, we yelled the words; our combined desire. "Be vanquished!"

A blast fired out of the tip of the blade, striking Amethyst dead on. A glow emanated from her stomach. It grew in intensity and brightness until it burst through her gown. In a startling eruption of flames, she ignited. The fire trailed up her arms and down her gown. It sizzled, alighting into her hair, and exuded a black smoke reminiscent of burning tires. Before us, where the Necrothyst had stood, was a bent and burning figure.

The sound of her screams sent chills up my spine and made the hairs on my arms stand on end. She cursed at the clouds, swearing her revenge on both us and the devil. I breathed, and she was gone. No ash...no echo of her threats...Simply gone.

Overhead, the dark clouds parted and a gigantic angel appeared directly in front of the moon. His wingspan looked to be a half mile across, and his eyes burned like brimstone from the deepest pit of Hell. From behind his ears, long curled horns wound around the side of his shadowy face. The light of the moon silhouetted his features, masking his identity. He slowly hovered and moved our way. **"You have robbed me of my prize. You destroyed her before I could extract the souls she collected."** The voice roared in anger.

"Arland, get out of here!" Mr. Dark screamed in my mind. *"Do you know who that is? You can't be thinking of facing him...are you crazy? If you do, you'll die. Run, hide!"*

The voice in my head couldn't deter my actions. We were too far into this to stop now. Whatever lay ahead, I had to face him. Even with my gift tuned up and running at Mach six, the future remained an enigma; I couldn't see it clearly. Whatever it was...it was my destiny...what I was born to do. This was the defining moment of my life. When Amethyst vanished, we had dropped our weapon, and it became three blades again.

I pointed Gabriel's sword at the approaching horror. Tuck, to my left, again laid the metal spearhead tip on it, and Jimmy, to Tuck's left, crossed our weapons with Saint Michael's sword. Again, the staff appeared, and we held onto it for dear life.

Behind me, I heard Roger shout, "Is this the day the Morning Star is chained—bound for a thousand years?"

I hadn't noticed, but time had restarted. Cars again moved and all my friends scattered across the lawn were pushing up to stand.

The dark angel, hovering above, stopped his descent.

"These holy weapons were forged for your downfall. Like the Creator himself, the three are now one. Do you dare challenge the power of the three as one?" I yelled. "Can you hear their whispers as I can? They tell me *your time is nigh.* They desire your submission, your defeat, your blood, and your death."

I chanced a glance back at Roger. There, to my surprise, all the Champions stood lined up shoulder-to-shoulder with hands clasped together in unity. Behind my friends stood a second row of Champions, warrior angels, all outfitted with sparkling armor. Together, they stood at the ready—unflinching and stoic. They were prepared for battle.

Flower called out to the sky, "Prince of Darkness, your fate is written and sealed in *the Book of the Lamb*. Will He open that book today? Is this the day you suffer your greatest defeat?"

The dark prince held his arms outstretched, side to side, and from his fists, green and violet sparks shot through the clouds. Colorful fire, electric arches, and a spectacular array of lightning flashed from his tight fists. When the flashing ceased, and the sound of booming stopped, the dark *Prince of the Fallen*, had vanished.

Clouds cleared from the sky, and those that were left became white fluffy cumulus vapors. No storm, and no sign of angelic intervention. Only the moon and stars ruled the night.

Flower looked around in bewilderment. "I have the distinct feeling we will see him again."

Tuck pulled her gun and waved it about, hunting for a target. "Where'd he go? I wanted to put a shell in that oversized devil mug, just for fun."

Roger waved his angelic book in Tuck's direction. "Cowgirl, you've got too big for your britches. Can't ya tell when the battlin's done?" he scolded. "Big, mean, and scary has left the building."

Tuck looked puzzled. "Roger, we ain't in no buildin'. I don't get it."

Rebecca ran a hand over the razor tipped blade at the end of the swordstaff. "This is way cooler than those daggers I've been using. Can I borrow it sometime?"

Tuck smiled. "We'll see. Who knows?"

"Way cool, I'd say." George rushed over to Tuck's side. "Where'd you get a thing like that?" As he spoke, the swordstaff became three weapons again. "Wow, I'd like to find out how that works. Pretty sure I'd get the blue ribbon at the science fair if I could pull off a transformation like that."

Just as they had separated, the three weapons vanished.

Sarah stood, straightened her black miniskirt, and pulled her twisted sweater into place. "Oh, how rude!" she exclaimed before pushing strands of hair back, away from her face, and trying to put the bouffant back in to her wind swept hairdo. She looked more disheveled than I'd seen her in years.

Flower went to her, and possibly led by her healer's instinct, helped Sarah over to sit on Stoney's porch, or what was left of it.

Roger gave a loud hoot. "Tuck, if you stopped saying things only my granny can understand you might actually fit into this century."

"Bucko, I ain't tryin' to fit in...and I sure ain't wearin no dad-gummed miniskirt."

"Thank the good Lord for that. I don't want to go blind from the glow off of your lily-white legs."

Tuck delivered a hard knuckled swing at Roger's nose. He dodged, but his retreat landed on Jimmy's toes.

With a solid thud, he socked Roger in his upper arm. "Numbnuts, shut up." Jimmy demanded.

CHAPTER FIFTY-TWO

Christmas Day

In the east, an orange glow appeared on the horizon.

It had been too long since I either ate or slept. Hunger and fatigue fell on me like a ton of bricks. Handing Stoney Saint Gabriel's Sword, I staggered into his house. Roger met me inside.

"Oh, no! Not again. I can't take another bout of verbal sparring with Roger's infectious wit. You're on your own. I'm leaving! You can go at him all you want to, but without me," Mr. Dark's inky shape skittered across the floor and disappeared under the front door. I went to the window and watched as he slid from one dark hiding place to another until I lost him in the haze of twilight.

A stray dog sniffed at the area he had inhabited. *"Scat, hound."*

Gazing through the glass, I said, "You know I can still hear you."

"Oh shit," he replied and fell silent.

The phone rang. Stoney answered it and called out for Rebecca. "It's your aunt," he said as he handed her the phone.

"I guess she tracked me down. Time to face the consequences." Rebecca put the phone to her ear. "Hello, Tia. ... What, you got a call from who? *Los funcionarios*? ... He explained that I was selected at the last minute to go on an excursion sponsored by the principal and the school nurse. ... Oh, yes, the Spanish teacher was there, too. ... Yes. ... Yes, Tia." Her eyes widened and cut to the side. "I know. I should have told you before I left. ... What? He said I got an award for my outstanding participation. ... Uh, what? The award is for how much? ... Tia, that will; that will... Yes, I Know. ... I promise, in the future I will remember to tell you when school related events are on my calendar. ... *Tia, Estas enojada*? Are you mad?" Rebecca breathed a sigh of relief. "You're not? I'm so glad. ... Yes, that's good. ... Well, I'm celebrating our success over here at the Spanish Teacher's house. I'll be home soon. *Feliz Navidad, Tia.*" She hung up the phone.

Stoney smiled. "I told you the council would do something to fix it. They didn't even lie—did they?"

Rebecca shook her head. "Not really." She paused. A tear fell down her cheek. "I don't believe it. The man who called my Tia said my award was two hundred fifteen dollars and it would be sent via cablegram. That is exactly how much Tia is behind on the rent."

"What a coincidence." Stoney replied.

Roger walked my way, and I turned to look out through the window.

"I suppose you want me to mop up after you, this time." Roger's voice was filled with animosity. Or was it impatience? I was way too tired to try to discern his mood.

"Friend Roger, are you alright?" My concern was mirrored in my face. "You insist on antagonizing Tuck for no reason. Did you get infected with another supernatural malady?"

"Of course not. She's been picking a fight with me since we met." Roger shrugged his shoulders. "I was just giving her a taste of her own medicine."

"Roger, you have a whole lifetime ahead of you...a life that doesn't include a certain blond young man who you once called friend," I said.

"Arland, what are you talking about? You sound like you're leaving," he replied.

"In time...I will." I crossed my arms and smiled. "I've learned that friendships are like treasured memories. What they were...was precious, but they...transform."

"No...no... The word is *transcend.*" Roger laughed. "Actually, all kidding aside, I stepped over here to offer my assistance with your next adventure."

My eyes cut his direction. "And what adventure might that be?"

"Well, I just thought the Wisdom of Solomon might help you fill out the papers the insurance company will be sending you about your house fire."

I considered his offer. "Good point," I replied. "Expect my call."

After plopping down on Stoney's couch, I, at last, closed my eyes. Exhausted from the battle, sleep overtook me. Neither Mr. Dark nor a crazy wild dream interfered. There in deep slumber, I got more rest than I had since this fiasco began.

Later, when I stirred, what I saw was not what I expected. Most of my demon fighting team was sitting on the floor around Stoney's Christmas tree.

Roger and Tuck were happily exchanging insults. George and Rebecca were sharing a piece of cake and some kind of red punch.

Jimmy was sitting crossed legged as he examined our celestial weapons, and Rose was heading his way, carrying a tray filled with saucers full of cake topped with a fluffy white icing and more red punch.

Flower and Sarah were sitting in a couple of spot chairs, laughing like they were old friends.

Stoney was standing by the door, looking out at the hard morning light. Through the living room's picture window, I could see what he stared at. The dazzling morning sunlight threw long shadows across his battle marked yard.

I pushed myself up and off the couch, a task much harder than it should have been. I leaned on the window seal and said, “Looks like a glorious Christmas morning—Texas style, a chill in the air and lots of sunshine.”

Stoney gave me a sideways glance. “For a second there, I thought you were joking.” He gazed out through the glass. “This is exactly like the winters in Africa.”

“Do you miss being there? I mean, do you get homesick?”

“Maybe? But only on days when we have to vanquish five devils and Satan himself.” A wry smile crossed his lips.

I laughed. “Oh...you mean like today? Now who’s joking?”

“Revelry aside, being alone for too long is not good for the spirit.” He tilted his head to the center of the room. “I know you think because you have the team...you have everything you need, but it’s not the same as having that one person—your soulmate.” He smiled, as if he knew something I didn’t. “Don’t you think it’s about time you asked her?” He glanced over at where Sarah and Flower were chatting.

“What? Are you talking about Sarah? No, I have no feelings for her. Teenaged boys may think she is God’s perfect gift, but I passed that mark many, many years ago. To me, she is nothing more than a precious person.”

“No...No. That’s not what I mean,” Stoney emphatically stated. “I’m talking about Flower. You had stars in your eyes the first time you met her. I remember because I was there. This whole last year you have avoided having too much to do with her, but I can see how you look at her with that same school boy stare...and she at you.”

"My dear Stoney, you make too much ado about nothing." I kept my gaze focused out of the window. If I looked at Stoney, I might not have the courage to say what was on my heart. "I have always thought you and she were more than friends. I just never said anything about it."

"No, not us. As you know, we both have done work for the council...but we were never more than friends."

I stole a glance across the room to where Flower was sitting. She and Sarah were nodding my way and giggling, but it was Flower, punch cup in hand, who stood and headed straight for me.

"Arland," she said, "dear friend...." She cleared her throat and her tone shifted downward, almost as if she had changed her mind about what she was going to say. "Well, do you think the danger is truly over?"

Closing my eyes, I tapped into my prophetic gift. Nothing alerted me. No twinges ran along my spine. No tingling raised the hair on my arms and neck. And oddly enough, Mr. Dark was silent. "I think we've won this round, and dear girl, frankly, I don't know if I have another round in me."

"Last year, when we rescued all those people from Abaddon's imprisonment, you wanted to return to the Kansas commune, but after the school board promoted you to principal, you stayed. I think your real reason was something else. It was more for them than for anything." She gave a casual gesture toward the room full of teenaged demon fighters.

Stoney leaned on the doorframe and caught my gaze. “They are the most powerful team of Champions ever chosen by the angel council.” He turned toward the window. “They do not need your protection.”

My heart had already told me what Stoney had so concisely said. Inhaling deeply, I caught Flower’s gaze. “It’s true. They would be fine on their own.” I didn’t look away, and neither did she. “I might consider returning to your Kansas paradise if...if you would accompany me.”

Flower slightly swayed, drank a sip of punch, and said, “I might consider it, too.” Her eyes smiled and spoke more than her words.

We walked toward the Christmas tree. Her arm found its way around mine, and our fingers clasped together.

Sarah clapped, Tuck gave a *yahoo*, and Stoney patted me on the back.

Roger was about to make a comment when a knock on the door startled us all. Dee Dee stuck her head in the room. “Sarah? Sarah, I know you’re here. I saw the Camaro outside. Are you guys having a Christmas party?” When she saw Roger, her eyes lit up. “Baby-boo, you were nowhere to be found. I called Michael, and he said that he had no idea where you had run off to, but then, he was half asleep when I talked to him.” A huff changed her tone to a harsher note. “And I find you here...eating cake.”

“Dee Dee, I can explain—”

She put a hand up in his direction and addressed Sarah. “Did you know...? He missed our date last night? Nobody stands up one of the sirens! I mean nobody. Not the captain of the football team, and certainly not Roger Reynolds! Who does he think he is, anyway?"

Mr. Dark slid under the door and parked himself in a shadow under the couch. *"Hey what's going on? Looks like I made it back for the floor show. This is sure going to beat watching the neighbor's dog chase its tail."*

Dee Dee gave her head a quick tilt and patted her bouffant hairdo into place before popping a hip to the side like a model on a runway. With both hands on her waist, she faced Sarah. "Beth Finnely said that she saw Christmas fireworks coming from out this way, and Mr. Abara's house is the only one in the area. It had to be coming from here."

Her expression suddenly changed. She gave Tuck a second glance and I suppose it was at that moment when she realized Roger was sitting on the floor with a girl. She shot a scathing look at Roger and a load of daggers at Tuck. "I see what you've been up to, Mr. Reynolds. You're sitting with this cowgirl, and don't deny it." She crossed her arms and tapped her foot. "How many girls do you have on the string? I saw you driving down Main Street with Rebecca Villa...whatever her name is...sitting beside you! You....you two-timing creep! You're giving up all this..." Dee Dee pointed toward herself. "...for that?" She pointed at Tuck, who gave her a plastic possum grin.

"Honey, sweetness...I know what you think, but that's as far from the truth as possible. There was nothing I could do about... This isn't what it looks like... I wanted to call you, but I couldn't. I was—"

I jumped into the conversation. "He was working for me. I went to his house yesterday morning and convinced him to come with me. He is very capable, as you surely know." I changed my focus and motioned toward Tuck. "Where are my manners? Tuck, please, get Dee Dee some punch." Refocusing on Dee Dee, I continued, "I do apologize for keeping Roger so busy." I tried to alleviate her anger with a kind and gentle tone. "Truly, it was all unavoidable."

"Save it, Mr. B.! I'm not his baby-boo any more. He's showed me he doesn't really care for me." She gave Roger a look that could have chilled his soul. "And a siren doesn't give second chances. I learned that from Sarah." She faced her mentor, the original siren, and asked, "Are you staying here with these losers, or are you coming back with me?"

Sarah leaned on the arm of the chair, lifted her cup of punch, and said, "I haven't finished my drink yet. I'm staying."

A horrified expression crossed Dee Dee's face. "Staying?" Every muscle in her body quivered, and she stomped across the room to the door.

"Pumpkin," Roger blubbered, "I promise it's all on the up and up. I promise, I'll never ever be late again. Can you forgive me? Sweet Pea...?"

She popped her gum and replied, "Maybe, when Hell freezes over, but not in this lifetime."

She stormed out of the door, leaving Roger standing with his arms outstretched.

Tuck reached up and grabbed his shirttail and yanked him back to the floor beside her. "Roger, wake up! Ya don't need a bimbo like that. She's spilled milk straight from the churn. Hang on a while. I bet ya there's someone out there who can make your little heart skip a beat or two." She shoved the drink she had poured for Dee Dee in his hand. "Here...sit, drink, and stop snivelin'. You're getting my cake all salty." She poked a bite of cake in his mouth from her fork. "You need someone with fortitude, character, and if you're lucky, she'll be able to shoot the corner off the queen of hearts from fifty feet away."

"How exciting!" Mr. Dark's humor lacked any form of social grace. *"Was that the opening act? Wait. Arland, are you holding Flower's hand? Did I miss something? Answer me!"*

I smiled to myself and patted Stoney on the back. "Don't get me wrong, Stoney. This fruit cake is delicious, and I appreciate you having saved it for Christmas...but I'd like some real food. Are there any of those burgers left?"

Jimmy sheepishly looked up at me. "Sorry, Mr. B., I had seconds."

Rose pushed him and said, "Seconds? You had thirds."

Flower smiled, a twinkle glinted in her eye as she said, "There's always McDonald's."

Made in the USA
Middletown, DE
18 March 2024

51223409R00215